THE DEAD REMEMBER

DETECTIVE INSPECTOR MARC FAGAN

JASON CHAPMAN

OFFWORLD
PUBLICATIONS

© Offworld Publications March 2024

All rights reserved. No part of this publication may be reproduced, stored on a retrieval system or transmitted in any form or by any means, electronic, mechanical, photocopying, recording or otherwise, without the prior permission of the author, producer, and publisher.

Author's notes

This is the part where I tell you the story you are about to read is a work of fiction. But those who remember, will know the miners' strike of 1984 – 1985 is anything but fiction. In a recent Channel 4 documentary series the miners' strike was once again brought into the public eye. Highlighting the struggles of those who were caught in the middle. Those who worked, those who walked out. The women who supported the strike. And the communities who were divided by political conflict.

This novel is a work of complete fiction. The names, characters and incidents portrayed in it are the work of the author's imagination. Any resemblance to actual persons, living or dead, events or localities is entirely coincidental.

Some geographical locations mentioned in this story did not exist in 1985. And have been changed to enhance the story. The Battle of Six Bells never happened. The role of Secretary of State for Wales, isn't being assigned to a Senedd Member.

I have in no way favoured any point of view. I have represented all parties on an equal level.

Obscene language and violence warning

This story contains language that some will find offensive. Also, scenes of violence some will find upsetting.

Acknowledgements

Many thanks to my beta readers who have been of enormous help with this project.

The miners, united, will never be defeated

Heart and Coal
by
Andrew Challis

In the valleys of South Wales, unfolds the tale of 84,
Solidarity through adversity, defiance dripped from every pore.

Proud banners raised up high, miners' brave struggles untold.
Fighting for their rights, in defence of Welsh black gold.

Through wind and rain, strong side by side.
Their undying resolve, brothers' hand in hand.

Within the depths of the pit, both day and night,
Determination reigned; proud miners unite!

Prologue

Blaenavon – South Wales - 1985

'Hiya mam.' Bryn Collier greeted loudly as he stepped into the kitchen.

Beatrice Collier smiled back at her eldest son. 'Hiya love, how's that new flat?'

'It's brilliant mam, enormous inside. It's a shame you can't manage the stairs. Me and Donna wanted you to come round for Sunday lunch in a few weeks.'

'Ah, sorry love, but the doctor said I can't climb too many stairs.'

'That reminds me, I'll finish the back room for you on the weekend. Then we'll come round and cook Sunday lunch for you.'

'Thanks love.' Beatrice kissed her son on the cheek. 'Sit yourself down, I'll make you a bacon butty.'

Bryn's two younger brothers were already seated at the table. He sat down and glanced out of the kitchen window. 'Crossing the pickets on Monday, are we, boys?'

'You know we are.' Alwyn Collier responded. 'I'm sure your mates will give us a warm welcome at Six Bells when the bus arrives. With the usual bricks and bottles.'

'You made your choice crossing the pickets. It doesn't have to be like that.'

'And what other way should it be?'

Beatrice placed a bacon sandwich in front of Bryn. 'You boys shouldn't be talking shop at the breakfast table. Your dad never did.'

'Those were different times, mam.' Bryn said.

'Your dad walked out and supported the unions back in 1972. He marched on London. Your great grandfather took part in the

Tonypandy riots. His brother, your great uncle Samuel, was killed in the riots. It's the same no matter how many years have passed.'

Alwyn shook his head. 'No, Bryn is right. We live in modern times now, mam. More selfish times.'

'What's that supposed to mean?' Bryn asked, dumping tomato sauce on his bacon butty.

'Not all of us are about the National Union of Mineworkers. Some of us just want to work. We're not interested in politics.'

Bryn glanced at his brother before biting into his sandwich. 'Even if it means the closure of more pits? Including the Six Bells.'

'No one knows anything yet. All we've heard so far are rumours spread by you and Lloyd Bevan.'

'Thatcher will shut every pit in Wales. She doesn't give a fuck about the working class. Ian MacGregor is drawing up plans for the closure of pits throughout the Valleys.'

'Language!' Beatrice scalded her son. 'You're not in the pub now. You're in my house. I'll have none of that sort of talk under my roof.'

'Sorry mam, emotions are running high at the moment with the strike.'

'They're always running high with you and the other union members.' Alwyn mocked his older brother.

'What have you got against the union, exactly?'

'The people running the union, that's my problem. We can't fart without their permission. That dick of a convenor, Lloyd Bevan, is a typical example. Every time management pisses him off, he gets everyone to stop the job. It costs money to stop work. He is aware of that, isn't he? He's too stupid to know he'll cause the pit closure, not Thatcher and MacGregor.'

'That's because management at the Six Bells are a load of fucking arseholes.' Bryn glanced at his mother, who planted her hands on her hips. 'Sorry mam. Lloyd is just looking out for Union members. You should rejoin the union.' Bryn glanced at his youngest brother. 'Dafydd should be a member of the union. It's the only way we'll beat the Tories.'

'You sound like Scargill now. And that dick, Bevan.'

'Scargill is rallying the miners across the country. We have the opportunity to bring Thatcher and her jackboots to their knees.'

'But he should have held a ballot before telling the miners to down tools. Instead, he just went off on a rant. Ordering miners to strike. That's why the Labour Party won't support him.'

'What choice did he have?'

'Scargill should have consulted Kinnock before organising a mass walkout. The Labour party has to be consulted before any major decisions are made.'

'Bollocks.' Bryn scoffed. 'Kinnock will be the downfall of the Labour party. He's just advised those who want to work should keep crossing the picket lines. I thought Labour was all about supporting the Unions. Not stabbing them in the bloody back.'

'You lot need to wake up and smell what Lloyd Bevan and Scargill are shovelling. Don't you see? They're trying to do exactly what they did ten years ago under the Heath government. But it won't work this time. Thatcher has been planning for this ever since she took office. Within ten years, the unions will be destroyed.'

'There's the defeatist brother I know.'

'It's not defeatist, it's bloody reality. Scargill has split the union down the middle. Thatcher saw this coming. The National Coal Board has been stockpiling coal for the last three years. They knew you silly sods would try something like this sooner or later. Industry hasn't been affected in the way the unions want. The longer this strike continues, the more chance the government has of breaking you. Three years of stockpiling Bryn. Are you planning to go on strike for that long?'

'We'll stand united, no matter what.'

'D'you even hear yourself, Bryn? We'll stand together no matter what. Even when support runs out. Even when the food parcels run out. There hasn't been a food delivery in Blaenavon for nearly six weeks.'

'There are families up and down the Valleys who are in more need.' Bryn countered.

Alwyn pointed at his mother. 'And what about our mam? If it wasn't for me crossing those picket lines, we would all be in the shit. I'd like to know how you're managing. How is it you can move into a nice new flat when you've been on strike for nearly a year?'

'I've made sacrifices.'

Alwyn let out a snort of derision. 'What would you know about sacrifice? How long do the unions think they can keep this up? A year, two years? And then what? What if you succeed? What d'you get out of it?'

'A union that can never be defeated, that's what.' Bryn replied in a defiant tone.

'You're all living in fairy la la land. Don't you see the changes that are taking place? Industry is changing. Switching from coal to gas. That's what Thatcher wants. In ten years, there'll be hardly any coal fires left in our homes. We'll all be dependent on gas.'

Bryn rolled his eyes. 'Here we go, the intelligent one in the family goes off on a rant of his own.'

'You and the unions are blind to what's going on. Industry in the UK is being dismantled. China is opening its doors to the west. Offering companies a chance to build factories out there and run them for a fraction of the cost. No more striking workers, no more trade unions. An obedient workforce who does what they're told. This cold war isn't even going to last. Russia and America are talking more.'

'So what, we just bend over and take it up the arse from Thatcher's government?'

Alwyn stared back at his brother. 'The end is coming for the unions, Bryn. Scargill is hammering in the final nails as we speak. He's going up and down the country, delivering speech after speech. Labour has deserted him. Don't you see Bryn, Scargill has already failed, and he doesn't even realise it. Scargill has been wanting to call industrial action since he took over the NUM. He's fighting a lost cause. And so are you. The news has been speculating this strike might be over in a few weeks.'

Bryn looked at his youngest brother. 'What about you Dafydd? The boys are really missing you down the pub.'

'Dafydd has responsibilities.'

'Oh yeah, that slut from Abergavenny you've got up the poke.' Bryn grabbed the remains of his sandwich and stood.

'Bryn, don't be like this love. Come on, you're all brothers. Your dad would have never wanted you arguing like this.'

Bryn glanced at his mother. 'You're right mam. Dad would never have wanted this. He'll be spinning in his grave now. He'd have wanted us to be united. Instead, I have two bloody scabs for brothers. You've bought nothing but shame on this family.' Bryn headed out of the kitchen door.

'I'm not trying to get involved, Alwyn, but why can't you listen to your brother?' Beatrice said with a despairing tone.

'Just because he's the eldest, mam, doesn't mean he's right. If I'd have joined the unions and walked out, there'd be no food in the cupboard. And you'd be out on the street because we'd have no money to pay the rent.'

CHAPTER 1

**Pen-Ffordd-Goch – Keepers Pond – Monmouthshire.
Present day**

Detective Inspector Marc Fagan stared across the tranquil waters of the Keepers Pond. An area popular with hill walkers, dog walkers, and those who enjoy the majestic beauty of the Welsh countryside. The pond was built in the early 19th century to provide water for Garnddyrys Forge, which started production in 1817. The forge was dismantled during the 1860s. The body of water gained the name Keepers Pond, because the gamekeeper of the grouse moors lived in a cottage nearby. The Black Mountains beyond spanned in all directions. Reminding Fagan of the natural beauty the South Wales Valleys offered. The Sugar Loaf mountain towered above the surrounding hills. Resembling a dormant volcano, ready to erupt. During his thirty-eight-year exile in Liverpool Fagan would reminisce back to his youth. He would often climb the Deri mountain that overlooked Abergavenny. Fagan and his childhood friend, Graham Walker, spent the long summer holidays exploring. Picking wineberries that grew on the slopes of the mountain side. Following his assault on Benny Nelson and just before he left Abergavenny Fagan climbed the Deri one last time. Saying his goodbyes to Rebecca and Graham as he stared across the valley.

The car park near the pond had been closed to the public. Further on up the road leading to Blaenavon, a group of early morning walkers huddled in a group. Watching the small army of CSI investigators swarming around the water's edge. A snapper was taking pictures of a body that had been hauled from the pond and placed on a forensic mat. Two CSIs were struggling, trying to pitch a forensic tent. A powerful wind swept across the landscape. A small inflatable boat was on the pond. A police diver tumbled backwards into the water.

Fagan parked his car on the side of the road. He walked up over a small embankment and followed the path that circled the pond. Detective Sergeant Sean Watkins stood by the body, talking to a CSI.

The snapper continued to take pictures.

'Morning boss.' Watkins greeted, sipping from a Costa cup.

Fagan scrutinised Watkins' coffee. 'You get me one?'

Watkins looked back like an innocent child. 'Well, uh, I thought you would have got one on the way up here, boss.'

Fagan smiled and winked at him before looking down at the body. The man was dressed in a smart suit. His face bloated from hours of being in the water.

'Already got an identification.' Watkins revealed, holding up an evidence bag with a driver's licence. 'Sixty-eight-year-old Alwyn Collier.' He pointed at another photo ID that was placed on the mat alongside the body.

'Name rings a bell.' Fagan remarked.

'According to his ID, Collier is the Senedd representative for Blaenau Gwent. And the Shadow Secretary for the Environment.'

A CSI was examining the body.

'Suicide by drowning?' Fagan stated.

The CSI pointed at the top of the cheekbone. 'There's bruising just under the eye socket. This man was assaulted before he entered the water.'

'So he wasn't alone at the time of death.' Fagan surveyed the surrounding landscape. 'No CCTV anywhere. If he was attacked, our suspect could have driven off in any direction. There are roads all over this area. Narrow roads, no CCTV for miles. Perfect place for a murder. Any idea how long the body has been in the water?'

'Several hours, I'd say about midnight.'

'There's plenty of boy racers that come up here late at night.' Watkins suggested.

'Yeah, and most of them are uninsured and won't be of any help.' Fagan pulled his phone from his pocket and activated a map. 'There are several roads that lead away from this area. Our attacker could have driven towards Govilon. Either heading back towards Abergavenny, or turning left and heading to the Heads of the Valleys road.'

'If our attacker had access to a vehicle?'

'He could have travelled to this location with Collier, who may have had a vehicle.'

'What were they doing up here this time of night?'

'Collier was a politician.' Fagan looked around. 'Up here late at night. Conjures all kinds of theories, doesn't it?'

'A sexually motivated murder, boss?'

Fagan shrugged. 'Your guess is as good as mine, Sean.'

'I should imagine there's a few houses that have CCTV along the road through Govilon.' Watkins said.

Fagan studied the map on his phone. 'Our attacker may have headed towards Blaenavon. Perhaps turning off towards Brynmawr to avoid CCTV at the Texico garage on the way into Blaenavon. But the minute he would have got to Brynmawr a traffic camera would have spotted the vehicle.' Fagan glanced towards a junction opposite the turnoff to the pond's carpark. 'The suspect could have taken that road which leads into Llanelli Hill.'

'That road also leads to several other locations.' Watkins pointed across the valley. 'Our killer may never have driven through Llanelli Hill. You can also get back down to the Heads of the Valleys road from here without driving through the village. Eventually, our attacker would have come into contact with a traffic camera or other form of CCTV. It's impossible for anyone to stay off the grid regarding cameras.'

Fagan pointed towards two radio transmitters that towered over the landscape. 'They could have driven past the radio masts. Following the road down the mountain, emerging out on Gypsy Lane, between Llanfoist and Llanellen. Or they could have turned off and come out on the main Pontypool road. You can also get to Llanover from here. It's a maze of narrow roads in that direction. It's possible they could have avoided all main roads that have traffic cameras.'

'Even if they were picked up by camera, it's a lot of cameras to check. Plus, the average speed cameras on the main dual carriageway on the Heads of the Valleys are switched off after ten o'clock at night. I checked last year following a fatal accident. They're not turned on again until six in the morning. We're looking at hundreds of vehicles. There was also an Ariana Grande concert in Cardiff last night, which would have meant more traffic.'

Fagan looked down at Collier's body. 'So, our assembly member travelled to this spot, was murdered, then dumped in the Keepers Pond.'

'Spur of the moment killing, boss?'

'Maybe.' Fagan knelt down for a closer look at the body. He glanced at the CSI. 'You say Collier was assaulted before he went into the water?'

The CSI nodded. 'The bruise on the cheek is consistent with a punch. Our attacker was right-handed by the looks. Collier could have been near the water's edge and fallen in. Or the attacker could have rendered him unconscious and dragged him to the pond before dumping him.'

Fagan looked back towards the road. 'What about tyre marks?'

'Nothing but donut tracks left by boy racers.'

Fagan inhaled the fresh mountain air. 'First things first. We contact his nearest and dearest and let them know he's been found.'

'Boss.' Watkins pointed across the pond.

The diver had surfaced and was clutching what appeared to be a satchel.

Fagan slipped on a pair of latex gloves.

The diver hauled himself over the side of the boat that headed back to shore.

A CSI took the satchel and laid it on the mat next to Collier's body.

'It's definitely Collier's.' Watkins pointed at a small brass plaque fastened to the front of the expensive-looking satchel. 'It's got his name stamped on it.'

Fagan unfastened the satchel clips and reached into the compartment. He pulled out a bundle of fifty-pound notes.

Watkins let out a whistle. 'Got to be a few grand there, boss.'

Fagan pulled out four more bundles of notes and placed them next to the satchel. 'That's a lot of money to be withdrawing from a bank.' He lifted the satchel and peered inside. 'Doesn't appear to be anything else in here. But forensics will tell us more.' He looked out across the pond. 'The body was found near the edge of the pond. But the bag was thrown into the pond itself. Suggesting our attacker threw this in after he murdered Collier.'

'Why leave the money?' Watkins asked. 'That's a lot of dosh to just chuck into the middle of a pond.'

'At least we know his purpose for being here wasn't honest.' Fagan gathered his thoughts. 'So Alwyn Collier, Senedd member, is found dead in the Keepers. Also found with the body is a large quantity of money.'

'Blackmail, boss.'

'If this is blackmail, then why throw the money into the middle of the pond? Our victim arrives at this spot. He's got a lot of money in cash. There's an altercation. Collier ends up in the water. Then the cash is thrown into the pond. Makes little sense, does it? If Collier was out here to meet someone to give them money, then what went wrong? Why did our suspect throw the money in the Keepers?'

Watkins looked down at the bank notes. 'Perhaps there was a reason the money was thrown into the centre of the pond.'

'Great minds think alike, Sean. That just crossed my mind Collier came out here with all this cash, intending to give someone the money. His attacker wasn't interested in money. They murder Collier and toss the cash into the pond.'

'I hate to run your theory down, Inspector Fagan, but the bruising around the eye socket isn't that severe.' The CSI explained.

Fagan looked down at Collier. 'He's overweight. I'd say around twenty stone. I bet he's got a tonne of health problems. Diabetic, heart problems, take your pick.'

'A full autopsy will reveal what happened to him.' The CSI

explained.

'Boss.' Watkins distracted Fagan's attention.

Fagan drew a breath. 'Shit, this is all we need.'

A Land Rover Freelander pulled into the carpark. Chief Constable Paul Griffiths climbed out and approached the crime scene. He looked down at the body. 'Christ, I was hoping someone was taking the piss when I got the call. Any idea what happened?'

'We've reason to suspect foul play, sir,' Fagan explained. 'It looks as if the victim was assaulted and dumped in the pond.'

Griffiths pointed at the body. 'Do you know who this is?'

'I believe he's a Welsh Assembly member, sir, for Blaenau Gwent.'

'And about to be bumped up to Welsh Secretary.'

'I'm afraid I don't follow politics much, sir.'

Griffiths shook his head, staring at Collier's body. 'When this gets out, the media will go into meltdown.' He looked at the money laid out by the side. 'How much?'

'Haven't counted it yet, sir,' Watkins said. He stooped over and picked up one of the bundles, weighing it in his hand. 'I reckon each stack has around ten grand.'

'Fifty thousand pounds.' Griffiths sighed. He looked around. 'If this is foul play, which direction do you think our murderer fled?'

'We've just been discussing it, sir,' Fagan said. 'There are roads all over this mountain side. I don't think our murderer is going to go anywhere they could have been picked up on CCTV. My best guess would be Llanover, sir. It's possible to drive from here to Llanover without CCTV spotting you.'

'What about the money and the satchel?'

'it's anyone's guess at the moment. The money obviously serves a purpose..'

'What's your next move?'

'We will visit his closest relatives and go from there.'

Griffiths nodded. 'I will handle the media side of things.'

CHAPTER 2

Market Road – Nantyglo

'I hate this part of the job.' Watkins admitted as they climbed out of the car.

'I know.' Fagan agreed. 'I've lost count of how many times I have had to do this. Every time seems harder than the last.'

The Collier family lived in a spacious bungalow with a large area at the front for parking. A field backed onto the property. Two ponies wandered the field grazing. Three cars were parked up in the spacious driveway. A black BMW, Audi sports car and a white Tesla. A horsebox and a large mobile home were also parked up.

Fagan scanned the immediate area. 'Nice part of the world, if you can afford it.'

'Yeah.' Watkins said, looking at the mobile home. 'Being a member of the Senedd has its perks.'

The front door to the bungalow opened. A woman in her mid sixties hurried out of the house, followed by a much younger woman.

'Mrs Collier?' Fagan reached into his inside pocket, pulling out his ID. 'I'm DI Fagan. This is DS Watkins. We're with Gwent police.'

Elizabeth Collier stared back. Her face already told the story of a woman preparing herself for the worst news.

'What's happened?' The younger woman stepped in front of Elizabeth.

'Sorry you are?' Watkins asked.

'Susan Collier. What's happened? Where's my dad?'

'I think it's best if we talk inside.' Fagan suggested.

Elizabeth took a few moments to respond. 'This way.'

Fagan and Watkins were shown to a spacious living room.

Collier's wife sat on a luxurious leather armchair, clutching a handkerchief.

Susan entered the living room with a tray.

'When was the last time you saw your husband, Mrs Collier?' Fagan asked.

'First thing yesterday morning. Alwyn gets up at six every morning.'

'Did he have breakfast?'

Elizabeth composed herself. 'Yes, he had a piece of toast.'

'How was he?'

Elizabeth shrugged. 'Nervous, on edge. It was going to be a stressful day at the Senedd for him.'

Fagan hesitated before speaking his next line. 'I'm sorry to bring you terrible news, Mrs Collier. Early this morning a body was discovered in the Keepers Pond near Blaenavon. The body has already been identified as your husband, Alwyn Collier.'

Elizabeth closed her eyes. Susan held her close and cried.

'On behalf of Gwent police, I'd like to convey our deepest sympathies, Mrs Collier.'

'What happened?' Susan cried through her sobs.

'We don't know the precise details of his death. At first glance he appears to have fallen into the pond and drowned. However, exanimation of the body at the scene indicates he might have been assaulted prior to his death.'

'You're saying someone murdered him?' Elizabeth asked, looking at her daughter.

Watkins nodded. 'Your husband has been taken to Prince Charles hospital in Merthyr. You will be required to give a formal identification as soon as possible.'

'I'll go with you, mam. I'll make sure you don't have to do this alone.' Susan cuddled her mother.

'Could you talk us through what happened yesterday first thing?' Fagan asked.

'Alwyn got up at six, as usual. He got dressed and went down for breakfast. I got up and had a cup of coffee with him.'

'And you say he was on edge?'

Elizabeth blew into a handkerchief, nodding.

'I noticed three cars in the driveway. Did one of them belong to your husband?'

'Yes, the Tesla. Alwyn was a campaigner for the environment.'

'Why didn't he drive to the Senedd yesterday?'

'I don't know.' Elizabeth sobbed.

'Our dad always took his car to work. He hated taking the train. I asked him why he was catching the train to Cardiff and not driving. He didn't say anything. Just grumbled about having to do it. The train drivers have been on strike lately. I remember dad being furious about it the other week. He even raised the issue on the Senedd floor.'

'How did he get to the train station from here?'

'I took him.' Susan revealed.

'What time was this?'

'Around quarter past seven. He had to be on the train for a quarter to eight.'

Fagan focussed his attention on Elizabeth. 'Did he contact you when he got to the Senedd?'

'He phoned me when he reached Cardiff Central.'

'How did he seem?' Watkins asked.

'He was still agitated. It was going to be a long day for him. He was due to appear in front of a committee at three o'clock.'

'What kind of committee?'

Elizabeth and Susan glanced at each other.

'Mrs Collier, is there something you wish to tell us?'

'My father was being asked to step down as Senedd member.' Susan revealed.

'Why was this?'

'There'd been rumours he'd been turning a blind eye to the behaviours of certain members of staff. One of his senior advisers was under investigation for bullying, harassment and misogyny. The newspapers were constantly harassing my father last year.'

'Must have put him under a lot of pressure.' Fagan said, looking at Elizabeth.

Elizabeth nodded. 'Alwyn wasn't a healthy man. He had problems galore. He had diabetes and had heart problems. He was on a course of medication.'

'Did he have any alcohol issues? Politicians are often seen as heavy drinkers.' Fagan felt guilty asking the question.

'Yes.' Elizabeth confessed. 'Alwyn was receiving treatment for alcoholism. He'd been sober for two years. He was attending weekly meetings. Only the family knew. But a member of his local group went to the press and said he was a recovering alcoholic.' Elizabeth paused. 'The papers would knock on our door and bombard him with questions. Alwyn wasn't exactly popular around here?'

'Why was that?'

'No one wanted us living around here. Alwyn was head of the Conservative party for the Senedd. The Tories are hated around these parts.'

Fagan spotted a wedding photograph. 'How long have you been together?'

'Thirty-five years.' Elizabeth replied. 'We met at the job centre, of all places. Alwyn was a miner at the Six Bells Colliery. When the pit closed in 1988, the men were put through a retraining program. I was working at the job centre when Alwyn strolled in, looking to be retrained. He was also studying at a local college. Dark times back then.'

'Why is that?'

'The miners' strike affected everyone throughout the South Wales Valleys. Not just the miners, but their families. We'd get a lot of former miners at the job centre who would kick off. Some of them had been down the mines for most of their lives. Now they were having to deal with unemployment.' Elizabeth reflected. 'A lot of the wives used to come into the job centre and have a go at us. Accusing us of not giving a toss. I didn't hate these people. I felt sorry for them. Their livelihoods had suddenly disappeared. But, because I worked at the job centre, I was seen as the enemy. Undermining the local communities by stripping miners of their dignity. Offering them more menial jobs. When we got married in 1990, we moved to Neath. That's when Alwyn first got interested in politics. He ran for local councillor and won a seat.'

'Why wasn't Alwyn popular with locals?'

'He worked through the strike. Back then, if a strike was

called, the unions would automatically expect you to walk out. Alwyn was a union member to start off with. Then he became disillusioned. He used to say there was a fine line between strike action and total anarchy.'

'How long have you lived in the area?'

'Since 2018.' Elizabeth replied. 'After nearly thirty years of living in Neath, Alwyn decided he wanted to be closer to home. When he first won his seat in 2007, he was determined to return home.'

'Home being?'

'Blaenavon.'

'But you're a valley over from Blaenavon.'

'Yes.' Elizabeth said. 'Alwyn wanted to move into the house he spent his childhood. Llanover Road in Blaenavon. He even offered the owner of the property over the odds for their house. But they wouldn't budge. So we settled for this place.'

'What kind of trouble have you had with the locals?'

'When we first moved in, it was awful. We had our cars damaged within weeks of moving in here. Alwyn had scab sprayed on his car. One time, a group of kids came up here and threw a brick through our window. Alwyn caught the child who had done it. The boy told the police that he was told to come up here and throw a brick through our window. Because a wicked man had moved here. The boy was only ten years old, for Christ's sake. He was told that Alwyn was an evil man and had done bad things in the past. He never told the police who had told him to attack our house. I remember telling Alwyn it was a mistake to move here. The locals would never accept him.' Elizabeth inhaled. 'But Alwyn was determined to make it work. He wanted to heal the wounds of the past. Namely, the miners' strike. There's still a lot of hatred regarding pit closures back in the eighties and nineties. Older people who remember the strike say the Tories were to blame.'

'Do you still get any trouble?'

'Occasionally. The odd car will drive by and shout scab bastards out of the window. Most of them are too young to know what the miners' strike was all about. I have told Alwyn on several occasions, we need to move.'

'Did Alwyn have any siblings, brothers, sisters?'

'He has two brothers. Alwyn is the middle of three boys. His older brother Bryn lives over at Garndiffaith.' Elizabeth paused. 'He coaches a team at the rugby club. But they haven't spoken in years. Since the miners' strike.'

'What about his younger brother?'

'Dafydd passed away many years ago. Alwyn doesn't like to talk about it.'

'Did Alwyn have many enemies on the Senedd floor?'

'Huh, take your pick,' Susan released a snort of derision. 'He would always say there were backstabbers everywhere. Making out he was another gravy train politician. Our dad wasn't like that. He wanted to make a difference.' She looked out of the window at the Tesla parked in the driveway. 'Dad was an environmentalist. He wanted a wind farm on the mountain over the way there. The project could have provided power throughout the Valleys. But his plans were blocked by the Senedd. They said it would be too costly and it would be an ugly blot on the landscape. Dad's main project was the Severn Barrage. He'd been campaigning for the past ten years.'

'What is that?' Watkins asked.

'it was a project that could have generated power for all of Wales. Dad was a huge supporter of the project. I even helped him design the presentation when he first proposed the idea to the Assembly nearly ten years ago. In 2016 it was kicked into touch. The Senedd claimed it would be too costly and would take years to recuperate the money they would have to spend. Then last year when the energy crisis kicked in, dad had another go at reviving the project. At first, the Senedd had renewed interest. But it all came to a halt in September last year. The Senedd closed it down for the second time. Our dad was devastated. Then came the calls for him to step down as assembly member because of bullying accusations.'

'I tried talking to him about what was going on,' Elizabeth said. 'But he wouldn't speak to me about it.'

'Has he been acting unusual lately?'

'Yeah.' Susan answered for her mother. 'Ever since the Severn Barrage project was scrapped for the second time. And the repeated calls for him to step down from the Senedd altogether. And don't get me started on that poor excuse for a First Minister.'

'Why is that?'

'He was the worst of the lot. He would constantly humiliate our dad on the Senedd floor. But dad clung on. He truly believed in everything he stood for.'

Fagan refocussed his attention on Elizabeth. 'You say he contacted you when he arrived at Cardiff Central? What about after?'

Elizabeth shook her head. 'Nothing. He turned his phone off. I tried to ring him several times during the afternoon. But he didn't answer.'

'Did you consider contacting the police when he didn't arrive home last night?' Watkins asked. 'After all, he was a member of the Senedd. It must have raised a few red flags when he didn't contact you.'

Elizabeth glanced at her daughter. 'It wasn't the first time he stayed out overnight.'

Fagan sensed rising tension in Elizabeth's tone. He closed his notebook. 'We appreciate you talking with us today. You will have to give an official identification that it's your husband at the Prince Charles.'

Elizabeth clutched her daughter's hand. 'Of course.'

'There'll be a family liaison officer visiting you later on today to see to all your needs. Because your husband was a public figure, we'll arrange for a couple of uniforms to stand outside your gates. You need to prepare yourself when the news of Alwyn's death is released to the press. People can be quick to judge. I suggest you stay off social media. You might even want to suspend your accounts for several weeks. Is it just you and your daughter?'

'No, I have one brother.' Susan looked at her mother. 'Our relationship is estranged.'

'Estranged?' Watkins said.

'We haven't had contact with Aron for five years.'

Fagan decided not to push for more information. He stood up. 'We'll give you time to grieve your loss, Mrs Collier. However, as soon as its possible, you need to visit the Prince Charles in Merthyr to identify your husband's body.'

Susan showed them to the door.

Fagan watched as Susan drew the curtains to the living room window.

'What do you reckon, boss?'

Fagan blew out through his cheeks. 'Looks like we're going to be up to our necks in shit again. We'll head back to Newport and grab Andrew for an analysis. I'll contact Stacey and assign her to the role of FLO. See if she can get some more info.' Fagan looked at the closed curtains. 'Something tells me this is going to be one of those cases.'

CHAPTER 3

Abergavenny Police station - 1985

Sergeant Bob Benson sprang to his feet, spotting Chief Constable Gordan Merlyn as he strolled through the entrance. Benson brushed the crumbs away from an egg custard he had just bought from Pinches bakery just around the corner. 'Good afternoon, sir.'

Merlyn spotted the sergeant's stripes on his uniform. 'I take it you are Sergeant Bob Benson?'

'Yes, sir.' Benson nodded stiffly.

'Is there somewhere we can talk?'

'My office is out back, sir.'

'I need to speak to you regarding a matter of importance.'

Benson nodded before looking over at Constable George Walker, who was typing up a report regarding a spate of burglaries. 'George, man the front desk. And get Mavis to put the kettle on.' Benson smiled at Merlyn. 'This way, sir.'

A woman set two cups of tea down on Benson's desk before hurrying out of the door.

Merlyn sipped from his cup. 'What are your thoughts on the miners' strike, Bob?'

'I watched the news last night, sir,' Benson replied. 'A rabble looking for a fight, if you ask me.' He drank from his cup. 'I see one officer covered in blood, being carried away by fellow officers. It's a disgrace our officers are being injured at the hands of a group of violent thugs. I remember the strike ten years ago. The government shouldn't have caved to these unionist bastards. I was glad to see the back of Heath and his government.'

Merlyn smiled. 'The current goal of Mrs Thatcher's government is to break the striking mineworkers. There are several initiatives currently underway, designed to destroy the morale of the striking miners. One initiative is cutting social security allowance to those who are currently involved in strike action.'

Benson grinned. 'Starve the bastards into submission. That's what I say.'

'What started in the North of England has filtered down to the South Wales Valleys. There is growing evidence that support for the miners in the north is gathering momentum in our part of the world. There have been several rallies in Newport, Cardiff, and Swansea. These rallies have been peaceful for now. Mostly made up of the wives of miners and their children. They have even formed a group. Women against pit closures. However, there are growing reports that striking miners throughout the South Wales Valleys are planning some kind of action.'

'What kind of action?'

'Similar to what happened in Orgreave last June. It is my duty, as Chief Constable of South Wales police, to make sure these union militants behave themselves, if you catch my drift.'

'I fully understand, sir,' Benson stated positively.

'Last week I attended a meeting in London of all the chief constables throughout the country. Police forces in England and Wales have been put on high alert. It would seem that Mr Scargill has been rallying a lot of support for the mineworkers. What I don't want is support growing for this rabble of strikers on my patch.'

'I fully agree with you, sir.'

'Over the last several months, intelligence organisations have been covertly gathering information regarding the activities of various union groups. One particular area of concern is the Six Bells Colliery near Abertillery.'

'Can you divulge where this information is coming from, sir?'

'The government has agencies that have infiltrated the National Union of Mineworkers up and down the country. These include Special Branch and MI5. The Special Demonstration Squad has also successfully infiltrated several miners' organisations throughout the South Wales Valleys.'

'I'm sorry to interrupt, sir. The Special Demonstration Squad?'

'It a deep covert unit that's been in operation since 1968. Their goal is to infiltrate organised groups and gather intelligence. They were first established to gather intelligence on minor groups like women's movements and *people of colour*. However, because of the events of the past several months, the branch has extended itself to include trade unions that could pose a threat to social order. The National Union of Mineworkers is top of their list at the moment.'

'Sounds like a bold and ambitious strategy, sir.'

'We have also recruited miners who have volunteered to assist our men on the ground.'

'You say you've recruited mineworkers?' Benson sounded surprised.

'Yes. They have provided valuable intelligence regarding various miners' groups. One of the Prime Minister's goals is to split the mining communities down the middle. To induce divisions within local union groups. One of these initiatives is to pay striking miners to relay information regarding the plans of the unions, or any splinter groups. This plan has been very successful in the North of England.' Merlyn cocked a smile. 'Stupid bastards don't even realise they are being used as pawns in the destruction of the unions. The names of these mineworkers are being kept under strict wraps.'

Benson nodded. 'If you ask me, sir, the unions have had it good for too long. It's time someone dealt with this rabble.'

'I am currently touring the police stations throughout the Valleys and Abergavenny was high on my list. I have also had a look at your record, Bob. You have spent a considerable length of time as a desk sergeant. May I ask why?'

'Abergavenny has been my home, sir. I have never really been ambitious enough to rise above the role of duty sergeant.'

'A commendable answer. One which gives me faith in your ability to offer you a role in putting down any incidents that may happen in the coming days at the Six Bells Colliery.'

'So you are expecting trouble?'

'There have already been several incidents in Abertillery and in Six Bells and the surrounding villages. Because of these incidents, there will be a significant increased police presence within local communities. You know, to show any militant trouble makers that South Wales police will deal with any violence.'

'A wise strategy, sir.'

'We have several operatives working in that area. One of these men is a former police officer who used to serve under you. He's been bumped up to detective sergeant in the Special Demonstration Squad. Owain Lance.' Merlyn revealed.

Benson smiled broadly. 'I always knew that boy would do me proud. He's an outstanding officer, sir.'

'Lance suggested I should call in on you and offer you a position of Police Unit Commander.'

Benson was taken aback by the offer. 'That sounds an important role for a lowly desk sergeant like me, sir.'

Merlyn dismissed Benson's doubt. 'Nonsense Bob. I think this would be the perfect role for an officer with your credentials. We have four thousand police officers in reserve. They will be deployed throughout the coming weeks to all villages in an around Abertillery and Six Bells.'

'That's quite a large number of men, sir. Those outlying villages around that area are quite small. To see such a large number of men deployed throughout the local communities could be seen as a provocative move on our part.'

'That's exactly my thinking, Bob. You'll be working with other unit commanders. Planning a strategy for tackling violence that may break out. Yesterday I received an intelligence report that striking miners from other pits in the South Wales Valleys will be descending on Six Bells. The date isn't set yet, but we think they're planning their rally for St David's Day. They intend to get the remaining miners to walk out with them. There have been a few incidents at petrol garages in that area. Drivers blockaded by small groups of striking miners. We have several reports that workers from other industries will be part of the demonstration. Workers at the Hoover factory in Merthyr have voted to join the picket lines. Other factory workers are also coming forward and showing support. Buses from all over the Valleys are due to pour into the area. They are coming from far and wide. The Six Bells pit cannot be allowed to fall to these militant bastards.'

'Do you have a plan, sir?'

Merlyn stood and walked over to a bookshelf, plucking a dusty road atlas from the shelf. He opened up the atlas. 'We'll have rolling roadblocks and checkpoints all the way up the Heads of the Valley road coming from Abergavenny. There'll be a checkpoint at Black Rock. Then we'll have regular checkpoints on the new road that runs from Brynmawr to the Six Bells Colliery. According to our ground intelligence picketing miners have been stationed all along the old road. Stopping traffic to see if cars contain volunteer workers heading towards the colliery. We've had reports from drivers who use that road regularly. They have been stopped and intimidated by striking workers from Six Bells and other collieries.'

'Bastard militants, sir.'

Merlyn glanced at Benson. 'Indeed, they are, sergeant. There are several pubs along the old road running through Blaina, into Six Bells. The Coal Shed inn at Six Bells is a particular favourite with striking workers. It's a literal bottleneck on that part of the road. Very difficult to drive through when you have dozens of men blocking the road. Vehicles have had their windows smashed, trying to avoid picketing workers. You'll be stationed in that area. We will give you four hundred officers. You will disperse your officers throughout the area. A show of force should deter any striking miners who wish to cause disruption. I'm not expecting trouble, but you never know.'

'Supposing this demonstration goes ahead on St David's Day. How many miners do you think will turn up at this rally?'

'We're expecting at least two thousand people to attend. Not everyone will be striking workers. There will be women and children amongst them. This will make it very difficult for our officers to take action should any violence occur.'

'As far as I am concerned, anyone who tries to attack our officers is a potential target.'

Merlyn grinned. 'I like your attitude, Bob. You are to meet with Owain Lance, who will supply you with ground intelligence. He's infiltrated the miners' union. Gained their trust. He's using an alias. But he cannot reveal his identity. These miners are fanatical and unpredictable. There have been reports of working miners who have been dragged from pubs and severely beaten.'

'I'll make preparation to organise officers to patrol that area, sir.'

'You'll have to meet Lance somewhere that the miners won't use.'

'I have just the place, sir. The Agincourt hotel just outside Monmouth. It's far from the Valleys. No one will bother us there, sir.'

'Good, you'll meet up with Lance tomorrow night. He will brief you on the current situation. We need to show strength in the Valleys, Bob. We cannot let these militant idiots win. You are to use whatever force you deem necessary to put down any demonstrations that turn ugly.'

CHAPTER 4

Newport Central police station
Present day

'Nice one Andrew.' Fagan plucked a custard slice from the box of confectionaries Brooks bought from Greggs.

A photo of Alwyn Collier was stuck to the whiteboard. His profile picture was an official photograph from his assembly webpage.

'So what do we know about the deceased?' Fagan asked, before biting into his custard slice.

Watkins stared at his laptop. 'Alwyn Collier, sixty-eight years of age. Been an assembly member since 2007. He's the shadow minister for the environment and climate change. Also in line for the job of Welsh Secretary.'

'I thought that position always went to an MP?'

Watkins scrolled down. 'Apparently, the law is changing. He's met all kinds of people through the years. There's a picture here of Collier with Greta Thunberg?'

'Who?' Fagan asked.

'You know, that young girl who's always banging on about global warming.'

'I remember the stare she gave Trump.' Brooks remarked, smiling. 'At that climate change conference. If looks could kill.'

'He's also met David Attenborough,' Watkins mused.

'Everyone knows him.' Fagan said, glancing at Watkin's laptop.

'Very much a campaigner for the environment.' Watkins continued. 'According to his bio, Collier was a former coal miner at the Six Bells Colliery. He was made redundant in 1988 when the pit shut. Met his wife in the same year, and married her two years later in 1990. They moved to Neath in the same year. Collier got involved in local politics and won a seat in the local council.

He ran as a Conservative.' Watkins switched web pages. 'Collier was interviewed by Wales on Sunday two years ago, looking back on a life in politics. He reflected on the miners' strike. Collier worked through the strike and had to face daily attacks from miners who were on strike. When the pit closed, he used his redundancy money to buy his mother's house and attend further education.'

'My grandad was a miner.' Brooks revealed. 'At the Tower Colliery. He went on strike back then. Just about every miner throughout the Valleys walked out.'

'But not Collier, it seems.' Fagan mused.

Watkins continued. 'According to this article, Collier spoke about his decision to go into politics. He transitioned into the realm of local politics in 1991, seeking to heal the scars left by the 1984 strike and the community's need for growth. In 2007, Alwyn Collier achieved a significant milestone by winning a seat in the Welsh assembly. Again, representing the Conservative Party. He represented the constituency of Neath. In 2016 Collier stood in the Senedd election and won the seat for Blaina Gwent. In 2018, he moved from his home in Neath to Nantyglo. A move that was to prove controversial for his political career and personal life. Collier states, his move was a testament to his commitment to the goal of reuniting the communities split during the miners' strike. Throughout his political journey, Collier remained dedicated to his mission of healing the wounds inflicted by the miners' strike.'

'Collier's wife mentioned that following the move to the Valleys, their home was attacked.' Fagan interrupted.

'Not surprising, given what he represented during the strike.' Brooks said.

Fagan looked at him. 'Why is that?'

'He was a scab for starters. Those who worked through the strike were hated. Collier moving back to the Valleys probably pissed a lot of people off. My grandad would talk about the miners' strike as if it were yesterday.'

'Is your grandad still about?'

Brooks shook his head. 'He died last year.'

Fagan mulled over the information. 'So Collier was a former miner. He worked through the miners' strike. No doubt making a lot of enemies back then. Went into local politics, representing the Tories.'

'Probably another reason people didn't want him moving back to the Valleys.' Brooks said.

'What else does it say about his political career, Sean?'

Watkins focussed on his laptop. 'In 2017, Collier was elected as leader of the Conservative party for the Welsh Senedd. In May 2022, a leaked report to the South Wales Argus revealed party members were unhappy with Collier's leadership. Several allegations of bullying, harassment and misogyny had been made against his senior adviser, Geraint Taylor. Several Instagram messages had been leaked to the South Wales Argus. Detailing how unhappy party members were with Collier's leadership. Further controversy was to come when another senior adviser to Collier was convicted of creating indecent images of children. Sixty-five-year-old Falon Barret was given a two-year sentence and was placed on the sex offenders' register.'

'Stop there Sean.' Fagan interrupted for the second time. 'Falon Barret, did you say?'

'Yes, boss.'

Fagan tapped the name into the police database on his computer. 'Falon Barret was arrested last January for possession of indecent images of children. He was also charged with producing indecent images of children and distributing them.' He paused for a moment. 'He's currently serving time in Usk prison.'

'I found that article on Geraint Taylor, boss. Says here he was dismissed from his post in December 2022. Following a string of allegations of bullying and misogyny. Taylor appeared before a committee and was sacked from his post.' Watkins switched to another article. 'This gets juicy. Collier was exposed in 2019 for having an affair with a fellow assembly member, Victoria Armstrong.'

'He was exposed?' Fagan questioned.

Watkins nodded. 'CCTV images leaked to Wales on Sunday captured Collier in a passionate clinch with Armstrong.'

'Looks similar to the scandal that broke about Matt Hancock.' Fagan shoved the last of his custard slice into this mouth and gulped down his coffee. 'Right, let's focus on the man himself. Collier was a former miner who went into politics following the closure of the Six Bells pit. Moved back up to the Valleys amidst controversy. Anything else about his personal life?'

Watkins continued to read from the screen. 'Behind the public persona, Alwyn Collier is a family man. Married to Elizabeth, he is the father of two children. The scars of the 1984 strike extended beyond the political sphere, as he found himself estranged from his older brother. A consequence of their differing positions during that pivotal time. The strike also claimed the life of Alwyn's younger brother, Dafydd, a loss that undoubtedly left an indelible mark.'

'Collier had two brothers. I seem to recall his wife telling us he hadn't spoken to his older brother in decades. But she didn't say his name.'

'She didn't boss, no.'

'That will be the result of the miners' strike again.' Brooks mentioned. 'There were loads of families split apart by the strike. A lot of them still aren't talking.'

'Which means one of his brothers supported the strike. And Collier worked through the strike.' Fagan glanced at Watkins. 'That article states the strike claimed the life of Collier's younger brother, Dafydd.'

Watkins tapped the name into a search engine. 'Here we go, boss. Nineteen-year-old Dafydd Collier was killed on the way to work on 1st March 1985. The taxi he was travelling in was hit by a metal scaffolding pole dropped from a footbridge. A taxi driver, fifty-three-year-old Sean Price was also killed. Four men were arrested following the incident.' Watkins glanced at Fagan. 'You're going to love this, boss. The four men arrested were Martin Cooper, Amlod Llewellyn, Bryn Collier.'

'Right, so we now know the name of the other brother, Bryn Collier. Who's the fourth man arrested?'

'You ready for this, boss?'

Fagan gulped down the last of his coffee, nodding.

'Lloyd Bevan.'

'You're joking. Lloyd Bevan, as in the First Minister for Wales.'

Watkins nodded. 'That's what it says here, boss.'

'Everyone hates that bloke at the moment.' Brooks said. 'Ever since he introduced the twenty miles an hour speed limit. There are even rumours he wants to introduce a fifty mile an hour speed limit on the main roads.'

'So, they were all arrested following the accident. What happened after that?' Fagan asked.

Watkins studied the screen. 'They were tried at Cardiff Magistrate's court in October 1985, but were acquitted because of lack of evidence.' Watkins scanned the article. 'According to their defence lawyer.' Watkins looked at Fagan. 'Malcolm Barry. The police investigation was flawed. Three days after the trial started, they were acquitted.'

'So Lord Barry, who lives out by Skenfrith Castle, was their defence lawyer. I see he's wriggled himself out of having any involvement with the murder of Robert Turner.'

'Slippery bastard.'

'He is one slippery bastard.' Fagan agreed. 'What about the case involving Dafydd Collier and Sean Price?'

Watkins carried out a quick search on the police database. 'Still a cold case, boss. According to police records, the case was shelved in 1995 because of insufficient resources to carry on an investigation. No one has touched it in nearly thirty years. The police files on this case aren't exactly full of information. A lot of the information is missing.'

Fagan leant back in his chair, rubbing his hands together. 'Looks like another can of worms, boys. What do we have so far? One cold case from nearly forty years ago, and the murder of Alwyn Collier last night.'

'You think there could be a connection between Collier's death last night and the death of his younger brother forty years ago?'

Fagan considered Watkins' question. 'At this moment, anything is possible. Collier was a high-profile assembly member. We'll pull the case on the murder of Dafydd Collier and Sean Price out of mothballs, but keep it on the back burner.'

'What's your thinking there, boss?'

'I'm just curious to see who crawls out of the woodwork. If it shows up on anyone's radar that we've pulled the case out of mothballs. For now, let's focus on the murder of Collier.' Fagan got up and marched over to the whiteboard. He pointed at Collier's picture. 'Sixty-eight-year-old Alwyn Collier found in the Keepers Pond last night. According to the initial examination, Collier had been assaulted.'

Brooks' phone pinged. 'Forensics have counted the money in the satchel they fished from the Keepers. In all fifty grand.'

'A lot of money to be carrying in a satchel.' Watkins remarked.

Fagan nodded. 'What did you make of Collier's wife and daughter?'

'On edge, I would say, boss.'

Fagan nodded. 'I got the impression not all is well in paradise. According to the daughter, Collier caught a train to Cardiff Central, instead of driving.'

'His daughter also mentioned Collier complained about taking the train.'

'His wife said he phoned her when he reached Cardiff Central. But after that, he went dark. He was due to meet with a committee.' Fagan inhaled. 'Shit.' He cursed, staring at the lack of information on the whiteboard.

'What's up, boss?'

Fagan looked back at Watkins. 'Politics, that's what. Collier was an assembly member. A man with a past by the looks. What's the betting we'll be bogged down with political bullshit?' Fagan gathered his thoughts. 'His wife also mentioned it wasn't the first time he stayed out overnight. Did you notice how agitated she became mentioning that fact?'

Watkins nodded. 'He was exposed in the media for having an affair with another assembly member?'

'At sixty-eight?' Brooks sounded doubtful.

'Oi, us older ones can still get it up, I'll have you know,' Fagan playfully scalded Brooks. 'Just because Collier was in his sixties doesn't mean he didn't have lead in the old pencil. You youngsters make out you're the only ones getting laid. I'm nearly fifty-eight, but I can still keep it up with the best of them.'

Both Watkins and Brooks laughed.

Fagan looked at the whiteboard. 'So Collier arrives at the station. I'm assuming after he phoned his wife he went straight to the Senedd.'

'The train from Ebbw Vale arrived in Cardiff at eight forty-two.' Brooks was trawling train timetables.

'Let's start pulling credit card records and his phone usage.' Fagan suggested. 'We need to pull all CCTV from Cardiff Central to see if he's anywhere on camera. Find out if there is any CCTV footage of Collier at the Senedd. Did the Senedd send a car, or did he catch a taxi or Uber? There's a shed load of information to trawl through. Did he have an office at the Senedd? If he did, then he'd have a personal assistant. He would have had a schedule for yesterday, so we need a list of all meetings he attended.' Fagan pondered the moment. 'He was due to attend some kind of committee hearing in the afternoon. We need to find out more about that. Because of who he is, Griffiths will probably give us extra bodies on this. The last thing he wants is a dead assembly member on his patch. Andrew, get hold of Stacey and tell her to get out to the Collier's house this afternoon. Hopefully, a couple of uniforms will be guarding the house by now.' Fagan walked back to his chair and threw his jacket on. 'Sean, you're with me.'

Watkins stood and grabbed his jacket.

'Andrew, I want you to pull that case on Collier's younger brother and the taxi driver who were killed in 1985. Do nothing else on record. See what you can find out through the media, Google or Wikipedia. Also grab as much CCTV footage as you can from Cardiff Central.' Fagan grabbed a jam doughnut out of the Greggs box. 'Sean, you're driving.'

Watkins grabbed a chocolate éclair. 'Where we off, boss?'

Fagan munched on the doughnut. 'The Senedd building in Cardiff.'

CHAPTER 5

Blaina – South Wales – 1985

Tara Jones entered the living room, holding her baby. 'What are you doing?' She asked her husband, who was tying his bootlaces.

'What's it look like I'm doing? I'm going to work,' Malcolm Jones replied.

A look of panic flashed across Tara's face. 'You can't go to work, Mal. Lloyd will have your guts for garters if you cross the picket lines.'

Jones looked at his wife. 'What bloody choice do I have, eh, love?'

'You stand with the boys on the picket lines. That's what choice you have. If you go to work, we'll be labelled as scabs. I'm helping Donna later on today. We're organising the girls for a rally in the park later this week. If Donna finds out you've gone to work, she'll have a hissy fit. The girls will bloody chastise me. I've done a lot for you boys over the last several months. I've worked really hard.'

'Well, I'm sorry, love, but situations change.'

'Mal, listen to me. If you cross that picket line, then it'll be over for us. We'll have to move from this area. Look at what happened to Tracy and John. When he crossed the pickets, the boys put him in hospital. They moved away last week because no one would tolerate scabs living in the community. I don't want that. Mam and dad won't talk to us if you go down the pit. I don't want to undo the hard work I've put into the cause over the last year.'

'Jesus, Tara, can you even hear yourself sometimes? The cause is a load of bollocks. Everyone is talking about going back to work. They reckon the strike is going to be over in a few weeks.

Thatcher isn't going to budge.'

'Thatcher will break, eventually.' Tara was steadfast in her opinion. 'The miners will get what they deserve. If you go back to work, then you're just letting her win.'

'For Christ's sake, Tara, Thatcher won't budge, and neither will Scargill. It's not about the miners anymore, it's about those two and their bloody egos.'

'But you can't go back to work, Mal. All you're doing is letting everyone down.'

Jones threw his arms in the air. 'Tell me what I'm supposed to do, then. How I can fix all this?'

'We fix this by standing together. Solidarity, that's what will get us through this.'

'Will solidarity put food on the table? Will solidarity pay the bills? Jesus, d'you know who you sound like when you go on about solidarity? That twat of a brother of yours, that's who.'

'Don't call Lloyd a twat.' Tara raised her voice. 'He's done a lot for you over the past year.'

The baby whimpered.

'Come on, love. You even said he can get obsessive. I'm tired Tara. I'm tired of the struggle. I'm tired of having no money, no food in the cupboard.'

'We're all tired, Mal.' Tara cut her husband off. 'Tired of Thatcher and her fucking jackboots. Trying to destroy the working class. And the mining communities throughout the Valleys. We can't let her do that.'

'She's the bloody Prime Minister. She can do whatever she wants. And right now, she wants to shut as many pits as possible.'

'The miners won't allow that?'

Jones pointed at the television. 'You need to stop watching Scargill on the news.'

'He's only looking out for the welfare of the workers.'

'Jesus fucking Christ, Tara. You're getting sucked into the lies he's spouting. Scargill doesn't give a shit about the miners. All he wants to do is create chaos. He'll end up destroying the NUM. More people are seeing right through him. All the rallies he's attending. Pretending to give a shit about the working class. All he's doing is feathering his own nest.'

'Have you been talking to that dickhead, Alwyn Collier? Is that what this is all about? The scab bastard who's been crossing the picket lines for the past several months. Lloyd has got his eye on him. Him and the boys are going to teach that fucking scab a lesson he won't forget in a hurry.'

'So now it comes down to this, does it? Your brother having to resort to violence. He's no better than the police bastards. Look what they did to the miners at Orgreave.'

'You better not walk out that door,' Tara seethed.

Jones glared back at his wife. 'Don't you understand? It's over!' He yelled.

The baby screamed.

Tara nursed her son, trying to calm him down.

'We've no fucking money left. What are we supposed to do, live on fresh air? The aid packages from your brother stopped weeks ago. Your mam and dad can't help us. Neither can mine.' He looked at his screaming son. 'We haven't eaten in two days. You're about to run out of baby food. No one is going to help us. We are on our own. We can't go on living like this. It's killing us.'

'It will get better,' Tara insisted.

'When?' Jones exploded. 'We need it to get better now. Not whenever this fucking dispute is over.' Jones stood and walked over to his wife. 'I thought the strike was worth it at the beginning. I know what's at stake here, Tara. I know Thatcher wants to destroy our way of life. But what power do the miners actually have? If the pits are no longer making money, they're bound to close.'

'I promise you, Mal. If you go down that pit, I will tell Lloyd and the boys.' Tara warned.

Jones turned and walked over to a sideboard, grabbing a pile of letters. 'Look at this, Tara.' He waved the letters in front of her face. 'This is what's happening now. The electricity board is going to cut us off because we're behind on payments. The water rates people are going to cut us off if we don't pay the bill. The council is going to evict us if we don't have the money for rent within the next few weeks. Rediffusion is coming tomorrow to take the video recorder and telly because we owe them. The washing machine people are coming next week. We've got bills from Littlewoods catalogue. We've got bills from just about everyone demanding money. Our social security has been refused because of the bloody strike.' Jones gritted his teeth. 'Pretty soon, this house will be empty and we'll have to sit on the bloody floor. We've no fucking money, Tara. And you're threatening to go to Lloyd and tell him I'm going back to work.'

'What about the promise you made the boys?' Tara argued. 'You promised to stand with them. It's all about solidarity.'

'Jesus fucking Christ, will you stop saying that!' Jones screamed. 'What about solidarity between man and wife? What about standing together as a family?'

'Mam, dad, why are you shouting?' A young girl appeared in the living room doorway.

Tara turned to her daughter and smiled. 'Hey sweetheart, you shouldn't be out of bed this early in the morning.'

'I heard you shouting.'

Jones smiled at his daughter. 'Go back to bed, scamp. Me and mam will try to be quiet.'

Tara handed the baby to her daughter. 'Take your baby brother upstairs, please, sweetheart.'

Jones listened as his daughter climbed the stairs and closed the door of her bedroom. He pointed towards the doorway. 'Can't you see what this is doing to the kids? Arwen can tell when something is up. She's old enough to understand we're under pressure.'

'It's only you doing the shouting, Mal. The rest of us are remaining calm.'

'Let me ask you this. How long d'you think we can hold out?'

'As long as it bloody takes.' Tara answered.

Jones waved the bills in front of her. 'See, that's your brother talking. As long as it takes. When will that be? After they've cut off the electric and water. Or when the council evicts us. Or will it finally sink in after they take the kids into care? That's what's going to happen if we don't deal with this shit now. We need money.'

'Oh right, okay then, let's forget the cause and think of ourselves. Instead of the boys who are fighting for a better wage packet.'

'Jesus, you don't see it, do you? All you see is what Lloyd sees. Tell me, Tara. Is his opinion more important than feeding our kids?'

Tara stared back at her anguished husband.

'Are you even going to answer the question? What's more important, Lloyd's opinion, or the welfare of our kids.'

'That's not fair, Mal.'

'What's not fair? Me asking you to make a choice between feeding our children, or supporting that militant brother of yours.'

Tara planted her hands on her hips. 'Now you sound like that heartless bitch, Thatcher.'

'Fuck off, don't be absurd.'

'It's not me who's being absurd, Mal, it's you. If you go down the pit this morning, you will undermine everything the boys have worked for.'

'But what have they fucking achieved? Nothing, that's what. There wasn't even a proper ballot to strike. Those fuckers at Cortonwood just walked out on Scargill's orders. Even Kinnock has criticised Scargill for what he's done.'

'You can't turn your back on the boys, Mal. If you do that, no one will speak to us again.'

Jones sighed. 'Can't you see the damage this is doing to us, Tara? We are arguing every single day now. I don't want to argue anymore. I am tired of arguing. We're on our knees. If you have a better solution to our money problems, then I'm all ears.'

An expression of apprehension appeared on Tara's face.

'What?'

'I'm going to get some money today.'

'Where from?'

'Dale Clint said he would tide us over until we get back on our feet. Until the dispute ends.'

Jones slumped down on the sofa, burying his head in his hands. 'Fucking hell.' He rocked back and forth. 'Fucking hell.

Why did you do that, Tara?'

'He said we can repay him slowly. He's giving out money to a lot of the families who are struggling.'

'Dale Clint is the biggest loan shark in the Valleys, you stupid bitch! D'you have any idea what you've done?'

'I can get a part-time job. You can look after the kids while you're on strike. It will help pay him back.'

'How much are you going to borrow?' Jones demanded to know.

Tara hesitated before answering. 'Two hundred quid.'

'Two hundred fucking quid!' Jones exploded. 'Do you know the interest he'll charge you? He'll want a thousand quid back.'

Tara shook her head. 'No, Dale only wants five hundred.'

Jones gritted his teeth. 'It doesn't fucking matter, Tara. Whether it's two hundred or a thousand.' Jones pointed at the pile of bills. 'We're up to our necks in debt. And now you pull this shit. We already owe hundreds to everyone. Water, electric, rent, Rediffusion, catalogues. What we don't need is for you to go to Dale Clint, asking for a handout. Knowing full well we can't afford it.'

'The money I get today will help get us through the next few weeks. It will get us some food.'

'What good is it if the council boots us out for not paying the rent, Tara? There are bills that need to be paid. The only way we're going to get back on our feet is for me to go back to work.'

'You can't just turn your back on the boys, they need all the support they can get.'

'What about support for us, Tara? Have you thought about that? What about support for our family? I was in the pub last night talking to a few of the boys. More of us are getting fucked off with the situation. Now you've just made things worse by going to that twat Clint and lending money off him. Gary Trinder lent money a few years back. When he couldn't afford to pay it back, Dale went to Gary's place with his brother Derek and smashed him up. Gary used to be one of the boys. Now he's too afraid to go out the door. If you borrow money off the Clint brothers, it won't be you they'll come looking for when we can't pay them back. It will be me.' Jones pointed at himself. 'I have tried everything to take care of this family over the past several months. I'm out of options. I'm at the end of my tether. We can't go on like this.'

'And what am I supposed to tell mam and dad? How am I going to explain this when they see you going into work? There are people grassing up miners who are going back to work.'

'I know the risks, Tara. It's not like I'll be walking to work. Dickie Green and a few of us are meeting a bus.' Jones threw his donkey jacket on. He looked at his wife. 'I'm not doing this because I don't believe in the cause anymore. I'm doing it because I've no other choice.'

Tara glared back at her husband, folding her arms. 'Don't expect tea to be on the table when you get home.'

'How can you have tea waiting for me when we've no food in the cupboard?' He turned and opened the front door.

CHAPTER 6

The Senedd – Cardiff Bay
Present day

Fagan watched a crowd of journalists armed with TV cameras and smartphones, swarming around a man standing on the steps of the Senedd building.

Watkins checked his phone. 'Looks like the cat is out of the bag about Collier, boss. Griffiths made an announcement half an hour ago.'

'Why the bloody hell did he do that? I doubt if his wife has had time to identify the body yet.'

'Collier and all the assembly members have offices in that building.' Watkins pointed at a building further on down the water's edge. 'His personal assistant's name is Tracie Morris.'

Fagan looked around the bay. The afternoon sun reflected off the water. 'Nice area to work. This place used to be derelict.'

Watkins' phone pinged. 'Talking of Stacey, boss. She's with Collier's wife and daughter at the Prince Charles in Merthyr. They're about to make the formal identification of Collier's body.'

'Let's go and have a chat with Collier's PA. Perhaps she can shed light on his movements yesterday.'

Fagan and Watkins took several minutes to gain access to the Senedd office building. Despite showing their IDs a stern-looking security guard made three phone calls before allowing them access to the rest of the building.

'I bloody hate private security firms.' Fagan grumbled. 'They're a law unto themselves. And half their staff couldn't guard a local Spar shop, let alone a building like this.'

Tracie Morris was sitting at her desk. She'd been crying. A colleague who was comforting her spotted Fagan and Watkins as they approached.

Fagan pulled his ID from his pocket. 'DI Fagan, DS Watkins, with Gwent police.'

Tracie's companion scrutinised their ID. 'How come you're from Gwent police? I thought South Wales police would handle this.'

'Mr Collier's body was found on our patch,' Fagan answered.

Tracie began sobbing again.

'We need to speak with you about the last time you saw Mr Collier,' Watkins said.

'Tracie is in no fit state to talk.'

'I'm sorry you are?' Fagan looked at the woman.

'Tanya Glover.'

'Considering what's happened, Tanya, I'm sure you know this is a difficult time for everyone. Particularly for those who were close to Mr Collier. Were you one of those people?'

Tanya showed frustration at Fagan's question. 'Look, I know you have a job to do. But as you can see, Tracie can't talk to anyone at the moment.'

'With all due respect, Ms Glover.'

'It's just Tanya.' She cut Fagan off. 'Just Tanya, do you understand? I hate that Ms, Miss and Mrs crap. I'm just Tanya.'

Fagan could tell she was trying to be obstructive. 'I will say this once, *Tanya*. Either you let us speak with Tracie or I'll call security and you'll be frogmarched out of this building. I'm looking for a murderer, and frankly, you're in my way.'

Tanya stared back for a few seconds. 'Fine, but if I hear any of you have been abusive towards Tracie, then I'll make sure you're both strung up.'

As she marched away, Fagan looked at Watkins, rolling his eyes. He focussed his attention on Tracie. 'Is there somewhere you'd feel more comfortable talking, Tracie?' He spotted an official photograph of Collier on the wall. 'Does this building have a canteen or is there a café nearby we can talk? I'm sure you don't want to be in here.'

Tracie nodded.

Fagan savoured the taste of the coffee he had just paid

thirteen quid for. The seagulls screeched overhead. They had found a small coffee shop on the waterfront. Although the coffee was good, Fagan guessed the café owners were charging more for the view than the coffee. He spotted Tanya, who stood several hundred yards away, watching their every move.

Tracie picked up her cup with a shaking hand.

'I'm going to ask you a series of questions regarding Mr Collier's movements yesterday. Is that okay?' Fagan asked tentatively.

Tracie managed a nod.

'Could you tell me when Alwyn first arrived at his office yesterday?'

'Around half-past nine, I think. Yeah, I remember now, because he was annoyed at being half an hour late. Alwyn always arrives at the office early.'

'Did he give a reason why he was late?'

'No. But he was annoyed that he had to catch the train into Cardiff.'

'What was his schedule yesterday morning? Can you remember?'

Tracie thumbed the screen on her phone. 'The first thing he usually does when he gets in is go through his e-mails. Then at ten o'clock he had a meeting with Delwyn Horlor.'

'And who is he, Tracie?' Watkins asked.

'Delwyn is the assembly member for Torfaen.'

'Do you know what their meeting was about?'

'They were discussing a proposed congestion charge the First Minister is planning for the city centre. Alwyn was opposed to it.'

Fagan jotted down notes. 'How long did the meeting last?'

'About two hours, I think. There was a lot to discuss.'

'Does Mr Horlor have an office in the same building?'

'No, he's head of the Unite union for Wales. He has an office on Cathedral Road.'

'After he had a meeting with Mr Horler, where did he go?'

'I think he went to lunch, but I can't be sure. Alwyn was a creature of habit. He always had lunch in the canteen. But yesterday he didn't.'

'How do you know this?'

'Another assembly member he usually had lunch with turned up at the office and asked where he was.'

'Who is this other assembly member?'

'Victoria Armstrong, they have lunch daily. However, yesterday Alwyn disappeared for a couple of hours. I tried to ring him because he was due to appear in front of a committee yesterday afternoon.'

'But he didn't?' Watkins speculated.

Tracie nodded. 'Yes, he did.'

'What was this committee meeting about?'

'The committee was asking for Alwyn to resign because of several incidents involving bullying and inappropriate behaviour of his senior staff. There was also an incident resulting in one of his staff being arrested and charged with indecent images of children. Alwyn had to face the committee and answer questions about his handling of the events.'

'The man convicted of downloading indecent images. Would that be Falon Barret?'

Tracie nodded.

'How well did you know him?'

'Not all that well. I used to steer clear of him. A lot of us girls did. He used to creep a lot of people out.'

'What about Geraint Taylor? Did you have anything to do with him?'

'I had to deal with him on a daily basis. I lost count of the number of times he made a pass at me.'

'Do you know how old Taylor is?'

'In his mid-forties. But he acted like someone in his mid-twenties.'

'Did Taylor show any interest in other women in the Senedd?'

Tracie nodded. 'It had been going on for about eighteen months. Geraint would try it on with just about anyone who walked into the building with a skirt on.'

'I take it people reported him?' Watkins enquired.

'Repeatedly.' Tracie replied.

'Was Alwyn aware of what was going on?'

'Yeah, but he never seemed too bothered about it. He made a comment once. Boys will be boys. But as time went by, Geraint's behaviour got worse. Not just the way he would come on to the women. But also the way he treated everybody. I know two people who quit their jobs because of that bloke. He even told me once that he was untouchable, and no one had the balls to take him on.'

'What eventually forced him out?' Fagan asked.

'We all wrote a joint letter to Alwyn, raising our concerns. Alwyn said he would look into Geraint's behaviour and address the issue. But nothing came of it. To be honest, some of us thought Alwyn was too scared of Geraint to do anything. When the issue wasn't addressed, a letter was sent to the First Minister.'

'Lloyd Bevan?'

'Yes.' Tracie said. 'At first, we thought he was going to ignore us. But then Lloyd had us all in a meeting. He gave us a chance to air our concerns about Geraint. A few weeks after that, Geraint stepped down from his post. He didn't even seem to care.'

'What was your relationship with Alwyn like?'

'It was good.' Tracie sipped from her mug. 'Four years ago, when I first got the post, I hardly saw Alwyn in person because of the pandemic. I even had the job interview through Zoom. Alwyn was in self-isolation because of his health. When the lockdown finally lifted, Alwyn would buy me lunch every day. He hated the lockdown. Alwyn said people had become more divided than ever.'

'Did Alwyn ever mention having brothers?'

'Once.' Tracie revealed. 'He had a little too much to drink at the Christmas party last year. We were walking along the bay.'

'Just the two of you?'

'Yes, but I didn't fancy him, if that's what you're thinking.'

'It didn't even enter my mind, Tracie.'

'I'm sorry, it's just because I was his personal assistant. You know what people are like. The minute they see you laughing and joking with your boss they make all kinds of things up.' Tracie glanced further up the bay where Tanya was standing.

Fagan looked in the same direction. 'You were saying about

Alwyn mentioning his brothers.'

Tracie nodded. 'Alwyn never used to drink. I knew he was a recovering alcoholic. But last year he did have a drink. That's when he told me about his younger brother, Dafydd. He was killed years ago. Before I was born. Alwyn started to cry when he talked about it. Said it was all his fault. He said he'd let his mam and dad down.'

'What about his other brother, Bryn?'

'When he mentioned his older brother, he became angry. He said he deserved to be rotting in jail.'

Fagan scribbled away. 'What about this committee he was due to face yesterday? Do you know what the outcome was?'

'No.' Tracie shook her head. 'He never returned.'

'Do you know who sat on this committee?'

'It was supposed to be a closed affair. But I know that Lloyd Bevan headed up the committee. Him and Alwyn were bitter rivals. They hated each other. Lloyd would often criticise Alwyn on the Senedd floor. One of the girls once told me they worked together at a coal mine a long time ago and had a massive falling out.'

'Was Alwyn popular on the Senedd floor?' Watkins asked.

'Yeah, he was popular with the younger assembly members. But most of the older ones didn't like him. I heard one of them arguing one day last year. Michael Davies, Assembly member for Monmouthshire, was having a massive argument with him.' Tracie paused, recalling when she saw them arguing. 'He burst into Alwyn's office one day last year. Michael called Alwyn a scab. I asked Alwyn what Michael meant by calling him a scab. Alwyn said it was nothing and that it was a long time ago.'

'Alwyn obviously met a lot of people during his time as Assembly Member?'

'Yeah, Alwyn was huge on environmental issues. He was always campaigning for the environment. He met Greta Thunberg last year when she visited Wales.'

'Must have got a lot of mail. Including hate mail?'

'Well, yeah. Alwyn said it came with the territory of being a politician. We'd get the odd occasion when someone would phone in pretending to be someone else, then go off on a rant. Whenever Alwyn was out and about on public engagements, he'd get heckled. But he was used to that sort of thing. It was like water off a duck's back. We had a spate of incidents last year where someone was sending letters with human shit in them. They had the assembly address on the front of the envelopes. But instead of Alwyn's name, it always had the Scab of Blaina Gwent Assembly Member. It made me sick the first time I opened the first letter. The person who sent the letters would use a jiffy envelope.'

'Besides the faeces, did they contain anything else?'

'Usually a letter calling Alwyn a scab and a traitor to the cause.'

'Cause?'

Tracie shook her head. 'I had no idea what it meant. I'm guessing it had something to do with when Alwyn was a miner.'

'How many letters did he receive?'

'Ten in all. Over a six-month period.' Tracie replied. 'Alwyn involved the police, but they weren't interested. They said unless the letters contained something threatening to life, like a bomb, there wasn't much they could do about it.'

'Did Alwyn ever receive death threats?'

'Not what I'm aware of. But sometimes Alwyn was very secretive.'

'Can you think of anything else that might help us with our enquiries?' Watkins asked.

Tracie thought for a few moments before remembering something. 'Last month, he had his satchel stolen.'

Fagan recalled the satchel recovered from the Keepers. 'Where from?'

'It was on the train on the way into Cardiff. He reported it to the police.'

'When was this exactly, Tracie?'

'Nearly four weeks ago.'

'Do you know if the satchel contained anything of value?'

'No.' Tracie shook her head. 'But Alwyn was annoyed because the satchel contained a speech he was about to deliver to the

Senedd.'

Fagan closed his notebook and finished his coffee.

'Do you have any idea who murdered him?' Tracie asked.

'Not as yet. But I have a team working flat out to find out who did this.'

'I saw it on my Facebook feed. He didn't deserve what happened to him. His wife and daughter must be devastated.'

Fagan nodded. 'Yeah, they are.'

'I need to get back to the office. I need to tie up Alwyn's affairs.'

'Thank you for talking to us, Tracie.'

She hurried out of the door.

Fagan watched as she walked back towards the office building. Tanya was waiting for her. Even from a distance, Fagan could see Tanya was giving Tracie an intense interrogation.

'What you reckon, boss?'

Fagan sighed. 'I reckon we're going to spend the next week up to our necks in political bullshit.'

'I noticed Tracie mentioned Collier had lunch with Victoria Armstrong daily. Might be why his wife got funny when she mentioned he stayed out overnight on the odd occasion.'

'We'll have to interview Armstrong sooner or later.' Fagan glanced at his watch. 'Come on, let's go and see this Delwyn Horlor.'

CHAPTER 7

Unite Union – Cathedral road – Cardiff

Fagan and Watkins introduced themselves.

'I had a feeling you boys would knock on my door.' Delwyn Horlor said. 'Everyone is devastated about what's happened.'

'According to Alwyn Collier's schedule, you had a meeting with him yesterday morning.' Watkins said.

Horlor nodded. 'Yes, we met here. Had a late breakfast together in the cafeteria.'

'How did he seem?'

'On edge, frustrated. All the things associated with a man who was about to see his political career go down the toilet.'

'So you're aware Mr Collier was due to face an investigative committee?' Fagan stated.

'Everyone knew about it. Even though it was supposed to be behind closed doors.'

'Why behind closed doors?'

'I don't know the ins and outs. Despite our meeting yesterday, Alwyn was still secretive about the hearing.' Horlor explained. 'It was no secret Lloyd Bevan wanted him out of the Senedd. They would constantly face off against each other on the Senedd floor. It was a political pantomime between them. Often coming to heated debate.'

'Did it ever come to blows off the Senedd floor?'

Horler took a deep breath. 'I wouldn't say blows, but they had their fair share of screaming matches.'

'They hated each other?'

'I'd say it was more of a case of Bevan hating Collier.'

'Why do you think that was?'

'Lloyd and Alwyn had a long history. They worked together at the Six Bells pit up the Valleys.'

'We've talked to Collier's assistant. She said Collier was often referred to as a scab by other members of the Senedd.'

'Yeah.' Horlor admitted. 'Alwyn didn't have many friends amongst the older assembly members. Some of whom are former coal miners.'

Fagan glanced at a black and white framed photo of Horlor with Arthur Scargill. 'Including you.'

Horlor turned and studied the picture for several seconds. 'The good old days, or the bad old days. Depending which way you want to look at it. That picture was taken at the pit where I worked. Just before the strike broke out in 1984. The strike to end all strikes, as some of us called it.'

'Did you walk out with the rest of the miners?'

'I did.'

'How long were you on strike for?'

'I stuck it out till the bitter end. I was young and still living with my parents. We were out for nearly a year. Before returning with our tail between our legs.' Dafydd should be a member of the union

'Why do you say that?'

'The strike achieved nothing for the miners. But for the Thatcher government, it spelt the end of the unions and the working class. Thatcher was determined to crush every last one of us.'

'Collier worked through the strike, didn't he?'

'Yes.'

'Did you hold a grudge because he worked?'

'Good Lord no. Life is too short to hold grudges, DI Fagan. The recent pandemic taught me that. Unfortunately, that wasn't the case for Alwyn Collier. Lloyd Bevan was a staunch union supporter, amongst other things. Many people hated Alwyn for working through the strike. Bevan made it no secret that Alwyn was a scab.'

'Other things?' Watkins said.

'Lloyd is very passionate about what he believes in. He's been spearheading a referendum ever since he was elected First Minister in 2018. Wanting to break away from the government in

London. He's due to give a speech this week about the referendum. Ever since Nicola Sturgeon stepped down, Bevan seems more determined to succeed, where she failed.'

'How would you describe your relationship with Collier?'

'We were friends both on and off the Senedd floor.'

'This is despite you being opposite on the political stage.' Fagan remarked.

Horlor pursed his lips. 'Despite what most people might think. It's possible to have a friendship with someone despite their political views.'

'Have you been friends for long?'

'About ten years. Before becoming an assembly member, I was a lowly councillor in my local constituency.'

'Where was that?'

'Pontypool.' Horlor answered. 'When the Senedd elections came around, I was encouraged to run for assembly member. I'll be honest, I never expected to win a seat. But here I am.'

'What was Collier's relationship like with other members of the Senedd?'

'Alwyn got on with the younger Senedd members. Bevan hated him the most. Lloyd would constantly remind Alwyn how much of a traitor he was during the strike.'

'But that was forty years ago.' Fagan pointed out.

Horlor nodded. 'Many of Lloyd Bevan's party members are from the Valleys. They were miners during the strike or they're from mining families. Fathers and grandfathers who were miners.'

'Did anyone have a problem with you being friends with Collier?'

'Yes, unfortunately. Even though I'm Labour, I don't toe the party line like the others. I serve the people, not the inward interests of the Senedd.'

'How do you mean?'

'Bevan's determination to hold a referendum borders on obsessive. He expects all the assembly members to fall in line and support him. I guess it's a throwback to his days in the National Union of Mineworkers. Bevan was a union convenor. He had a lot of influence over the miners back in the day. However, I have no intention of supporting a referendum next year. Bevan is only campaigning for his own self-interests and not the interests of the Welsh people. I don't agree with the UK government on most of their policies. But holding a referendum to break away from the UK government serves no one's interest.' Horlor smiled. 'I'm sorry. I have been rehearsing that speech so many times.'

'What was your meeting about yesterday?'

'We discussed the Senedd's proposal for a congestion charge in the city centre. But Alwyn was very much against it. And so was I. Motorists are hard pressed at the moment, given the cost of living. The last thing they need is to have to pay to drive through this city. However, Bevan had the backing of most of the Senedd. So it's only a matter of time now.'

'Did he mention the committee he was due to appear in front of?'

'Yes, but like I just said. He didn't go into any specific detail. I could tell it weighed heavily on his mind. He knew Bevan was gunning for him. Alwyn had been a constant thorn in Bevan's side since he was elected First Minister back in 2018. Bevan only won by a narrow majority. Alwyn was about to take on the role as Secretary of State for Wales. Another reason why Bevan hated him.'

'Were you aware of the bullying accusations regarding Collier's senior staff?'

'I was aware of it, yes. But to be honest with you, DI Fagan, I believe Alwyn was being set up.'

'Care to explain?'

'Have you got the rest of the week?' Horlor threw a question back. 'The Senedd has always maintained the image that it's a beacon for democracy and fairness. Ever since Bevan took office, it has been anything but. I've even thought about resigning a few times.'

'Have you ever been the victim of bullying?'

'Definitely not. I'm too old to put up with that kind of thing. Everyone knows it on the Senedd floor.'

'What about others?'

Horlor took his time answering, before nodding. 'There is a culture of bullying, misogyny and prejudice at the Senedd. I have raised the issue frequently. But my concerns have always been ignored. I can tell you that most of the bullying is from Lloyd and his staff. They expect you to fall in line and accept the way they deal with things. If you have any complaints, they are handled by his personal assistant, Tanya Glover.'

'We encountered her earlier on.'

Horlor let out a snort of derision. 'Don't let Tanya catch you using the term *her* as a description. It's them, or they. Or as Tanya likes to say. *It's them, they or the highway*. She's a nasty piece of work who likes to collect dirt on everybody. And those who are clean, she'll do everything she can to manipulate them. She's manipulated some of the female Senedd members into bed, and blackmailed a few of them. She is one of Lloyd's most staunch supporters of the referendum. She's bulletproof. There are people who have tried to get dirt on her. But like shit on a wet shovel, Tanya slides right off.'

'Getting back to Alwyn Collier. How was his behaviour yesterday when you had a meeting with him?'

'He was on edge and nervous about having to face the committee. I advised Alwyn he should fight whatever trumped up charge Lloyd was trying to accuse him of.' Horlor paused. 'He did say one thing that made me think. He said he was being forced to play a trump card earlier than he expected.'

'Do you know what he meant by this?'

'No, sorry.'

'How regularly did you and Mr Collier meet?'

'Twice a month.' Horlor answered. 'We'd always meet here. Alwyn felt every time he had lunch in the canteen at the Senedd offices his every move was being scrutinised. Especially when he had lunch with Victoria Armstrong. The female assembly member he was exposed for having an affair with.'

'Did he ever mention hate mail he had been receiving?'

'Yes, he'd sometimes complain about the number of letters he would get in the post. Calling him a scab. Then there were the series of parcels he was getting last year containing human shit.

Alwyn went to the police about the matter. But nothing was done about it. It left him a little disgruntled with the police.'

'Do you know much about Mr Collier's past? Regarding family members?'

'If you're talking about what happened to his brother Dafydd, only what I have read over the years. Alwyn wouldn't talk about it. In 1985, his youngest brother was killed in a road accident. It was on the day of the Battle of Six Bells.'

'Battle of Six Bells?' Watkins asked.

'It was also known at the miners' last stand. It happened on St David's Day 1985. About two and a half thousand picketers marched on Six Bells Colliery. The police had twice that amount. We were hemmed in. It was total chaos.'

'You were part of it?' Fagan questioned.

'Yes. I also bared witness to the Battle of Orgreave. At Six Bells, I saw what was going to happen. A few of us decided it wasn't worth getting arrested. So we abandoned the march. By lunchtime the police had contained most of the miners in a small area. Hundreds of men were dragged away and slung into cells. There were stories of police brutality. Miners getting the shit kicked out of them. By the early afternoon it was all over. The demonstration had been quashed, and the police had won a final victory against the miners and the unions. However, a few diehard unionists decided to make one last stand. They escaped the police and headed towards a bridge that spanned a main road. A taxi was travelling along the road, escorted by two police vehicles. As the car was about to pass under, a scaffolding pole was thrown from the bridge, hitting the taxi. The driver was killed outright. Apparently, the pole smashed through his chest. The car then flipped over and rolled several times. Alwyn's brother Dafydd was in the front. He wasn't wearing a seatbelt. Neither were the two men sat in the back. All three passengers suffered serious injuries. Dafydd hung on for a few days, but he died of his injuries.'

'They arrested Alwyn's brother a few days later, in connection with the incident.' Fagan said.

'Yeah.' Horlor nodded. 'Bryn Collier, Martin Cooper, Amlod

Llewellyn, and our beloved First Minister, Lloyd Bevan, were all arrested. They spent six months in jail before they went to trial. But the trial collapsed. And they were acquitted.'

'Did you ever meet Alwyn Collier outside of work?' Watkins asked.

'Yes. We would meet twice a year in Blaenavon at the Rifleman's arms. We were part of a small group known as the Valleys Colliery Union.'

'What is that?'

'Just before the strike ended, Alwyn started a local union. A lot of the miners had become disillusioned with the strike and the NUM. So Alwyn set up a new union for the miners who wanted to still be part of a union. As the pits closed across the Valleys, members of the union were given a redundancy package and a lump sum paid out by the union. It was quite a good package. But those who remained in the NUM were furious.'

'When was the last time this Valleys Colliery Union met up?' Fagan asked.

'Six months ago. We're due for another meeting in the next few days. I cannot attend, unfortunately.'

'How many in the organisation?'

'Just a handful now, about twenty. There were several thousand of us back in the day. But once the boys had their payout, they left the union.'

'Have you ever met his brother?'

'A few times over the years. Bryn Collier lives in Torfaen, Abersychan. He's chairperson at the Garndiffaith rugby club.'

'Collier's wife said that Alwyn and his brother haven't spoken for years.'

Horlor nodded. 'I've heard that. It was because of what happened to their youngest brother, Dafydd. And because Bryn was out on strike and Alwyn worked through it.' Horlor paused. 'Are you allowed to reveal any details of how Alwyn died?'

'I'm afraid not.'

'I can't think of anyone who hated him enough to kill him. But then again, you don't know these days.'

Fagan closed his notebook, glancing around Horlor's office. 'I see you're still a major supporter of the union.'

Horlor smiled. 'The unions are not what they used to be. But we are still fighting for the rights of the workers. We live in turbulent times Inspector Fagan. The scars of the miners' strike and Thatcher's policies have yet to heal. And now it's happening all over again.'

'How so?'

'Port Talbot Steelworks. The cornerstone of South Wales industry. Another mass layoff and another thriving community about to fall. Under another Tory Government.'

Fagan stood. 'We'll be in touch if there are any developments.'

Horlor stretched out his hand. 'I appreciate you coming in today, DI Fagan, DS Watkins. I just want to take this opportunity to say that not everyone still holds grudges against the police.'

'Care to elaborate on that statement?'

'Alwyn had a past. You're about to enter a world where prejudice against the police is still rife throughout the South Wales Valleys. There are many former miners who have never forgiven the police for what happened at Orgreave and Six Bells.'

'Thanks for the warning.' Fagan said.

CHAPTER 8

Agincourt Hotel–Monmouth - 1985

'Evening, sergeant Bobby.' Mickey Mercury greeted, spotting him walking through the main entrance. 'You're the last person I'd expect to see on a Monday night. This hotel is usually a weekend thing for you, isn't it?' Mercury winked at him.

'I'm here on police business, Mickey,' Benson stated.

'What a shame.' Mercury smiled. 'I was hoping to introduce you to some delicious delights.' Mercury nodded at a group of young men who were walking towards the lift.

One of the men turned and smiled at Benson.

'I'll see if I can come after I am finished.' Benson said, staring at the attractive young man.

'Well, don't be too long, darling. I wouldn't want to exhaust them all before you had some fun.' Mercury glided towards the elevator.

As the lift doors slid shut, the young man who had smiled at Benson gave him a suggestive wink.

Benson entered the sparsely populated bar, spotting Owain Lance in a darkened corner of the room, sitting with another man. He ordered a pint from the bar before joining the two men.

'Thanks for coming, sir.'

'Owain, how many times have I said? You don't have to call me sir.'

Lance smiled back at the fifty-three-year-old sergeant. 'This is our contact from MI5.'

'MI5?' Benson questioned. 'I thought it was just you and I meeting tonight.'

'Detective constable Lance is part of the Special Demonstration Squad.' The MI5 contact explained. 'Which is under the umbrella of the intelligence services. We have been monitoring events up and down the country. The SDS has hundreds of operatives who have infiltrated the ranks of the miners' union and other groups which have come out to support the strikers. Over the past several months there have been clashes with police forces up and down the country. The incident at Orgreave drew unwanted sympathy for the unions regarding police tactics.'

Benson savoured the taste of his pint. 'Those militant bastards had it coming. The entire country is fucked off with this miners' strike.'

'Mrs Thatcher is confident the strike will soon peter out. More miners are defying the picket lines and returning to work. Support for the strike is running out.'

'It's happening everywhere.' Lance continued. 'Splitting communities down the middle. Especially across the South Wales Valleys.'

'Well, it should be entertaining to watch those silly bastards give up and go back to work with their tail between their legs.' Benson taunted.

'Not a fan of the working class, are we, Benson?' The operative asked.

Benson supped on his pint. 'Some of them are okay, in small doses.'

'The officers assigned to you will concentrate their patrols in the Six Bells area. We are expecting resistance from the miners as more of their colleagues go back to work. We are particularly interested in the hardliners who refuse to budge. Scargill is counting on the core of these militants to carry on striking and cause as much disruption as possible. Almost twelve months have passed and the coal has kept flowing to the power stations. This is despite the best efforts of the miners' union to blockade coal storage facilities around the UK.'

Benson finished the last of his pint. 'So what's your role in all this, Owain?'

'My job was to infiltrate the mining community in the Six Bells area. The operation started last September. I had to give myself enough time to settle into the community and form friendships with workers at the Six Bells Colliery. My goal was to identify key members of the local miners' groups. I am posing as an odd job man. I have made connections with a lot of prominent union members who wield a lot of power within the community. When they walked out to support the miners in the North of England, there have been many incidents where those who remained working at the colliery have been attacked. Some of these militants have been using underhanded tactics to intimidate the workers. These include acts of violence and damage to vehicles and properties in an effort to stop workers from going to work. Local bus companies have had to put protective mesh on their buses in areas where support of the strike is strongest. These buses often get attacked while travelling back and forth the collieries.'

The MI5 operative looked at Benson. 'You will be given four hundred officers to ensure order is maintained in the Six Bells mining community. I must warn you. These men won't be swayed when the police turn up. We are expecting it to get ugly. There is a rally that is being planned at the Six Bells park in the coming days.' He looked at Lance. 'Your colleague has been profiling individuals who might cause trouble at the demonstration.' The man reached into a briefcase and handed it to Lance.

'I'll start with the foot soldiers. First up is Martin Cooper. Twenty-nine years of age. Cooper is known locally as the gas lighter. He's particularly fond of starting trouble between striking miners and working miners. Cooper has been spotted at pubs around the area over the last several months. Where skirmishes have erupted between the police and locals. Cooper has a record for public disorder and damage to property. In June last year he travelled up to Orgreave where he took part in the demonstration. He was arrested and charged with affray.'

'A nasty series of events,' Benson stated. 'The police were right to go in with horses, and trample those bastards.'

'The Chief Constable of South Wales police is concerned a similar incident might happen at the Six Bells Colliery. The National Union of Mineworkers has been deploying demonstrators throughout South Wales. The steelworks at Port

Talbot have been blockaded several times over the past three months. Because there is coal still coming from the Six Bells Colliery, there has been talk of a major operation by striking miners to halt the flow of coal. Martin Cooper has been spotted at a pub called the Coal Shed Inn at Six Bells. This establishment is used as a meeting place for the striking miners. I have attended several meetings over the past two weeks. The strikers are planning a demonstration in the next few days at the Six Bells park.'

'You will deploy your officers. To make sure the coal production at Six Bells continues.' The MI5 contact revealed.

'How many will be at this demonstration at Six Bells park?'

'The miners' union is expecting anywhere between fifteen hundred to three thousand.'

Benson glared back at the man. 'Are you bloody joking? How the hell are my officers going to fend off that many?'

'We'll have reserve officers who can be transported to your area within the hour.'

'It'll only take an hour for our arses to be kicked. That's too long to hold out against those kinds of numbers.'

'Relax Sergeant Benson. This will not be like Rorke's Drift. The rolling roadblocks across the Valleys will be stopping any coaches coming to that area. Our ground intelligence is confident you will cope with the gathering.'

'How are you getting ground intelligence?' Benson directed his question at Lance.

'There are a few striking miners that have cooperated with the South Wales police. They have received financial support for information they have given us.' Lance opened up another file. 'Next up is Amlod Llewellyn. He's the go to man in the Valleys if you want anything stolen, or if you've got something to sell. Llewellyn has a record for handling stolen goods. He's also suspected of arson. He runs back and forth to various collieries throughout the South Wales Valleys. Keeping striking union officials up to date with the latest developments. Llewellyn isn't as dangerous as Cooper, but he's a slippery bastard none the less.' Lance picked up another file. 'Next on our list is Bryn Collier. He's one of the staunchest members of the NUM in the Valleys. Many of the workers currently on strike won't move until Collier gives the go ahead. It was Collier who led the miners out on strike in March last year.'

Benson studied the file.

'Collier is the local version of Scargill. Collier has two younger brothers, both of them are still working.'

'I bet that makes for interesting conversation around the dinner table.'

Lance handed Benson a file. 'Last is a man called Lloyd Bevan. He is the glue that holds the four of them together. He's a strategist, this one. Brilliant at organising demonstrations. Most of which are peaceful. Like Collier he commands a lot of respect. Bevan is a fourth generation coal miner. He has been spotted over the last several months all over the country, attending mass rallies. He is the ambitious one in the group. He's been a union convenor for over ten years and has been working at various pits for nearly fifteen years. Bevan has been on the watchlist of various security services for some time.'

'Together, these four men are capable of causing a lot of disruption.' The MI5 contact continued. 'Ground intelligence has informed us large numbers of workers from other factories are planning to join the miners at a larger protest. Which we believe is happening on St David's Day. Bevan has organised a rally you will be policing in the Six Bells Park. Most of your men will be in reserve further on up the main road toward Brynmawr. We'll have spotters in the area who will inform us the moment they think it will kick off. Bevan will encourage the demonstrators to march to the pit.'

'I don't think they'll have the balls to start anything,' Benson said confidently.

'There's a meeting at the Coal Shed tomorrow night.' The contact revealed. 'We don't expect you to just storm in and arrest everyone. But you need to show your face around the valley. Make sure everyone is familiar with you.'

'Mark my words, everyone will be familiar with me.' Benson smiled.

CHAPTER 9

Newport Central Police Station
Present day

Fagan studied the whiteboard. 'What have we found out so far?'

'I pulled a load of CCTV from Cardiff Central train station.' Brooks said. 'I also got CCTV from the Senedd building and Collier's office building. He's captured multiple times on their camera system. Thanks to the facial recognition system operating around Cardiff, we can track his movements throughout the day.'

'Nice one Andrew.' Fagan complimented.

Brooks walked over to a large TV screen with his laptop. The screen contained multiple images of Collier. 'The first CCTV image of Collier was taken at eight forty-four yesterday morning. As he's getting off the train. He then scans his phone at the ticket terminal before buying a newspaper. He exits the station and gets into a car. The car is a registered Uber vehicle. I've already run the plates. The vehicle is registered to a Roman Belous, a Ukrainian national. He's been in the country since April 2022, moved here with his family following the Russian invasion. He was an Uber driver back in Ukraine. Set up his Uber business in November 2022.'

'Not worth talking to.' Fagan remarked.

'The car drops Collier off at the Senedd's office building at about nine o'clock.' Brooks pointed at the screen. 'Collier is seen again at around twenty-five past nine exiting the building.'

'I'm guessing he was on his way to meet Horlor.' Watkins suggested.

Fagan nodded.

'The car that picked up Collier is another Uber. Registered to Olaf Panek.' Brooks continued. 'He's a Polish national.'

Fagan repeated his previous comment. 'Not worth talking to.'

'The car is picked up on multiple traffic cams. It drops him off at the Unite Union headquarters on Cathedral road.'

'Where he has a meeting with Delwyn Horlor.'

'Collier books another Uber car back to the Senedd.'

'He doesn't return to his office?' Fagan queried.

'No.'

'Check with the Senedd, Sean. I want to know if there were any sessions yesterday.'

'This is where it gets interesting.' Brooks stated.

'How do you mean?'

Brooks pointed at a CCTV image on the screen and hit play. 'Collier is seen leaving the Senedd building around midday and jumping into a black Mercedes.'

'What's the mystery here, Andrew?'

'The plates are false, sir.'

Fagan raised an eyebrow. 'Really.'

'The plates on the black Mercedes don't register with the DVLA.' Brooks tapped the screen. 'Collier is picked up at the front of the Senedd building. As you can see, the driver of the vehicle doesn't get out and open the door.'

Fagan squinted at the image. 'It's a clear image. But the driver's face is obscured.'

'The next bit is absolutely bonkers, sir. The car heads towards Pierhead Street. It drives down Pierhead Street and stops at the lights. The Mercedes then turns left onto Caspian Way. It stops again at lights on the Queens Gate roundabout. Watch this next bit. It's insane. This was picked up on one of the traffic cameras monitoring that area.'

Fagan stared at the screen. The black Mercedes waited patiently at the lights. Three more black Mercedes suddenly came into view. Stopping short of the roundabout's exit where Collier's car was waiting.

'What the bloody hell is going on there?' Fagan watched as traffic behind the three cars slammed on their brakes.

The black Mercedes at the traffic lights pulls out at speed before the light turns green. Followed by the three other cars.

'They all take the first exit off the Queens Gate Roundabout and head down the Cardiff Bay Link road. I checked with traffic in that area. All the cameras in the Queens Gate tunnel are undergoing maintenance.'

Fagan rolled his eyes. 'Of course they are.'

'All four Mercedes exit the tunnels and are picked up again by another traffic cam. Single file formation.'

'Looks like a diplomatic convoy.' Watkins remarked.

Fagan nodded thoughtfully.

'All the vehicles have exactly the same number plate.' Brooks revealed. 'The lead car takes the first exit after the tunnels. I've tracked its movements. It's picked up one more time on Ferry road.'

'What's in that area?'

'It's a mixture of flats, retail parks and leisure centres.'

Watkins stared at Google maps rattling off a list. 'You have the Cedar tree pub. There's Asda, JD Sports, Pets at Home, MacDonalds, Sports Direct, Home and Bargains and Ikea Cardiff. There's a maze of roads through that area, boss. The Mercedes could have gone anywhere.'

'The other three cars continue along the Cardiff Bay link road.' Brooks continued. 'The second car then turns off the next junction and is picked up on Leckwith Road. Nothing after that.' Brooks tapped the screen again. 'The third car takes the next exit emerging on to the Culverhouse Cross roundabout. Then turns on to Culverhouse Cross Road west. There are a lot of car showrooms in that area.'

'What about the fourth car?' Fagan asked.

'It carries on until it reaches the M4. It then heads towards Swansea.'

Fagan considered the CCTV evidence. 'Right, so a car picks Collier up. Drives away from the Senedd. Its then met by three other identical cars with false plates. They enter the Queens Gate Tunnel. No cameras in the tunnel. After that they all split up. While in the tunnel the cars switch places. Which means Collier could be in any of those cars.'

'There's more.' Brooks revealed. 'The next time Collier is seen on CCTV is around two thirty. He's dropped off by the Senedd office building by a white BMW. As with the black Mercedes the plates are false.'

Fagan watched the CCTV image of Collier getting out of the BMW and hastily making for the office building. 'Another car with false number plates. This is looking more like a bloody spy thriller than a murder investigation.'

'According to Tracie Morris, Collier was due to face a committee yesterday afternoon.' Watkins said.

'Yeah.' Fagan nodded. 'We need to find out more about that committee. What was the outcome? Was he booted out of the Senedd?'

'Collier is picked up on CCTV again around five o'clock exiting the Senedd offices.' Brooks pointed at the TV. 'He jumps into an Uber that drives to Cardiff Central. They emailed me this image of Collier standing on Platform Two. He gets on the five forty train to Manchester Piccadilly.'

'Where does that train stop?'

Watkins scanned through Trainline. 'Newport, Cwmbran, Pontypool, Abergavenny, Hereford and loads more stops until it reaches Manchester.'

'He could have got off between Newport and Abergavenny.' Fagan speculated. 'He gets off the train and somehow ends up at the Keepers.' Fagan considered his options. 'Collier was due to face a committee yesterday afternoon. He wasn't very popular on the Senedd floor with the older members. This is because of his history with the miners' strike.'

'Tracie also mentioned he had his satchel stolen a few weeks back.'

'I'll bet it's the same satchel that was found with fifty grand in it. That's more of a coincidence that happening. It's looking more likely Collier was being watched.'

'Who by?' Brooks asked.

Fagan shrugged. 'It could have been anyone. We know he was getting human faeces sent to him last year. And the envelopes were addressed to the Scab Bastard of Blaina Gwent. Sean, run Collier's name through the police database. Collier's assistant said he went to the police regarding the incident.'

'Whoever it was sending those letters knew about Collier's past.' Brooks said.

'But is there a connection between the incident last year and what happened to him last night? The next step is to find out about the committee he had to face yesterday.'

'Got him, boss.' Watkins announced. 'According to police records. Collier contacted South Wales police last April about the incident. He'd been sent ten packages. All containing human faeces.'

'Hang on a sec.' Fagan interrupted. 'If it was human faeces, then it should have pinged on the DNA database.'

Watkins took a moment to come back with an answer. 'No, boss.'

'No DNA match?'

'No, as in the case was shelved after the sixth package was sent.'

'So there was no DNA test carried out?'

'No. South Wales police shelved the case after they concluded there was no case to investigate.' Watkins stared at the screen.

Fagan noted the look on his face. 'What?'

'Collier made a complaint last September. He claims the police refused to carry out a proper investigation. It also says here Collier's home was targeted. Someone dumped a lorry load of manure on his driveway.'

'I'm surprised his wife didn't mention it this morning when we interviewed her. Was his complaint dealt with?'

'Yeah,' Watkins replied after several seconds. 'But according to this, South Wales police were cleared. There was no evidence to suggest they didn't carry out a thorough investigation.'

'What we need is a starting point. Andrew, I want you to contact Transport for Wales and get them to release CCTV from Pontypool and Abergavenny. Pontypool is a little closer to Blaenavon, so it's a safe bet he got off there. Check all the local Uber drivers and taxi firms in Pontypool. See if they picked up his fare.'

'That's quite a big ask, sir.'

'I know, but we have to fill in as many gaps as possible here. We know Collier disappeared for over two hours yesterday. The Mercedes and the BMW with false plates suggest Collier was involved in something. The question is, what? No one drives around in cars with dodgy number plates, unless they're up to no good.'

The door to the office opened and Griffiths stepped through the door. He was followed by another man. Chunky around the shoulders. Wearing a suit that looked like it belonged in the seventies.

'Good afternoon, sir.'

Griffiths skipped the pleasantries. 'I need a situation report on the progress you're making regarding Alwyn Collier's murder.'

'It's slow going at the moment.'

'It looks to me like you've been sat around all afternoon with your thumbs up your arses.' The man with Griffiths barked.

'This is Detective Chief Superintendent Clive Warren.' Griffiths introduced. 'He will be the lead investigator on the murder of Alwyn Collier.'

'I don't understand.'

Warren stepped up to Fagan. 'He means, I'm in charge. Do you understand DI Fagan?'

Fagan stared back at him. Warren was the sort of officer that could terrify the junior officers. But Fagan had been too long in the force to put up with that bullshit. 'I understand perfectly, sir.'

'Right then, you lot, listen up. Gwent Police and South Wales police have a long history of cooperation. I expect the same from you. We have set up an incident room in Cardiff. All information you gather will be analysed in Cardiff. Anything you have discovered so far will go to Cardiff.'

'Collier lived in Nantyglo.' Fagan pointed out. 'Which means he lived on our patch.'

'Are you saying South Wales police have no jurisdiction, DI Fagan?'

'No sir, this isn't America.'

Warren cocked a smile. 'You're not fucking me about, are you, Fagan?'

'No, sir. I don't take part in dick measuring contests.'

'Good, because I've no tolerance for that kind of shite. Now, instead of standing there with your thumb up your arse, tell me what you know so far.'

'I'll leave you gentlemen to it,' Griffiths said, before making a hasty retreat.

Fagan contained his temper enough to give a short briefing.

'How can you be sure if Collier got off the train at Pontypool or Abergavenny?'

'Both locations are close to Blaenavon.'

'But he could have met someone in Newport or Cwmbran,' Warren argued. 'Just because Collier ended up face down in the Keepers doesn't mean he didn't get off the train at the other two stops. I want all CCTV pulled from the other two stations.'

Fagan glanced at Brooks and nodded. 'Do as DCS Warren asks, Andrew, please.'

'What did you make of Collier's personal assistant?'

'Nothing really, sir.'

'You don't think she knows more than she's letting on?'

'Why would I think that?'

'You and Watkins interviewed her, didn't you, for Christ's sake?'

'We did, sir. But Tracie Morris didn't register as suspicious. The woman was extremely upset by his death.' Fagan glanced at Watkins. 'Myself and DS Watkins carried out a thorough interview. Morris told us Collier wasn't liked by the older members of the Senedd.'

'So what you're saying, DI Fagan, is that every Senedd member above a certain age is a potential suspect.'

'No sir. But we need to interview members of the Senedd that had contact with him a week prior to his death. I have already spoken to one Senedd member. Delwyn Horler.'

Warren put up his hand. 'Let me get this straight. You want to pull members of the Senedd in for questioning?'

'What I'm saying is we should question Senedd members to find out if they noticed anything strange in the past few days. Collier had a lot of hate mail. Including human faeces sent in jiffy envelopes to him last year. Apparently, the investigation was shelved. Collier put in a complaint to the Independent Office for Police Conduct. They ruled that there was nothing to pursue. What I would like to know is why the investigation was shelved?'

'Someone sending shit through the post, DI Fagan, is not worth investigating. Do you have any idea how many times this happens to those dicks sat in Parliament in London? None of them know their arses from their elbows. They only give a fuck about themselves.'

'Collier was also due to face in investigative committee yesterday. Regarding the conduct of his staff. One of which is now a convicted paedophile.'

'I haven't got my head stuck in the fucking sand, DI Fagan. I am aware of Collier's circumstances.'

Before Warren could say anything else, Fagan jumped in. 'Then I suggest, sir, we interview Lloyd Beven in the morning. As he was due to head the committee.'

'Are you aware of the implications, DI Fagan? We can't just pull the First Minister in for questioning. What do you think the media is going to do if we do that? They're already having a meltdown over Collier. It's all over the news. Just about every network is camped up on the Keepers Pond.'

'I'm not saying we pull him in, sir. We interview him at the Senedd's offices.'

Warren's tone mellowed. 'Okay, I'll go along with that. But you and I will interview him, and no one else.'

'Fine by me, sir.'

Warren glared at Watkins and Brooks. 'In the meantime, your little minions here can do all the legwork. I want CCTV pulled from Newport and Cwmbran. And I want all notes and leads you have shipped down to Cardiff.' Warren looked at Fagan. 'I'll see you back here tomorrow at nine. Be here on time, DI Fagan, or I'll have your guts for garters.' He then headed towards the door.

'What an absolute twat, if you don't mind me saying sir.'

Fagan couldn't stop himself from chuckling. 'No, I don't mind, Andrew. And yes, he is a twat.'

'What happens now, boss? I've been put on the back burner

and now that dick is in charge.'

Fagan gathered his thoughts. 'I want you to meet up with Stacey tomorrow. Find out everything you can about Collier and his family. His wife mentioned that Collier and his son are estranged. See what you can dig up.' Fagan glanced towards the door Warren had walked through. 'I've a feeling there's a cuckoo in the nest.'

'How do you mean, boss?'

'It's not very often officers with Warren's rank head up an investigation. It does happen, but usually when there's something about to be uncovered that could cause embarrassment in the public eye. Since this is about politics, I'll bet someone doesn't want to be exposed for dodgy behaviour or activities. Collier got into a car with false plates yesterday and disappeared for over two hours. That in itself raises a lot of red flags. We'll finish up here, then call it a night.'

CHAPTER 10

The coal shed Inn–Six Bells–1985

Lloyd Bevan and Bryn Collier strolled through the entrance to the pub. The dimly lit room plunged into silence as they approached the bar. Thick cigarette smoke created a hazy fog, adding a tense atmosphere to the centuries old pub.

'Two pints of Albright please, Taff.' Collier requested, in a voice that sliced through the tense silence.

Bevan turned to the assembled miners. He picked his pint off the bar and consumed half of it within a few seconds. 'Right, let's get straight to the point, shall we, boys. How many of you have doubts about this strike? Come on, don't be afraid to speak up. I know most of you well enough.'

The room remained eerily silent.

'It fills me with pride to see you boys have no intention of going back to work.' Bevan scanned the room. 'I know there are absent faces tonight. And those who have stayed away have joined the ranks of the scabs.'

Martin Cooper stood, holding his glass high. 'Scab twats should all get their fucking heads kicked in!'

Murmurs of agreement rumbled through the bar.

'I don't hear all that much enthusiasm for Martin's idea.'

'And then the papers will make us out to be a bunch of twats, won't they?' Another man spoke up.

Bevan locked eyes with him. 'Is that what you're worried about? Our reputations. You're not worrying about the prospect of our livelihoods being under threat.'

'We know what's at stake, Lloyd. You've been telling us for nearly a year.'

'Okay then, let's take a step back, shall we.' Bevan said. 'How many of you in this room have been approached by the National

Coal Board and offered an incentive to go back to work?'

After several seconds of blank expressions, hands went up.

'I see,' Bevan stated. 'How many of you have been tempted to take their offer?'

Hands stayed up.

'Thing is, Lloyd, you can't blame some boys for returning to work. This strike has been dragging on nearly twelve months. That bitch in Downing Street will not budge. And neither is Scargill. They're at loggerheads. The Tories have planned for this. The question we need to ask ourselves is, how long can we hold out? We have to be realistic about things.'

Bevan finished the rest of his pint and handed it to the barman. 'You want realism, Dicky. I'll tell you what realism is. It's every pit across the South Wales coalfields being shut within five years. Is that realistic enough for you?'

'We all know what Thatcher is trying to do, Lloyd. There's no need to give us one of your grand speeches.' Dickie Morgan stated. 'All we want to know is, how long the NUM is planning to go on for?' His gaze swept the room. 'I know there are boys that have gone back to work. But it's not because they've betrayed the cause. It's because they're desperate. They kicked Nicky Symons out of his house last month. Because he couldn't pay his rent. He shacked up with his sister for a week. But the council found out and turfed him out again. Nick has four kids. They are living in a hostel now. And social services are threatening to take his kids away. The reason he's not here tonight is that he's too bloody terrified to tell you he wants to go back to work. You don't give a shit what happens to Nick or anyone else.'

Collier pointed at Morgan. 'Don't make us out to be bastards like the government.'

'Most of the boys who have gone back to the pit thought the strike would only last for a few weeks. But it's been nearly a year, Bryn. Everyone is at breaking point. Plus, there are rumours about you and Loyd.'

'What rumours?'

'Taking back handers off the NUM to keep us out on strike.'

'That's the press trying to make us out to be tossers.' Bevan stated.

Morgan continued. 'There hasn't been a day gone by where I haven't heard of someone getting a hammering for breaking the picket lines. Do you know who I spoke to last week? Robbie Marshman's mam. Three weeks ago, someone saw Robbie talking to Alwyn, your brother.' Morgan pointed at Collier. 'A couple of days later, Robbie was just having a pint in the Vivian up the road, minding his own business. A group of boys dragged Robbie out and kicked the shit out of him. All because someone saw him talking to your brother. Robbie isn't even a miner. He works at the Royal Ordinance factory just outside Monmouth. Why did he deserve a kicking? Are we not allowed to talk to whoever we want now?' Morgan's eyes swept the room. 'When this strike first started, this bar was standing room only. Now it's down to less than half. All that's left are die hard unionists.' Morgan threw a glance at Collier and Bevan propping up the bar. 'Youngsters who are living with mam and dad. And us dinosaurs who are at the end of our time. I'm due to retire in less than six months. I have worked my arse off. And yes, I own my house. I don't have to worry about a mortgage or rent like the rest of the boys. I can afford to stand with you because my Lesley has a well-paid job. But if this strike isn't over when I clock off for the last time, don't expect me to continue to support you.'

'Not willing to make one last sacrifice for us then, Dicky.' A young miner in his early twenties glared at Morgan.

Bevan bowed his head. 'Fuck!' he swore under his breath.

Morgan rose to his feet and strolled towards the youth. 'You haven't even been at Six Bells for twelve months. How dare you fucking lecture me about sacrifice. You've no idea what that word even means. I have worked at Six Bells for nearly forty-four years. I have worked there as man and boy. Started in 1940 when I was fifteen. D'you want to know the true meaning of sacrifice? It's scrambling through rubble in pitch darkness, choking on coal dust, barely able to breathe. Knowing full well my dad and my brother were caught up in the explosion that killed forty-five miners in 1960.' Morgan's voice trembled. 'My mam wouldn't let me go home until I had found their bodies. She wouldn't let the rescue team locate their remains. It had to be me. And when I finally found my dad and my brother, I saw they died in each other's arms.' Morgan broke down and sobbed.

Bevan walked over to Morgan and put a comforting hand on his shoulder.

Morgan glared back before pulling away. 'Tell them Lloyd! Tell the boys in the room why my dad and brother died that day!'

'Please don't do this, Dick.'

'Not going to say anything, Lloyd? Then, I'll explain, shall I.' Morgan looked around the room. 'My dad and my brother should have been on the afternoon shift that day. But Lloyd's dad pulled a sickie that morning. So he phoned our dad and asked him to cover. My dad, being the loyal friend he was to your father, said yes. My brother, who wanted to learn my dad's job, offered to do the extra hours just to bump up his training. I even offered to go with them. But dad insisted I start the afternoon shift as usual. I remember watching my dad kiss our mam goodbye, asking her to cook that ham she'd bought the day before. That's the last time we saw them alive.' Morgan glared at Bevan. 'But why was your dad sick, Lloyd? Because he got pissed as a fart the night before. He was too hungover to come into work the next morning. So he asked our dad for a favour. Why d'you think our mam never spoke to your dad after that day?'

All eyes in the room focussed on Bevan.

Morgan looked back at the boy, who had made the comment. 'So you see, I have made my sacrifice. And if all the mines have a future with people like you working in them, then the coal industry is fucked.' He walked towards the pub entrance, stopping short. 'I'm going back to work first thing in the morning. I don't give a shit what any of you think about me. I'm not doing it because I'm a scab. I'm doing it to honour my dad and my brother. If any of you even come near my house or anything happens to me, then I will grass the lot of you up to the police.' Morgan turned and left the pub.

Cooper marched towards the entrance. 'That twat can think again if he thinks he's going back to work.'

'For fuck's sake Martin, sit down.' Collier ordered.

Cooper pointed at the entrance. 'You heard what Dickie said he's going to do. He's fucking going back to work in the morning.'

'So what are you going to do? Chase after a sixty-four-year-old man and kick the fuck out of him. And incidentally, he's right about one thing, Robbie Marshman. I know you were in the Vivian that night talking to Robbie. I also know you grassed him up for talking to my brother because you were in the pub that night when they were having a conversation. I thought you and Robbie were mates. Where were you when those boys dragged him out of the Vivian and kicked the shit out of him? I'll tell you something else, shall I? Those boys weren't even miners. Some fucking mate you are, leaving him like that.'

Cooper slumped down in his chair, assuming a sulking position.

'So what are we going to do about the scabs?' A man asked.

'We'll convince them that by standing with us, we have a better chance of winning this fight.'

'I hate to piss on your chips, Lloyd, but Dickie Morgan was right. Most of the boys who've gone back to work had no choice. At the beginning of this strike there was plenty of help. Now there's virtually no help. I've eaten through all my savings to stay afloat. I've had to support two brothers who walked out with us.'

Their conversation was interrupted. Everyone focussed their attention on the five uniformed police officers that entered the bar.

The lead officer took up position by the bar. He scanned the room. 'Enjoying a night out at the pub, are we lads?' He boomed. 'My name is Sergeant Bob Benson. I have been assigned to this area to keep law and order.'

Bevan and Collier glared back at Benson.

'Every one of you in this room is a militant bastard.'

Cooper jumped to his feet. 'Fuck off Sergeant Porky Pig. You have no right to come in here.'

Benson stared him down before glancing at the four officers. 'Arrest this man for being abusive towards a senior police officer.'

The uniforms marched toward Cooper. One of them unclipped handcuffs from his belt.

Three men stood and blocked their path.

Benson clapped his hands together, rubbing them. 'And there was me hoping you were going to behave. Looks like the cells will be full tonight. Anyone else want to spend the next few days in a cell?'

Collier stood toe to toe with Benson. He looked at Cooper. 'He's right. You've no reason to be in here, other than intimidation.'

Benson looked at the men blocking the uniforms' path. 'It's not my men who are being intimidating.'

Collier glanced at the men. 'Sit back down, boys. There'll be no trouble in here tonight.'

'And there'll be no trouble any other night, or day, for that matter.' Benson stated. He looked at the four officers. 'Come on, men. Let's leave this shithole.'

'You see what we are facing here, Lloyd?' One miner growled angrily, pointing towards the door.

'Calm down Stuart. All the police want to do is wind us up. Try to provoke us into doing something.'

'What are we going to do, Lloyd?'

'Look, we've got five hundred boys being bused in tomorrow. We're all meeting in Six Bells park for a rally. Then we'll march on the pit. There'll be a lot of support for us. We're also planning another major rally for St David's Day. We'll have at least three thousand men who will come.'

'And what if the police provoke us tomorrow at Six Bells park?'

Bevan looked back at him. 'Then we fight the bastards.'

CHAPTER 11

The Cantreff – Abergavenny.
Present day

'Evening Fagan, the usual is it?' Jackie Mills reached for a pint glass.

Fagan walked up to the bar. 'I'll start with a double.' He pointed at a bottle of brandy.

'Been one of those days, has it?'

Jamie Evans joined Fagan at the bar.

'I hope Daisy knows where you are.' Fagan grabbed the glass Jackie placed in front of him and knocked it back.

'Daisy is out with her friends. So I thought I'd pop in and see if you were here.'

'I can't tell you anything about what happened at the Keepers. I'm afraid, Jamie.'

'There's no need. It's all over the BBC Wales news. They've shut off the road to the Keepers. Loads of people are pissed off, because they're shutting the Heads of the Valleys at ten o'clock for road works.'

'They're always shutting that bloody road.' Jackie complained.

'I was talking to Terry earlier. He said he picked up Alwyn Collier from the train station last night and took him up to Blaenavon.'

Fagan looked at Evans. 'Terry as in Terry's taxis?'

Evans nodded.

'Was Collier carrying anything?'

'I don't know. Terry didn't go into any specific details.'

'Where did he drop him off?'

'Outside the church at the bottom of High Street.'

'I want you to text Terry and tell him to contact the incident room in Cardiff. He needs to tell them everything.'

Evans was already thumbing the keypad on his phone. 'Done.'

'Everyone has been talking about it on Abergavenny's Facebook page.' Jackie said.

'I've been following Blaina Uncut today.' Evans mentioned.

'What's that?' Fagan asked.

'It's a Facebook page for Blaina. The comments posted have been a little aggressive.' Evans scrolled through their Facebook feed. 'Here's a few comments people have been posting. The only good assembly member is a dead assembly member. Once a scab, always a scab. The scab had it coming to him after betraying the miners back in 84. Rot in hell, you scab bastard. Alwyn Collier was a traitorous scab. Hope he enjoys eternity in hell.'

'Jesus, people can be so nasty on social media.' Jackie stated.

'It's called free speech, Jackie. Everyone is entitled to it.'

'That's not free speech, Jamie. That is just being nasty. Most of those people who've posted those comments don't know who that man was. They don't realise the damage they've done. He had a family who loved him. A wife and two grown up kids according to his page on the Senedd website. Think about what they must be going through right now.'

'This is why I don't do social media.' Fagan commented. 'It's all a load of bollocks. People posting when they're going to bed or having a shit. Some people are too stupid to know they're coming across as dicks.'

Evans stared at his phone. 'Plenty of politicians sending their respects. The Prime minister said he would do everything in his power to find out those responsible. Lloyd Bevan said that Alwyn Collier was a valued member of the Senedd and will be missed by all.'

'I hate that bloke and his stupid twenty mile an hour speed limit.' Jackie moaned. 'They reckon it's caused a lot of damage to the tourist industry in Wales. No one wants to drive at those speeds. Have you seen the potty signs they have on the way to Crickhowell? One minute it's sixty, then it's twenty, then it's thirty. And Bevan has been moaning about Welsh independence. He's worse than Sturgeon. So they think someone murdered him?'

Fagan nodded. 'It's only a matter of time before the press reveals all the grizzly details.'

Evans continued to stare at his phone. 'This is all about the miners' strike.'

'How do you mean?'

'No one seems to be focussing on the fact that he was an assembly member. The news has been repeating itself all day. He was a former miner and his brother was killed in 1985.'

'I wonder if this is something to do with Sean Price.' Jackie considered.

The name jogged Fagan's memory. 'The taxi driver killed up the Valleys.'

Jackie nodded. 'He worked for Lewis' taxis back then.'

'I bought a black cab from Lewis when I started up my taxi business.' Evans revealed. 'They had a few of them. But it became too expensive to run.'

'Sean Price was killed outright when a pole went through his windscreen. Alwyn Collier's brother was sat in the front.' Jackie carried out a quick search on her phone. 'According to Wikipedia, a few days after the accident, Dafydd Collier died of his injuries. I remember our nan organising a collection for Sean's funeral. Loads turned up.'

'I was doing time in Usk, when the miners' strike happened.' Fagan recalled.

'I'd have a chat with Sean's son, Adam Price. He's been campaigning for years to get justice for his dad. His mam died last year.' Jackie switched to Facebook. 'He posted on Abergavenny's Facebook page today. *The last chance for justice for dad died last night. Alwyn Collier knew more about my dad's murder, but he wouldn't tell*.' Jackie switched back to Wikipedia. 'Four men were arrested. But were later acquitted. They also reckon the police investigation was flawed. Some of the officers signed false statements.'

'It was the 1980s.' Evans said. 'A lot of bent coppers back then.' He glanced at Fagan, who was glaring back at him. 'But not now, mate. I'm sure all coppers are straight these days.'

'I remember our nan organising collections for the miners' strike.'

'There's a lot about the miners' strike still to be revealed.' Evans remarked, glancing at Fagan. 'I tell you who you should speak to.'

Fagan swigged from his pint. 'Who?'

'Know it all Nigel. He wrote a book on the miners' strike about ten years ago.' Evans held up his phone. 'It's available on Amazon.'

Fagan read the title. 'The Rape of the Working Class. A controversial title.'

'It's a play on words. Another author wrote the Rape of the Fair Country.'

'Our nan knew the bloke who wrote that book,' Jackie said, looking at her phone. 'Alexanda Cordell. He used to drink in here.'

'Where does Sean Price's son work?'

'Morrisons.' Jackie replied. 'On the pizza counter.' She glanced at a clock on the wall. 'He'll be there now. Morrisons shuts at ten. This is the best time to catch him.'

Fagan drained his glass.

'This has to be about the miners' strike.' Evans said. 'Many people are still pissed off with what Thatcher did back in the eighties. Loads of miners lost their jobs in the Valleys. A lot of them didn't work again. I pick up a lot of fares from the Valleys. People still talk about the strike as if it were yesterday.'

Fagan stepped away from the bar. 'I'll see you lot for quiz night.'

Morrisons–Abergavenny

The café was closing. Fagan convinced the store manager to let them have a table. A member of staff from the canteen had made them coffee.

Adam Price stared at Fagan's ID for several seconds before handing it back. 'The last thing I was expecting was plod calling. Am I being considered as a suspect?'

Fagan sipped coffee from his mug. 'Why would you think that?'

Price took a deep breath. 'I'm a bit paranoid when it comes to this sort of thing. I was thinking about it today when I saw it on the Welsh News.'

'I'm not here officially, Adam, so you don't have to worry. Can you tell me about what you remember the day your dad died?'

'1985. I was in school. Mr Holder's English class, to be exact.'

Fagan remembered the name, grinning. 'I remember Mr Holder. Not the kind of teacher you'd want to piss off.'

Price nodded. 'I saw him throw a boy across the classroom once and beat the shit out of him.'

'Hard teachers back then at King Henry.' Fagan paused. 'What happened?'

'Don Prosser, the Middle School headmaster walked into the classroom with a copper. He called me out of the class. It must have been about three o'clock. Prosser let us have his room. There was another copper waiting. That's when they told me what happened to dad. I remember thinking, they're playing a joke on me. Then they took me home. The house was rammed with family. All dad's brothers and sisters were there. Plus our mam's family. Both sets of grandparents. You couldn't move in the house. Both mam and dad had massive families. Later that day our mam went to the Prince Charles in Merthyr to identify dad's body. Both grandads went with her. We were a very close family.'

'Must have been hard on your mam.'

Price nodded. 'The following day, she collapsed and was rushed to Nevill Hall. She had a miscarriage. Mam was five months pregnant. She was carrying twin girls. Later in life she would say that three of our family died that day.' Price composed himself. 'She, uh, died of cancer last year. Never got to see justice for dad.'

'Jackie Mills from the Cantreff said that you've been campaigning for years to get justice for your dad.'

'Hasn't got me very far, has it. I get five minutes of fame every ten years when the anniversary comes around. It's the fortieth next year.'

'Have you ever met Alwyn Collier?'

'Yeah, ten years ago when there was an event to mark the thirtieth anniversary of his brother's death. He first met mam when the men who were accused of the murders went on trial. That was a load of bollocks. They all got away with murder. Even though they were on that bridge.'

'But they were acquitted.' Fagan did his best to sound sympathetic.

'That's because the bloody police beat a confession out of one of the men. That's why the trial was thrown out. Lord snooty arse Barry up the road saw it as a defeat against Thatcher's attack dogs. Our mam never got over it. She'd go to the spot every year with flowers. Then she started to look into all the police corruption.'

'Your mam thought there were bent coppers behind it all?' Fagan asked.

'Yeah. The tossers who gave Martin Cooper a good hammering knew what they were doing. They knew if they could get him to confess, then they would be home free with a conviction. But because of what happened at Six Bells that day with the demonstration, the case fell apart.' Price stared at Fagan. 'They were all on that bridge that day. One of them threw that scaffolding pole.'

'Have you ever met any of them? You know, confronted them over your dad's murder.'

'Loads of times. But no one would ever tell me anything. When Lloyd Bevan became First Minister, it gave mam a nervous breakdown, almost. We couldn't believe how one of the men responsible for dad's death was now running the country.'

'Did you ever contact Lloyd Bevan about it?'

'Loads of times, but the man is bulletproof. I wrote to him last month and asked him if he had anything new to say about what happened to my dad. Given that its approaching thirty-nine years since he died. I mentioned my mam had died and I would carry on the fight for the truth.'

'Did he respond?'

'He sent me an e-mail expressing his sympathies for my loss.' Price let loose a snort of derision. 'He's not a popular First

Minister, is he? There's a petition to try to reverse this stupid twenty mile an hour speed limit. It's had half a million signatures and still he's ignored it. And then he keeps going on about Welsh independence. There's no way anyone is going to sign up to that. It would be a disaster. I saw him last week on the news, giving one of his speeches on the Senedd floor. Wales is for Wales. All the silly twats from his party stood up and applauded him.'

'Do you know much about what happened when they arrested the four men accused of your father's murder?'

Price nodded. 'Even the trial was flawed. That's why they threw it out. They never mentioned any of the coppers by name. It was always detective A or Detective B. I suppose they had to protect them.' Price remembered something. 'Ten years ago when we were marking the thirtieth anniversary of dad's murder I was contacted by this bloke. He claimed that information exists that could spark a retrial if it ever came into the public domain.'

'Did he say what kind of information?'

'Not really. I thought he was taking the piss. You know one of these conspiracy theorists.' Price drew a breath. 'But he knew certain things only the police would have known. The timeline leading up to dad's death.'

'But you do not know who he was.'

'No. But he was very official sounding.' Price finished his coffee. 'So, any clues about what happened to Collier last night? The news has been on about it all day. They said there were certain items found with the body but won't say what.'

Fagan drained the last of the coffee from his mug. 'It's very early days yet. We're hoping to find something soon.'

'None of the taxi drivers up the Valleys would take striking miners to work. The picketers would attack the buses as they drove into the pits. Dad supported the strike, but he was also desperate for money. Our mam was working at the sweet factory plus doing weekends in Coopers filters. His car was attacked, but he just ignored it. On the day he was killed he was on a high. Mam was pregnant and Lewis' taxis had just upped his money. We were planning to go out that weekend. But he never came home.' A single tear trickled down Price's cheek.

'I have to go, Adam. I appreciate you talking to me.'

'It's nice that someone has taken the time out to come and see me,' Price replied with a grateful tone. 'You're the first copper I've spoken to about dad's death in decades.'

Fagan placed a business card on the table. 'My contact details. Call me sometime.'

CHAPTER 12

Six Bells park 1985
Lloyd Bevan looked across the park. An expression of disappointment etched on his face.

Less than a hundred men had turned out to support the rally. A few of them were waving banners and flags. A line of uniformed police officers stood at the park's entrance. Some of them were clearly amused at the poor turnout.

'No fucker has turned up.' Bevan complained with a despairing tone. 'We look like a right bunch of wankers. I was expecting a few buses. There should be hundreds of us. I bet the fucking police have stopped them on their way in.'

'Bastards.' Martin Cooper seethed. 'I went round everyone's house yesterday and told them they had to be here.'

'You wait till I see those twats in the pub.' Amlod Llewellyn glanced at Cooper. 'We're going to be knocking a few heads together tonight. Don't they know what's at stake here?'

'It doesn't matter.' Bryn Collier clutched his megaphone.

Bevan looked at him. 'Bryn, are you fucking blind or what?' He waved his hand. 'No fucker is here, mate. There should be at least five hundred people here today. There's more fucking coppers than miners.' He pointed at the police sergeant who had walked into the pub the night before.

Benson stared back at the four men standing on the back of the flatbed van.

Bevan pointed at him. 'That fucker is hoping we're going to start a fight. Those pigs will arrest the lot of us.' He glanced at Cooper. 'I wouldn't start anything if I were you, Martin. Is that clear? The last thing we need is a few nights in the cells. We need to organise things for the rally on St David's Day.'

'As long as we stand together, there's more than enough of

us.' Collier's tone was calm. 'I'll make this speech. It should rally these men enough. Then we'll march on Six Bells and show those twats who run it, and to the scab bastards who have betrayed us. We're going to stand up to them no matter what.'

'There's a lot riding on this, Bryn. There should have been at least five hundred of us today.' Bevan reminded him.

'Let me talk to the boys first, before we make our next move.' Collier turned on his megaphone.

A piercing tone cut through the park, drawing everyone's attention. The small band of protestors gathered around the van. The police line watched from a distance.

'Thank you for turning up this morning, boys. We really appreciate it.' Collier's voice crackled through the megaphone.

Some protestors looked around, clearly disappointed at the turnout.

'I know how this looks, but there will be more people, I promise.'

'Bollocks.' One man shouted. 'No fucker has bothered to turn up today.' He pointed at the line of police officers. 'They're laughing their fucking heads off.'

A few of the uniformed police smirked at the group.

'Good turnout boys!' Benson shouted over to the miners.

Cooper glared back at Benson. 'I'd like to knock that twat's head off his shoulders.'

Bevan rolled his eyes. 'Jesus fucking Christ, Martin, shut the fuck up, will you.'

'He's trying to start a fight.' Cooper protested.

'No, it's you who wants a fight.' Bevan pointed at a man clutching an expensive camera. 'What's the betting he's from the local press? Or even worse, a national newspaper. How d'you think it's going to look if we kick off?'

'Anything has to be better than us having to take shit from that bastard pig.'

'Oi, Martin.' Collier barked. 'Lloyd is right. Don't start anything.' Collier refocussed his attention on the crowd. 'Look, I know there's not many of us. But that doesn't matter. Even a small group of men can make a big noise.' He pointed at the line of uniformed police officers. 'D'you know why they outnumber us? Because Thatcher is afraid. She is afraid we will win this fight.'

A few protestors nodded.

'We will continue to fight the oppressive Tory government, determined to destroy our way of life.' Collier fixed his gaze on Benson. 'You don't intimidate us. You may stand there looking smug. But I promise in years to come, you will be the ones who history remembers. We all recall what you bastards did last year at Orgreave. The police will be remembered as the attack dogs unleashed by the Thatcher government. Your only goal, to oppress striking miners and their families. We will support other collieries up and down Great Britain. Our only goal is to keep the pits producing the life blood this country has relied on for hundreds of years.'

'Arrogant militant bastard.' Benson said under his breath.

Collier pointed at the horizon, toward the Six Bells Colliery. 'For ninety-six years, the men of this valley have worked at Six Bells. We have sacrificed everything to keep that pit from shutting. We have had to endure hard times. Lives have been sacrificed. Everyone here remembers the disaster of 1960. Some of you were working in the pit. Scrambling through rubble to pull your fallen comrades out.' He swept a gaze across the crowd. 'The Iron Lady has labelled us as militants. But we are not soldiers or warriors. We are the men of Six Bells Colliery. We only seek a fair day's wage for a hard day's work. Yet Thatcher and her government, and Ian MacGregor, want to see us on the dole.'

A few of the miners shouted their support.

'D'you honestly believe after she's finished with the miners, Thatcher will stop there? This Tory government aims to destroy the working class. The car workers, the dock workers, the steelworkers. The working-class men and women in factories up and down the country know what's at stake here. All these jobs will go within the next ten to twenty years. Entire communities decimated because of Thatcher's so-called twisted dream of a capitalist society. We are witnessing this now. She is turning the miners against each other. There are those who have betrayed the cause. Those scabs who will happily stand idly by and watch

Thatcher and her thugs crush the unions. We will be left with a welfare state. Millions on the dole, forced to survive under a morally bankrupt government. The Iron Lady wants to crush the working class under her heel. This is not just about pits and factories closing. This is class genocide. Are you prepared for that?'

'No!' the crowd roared.

Collier pointed at the line of police officers. 'You should be supporting the unions, not opposing us.'

Benson smirked back at Collier. Hoping for a confrontation.

'We will not lose this fight. I promise you, brothers, the working class of the South Wales coalfields will stand tall against the Thatcher government. We will come out on top. We do not seek violent confrontation with the police. The men of Six Bells Colliery seek a better life. With better wages. So that our families will never go without. We do not want this strike to drag on. It's the Thatcher government who wants to prolong this strike, not us. Thatcher's plan is to squeeze the life-blood out of Wales. I would gladly return to work, as long as the government make a pledge to keep the pits open. The National Coal Board should be ashamed of themselves for allowing the government to come in and close pits across the county. The fat cats like Ian McGregor, who sit in their offices taking backhanders from a corrupt government who seek to destroy every union. Let me ask those of you who have turned out today, are you going to let that happen?'

'No!' the crowd shouted back.

'Are you going to let the government take away our livelihoods and our future?'

'No!'

'Are you going to let the government rob our children of their future?'

'No!'

'I know every man here today will be resolute in the face of hard times. I know the sacrifices you've made over the last several months. But the sacrifices you have made will be paid back tenfold. We will win this fight and the working class of the

South Wales coalfields will thrive for generations to come.'

The crowd of demonstrators erupted in cheers and whistles, defiantly punching the air.

Collier jumped down from the truck. 'Now, I want to see those banners held high. We'll march on the Six Bells Colliery and stand outside the main gates. The management and the scabs will hear the voice of the working class.'

A roar from the miners filled Collier with pride.

'Off we go then!' Collier yelled through his megaphone.

Benson ordered the uniform to block the park entrance.

Collier and Bevan led the march.

A chorus of men shouted in unity. 'The miners united, will never be defeated. The miners united, will never be defeated.'

'Should have brought riot gear, sarge.' A uniformed officer expressed his concern to Benson.

Benson looked over his shoulder. 'Stand your ground! Not one of these militant fuckers is leaving this park. Is that understood, constable?'

'Yes sarge.'

'The miners united, will never be defeated. The miners united, will never be defeated.' The approaching men chanted.

Benson stood defiantly in front of the line of uniforms. He glared at the approaching demonstrators. 'Draw your truncheons men!'

The line of uniforms unclipped their truncheons.

Collier held his hand up, signalling the crowd to stop. He approached Benson.

'If you think any of you militant twats are getting out of this park, then you can think again,' Benson growled. 'I want you all to disband and fuck off back home.'

'This is a peaceful march.' Collier stated. 'We have every right to make our voices heard.'

'You stupid twat.' Benson smirked. 'There are less than a hundred of you.' He glanced behind. 'I have two hundred men. That's two to one. I promise you, if any of you wankers take another step forward, my men will kick the shit out of every one of you. Every man will end up in a cell for the next few days.'

'Is that what the police are like these days?' Bevan shouted. 'A bunch of lapdogs who will do anything that bitch in Downing Street tells them to do.'

Benson looked over Bevan's shoulder at the men stood behind. 'Listen to me, all of you. You're fighting a lost cause. Give it up boys, no one has to get arrested today.'

Collier took a step forward, expressing a wry smile. 'If the cause is just and honourable, then these men are prepared to fight for their livelihoods.'

Benson released a snort of derision. 'You dull fucker, every one of you will spend the next week in a prison cell if you make an aggressive move.'

Bevan's attention was distracted. Chanting could be heard in the distance.

The line of officers looked beyond the park entrance.

'The miners united, will never be defeated.' A crowd shouted as they marched down Windsor road.

Collier took another step forward, smiling. 'Now it's you who are outnumbered. So what's it going to be?'

Benson glared at Collier. 'You militant twats make me sick. All you're doing is prolonging your doom. Don't you see? The days are numbered for you working class degenerates.'

Collier looked towards the photographer furiously snapping away at the two men stood face to face. 'I wonder what the newspapers will say tomorrow morning? Will they show the police beating the shit out of these men who just want a better way of life? Or will they show a peaceful march on Six Bells Colliery?'

The chanting was deafening from the chorus of demonstrators. 'The miners united, will never be defeated. The miners united, will never be defeated.'

Benson's nerve collapsed at the sight of overwhelming odds. He looked back at his men and nodded. 'Stand aside men!'

As Collier advanced, Benson grabbed his arm. 'You may have won this fight. But I promise you. If you fuckers try anything like this again, then we'll be ready.'

Collier pulled himself away from Benson's grip. 'Maybe, but

not today.'

The line of officers stood to one side and watched Collier and his followers march out of the park entrance.

Collier's girlfriend, Donna, smiled at him. 'Hiya, love. Sorry we're late.' She glanced at the crowd behind. 'I had to get half of these lazy bastards out of bed.'

Collier held Donna close. 'You're just in time.' He looked back at Benson, who was glaring back at him. 'Now let's stand outside the gates of Six Bells and jeer those scab bastards who are coming into work for the afternoon shift.'

CHAPTER 13

Llanover – 7:03am
Present day
Nigel Thomas yawned, opening the door.

'Morning Nigel.' Fagan greeted cheerfully, holding up a cardboard tray of coffee and pastries.

'Jesus Fagan, do you have any clue what bloody time of the day it is?'

'Yeah, it's just gone seven. I would have thought a man of your intellect would be up at all hours. Didn't you get the text I sent you last night?'

'No, I bloody didn't.'

'I sent it about ten o'clock.'

'I turn my phone off at eight Fagan. I have a spare phone for the kids. Just in case they need to ring me, or I need to contact them.' Thomas ruffled his hair, trying to adjust to the approaching morning.

'I brought a copy of your book, by the way. Started reading it this morning.'

Thomas yawned again. 'Come in and go through to the office. I'll get dressed.'

A few minutes later, Thomas returned. He plucked a croissant out of the box. 'So which book did you buy?'

Fagan produced his kindle. 'The Rape of the Working Class.'

Thomas bit into his croissant. 'I wrote that ten years ago to mark the thirtieth anniversary of the miners' strike. Wait, are you here because of what happened to Alwyn Collier? I was talking to a neighbour. They said there were police everywhere on the road leading to the Keepers from Llanover.'

'Collier was a former miner who worked through the strike.'

'It's commonly referred to as the strike to end all strikes.'

Thomas stood and walked over to a bookcase. He handed Fagan a paperback version of the book he had downloaded onto his Kindle. 'I was going to call it the fall of the working class. But then the author Alexander Cordell sprung to mind.'

'Rape of the Fair Country.' Fagan said.

Thomas nodded. 'He spent many years in and around Abergavenny.'

'Tell me about the miners' strike.'

'It all kicked off in 1984, when the National Coal Board announced they were going to shut Cortonwood Colliery, along with nineteen other pits across the North of England. The leader of the National Union of Mineworkers, Arthur Scargill decided he was having none of it. Everyone at Cortonwood downed tools and walked out.'

'Carried on for a long time, didn't it?'

'A few days short of a year. D'you think Collier died because of what happened back in the mid-eighties?'

'It's a lead I'm following. He wasn't a popular man on the Senedd floor.'

'He was the shadow environment minister for Wales, wasn't he?'

Fagan nodded.

'The miners' strike changed the course of history for this country. Maggie Thatcher was determined to break the working class and destroy the unions. They'd been a thorn in the government's side for decades. In 1972, the miners bought down Edward Heath's government when they went on strike. His cabinet had to meet by candle light to reach an agreement with the miners' union. Thatcher was determined this would not happen to her. The moment she took office, she set a plan into motion to dismantle the powerhouses of British industry. Coal, steel and the docks were on the top of her hitlist. Thatcher decided that cheap imports and a free market was the way forward for Britain. The only thing stopping her was the unions. Controlled by a powerful hardline leadership. When you look back, the 1980s were a battleground for many things. Class war being one of them. Thatcher hated the working class. Despite being the daughter of a humble greengrocer.'

Fagan bit into his pastry. 'I watched the film The Iron Lady many years ago.'

Thomas smiled. 'History according to Hollywood. When the miners walked out in 1984, Thatcher was prepared for it. The National Coal Board had been stockpiling coal to prepare for a looming strike. Pits had already been closed in previous years, which led to a backlash from the National Union of Mineworkers. When the National Coal Board announced they were shutting more pits in 1984, it was the final straw for Scargill. He ordered everyone to walk out.' Thomas paused. 'He walked right into Thatcher's trap.'

'How so?'

'He never called a national ballot for a strike. He just ordered everyone to down tools and walk out. That decision was the start of the downfall of the miners' union. There were those who reckoned he should have held a national ballot. But he didn't. By September 1984, a Supreme Court had ruled the strike as illegal. Thatcher was loving it. She was clever enough to know that without national support for a strike, then it would only be a matter of time before people turned on Scargill. But he was determined to keep the miners out. Most of the miners thought they'd only be out for a short amount of time. But after a month, it was clear the strike was going to go on for longer. Scargill dug his heels in and told the striking miners to stand their ground. At first, there was massive support for the strike. The public was pitching in collecting for the miners. As the summer drew on, soup kitchens sprung up all over the country. Helping those families who didn't have a wage coming in. Thatcher doubled down and was determined to break those supporting the strike.'

'What did she do?'

'She cut social security to those families who were striking. A controversial move on her part. But she was determined to win. By June 1984, the strike was on the news every day. I remember my dad being glued to the television. Screaming at Thatcher every time she appeared. And then in mid-June it all kicked off at Orgreave.'

'I've heard a lot of things about Orgreave.' Fagan said.

'The NUM sent around six thousand miners to blockade lorries, leaving a coke plant. Even Scargill himself attended the demonstration. What he didn't count on was the response from the police. The government mobilised an army of coppers to stop them. The miners thought the police were there to maintain order.' Thomas shook his head. 'It was a deliberate attempt to put down the demonstration and cut off the head of the unionist snake. That's what one witness I spoke to told me.'

'You've spoken to people who were there?'

Thomas nodded. 'I did a lot of research for the book I wrote. Went all over the country talking to everyone. Strikers, strikebreakers, and retired coppers.'

'What happened at Orgreave?'

'It was a slaughter.' Thomas rephrased. 'Not in a murderous sense. The police had battalions of riot police, dog handlers and mounted police to stop any strikers from blockading the coke plant. They sent in the mounted police to stampede the strikers when the lorries left the coke plant. The police cornered them in a field and charged them down on horseback.' Thomas picked up a tablet from his desk and scrolled through YouTube. 'Watch that.'

Fagan stared at the tablet, watching as mounted police charged down unarmed men. 'Jesus.'

'You never thought the police could do anything like that.'

Fagan gawped at Thomas. 'Not really no.'

'For years there have been calls for an official enquiry into what happened. Channel 4 recently screened a documentary series with new footage. Those who were there have been campaigning for an enquiry. But it's yet to happen. There were so many witnesses who saw police officers smashing unarmed men with truncheons. There are loads of videos. But nothing has been done.'

Fagan stared at the tablet, mesmerised by the video of police officers with riot shields.

'The Battle of Orgreave was a turning point in the strike. After June 1984 people got fed up with it. The collections dried up. The media published bad press about the miners. More images circulated of miners attacking convoys and buses. Robert Maxwell fought in Thatcher's corner. This made Scargill more determined to go on with the strike. After a while it became known as Scargill's strike. It was a battle for ideology in the Eighties, between the Thatcher Government and the working class. Thatcher won and the working class lost. Thatcher wanted a free market and to promote capitalism over socialism and communism. Cheap coal and oil imports. Now fast forward forty years later and look at where we are. A cost-of-living crisis. No one can afford to do anything. Hooray for capitalism.'

'Better that than live under someone like Putin.'

'And I totally agree. What I'm trying to say, Fagan, is that there are two types of people in this world. Rich and poor. All this bullshit ideology people subscribe to has been created to make people feel they're part of something.' Thomas sipped his coffee. 'Anyway, in the latter half of 1984, even the miners and their families were split down the middle. There were those who supported Scargill and wanted to continue the strike until the bitter end. And there were those who buckled under financial pressure. Miners drifted back to work. Especially as Christmas approached. Thatcher doubled down on her determination to break the miners' union. She cut benefits to striking miners and their families. It was a real struggle for some. She literally starved people back to work. For the diehards who carried on there was no persuading them to see sense. All they saw was Scargill and his ideology, and nothing else. When I researched the book, I travelled to Yorkshire to interview men who were part of the strike. There are still a lot of people who are bitter and twisted about what happened all those years ago.'

'I spoke to an assembly member yesterday. He mentioned the Battle of Six Bells.'

Thomas nodded thoughtfully. 'The Battle of Six Bells could be described as the day when the working class fell. It wasn't on the level of Orgreave, but it was definitely the last stand of the miners in the South Wales Valleys.'

'What happened?'

'Two and a half thousand miners and their supporters marched on the Six Bells Colliery,. The plan was to take the pit and hold it for a few hours. What the miners and their supporters didn't realise was that the police were more than ready for them. The government deployed four thousand officers to that area. In the months leading up to the incident the police had been laying siege to the villages up and down the Valleys. Entire communities were locked down because of the strike and what happened at Orgreave. Some described it as an occupation. The police knew about the demonstration. So they lured the miners into a trap. They let people into the area to join the demonstration. When the miners tried to take the pit, the police sprung their trap. There were a couple of hundred undercover officers who hid in plain sight. The miners never saw it coming. It turned into a pitch battle. By the time the miners knew what was happening they had been surrounded. Seven hundred and twenty miners were arrested. They were beaten, and slung in jail.'

'I spoke to Adam Price last night.' Fagan revealed.

Thomas nodded. 'Two men were killed that day. Adam's father and Dafydd Collier,' Thomas suddenly realised something. 'Shit, why didn't I see that?'

'What?'

'I met Alwyn Collier ten years ago.' Thomas held out his hand. 'Give me that tablet a sec. My memory isn't what it used to be.' Thomas carried out a quick search before handing the tablet back to Fagan. 'Four men were arrested after the incident. Martin Cooper, Bryn Collier, Amlod Llewellyn and First Minister Lloyd Bevan were on a footbridge where the accident took place. A scaffolding pole was allegedly dropped from the bridge, killing Sean Price instantly. The other three men in the car were seriously injured. Dafydd Collier died a few days later. The four men arrested were held for six months, then put on trial.'

'And were acquitted,' Fagan remarked, staring at the article Thomas had found.

'The trial still divides many people to this day. Following the arrests, one of the accused, Martin Cooper, was beaten so bad while he was in police custody he was rushed to hospital. The others were subjected to days of interrogation by the police. They were all forced to sign false confessions. When the trial came around, their defence lawyer, Malcolm Barry, wiped out the prosecution. The trial collapsed. Since then, there have been rumours that although they were acquitted, one of them was guilty of the murders. But because of what the police did, the whole trial turned into a farce. All the men who took part in the Six Bells demonstration had their convictions quashed. But it didn't stop the National Coal Board. They sacked four hundred miners just for taking part. Saved them money on redundancy packages. When I was researching the book, I contacted the police and asked them to release documents relating to the arrest of the four men arrested for the murders. They wrote back to me and said all the material relating to the arrests and interviews were lost.'

'A lot of bent coppers back then.' Fagan admitted. 'Different times.'

'Obviously there's something to Alwyn Collier's murder.'

'We haven't even got any suspects to question. I was just checking my e-mails this morning. No one has come forward with any vital information. Terry's taxis picked him up at the train station and dropped him off in Blaenavon the night he was murdered. But no one seems to have seen him after that.'

'I'd watch your back with this one, Fagan.'

'What do you mean?'

'There are now fourth generation families that haven't worked since the strike. In Yorkshire and throughout the Valleys. People have long memories. Especially in the Valleys. When I was researching the book, I came under fire from former miners who didn't like an intellectual like me bending the truth. Even though that wasn't my intention. Many still remember what the police did at Six Bells.'

Fagan looked at his watch. 'I better get to Newport.'

Thomas stared out of the window, watching as Fagan pulled out of his drive. He dialled a number on his phone. 'Hi, it's Nigel Thomas. Is there a place we can talk? Something has happened.'

CHAPTER 14

Blaenavon 1985

Alwyn Collier and Bryn Collier stood on opposite sides of the living room. The coal fire crackled gently in the grate.

'Sit down, the both of you.' Beatrice Collier said in a firm but motherly tone.

Alwyn and Bryn sat in armchairs, maintaining eye contact with each other.

Beatrice sat on the sofa. She stared into the coal fire.

The fire danced in the hearth, crackling and hissing. Its flames an intricate tapestry of crimson and amber as they leaped and swirled. Painting vibrant patterns on the walls. The scent of burning coal hung in the air. A comforting and familiar aroma for a family rooted in the mining traditions of their town.

Beatrice composed herself. She knew how much her sons hated each other. The strike had dragged on for nearly a year. She watched the news broadcasts every day. The TV was on, but the volume turned down low. Beatrice glanced outside. Snow was falling steadily. She smiled, recalling a memory. 'I remember when you boys would play in the snow outside on the street. Remember when your dad made that sleigh out of an old pallet?'

'I remember breaking my arm.' Bryn recalled, managing to smile. 'It's a wonder I wasn't killed outright.' He glanced through the window. 'It's a steep road.'

Beatrice looked at her eldest son. 'Alwyn ran back to the house to tell me and your dad what happened. We were so worried about you. You'd just recovered from that bad bout of chickenpox.'

Bryn looked at his younger brother.

Beatrice took a breath. 'Hasn't this gone on long enough?'

'Yeah, you're right, mam, it has,' Bryn said. 'It's about time people supported us, instead of stabbing us in the back.'

'No one has stabbed you in the back. You've done a good enough job of that already,' Alwyn stated.

'What's that supposed to mean, huh?'

'You don't get it, do you? There's only a small majority of you out on strike now. Most have gone back to work. Because they're tired of hearing the same old bullshit from the union.'

'The union has backed us all the way through this strike.'

'You really need to wake up and smell what Lloyd Bevan has been shovelling.'

'The NUM has supported the strikers throughout this dispute.' Bryn maintained.

'Have they? So tell me this, Bryn. Why are there families getting thrown out on their arses? Have you even seen what's happening out there? That's why everyone is returning to work. People are at the end of their tether. They've no choice. Don't you see? Public support for the miners has collapsed. Every day you lot are on the news. Being portrayed as thugs and troublemakers.'

'That's Thatcher's doing, not ours. Those who have gone back to work are gutless scab bastards.'

'Those so-called scab bastards you're talking about, including me, haven't gone back to work because we want to. It's because we'd have no bloody money. Let me ask you this. How have you been managing? I haven't seen you struggling. You haven't brought mam a food parcel since before Christmas.'

'Donna has been supporting me.'

'Oh yeah, that girl you barely know. I don't see her going out every day like the rest of us and grafting for a living. Yet the both of you have moved into that flat. How have you managed that with no wages?'

'We've had support from the union.'

'Bollocks.' Alwyn shot back. 'There's no way the union would support you like that. Unless.'

'Unless what?' Bryn demanded to know.

'Unless you've been taking back handers.'

Bryn sprang to his feet. 'Fuck you.'

'Calm down, the pair of you.' Beatrice ordered, pointing at Bryn. 'And you mind your language.'

Alwyn remained sitting. 'The rumours are already circulating, Bryn. Scargill's right-hand man, Roger Windsor, meeting with Gaddafi. It was all over the news last summer, for all to see. Then there's that copper who was shot dead outside the Libyan Embassy last April. What about her, Bryn? What about her family? You've aligned yourselves with the devil himself.'

Bryn was stuck for an answer.

'Haven't got anything to say about that, have you?'

'Piss off!' Bryn yelled back. 'Not all of us are privy to information.'

'Is that how you paid for that flat, with blood money? I know you've been meeting with Scargill and his cronies. There's rumours he's been slipping union conveners money just to keep the miners out on strike. All you've done over the past year is destroy families. For what, some pointless cause?'

'You call losing your livelihood pointless, do you?'

'Wake up, will you, Bryn. Look at what's going on out there.'

'I know what's going on. Thatcher wants to close the pits. It's you and the rest of your scab mates who have your eyes shut.'

'D'you honestly think coal is going to go on forever?'

'No, I don't. I'm not as blind as you think, Alwyn. I know the pits won't go on forever. But the way Thatcher is doing things is not right.'

'Finally, something we can agree on.' Alwyn shot back. 'I know she wants to destroy the working class. The miners are on the front line. We've borne the brunt of it from both sides. We've got to put up with you and your bloody mates calling us scabs, attacking us and the buses we take to work each day. Plus, we know the end is coming for all of us. It's you lot still on strike that don't see that. You silly bastards think in the event the government gives in to your demands, you'll have won. All Thatcher will do is regroup and have another go at ending the strength of the unions. But that's never going to happen. Because the government has won. The NUM is finished.'

'That's what this is all about, is it?' Bryn stated.

'What d'you mean?'

'Don't think I don't know about your little meeting.' Bryn folded his arms. 'Setting up your own union.'

Alwyn stared back.

'You think I didn't know? Well, think again. We have people everywhere. Checking up to see how far you scab bastards will go to stab us in the back.'

'It's not about stabbing anyone in the back. It's about giving back control to the union members.'

'We already have control.'

'If so, then why did Scargill order a walkout without the backing of the union?'

'Because of pit closures.'

'Yes, but he should have held a ballot. Not that it would have done any good. Thatcher saw this strike coming a mile off. She ordered the National Coal Board to stockpile coal three years back. Let me ask you this. Can the NUM last another three years?'

Bryn failed to answer.

'Your glorious leader of the NUM didn't have a plan when he ordered a walkout. And like bloody lemmings, the lot of you followed his orders. Now look at where we are, almost a year down the line. The soup kitchens are closing, Bryn. The food parcels stopped months ago.' Alwyn pointed at his mother. 'If it weren't for me and Dafydd, our mam would be out on the street. In some homeless shelter. Is that what you want for her? Is it Bryn?'

Bryn looked at his mother. Her face told the story of a woman torn between her two feuding sons. A woman who had seen change and upheaval over the last fifty-eight years.

'Dad grafted all his life down the pit. It ended up killing him. All the men of the South Wales Valleys have given their lives to the coal industry. Those who are retired struggle with their health because of black lung. Dad died of black lung.' Alwyn glanced at his mother. Tears streamed down her cheeks as she remembered her late husband. 'People are being thrown out on to the street. Children are being taken away from their parents because they can't afford to feed them. It's alright for the likes of me, you and

Dafydd. We've barely started our lives. We're still in our twenties and have yet to settle down. But what about those who are on the brink? The NUM is no longer supporting them because they've no money left in the pot. That selfish bastard of a union convenor is encouraging miners to stay out on strike.'

Bryn pointed at his brother. 'Lloyd is doing what's best for the miners. You scab bastards still working are undermining everything we stand for.'

'What's that, eh? Anarchy and chaos. Don't you get it, Bryn. This is the end. The end of everything. No more working class any more. No more striking workers. Thatcher has already broken the union. It's clear as the nose on your face!' Alwyn began to shout. 'But you and your militant pals are still out on strike.' He pointed at the TV set. A stern faced newsreader stared out from the screen. Images of police and miners engaged in pitch battles. 'You were lucky with the stunt you pulled yesterday. The thing that saved you was the women. If it would have been just men at that rally, it would have looked different. You're provoking the police into being total bastards. Every village up and down the valley has a garrison of coppers camped on their doorstep. You can't even walk down the street without being interrogated by a copper. Everyone is fed up to the back teeth of it.'

'That's Thatcher's doing. She's using the police to crush us.'

'And she's doing a good job, isn't she? You only have to look at what happened at Orgreave. Is that what you want happening in the South Wales Valleys?'

'If the sacrifice of the few can lead to the preservation of jobs, then yes.'

Alwyn tapped his finger on the side of his head. 'You and the rest of your union lemmings have been brainwashed. You're off your bloody heads if you believe in that kind of bullshit ideology.'

'What's the alternative?' Bryn screamed back. 'Lie down and let Thatcher walk all over us.'

'That's exactly what she's done. Don't you get it, it's over. Why d'you think I am setting up a new union? To break away from the National Union of Mineworkers, which has become toxic over the years. Thanks to Scargill and his small-minded ideology. Jesus, they should put him in a room with Thatcher and let them fight it out. That would be worth seeing.'

'You can't set up a new union.'

'I bloody well can. The last time I checked, we live in a free society. I've got loads of support already. There are men all over the Valleys who are fed up to the back teeth with the NUM.'

'Traitorous bastards, the lot of them.' Bryn seethed.

'That's enough foul language from you.' Beatrice interrupted. 'I will not have my sons turning this house into a war zone.'

'It wouldn't be like that, mam. If Alwyn and his mates joined the cause. Dafydd should also be supporting us.'

Alwyn shook his head. 'There's no bloody talking to you, is there? All you have is tunnel vision. You don't see any other option but to wage a pointless war.'

'And what's your solution, Alwyn? To betray the NUM by setting up a union for scabs.'

'I'm doing it to save our dignity.'

'Scabs know nothing about dignity.'

'You really think when this strike is over, they'll welcome you back with open arms? This is why I'm setting up a new union. To plan for the future. The National Coal Board will negotiate redundancy payouts with unions who don't cause disruptions.'

'Redundancy payouts. In other words, you're taking a bung from the National Coal Board.'

'No, I am not. How long d'you think the Six Bells Colliery will stay open for? After Thatcher is finished with the NUM, she'll close the pits. It's all about negotiating for a decent payout at the end.' Alwyn pointed at his mother. 'We could afford to buy this house for our mam. And still have plenty of money left over. If you let this strike drag on, then you'll get nothing when the end comes.'

'Better to have nothing than be a scab like you.'

Alwyn stood. 'Fair enough, Bryn. If you want to flush your life down the toilet, then I won't stop you. But if you think I'm going to end up with nothing, then you can forget it.'

CHAPTER 15

The Senedd – Cardiff
Present day

Warren shook Lloyd Bevan's hand. 'I appreciate you taking the time to speak with us, Lloyd. I know how busy you are.'

'It's okay, Clive. This is a terrible time for all of those concerned. Especially Alwyn's family. I sent my condolences yesterday when I heard the terrible news. I hope you're going to get whoever did this.'

'We are doing everything we can to apprehend those responsible for Alwyn's murder. We are planning to interview Senedd members who had contact with Alwyn in the days leading up to his murder.' Warren glanced at Fagan. 'This is DI Fagan with Gwent police.'

'Gwent police.' Bevan said. 'I thought this would be a matter for South Wales Police.'

'Mr Collier's body was found in Monmouthshire, which is under Gwent police territory. We are actively working with South Wales police to solve this murder.' Fagan explained.

'I'm sure the First Minister is aware of this, DI Fagan.' Warren said with a stern tone.

'It's okay Warren, the more police involved in this case, the better chance you have of finding who did this. So, how can I help you today?'

'We're going through the motions. Interviewing people in Alwyn's close circle. We'll try not to take up too much of your time.'

'A momentous week for you.' Fagan remarked. 'You're about to give a speech on a proposed referendum for Wales, aren't you?'

'DI Fagan, we are here to solve a murder, not have to listen to you babble on about general politics,' Warren groaned.

Bevan smiled and waved his hand dismissively. 'It's fine Warren. I've had many people asking me about the speech I'm planning to deliver on St David's Day.' Bevan fixed a stare on Fagan. 'These are exciting times for the people of Wales, DI Fagan. Their first vote on independence since the Senedd was formed over twenty years ago. It's been a long time coming.'

'And you think people will vote yes?'

'I think the people of Wales will make the right choice for this country. The pandemic and the failings of the current Tory government is a wake-up call for Welsh people. I am confident the people of Wales will usher in a new era.'

'But the referendum failed in Scotland. No one wanted to leave the UK. What makes you so sure?'

'DI Fagan, will you stay on track.' Warren seethed. 'We're not here to question Mr Bevan on the political dealings of the Senedd.'

'Of course.' Fagan said calmly. 'How well did you know Mr Collier?'

'I knew him fairly well. We have worked in the Senedd together for several years.'

'How would you describe your relationship with him?'

'I'd say it was amicable. We were on opposite sides of the political divide. Often engaging in lively debate on the Senedd floor.'

'What about in private, off the Senedd floor?'

'We'd talk about issues discussed on the Senedd floor.'

'Did you ever engage with Mr Collier on a more social level?'

'No.' Bevan answered. 'We never socialised.'

'Did you ever argue with Mr Collier about matters discussed on the Senedd floor?'

'Not that I remember.'

'DI Fagan, is there a point you wish to make here? Instead of prattling on,' Warren moaned.

'I've spoken to others about your relationship with Mr Collier and they paint a different picture. You have often been seen having screaming matches with him.'

'DI Fagan, I think you're done here.' Warren stood. 'We're sorry to take up your time, Lloyd.'

'Clive, please sit back down. DI Fagan is just being thorough in his investigation.'

Warren glared at Fagan. 'A little too thorough.'

Bevan pursed his lips. 'DI Fagan, my business is politics. There are always arguments. Alwyn Collier was a Tory representative. I represent The Welsh Independent Nationalists. So yes, there is a conflict of interests between both parties. Both on and off the Senedd floor. Did I argue with Alwyn off the Senedd floor? Yes, I did. But it wasn't because I hated the man. Certainly not enough to murder him.'

'I wasn't suggesting that at all, Mr Bevan. Can you tell me the things you used to argue about and how some of these arguments turned into screaming matches?'

'We are both passionate men, DI Fagan. Passionate in our beliefs and ideals. Because we were on opposite sides of the Senedd, sometimes our arguments used to spiral. I disliked the man because of what he represented.'

'And what was that?'

'A Tory, DI Fagan. Who, like his fellow Tory representatives serve themselves and not the people of Wales. I disliked the man because of his political standing. In other words, it was political, not personal. I am deeply upset by what has happened over the past twenty-four hours. The news media will be camped outside for the next few days. No doubt wanting to pin some of the blame on me.'

'And why would they do that?'

'DI Fagan, is this just a routine questioning, or an interrogation?' Warren interrupted.

'Clive, I just said it's okay. I have no secrets DI Fagan. Probably why I am not popular in the eyes of the media. What they cannot find, they simply concoct out of thin air. I don't align with the ideologies of the main political parties. I believe the people of Wales have a right to choose their own path, and determine their own future. Alwyn Collier represented the Conservative party. Those of us who have long memories remember what the Tories did to the South Wales communities during the eighties. Thatcher and her government destroyed the future of the working class. Men who had worked in the coal mines for generations. Alwyn Collier betrayed the communities of South Wales by working during the miners' strike.'

Fagan sensed the frustration in Bevan's tone. 'I understand that Mr Collier was due to face a committee. And that it was an ongoing enquiry into the behaviour of his staff.'

Warren shot Fagan a stern look.

Beven took time to answer. 'Yes.'

'Was this regarding his lack of action regarding the behaviour of some of his staff?'

'Yes. Alwyn wasn't what I call a strong leader. Considering he was the leader of the Tories for the Assembly, there were those who abused their power and he let them get away with it.'

'So you think his leadership lacked strength?'

'Yes.' Bevan replied. 'I could never understand how he was elected as the Welsh Conservative leader. But given the choice it was relatively easy for him to win the seat.'

'I would have thought it would have been harder for you, given that your party is neck and neck with Labour.'

'Times are changing, Inspector Fagan. The people of Wales are turning away from mainstream political parties. We are the majority party in the Senedd.'

'Is that why you are so keen to hold a referendum?'

'Can we please stay on topic, DI Fagan.' Warren sighed.

'Certainly. This committee was due to meet the day before yesterday at three o'clock?' Fagan continued.

'Yes.'

'The committee first met with Mr Collier three weeks ago. What issues were addressed?'

'Mainly his lack of action involving his senior staff.'

'What was the outcome of the meeting?'

Bevan seemed uncomfortable with the question. 'I don't see how the inquiry into Mr Collier's staff is connected to his murder. I've had to discipline several people about their behaviour over the years, DI Fagan.'

'I'm just trying to establish the facts behind Mr Collier's death. I have to cover all my bases, Mr Bevan. How many hearings were you going to have before you reached a decision?'

Bevan could not come up with an answer.

Fagan repeated the question.

'There was two.'

'The second one being the day before yesterday. The day he died.'

'Of course, yes. I believe I have already stated this.'

'Who sat on the committee?'

'I beg your pardon.'

'You were part of the committee, were you not?'

'Yes.'

'I assume your goal was to reach a verdict on Mr Collier's lack of action.'

Bevan inhaled. 'Yes, it was.'

Fagan shrugged. 'And?'

'And what, DI Fagan.' Bevan snapped.

'What verdict did you reach?'

'We could not reach a verdict.'

'Would you care to elaborate on why?'

'No, the hearing was held behind closed doors, DI Fagan. The reason being, we wanted to save Mr Collier any embarrassment in the eyes of the media. He was due to be appointed to Secretary of State for Wales. I felt it would be unfair to put this in jeopardy.'

'How many members sat on the committee?'

'There were six of us.'

'I'd like a list of names, please.'

'Why is this relevant, DI Fagan? I know every member of the committee personally. None of them had any kind of grudge against Collier. Certainly not enough to murder the man.'

'And I'm sure they'll testify to this when I get the chance to interview them.'

'DI Fagan, I think we are done here,' Warren interrupted.

Fagan threw him a sideward glance. 'With all due respect, sir. I am trying to conduct a murder investigation.'

'What you are trying to do, DI Fagan, is discredit a respected politician. Mr Bevan has been very open with his answers.'

'I take it you can account for your whereabouts the night Alwyn Collier was murdered?' Fagan continued.

'Of course I can. I was at a charity auction in Swansea.'

Warren stood. 'Let's go, DI Fagan, *now!*'

Fagan and Warren emerged out of the office building.

'Let's get one thing clear, DI Fagan. Lloyd Bevan is not a suspect in the murder of Alwyn Collier.'

Fagan pointed at the building. 'At what point did I even suggest that? We are day two into this investigation and still no closer to pulling in anyone that may be connected.'

'Then I suggest you pull your finger out of your arse and draw up a list. Get back to Newport and go over the case with your team. I will be there in the morning. I expect results.'

Fagan watched as Warren walked away. He called up Watkins' number. 'Sean, do me a favour.'

'Yeah, sure boss.'

'When we met with Collier's personal assistant yesterday. She said that Alwyn had his satchel stolen a few weeks ago when he caught the train to Cardiff. Find out when exactly and see if there is any CCTV footage available.'

'Sure thing.'

'Has Stacey found anything juicy about the family?'

'Collier was having an affair with another member of the Assembly. Collier's wife is still pissed off about it. Fifty-nine-year-old Victoria Armstrong. She's the Assembly member for Powys. She lives just outside Talgarth in a village called Cwmdu. Has a consultation surgery in Brecon, Talgarth and Builth Wells once a month.'

'Looks like we're going to be pulled pillar to post on this one, Sean. Get hold of her office and find out when she's available for a chat. I'm on my way back now.'

'How did it go with the First Minister, boss?'

'Don't ask.' Fagan sighed. 'There's something about that man. I can't quite put my finger on it.'

CHAPTER 16

Abertillery Working men's club–1985
Lloyd Bevan peeked through the curtain at the audience in the main dance hall of the club.

The landlord, who had supported the strike, had allowed them to meet up.

He smiled. 'Well, at least there's a good turnout tonight.'

'What exactly is the plan here, Lloyd?' Bryn Collier asked. His thoughts dwelled on the recent argument he had with his brother at their mam's house.

'What d'you mean?'

'The demonstration the other day was brilliant and all. But we need to take further action. We need to make a stand and let those bastards at Six Bells know we mean business.'

'That's what I'm about to reveal tonight. Don't worry, I've got a plan.' Bevan closed his eyes and said a silent prayer. He pulled back the curtain and stepped out in front of a grim faced audience of striking miners. 'Thanks for coming tonight, boys. Me and Bryn really appreciate it.'

Bevan's words were met with a wall of silence.

'I know it's been a hard year. And that some of you may have doubts about where we are going with this strike. But I promise you that a lot of work is going on at the top level of the union.'

'Like what?' A voice shouted from the audience.

Bevan took a moment to answer. 'The head union conveners are meeting with the National Coal Board to hammer out a decent pay deal for the miners.'

Collier shot Bevan a suspicious look.

'I am confident that a deal will be reached and that we can all go back to work.'

'How much?' Another miner asked.

'I don't have the figures yet. But I will speak with our regional union convenor later this week to get the figures. I think we are close to reaching a deal.'

'What about the rumours that the NUM is close to collapse and Scargill might have to abandon the strike?' another miner asked.

'What rumours are they?'

'Don't treat us like we're fucking idiots, Lloyd. Surely you read the papers and watch the news. They're saying that a prolonged strike by the miners cannot continue for much longer. The Daily Mirror reckons everyone will be back to work within two weeks.'

'There's no way that is going to happen.' Bevan said with a firm tone.

'What about the food parcels that you promised us last week?'

'We are working on that. I promise you'll see some packages by the end of the week.'

'Are you close to a deal or what?'

'Yes, we are.' Bevan insisted.

'What percentage d'you think the National Coal Board is going to offer us?'

'This isn't really about pay increases. It's about the pit closures that are happening all over the country. This is about saving our way of life. Our communities are under threat.'

'But if the government wants to shut the pits, there's nothing we can do about it, is ther?.' An audience member shouted.

'Is Six Bells going to shut?' Another man questioned.

A low rumble of murmurs rippled through the miners.

Bevan held up his hand. 'Six Bells will not shut. The pit will still be there in fifty years. Coal mining is a job for life.'

'When is this strike going to end?'

'It will end when we say so,' Bevan said loudly. 'When the government gives into our demands and stops threatening us with pit closures. We cannot let them win.'

'What more can the miners do, Lloyd? We've been out of work for nearly a year now. And there seems to be no progress made regarding our demands.' The man looked around the room.

'There aren't as many people here as there were last year. People are getting fucked off with the way Scargill is handling this. He doesn't seem like he's getting anywhere. All I see on the telly are grand speeches. But no one is listening anymore. Isn't it time to throw in the towel?'

People throughout the room nodded.

Bevan stared directly at the miner. 'Is that what you plan to do is it? To just roll over and die. Let the government and that bitch sat in Number Ten destroy our way of life.'

'Don't put me on the spot like that, Lloyd.' The man responded. 'This strike has been dragging on for a year. And still we are no further along the road with negotiations. Scargill is a complete waste of time. He goes on TV and defends his actions. Not the actions of the miners. All that man gives a fuck about is himself. Look around you. Everyone has returned to work. There are more men at work now. There's not enough of us to pose a threat.' The man waved his hand around. 'This is all that is left of us. Tell us how we can still make a difference.'

'We blockade the Six Bells Colliery. That's how we can make a difference.' Bevan answered.

The audience exchanged doubtful expressions.

'Blockade Six Bells.' The man's voice was laden with doubt. 'There aren't enough of us to piss in a jar right now. Let alone organise a full march on Six Bells. We need a massive number of men to do that.'

'And we'll have it.' Bevan stated. 'Me and Bryn are going to Port Talbot to meet union officials. I spoke to a union convenor yesterday. He's promised five hundred men to join us. There are also workers at the Hoover plant in Merthyr. They have pledged two hundred workers. There are supporters coming from all over the Valleys. We have men coming from Coopers Filters in Abergavenny. There are workers from Lucas Girling in Cwmbran. We even have over a hundred men coming from the Royal Ordnance factory near Monmouth. We'll have two thousand workers at the Rally. Plus, we'll have the support of the local communities.'

'If we have two thousand men. You can guarantee plod will

have twice as many. You know they'll be ready for us. If we try to set foot in Six Bells, then we'll all be arrested. It'll be a repeat of Orgreave last June. We all saw that play out on the news. The bloody police sent in horses to trample the miners. I'm not risking my neck if it's not going to get us anywhere.'

'If that's your attitude, then fuck off out the door and join the rest of the scab bastards that have betrayed us,' Bevan said, pointing at the entrance.

'Jesus, you sound just like Scargill.' The man stated. 'We have stuck with you on this strike. We have followed your orders. But you have to face facts. The government has won. I am a week away from getting kicked out of my house. You need to resolve this within the week.' The man pointed at Collier and Bevan. 'If I get kicked out of my house because I can't pay the bloody mortgage in the next few weeks, then I am blaming you.'

'And that's exactly what Thatcher wants. Us fighting amongst ourselves.'

'We've been doing that for a year. Just in case you haven't noticed, Lloyd. Turning against family, long time workmates and colleagues. We've been all over the country turning up at protests. A few of us were at Orgreave. I spent three days in a prison cell because of what happened up there. Yeah, I'll keep standing by you. But I can't do it forever. If the coal board doesn't give in to our demands soon then we'll all be going back to work.' The man looked around the room for supporting nods, but saw none. 'You lot are full of shit.' He pointed at Collier and Bevan. 'You'll slag them off behind their backs about the strike. But when they're here in person, you'll all pretend to support them. I've spoken to everyone in this room. We're all fucked off. So what are you two going to do about it?'

'I just said, didn't I?' Bevan responded. 'We're organising a march on Six Bells.'

'But to do what?'

'To let the National Coal Board know they cannot shut the pits.'

'And then what? What's your plan after that? Hold another demonstration, and another. I'm sick and tired of it.' The man's agitation increased.

Bevan held his hand up. 'Right, let's just calm down here. We know what we're up against. So let me ask you this. If this strike ends in the next few weeks, you know that bitch sitting in Downing Street will have a field day. We need to make a stand.'

'It will be our last stand.' The man pointed out. 'Because I'm all out of patience with everything.'

'Fair enough.' Bevan stated. 'All me and Bryn ask is for you to hear us out for a few minutes.'

The man inhaled before sitting back down.

'We have support from workers all over the Valleys. It's just a case of organising everything.' Bevan looked at Collier. 'Bryn will explain our plan.'

Collier spoke. 'First, we have to deal with the police presence in the Valleys. For the past year, entire communities have been under siege from these bastards. The other day, when we marched on Six Bells, they were guarding the main entrance to the pit. When we march on the pit on St David's say we're planning several distractions to lure the police away from the pit. We know they won't totally abandon it. However. If we can decrease the numbers, then we may have a chance to get inside.'

'And then what?' A miner asked.

'We need several volunteers to scale the pit head's winding gear.' Collier said.

The audience looked at each other, shaking their heads.

'Look, I know it's dangerous. But I think if we have men positioned on the pithead's winding gear, then they'll have to stop operations.'

'And what about those working underground? If you have men on the winding gear, then they won't be able to come to the surface.'

'I'm not suggesting we station men on the winding gear all day long. Just a few hours. It will be enough to let the press know we mean business. Plus, we'll hang a banner. There'll be press there. So it will be all over the papers the following day. A banner on the pithead's winding gear will be our symbol of defiance.'

'But how are you going to lure the police away from the pit

entrance?'

'We are working through several ideas that will distract the police. The wives and girlfriends of the miners are organising a rally that will take place at the Six Bells park. What we'll do is make it look like they're marching on the colliery, then they'll occupy the police station. There aren't all that many police stationed there. Most of the police patrolling the valley are from other areas. If the women cause enough noise, the police will respond and pull resources away from the Six Bells. We're also going to spread gossip about demonstrations happening in other places like the Tower Colliery. The police will be thinly spread through the Valleys. We plan to station men at the Tower to make it look like there's going to be a major demonstration.'

'What about when the police make arrests?' An audience member asked with a concerned expression. 'I don't want to get arrested while you union officials take a back seat. Watching the demonstrations from afar.'

'No one is taking a back seat.' Collier seemed to take offence at the comment. 'We'll be there every step of the way with you. Me and Lloyd will lead the march on the Six Bells Colliery.'

'Where are we meeting up?'

'We'll meet up in Six Bells park. The women will already be there. When they march on the police station, the rest of us will march on the pit. The police will be totally confused. All me and Lloyd ask is for you boys to turn up and support us. I promise. This plan will work. We'll take Six Bells and occupy it for a few hours.'

CHAPTER 17

Newport Central police station
Present day

Fagan took a swig of coffee and focussed on the whiteboard. Watkins and Brooks walked into the room.

'Where have you boys been?' Fagan barked.

'Sorry, boss. We've been going over CCTV footage.'

'Anything?'

Watkins opened his laptop. 'I phoned Collier's assistant about the stolen satchel. Collier didn't notice his satchel was missing until he was getting off the train. Tracie said he spent an hour at the station with the police. But it was chaotic. They couldn't find the satchel or the thief. Cardiff transport police logged the theft. However, I checked with Cardiff Central. They scrub their footage once a month.'

'Which means there's no footage of Collier getting off the train or at the station. Shit, another dead end.'

Watkins grinned.

Fagan looked back at him. 'You've found something.'

Watkins nodded. 'I did a sweep of all the cameras near the train station. The BBC studios is located close to Cardiff Central. They scrub their footage every twelve months.' Watkins clicked on his mouse. 'Their cameras captured this image of a woman standing outside the main entrance.'

Fagan studied the image. A woman in a baseball cap was talking on a mobile phone. The tattoo on the woman's neck was very clear. The woman turned to face the camera, unaware that it was watching her. Fagan smiled. 'That's Tanya Glover. Lloyd Bevan's personal assistant.'

'Or just plain Tanya. That's her preferred pronoun.' Watkins mocked.

Fagan spotted the satchel she was holding. 'That looks like the satchel recovered from the bottom of the Keepers.'

'With fifty grand in cash.' Watkins added.

Brooks handed Fagan a sheet of paper. 'I've already checked her bank details and mobile data. On the morning that image was taken, Glover boarded a train at Newport station to Cardiff Central. Thing is, she doesn't live in Newport, she lives in Barry. I cross checked Collier's bank details.' Brooks pointed at the sheet. 'He booked a train from Abergavenny train station that morning. There were major works on the Ebbw Vale line, which meant the line was closed for three days. The train Collier boarded is the same train that Glover boarded at Newport.'

'So she gets on the train and steals Collier's satchel.' Fagan surmised.

'I checked with Collier's wife. She bought him that satchel as a sixtieth birthday present.' Watkins revealed.

'It has to be the same satchel.' Fagan studied the footage. Although there was no sound, Tanya was laughing out loud. 'Do you reckon this video is clear enough to get a lip syncing expert to have a look?'

'Probably.' Watkins answered. 'Do you want me to make a call, boss?'

Fagan nodded. 'Yeah. What about Glover's phone records?'

Brooks handed Fagan another sheet of paper. 'I ran a check. According to her phone records no phone calls were made from her phone at that time.'

'Which means she's using a burner phone.'

'You're right, boss.' Watkins clicked on the mouse. Another video file played. 'She's on the phone for less than a minute. Then she walks out of view of the camera. However, another CCTV camera picked her up a couple of seconds later.'

Fagan watched as Tanya tossed the phone into a litter bin. 'Yeah, it's definitely a burner phone.' He paused for a moment. 'Any records on her debit card about a phone purchase?'

'No, sir.' Brooks replied. 'However, she withdrew two hundred quid in cash that morning from a Sainsbury cashpoint in the centre of Newport.'

'Enough to buy a cheap burner phone and dispose of it.' Fagan looked at the whiteboard, considering his next move. 'Send a couple of uniform to pick her up. She's our first lead in this investigation.'

'Going to raise some red flags, boss. Her being Bevan's personal assistant.'

'Exactly.' Fagan smiled.

'I phoned Victoria Armstrong's personal assistant. She's at Talgarth Community Centre tomorrow and will talk to us.'

'Good. We'll see if Collier had any other skeletons in his cupboard. Anything about the cash found in the satchel?'

'Not yet, sir,' Brooks answered. 'I have checked Collier's bank account. There was nothing matching the amount found in the satchel. I also checked Tanya Glover's account. She's skint, lots of credit card debt.'

'So where did the fifty grand come from?'

'One more thing, boss.' Watkins said. 'Stacey had a long conversation with Collier's wife last night. There was an incident four months ago at their house. A man turned up and threatened to kill Collier. The police were called, and the man was arrested. But no charges were made against him.'

'You got a name?'

'Sixty-nine-year-old Martin Cooper.'

'Has he got form?'

'Yeah.' Watkins replied. 'A string of property damage convictions stretching back decades. A load of anti-social behaviour orders. Nine drink driving offences.'

'We'll pull Cooper in for questioning. I want to see why he turned up at Collier's house. That's two possible leads we have.' Fagan glanced at the whiteboard. 'At least it's a start. What about Collier's last movements the night he was murdered?'

'Still nothing, boss.' Watkins said. 'Uniform have been door to door in Blaenavon, hoping that someone saw Collier in the area the night he was murdered.'

'Anything new from Terry's Taxis in Abergavenny?'

'No, I spoke to Terry while you were in Cardiff. He said Collier hardly spoke to him when he picked him up from Abergavenny train station. He dropped him off in Blaenavon and headed back to Abergavenny.'

'Did Terry say which way he went?'

'No, boss. But he probably drove back over the Keepers.'

'Andrew, find out if Terry has a dashcam in his taxi and if he keeps footage.'

Brooks nodded. 'Will do, sir.'

Fagan looked at Watkins' laptop. 'I know it's a big ask, but I need to see if you can track Tanya's movements after she threw the phone into the bin. Also, find out if Cardiff council recycles their waste.'

'There's a lot of CCTV cameras around Cardiff centre, boss, that is a big ask.'

Fagan pointed at the laptop. 'Glover is Bevan's personal assistant. We need to do a background check on her. I want to know everything about her before we pull her in.'

'Think you'll turn something up, boss?'

'I'm sure of it. The woman was trying to be in control yesterday. She followed us to the café where we interviewed Tracie. What's the betting she's Bevan's minion?'

'She's out and proud.' Brooks said, staring at his tablet.

'What have you got, Andrew?'

'Thirty-eight years of age. Did her masters in philosophy at Oxford. She boasts about batting for both sides. But mainly likes women.' Brooks paused.

'What?'

'She said she prefers women, because they are often more submissive.'

'Well, that could be seen as politically incorrect.' Fagan remarked.

'She has a weekly radio blog called Cymru for Queers. She's outspoken on several issues, and a staunch supporter of independence for Wales. In a recent tweet, she said that an independent Wales will create more jobs for the LGBTQ community.' Brooks scrolled down the page. 'She's definitely big on the cancel culture and will push for a law to ban any critical speech against the LGBTQ community.'

Fagan stared at her image outside the BBC building. 'Why steal the satchel?'

'Collier's assistant told us his satchel contained a speech he was giving to the Senedd that day.'

'Is that really worth sealing?'

'Depends on what the speech was about.'

'What was Collier again? Shadow Secretary for the Environment.' Fagan tapped Collier's name into his computer. 'It says here Collier was pushing for more green energy production in Wales. His projects included the Severn barrage, a solar farm just outside Sennybridge, and a wind farm along the top of the mountains near where he lived. He was voted down on everything he suggested to the Senedd.' Fagan mulled over the information in his mind. 'A former coal miner who switches to green energy.' Fagan tapped Lloyd's name on his keyboard. 'This is interesting. According to this, Bevan was looking to regenerate the communities of south Wales by opening a certain number of coal mines.'

'Good luck with that.' Watkins said. 'Nearly all of them have been knocked down and filled in. It's like the steel works in Ebbw Vale. There are houses, a hospital and a college there now.'

'So they were at opposite ends of the energy production debate. Still, not enough reason to murder the man. So, why steal the satchel?'

'It was premeditated.' Watkins suggested.

Fagan pointed at the image of Glover on Watkins' laptop. 'You saying she planned to murder him?'

'Not exactly, but she wanted the satchel for a reason. If it wasn't his speech she was interested in, it had to be something else.'

'We don't know if it's just her involved in Collier's murder or other parties.' Brooks said.

'So she could have been acting on someone else's orders?' Fagan said.

Brooks nodded.

'But why go to all the trouble of boarding a train at Newport to steal the satchel? She could have had many opportunities to steal it when Collier was at the Senedd or in Cardiff. You saw her with Tracie Morris yesterday, Sean. When we turned up, she was cosying up to her.'

'Delwyn Horlor mentioned Glover was the manipulative type. And she had the power to lure straight women into bed.'

'A useful weapon to have at your disposal if you're the First Minister.'

Watkins and Brooks looked at Fagan with blank expressions.

'Think about it. Lloyd Bevan wants independence for Wales. He told me this morning his party has the majority of seats in the Senedd. I'm no expert in politics, but I'm sure if he wants independence for Wales, he's going to need backing from assembly members from the other political parties. Who do we have? The Tories, Labour and Plaid Cymru. Many of those assembly members are women. When we meet with Victoria Armstrong tomorrow, we'll find out if there is any juicy gossip.' Fagan got up and walked over to the whiteboard. 'So Glover steals Collier's satchel a few weeks back. She's clever enough to know that Cardiff Central scrub their CCTV once a month. She hangs onto the satchel and then stuffs fifty grand into it, before meeting Collier and murdering him.' Fagan frowned at the whiteboard.

'What's up, boss?'

'None of this makes sense. There's no connection between Collier and Glover. There's something we're missing. I reckon this murder has its roots in the murder of Collier's brother nearly forty years ago.' Fagan returned to his computer and tapped Martin Cooper's name into the police database. 'Martin Cooper was arrested at Collier's home about four months ago. According to Stacey, Collier's wife told her that Cooper threatened to kill Collier.' Fagan read from the Wikipedia page he had found. 'Martin Cooper was one of four men arrested for the murder of Dafydd Collier and Sean Price in 1985..'

'Similar to the Birmingham six.' Watkins mentioned reading from a webpage. 'The Birmingham Six were each sentenced to life imprisonment in 1975 following their false convictions for the 1974 Birmingham pub bombings. Their convictions were declared unsafe and unsatisfactory and quashed by the Court of Appeal on 14 March 1991.'

'These aren't IRA.' Fagan pointed out. 'However, Cooper was beaten and forced to sign a confession.' Fagan inhaled. 'More bent coppers.'

'He hated Collier enough to turn up at his house, threatening to kill him. Why?'

'Horlor told us that Collier worked through the strike in 1984. Cooper and the other three accused of murdering Dafydd Collier and Sean Price were strikers. Including his older brother, Bryn.'

'One of which was Lloyd Bevan.' Watkins pointed out.

Fagan looked at Brooks. 'Did you pull the file regarding the murders?'

'I did, sir, but I haven't opened it.'

'Okay, we'll put it on the back burner for now. Let's wait until uniform brings in Glover.'

'It's going to rattle Bevan when they arrest her and bring her in for questioning.'

Fagan smiled. 'That's what I'm counting on. If you shake the rotten apple tree for long enough, something is bound to fall.'

CHAPTER 18

The Agincourt Hotel – Monmouthshire 1985
Benson knocked loudly on the door of the hotel room that had been reserved.

Owain Lance opened the door and shook the hand of his former superior. 'Thank you for coming, sir. We've booked a room because of the situation on the ground within the Six Bells valley. I didn't want to be seen out in the open. There are rumours that the unions have informants everywhere.'

Benson stepped into the room. 'A wise move.' He spotted the MI5 operative who was looking at a map of the Six Bells area. The operative was with another man dressed in a police commander's uniform.

'Heard you got egg on your face the other day during the incident at the Six Bells park.' The operative casually remarked.

Benson was immediately on the back heel. 'My officers were not prepared. We didn't expect the strikers to have reinforcements.' He glanced at the police commander. 'I thought the Met would have been more of a help.'

'This is Commander Roger West.' Lance introduced.

'I'm sorry we didn't send more men to assist Sergeant Benson. This strike has dragged on for almost a year. Police forces throughout the UK have been overstretched. Fortunately, most of these silly bastards have gone back to work. We estimate there are only a small percent of miners now on strike. Most of these seem to be in the South Wales Valleys. So we are setting out a plan to counteract any action these unions have planned. We've been given an extra ten thousand police officers in case things get a little rough.'

'A good idea, sir,' Benson said. 'From what I experienced the other day, these militant bastards are itching for a fight.'

'The good news is, the government expects this strike to collapse any day now. Scargill and his deputies had a meeting last weekend to discuss a way forward. The government is confident they are close to ordering the miners back to work. The public is tiring of the constant public unrest. We will now focus our efforts on the areas that remain a problem. Mainly the South Wales Valleys. There have been a few skirmishes at the Port Talbot steelworks and Llanwern in Newport. Lorries have been held up frequently over the last few weeks. Several coke plants have been blockaded. The striking miners in this part of the world seem to be more dug in.' West glanced at Lance. 'He's been on the ground over the past few months providing valuable information to both police and the intelligence services.' West glanced at the operative. 'The intelligence services have several individuals on the radar at the moment. We mentioned these at our last meeting. Our MI5 contact is here to fill you in on more of what these men are about.'

The operative took charge of the briefing. 'What I'm about to tell you is a matter of national security. The union officials I mentioned the other night have a large following and are likely to cause a major disruption. It is our aim to monitor these individuals to ensure things don't get out of hand. What we don't want is another Orgreave happening. Because the number of strikers is dwindling, there's a possibility that they may try something desperate to gain support. Another thing going in our favour is dwindling media interest in the strike. Compared to a few months ago, the papers are no longer interested.'

'What's the plan?'

West walked over to a map. 'Sergeant Lance has provided us with vital intelligence. There's going to be a massive demonstration at the Six Bells Colliery on St David's Day. So the strategy we are going to implement is going to be the same we used in Nottinghamshire last year.'

Benson nodded. 'I believe the media labelled that area as Fort Notts.'

West smiled. 'It was a highly successful operation carried out by various police forces in that area. We are planning to use the same strategy in the South Wales Valleys.'

'That's a lot of roads to cover, sir,' Benson pointed out.

'Agreed. However, many of the roads are not suitable for large vehicles such as buses. Our intelligence suggests that a large number of men are due to arrive in coaches. These coaches will follow major routes. We know that NUM union officials had a meeting with the workers at Port Talbot steel works yesterday. They have pledged at least seven hundred men to the strikers. A lot of coach companies within the Valleys are sympathetic to the strike. They have been transporting miners from all over the Valleys to areas where there have been protests.'

'Can't we revoke their licences?' Benson asked.

West shook his head. 'There are too many legal ramifications. Plus, it would take too long. Our immediate goal is to stop support for the miners from getting access to key pitheads in the South Wales Valleys. The Six Bells Colliery is high on our priority list because it's being targeted. The first strategy in place it to stop any supporters coming from Port Talbot.' West pointed at the map. 'We'll be setting up checkpoints along the Heads of the Valleys road. Stopping any large coaches and other vehicles carrying over three people. They will be turned back or face arrest. There is a service station just off the motorway. This location is where large vehicles will be detained. They will then be taken back to Port Talbot under a police escort. Anyone traveling on these coaches will be ordered to disband or face arrest.'

'It will be enough to discourage these militant bastards from stirring up trouble, sir,' Benson said.

'Indeed.' West continued. 'We'll have several other checkpoints along the heads of the valley road. The Severn Sisters will be another area we will be stopping vehicles. If there are over three men in a vehicle, then they will be detained and questioned. Our officers will hold them for at least five hours before being sent on their way. Our key goal here is to starve the strikers of reinforcements who are planning to march on Six Bells. We'll have a checkpoint at Hirwaun near the Tower colliery.' West pointed to an area on the map. 'We'll also have a major checkpoint at Brynmawr at the roundabout where the new bypass starts. We'll have spotters at Nantyglo and Blaina. A lot of the local residents will turn out for this rally, which means a mixture of old fogies, women and children. Many will be wives and girlfriends of striking miners.'

Benson surveyed the map. 'What about all the side roads?'

'There's not a lot we can do about those. We'll have patrols out in the local communities along the mountain roads road. But even I am limited to the number of men and vehicles I can have. We are expecting people to get past our roadblocks.'

'How many demonstrators are you expecting at the Six Bells?'

'We estimate there could be at least two thousand demonstrators who will attend the rally. The area in which they plan to gather is very small,' Lance explained.

'Which makes it very dangerous. What we don't want is our officers being squeezed into a small area. So we are setting up checkpoints along the key routes.'

Benson looked at the operative. 'Remind me again, who are the union officials you have your eye on?'

The operative picked up a file containing documents and photographs. 'The first man on our list is Lloyd Bevan. He is the head union official for that area. He has been involved in several incidents throughout the UK. He was arrested at Orgreave in June and charged with public disorder offences. This has not deterred him from organising mass protests throughout the South Wales region. Bevan is a fanatic when it comes to this kind of thing. We have him under surveillance for several reasons. I'm afraid it's confidential as to the exact nature. It's a matter of national security. Bevan is the leader of a radical group known as Meibion Glyndwr. We believe they are responsible for firebombing multiple holiday homes owned by English residents. Bevan was arrested four years ago in connection with the firebombing of a property in Abergavenny.'

Benson recalled a memory. 'I remember.' He glanced at the police commander. 'I also recall Special Branch turning up and booting local police out of the area.'

West nodded. 'It was necessary. With the recent spate of

bombings by the IRA, we weren't sure if there was a connection.'

Benson pointed at the photograph. 'You think this group may be connected with the IRA?'

West shook his head. 'Meibion Glyndwr is a separate entity.'

The operative continued. 'Next up is Bryn Collier. He's the man behind Bevan's success. Bevan isn't much of a speaker. It's Collier who writes all the speeches at rallies. Collier is also a member of Meibion Glyndwr. Although there is nothing to connect him with any attacks, Collier is of special interest to us. Once again, for purposes of national security, I cannot divulge why. Collier is also the money man for the NUM in this part of the world. He's been seen at several rallies in the north of England with Scargill and Chief Executive for the NUM, Roger Windsor.'

'I remember seeing Windsor in the news last year. There were pictures of him meeting with Colonel Gaddafi in Libya.' Benson mentioned. 'Caused quite a stir in the news. It was only a few months after that poor woman police officer was murdered outside the Libyan embassy.'

The operative glanced at West. 'Next on our list is Martin Cooper. Or as we have labelled him, the Union attack dog. Cooper is a nasty piece of work. Offences ranging from drunken disorderly to public order offences. Cooper was also arrested at Orgreave last year. He's been known for attacking miners who have worked through the strike. He's very good at organising brawls. So we need to monitor him.'

'It's these three men that will be key in the rally they are planning.' West remarked.

'Well, it looks as if you have everything in hand. What will my role be during this demonstration?'

'You will be stationed at the Six Bells Colliery.' West revealed. 'You will have two hundred officers at your disposal. All your men will be fully equipped with the latest riot gear. This will be enough to deter the miners from attempting to take the colliery.' West looked at Lance. 'From what Owain has told us, it looks like they will launch a full assault on the colliery. They plan to take control and station men on the pithead winding gear. Your role is to stop this from happening. Police officers will be stationed at the gate and keep a twenty-four-hour guard at the pit.'

'I'll do my best to make sure they don't get in, sir,' Benson said with confidence. 'You say my men will be equipped with riot gear. What about the strikers? Are you expecting them to be armed in any way?'

The operative pointed at the picture of Martin Cooper. 'He is also a member of Meibion Glyndwr. We believe Cooper firebombed Nicholas Edward's home in Abergavenny four years ago. But again, we have no evidence to prove this. I am positive that Cooper will try something when the rally happens. If petrol bombs are used during the demonstration, then the fire brigade will be on standby. Hopefully, with all the checkpoints and sheer police numbers, it will be enough to deter anyone from starting trouble. But if they do, we'll be ready for them.'

Benson nodded. 'I will see this through. I'll make sure my men will protect that pithead.'

CHAPTER 19

Newport Central police station
Present day

Fagan stared at the cryptic text message he'd just received. It was from an unknown number, something that Fagan despised. But this text wasn't a spammer. It simply said. *'You're on the right path arresting Tanya Glover.'*

'Boss, they're ready for us. Glover has been briefed by her solicitor.' Watkins said.

Fagan snapped out of his trance, slipping his phone into his pocket.

'You okay, boss.'

'Yeah, just some nuisance insurance company trying to spam me.'

They both entered the interview room.

Glover fixed a stare on Fagan as he sat down. 'You're in deep shit, arresting me. I'll make sure you won't even get a job as a lollipop man when I'm through with you.'

'Really.' Fagan smiled, remembering a childhood memory. He went to Llantilio Pertholey infants' school. An old country school at the foot of the Skirrid mountain. George Watkins would pick Fagan up every morning in his panda car and drive him and his best friend Graham up to the old Mardy post office where they would meet up with other children. They'd walk to the foot of Poplars Road where a stout, red-faced lollipop woman would wait to cross them safely across the road. Fagan and Graham would spend money in the petrol station that was run by an Irishman they nicknamed Paddy. He'd give them free chocolate that mice had helped themselves to in the storeroom at the back.

Watkins started up the interview sequence. 'Interview with Tanya Glover. Present in the room is Ms Glover.'

'It's not fucking Ms,' Glover interrupted. 'Do you understand? It's just Tanya. I am not going to say another thing until you address me by my preferred pronoun.'

Watkins was unphased by Glover's rant. 'Present in the room is Tanya, and representing Tanya is *Tanya's* solicitor, David Smith. Interviewing detectives are Detective Inspector Marc Fagan and Detective Sergeant Sean Watkins. I would like to remind Tanya of the caution our officers issued. You do not have to say anything, but it may harm your defence when questioned something you later rely on in court. Anything you do say may be given evidence against you.'

'So come on then, what are you about to accuse me of? Because whatever it is, I didn't do it.' Glover said with a confident tone. 'When Lloyd finds out you've arrested me, he will have your guts for garters, the both of you.'

'Close to him, are you Tanya?' Fagan questioned.

'What do you mean, close to him? As in screwing him. A bit old for me. Although his wife isn't bad. Likes to experiment between the sheets. I love women in their sixties. They're so easy to seduce. And they're up for anything. Usually, you men are spent by the time you've hit sixty.'

'Are you having an affair with Bevan's wife, Tanya?' Watkins asked.

'Good god no, the woman is unbearable. It was just a night of fun,' Tanya answered in a casual tone. 'She keeps herself fit and was pissed sa a fart after a function in Merthyr one night. So I thought I'll have a slice of her.' Tanya closed her eyes, taking a deep breath. 'Tasted of honey. Screamed like a banshee when I went down on her.'

'Very open about your sexual relationships, Tanya.' Fagan remarked.

'It was consensual, before you accuse me of anything. Lloyd isn't exactly breathtaking when it comes to bedroom matters. Cheryl just wanted to feel like a woman again.' Tanya leant forward, interlocking her fingers. 'I gave her a night she'll never forget.'

'DI Fagan, how are Tanya's sexual relationships related to her arrest?' Smith enquired.

Fagan looked back at him. 'They're not. But Tanya seems eager to boast about a sexual conquest.'

'I don't conquer my sexual partners. I'm a person of equal opportunity. They give to me what I give to them.' Tanya shrugged. 'If they beg for more, then who am I to say no?'

Fagan could sense Tanya was trying to toy with him. He reached into an evidence box he'd discreetly placed under the table, pulling out the satchel.

'I'm showing Tanya a satchel that was recovered from the Keepers Pond on the morning that Alwyn Collier's body was discovered.'

Glover looked at the satchel.

'Tanya, have you seen this satchel before?'

'No.'

'Do you own a satchel similar?'

'No, I don't own a satchel. Is there a point to all this?'

'Last month, you boarded a train to Cardiff. You got on at Newport.'

Glover shrugged. 'So, I'm always in Newport. Some good LGBTQ clubs there. Plenty of action. Especially the straights.'

'Straights?' Watkins said.

'Men like you, looking for something different. You'll be surprised how many straight people bat for the other side. I've bedded more straight women than I can count.' Glover boasted.

Fagan pushed the satchel in front of Glover. 'I'd like you to look at this satchel, Tanya. Take your time. I'm in no rush. As you can see, it's got a very distinct clasp.'

'Why do I need to examine it? I have never seen this.'

'On the morning of the twenty-third of last month, you boarded the eight twenty-seven train to Cardiff.'

Glover shrugged again. 'If you say so. Like I just said, I'm back-and-forth Newport regularly.'

'Do you use the trainline app?' Fagan asked.

'What?'

'You know, the trainline app. Our people have already had a look at your phone.'

'Have you got a warrant?' Glover demanded to know.

'We have.' Fagan answered. He picked up a sheet of paper. 'It gives all your details about your activities on trainline.'

'I've nothing to hide. So if you think you can find anything on my phone that could get me charged with anything, then you're going to be very disappointed.'

Fagan read the information aloud from the paper. 'You caught the train at Newport on the day DS Watkins mentioned.'

Glover rolled her eyes. 'Bugger me. How many times do I have to spell it out to you? I regularly visit Newport.'

'The train you caught that morning was the same train that Alwyn Collier boarded. We have also gained access to his trainline account.'

'So.' Glover snorted.

'On that morning in particular, Alwyn Collier reported a theft while he was on his way to Cardiff. He reported it to the police.' Fagan picked up a tablet. 'In his statement, Mr Collier maintains his satchel was by the side of him until he reached Newport. He had just been through a speech he was due to give to the Senedd later that day. When the train arrived at Cardiff, Mr Collier noticed his satchel wasn't by the side of him. He also expressed anger that he put it in a position that made it easy for someone to steal it.'

'And you think I stole it? Is that what you're saying?'

Fagan looked at Glover, shaking his head. 'I haven't stated this.'

'So what are you trying to get at?'

Fagan tapped his finger on the evidence bag containing the satchel. 'Think hard, Tanya. Have you seen this satchel before?'

'No, I bloody haven't.'

'But you freely acknowledge to being on the same train as Alwyn Collier that morning.' Watkins said.

'I don't know.'

'What don't you know, Tanya?'

Glover took a few moments to answer. 'That I was on the same train as Collier. At that time of morning it's usually packed. I probably remained by the door.'

'After you got off the train, where did you go?'

'Probably to work if it was a Friday. Doesn't take Sherlock Holmes to figure that one out.'

'Did you get a taxi to the Senedd, Tanya?' Fagan asked.

Glover sighed. 'I don't know, I probably called an Uber.'

'From outside Cardiff Central?'

'Yes, I'm not going to walk to the Senedd, am I?' Glover's frustration grew.

Fagan pointed at the satchel. 'And you still maintain you've never seen this satchel before today.'

'Jesus bloody Christ. Check with Cardiff Central will you. They'll probably have me on CCTV somewhere. I know they have those facial recognition cameras dotted everywhere. And since I work at the Senedd, my face was probably picked somewhere in the station.'

'You're right, they would have Tanya. Only Cardiff Central scrub their CCTV at the end of the month. And since the incident took place last month, there'll be nothing to connect you with Mr Collier and the theft of his satchel.'

A smug look appeared on Glover's face. She leant back in her chair, folding her arms. 'Well, that's just unfortunate, isn't it. You can't accuse me of whatever bullshit you're about to pin on me.'

Fagan stared back at her for several seconds before calling up an image on his tablet. 'I'm showing Tanya a CCTV image taken of her outside the BBC offices located close to Cardiff Central train station. The time and date are clearly visible on the top right-hand corner of the image.'

An expression of terror flashed across Glover's face.

'As you can see Tanya, this image shows you looking directly at the camera located near the main entrance. Can I ask what you are holding with your left hand?'

Glover remained silent.

'The image is very clear.' Fagan pointed at the satchel. 'It's pointless denying it, Tanya. The clasp is the same as the one on the image. Our image analysis team has confirmed this.'

'Why did you steal the satchel, Tanya?' Watkins asked.

Glover became mute.

'Did you have anything to do with Alwyn Collier's murder?'

Glover shook her head rigorously. 'No way, you're not pinning this on me. I had sod all to do with that.'

'But you admit stealing the satchel.'

'No comment.'

'Tanya, listen to me,' Fagan said. 'I'll remind you of your caution. You do not have to say anything, but it may harm your defence when questioned something which you later rely on in court. Do you understand?'

'I didn't kill anyone,' Glover protested.

Watkins repeated his question. 'Why did you steal the satchel, Tanya?'

Glover glared at him. 'No comment.'

Fagan studied her mannerism. 'Who are you protecting, Tanya?'

'I'm not protecting anyone.'

'Then why did you steal the satchel?'

'No comment.'

'A large sum of money was found stuffed into this satchel the day Collier's body was found at the Keepers. Were you blackmailing him?'

'No.'

'Then why did you steal the satchel?'

'No comment.'

'Tanya, you are our only suspect at the moment. I know you're protecting someone. I will ask you again. Why did you steal the satchel?'

Glover pursed her lips. 'No comment.'

'Do you realise what you are facing here, Tanya? You will be charged with perverting the course of justice. This satchel is directly linked to the murder of Alwyn Collier. This is a very high-profile murder. It's only a matter of time before our press office releases your name to the press.'

'DI Fagan, you cannot coax my client into giving a statement like that,' Smith warned.

Fagan pointed at the satchel again. 'Why did you steal the satchel?'

Glover gritted her teeth. 'No comment.'

'Tanya, do you honestly think that you can distance yourself from this?' Watkins asked. 'We have you on CCTV outside the BBC offices. This satchel is the same one that was recovered from the Keepers.'

Glover rubbed her hands.

'Where were you on the night Alwyn Collier was murdered?' Fagan asked.

'Nowhere near the Keepers, that's where.'

'So where were you?'

'No comment.'

'Tanya, if you want to provide an alibi the night Collier was murdered, then you won't be implicated in his murder.'

'I wasn't at the Keepers. I don't even know where that is. I live in Barry, for fuck's sake.'

'And you regularly travel to Newport. You've just admitted this,' Fagan pointed out. 'On the morning Alwyn Collier reported his satchel stolen, you were on the same train.' He pointed at the image on the tablet. 'You were captured outside the BBC building, holding the same satchel that Collier reported stolen. The same satchel that was found near his body the day before yesterday. It's not looking good for you, Tanya.'

'No comment.'

The door to the interview room opened. Griffiths and Warren marched in.

'Chief Constable Paul Griffiths and Detective Chief Superintendent Clive Warren have just entered the room.'

Warren walked up to the recording machine, switching it off.

'You can't do that.' Fagan pointed out. 'There is a procedure that has to be followed.'

Griffiths faked a smile. 'I'm sorry our officers have detained you, Tanya. You are free to go.'

The smug look returned. Glover stood up. 'I'd like to lodge a full complaint.'

'Of course.' Griffiths' tone was submissive. 'I'll make sure someone takes a statement.'

Glover stood nose to nose with Fagan. 'It's you who's in a

world of shit, not me.'

Griffiths turned and followed them out the door.

Warren glared at Fagan. 'DS Watkins, you are excused.'

Watkins seemed frozen for a few moments before gathering up his notes and walking out of the room.

'You want to tell me what's going on?' Fagan could sense anger welling up.

'*Sir*.' Warren barked. 'I believe there is a chain of command in this room, DI Fagan.' Warren grinned. 'And I command it.'

'Drop the bullshit, will you, *sir*. You've just interrupted a vital interview. Not to mention breaking protocol.'

'No, Fagan. What I've just done is save Gwent police a lot of embarrassment.'

'That woman is connected to all this.'

'DI Fagan, your job is to apprehend the person responsible for the murder of Alwyn Collier.'

'That's what I was doing.' Fagan looked at the satchel. 'Tanya Glover stole this satchel last month. Someone has been targeting Collier.'

'Immaterial.'

'I beg your pardon, sir.' Fagan could hardly believe what he was hearing.

'It's vital we arrest the person responsible for Collier's murder.'

Fagan pointed at the door. 'And that's exactly what I was trying to do. Until you burst in and ended our chances of catching the murderer. I will be launching a full complaint.'

Warren's nostrils flared. 'If you want to see that nice pension you're sat on, Fagan, I suggest you do your job.'

'Is that a threat, sir?'

'I don't make idle threats, Fagan, I just keep my promises.' Warren turned and marched out of the door.

Fagan grabbed his phone off the table and keyed in a number.

'Fagan, my old mate. How the devil are you?' Wayne Tanner greeted in his broad Scouse accent.

'Not bad Wayne. Listen mate, I need a favour.'

'Here we go. Who have you pissed off now?'

Fagan smiled. 'Just the usual. I need you to run a name. Detective Chief Superintendent Clive Warren.'

'Jesus Fagan, that's a big fish.'

'I know. But you're the only one I trust who can run the name and stay under the radar. I want you to also run a check on a Lloyd Bevan. He's the First Minister for Wales.'

'Everything alright at your end? I see the news the other day about that politician turning up dead.'

'I'm smack bang in the middle of it. Someone is trying to muddy the waters down at this end.'

'Listen, Fagan, I've been meaning to get in touch with you. It looks like our old friend is back.'

'Who.'

'The foetus snatcher.'

The name froze Fagan to his core. 'It's been thirty years, Tanner. You sure it's not a copycat?'

'No, this is the genuine article. We've had two working girls who've turned up dead in the last three months. Both were murdered while they were heavily pregnant. The babies were cut out of their wombs.'

'Jesus.' Fagan gasped.

'He's yet to taunt you, Fagan, but I suspect it will only be a matter of time before you are pulled into this.'

'Who's heading up the investigation?'

'Our old pal, Jack Daw.'

'If they've pulled Jack out of mothballs, it must be serious.'

'I thought he'd left long ago.'

'No, Jack never left. He just melted into the background. It was horrific what happened to his girlfriend.'

'We all remember that. The grinder Jack had to go through, considering what she was. He's done well for himself. It's now Chief Detective Inspector Jack Daw.'

'Good for Jack. Keep me posted, Tanner. It's only a matter of time before I'm called up on this. Given my relationship with that bastard. Run that name for me as soon as you can.'

'No worries Fagan, I'll get back to you.'

CHAPTER 20

The Travellers Rest–Blaina–1985

Martin Cooper and three other men stood across the road, hidden from view behind a van. Watching as two men entered the pub.

'What's the plan then, Martin?' One of three other men asked.

'We go in and we drag that scab bastard, Malcolm Jones, out of the pub. Tell him he either joins us, or we'll kick the fuck out of him.'

The man nodded. 'Sounds good to me. Perhaps we should give a few of them a good kicking.'

'We don't know how many scab twats are in there. Lloyd told me to look for his brother-in-law. Fucker has joined the rest of the scab bastards.' Cooper grinned. 'But it wouldn't hurt to give a few of those scabs the beating they deserve.'

'Is this a good idea, Martin?' One of Cooper's associates questioned. 'The Travellers Rest has been marked as a safe pub for working miners. If we go in there and start a fight, then it will annoy Lloyd and Bryn.'

Cooper shot him a sidewards glance. 'I hope you're not looking at fucking off home.' His tone was threatening. 'We are at war with these scabs. So nowhere is mutual ground.'

The man decided not to add to Cooper's agitation. He knew Cooper had a reputation for turning on people on a whim.

'We'll go in and cause aggro, before dragging that scab bastard, Malcolm Jones, out of there. Give him the pasting he deserves for jumping ship.' Cooper waited several seconds. 'Come on, boys, let's have a little fun.'

'You okay Martin?' Lynn Williams asked.

Jones sipped away at his pint. 'I'm just a little jittery, that's all, mate. I've been arguing with the missus about going back to work. That's why I'm in here. She was calling me every name under the sun when I got home from work. We had a blazing row in front of the kids. The trouble with Tara is she doesn't understand what we're going through. She thinks we can survive on fresh air alone. I'm surprised that twat of a brother-in-law of mine hasn't been round to give me a kicking already.' Jones took another sip. 'I just feel a little guilty.'

'You've done nothing wrong, mate.' Williams gestured around the pub. 'We were all out on strike when it began. When it all kicked off last year, I hoped we'd only be out for a couple of weeks. We all thought that Thatcher would cave. By September, I'd gone through all my savings and ran out of money. It took me over a year to save the amount I had in the bank. Me and the wife were planning to go to Spain in the summer. She's been going on about it for months. Now we can't afford it. I'm piling in the overtime, but it will be another year before I can get the money I lost during the strike. It's okay for the likes of Bevan and Collier. They've been getting handouts from the NUM.'

'No one has seen a food package in weeks.' Jones said. 'They're getting more irregular. That's why I went back to work. I'll be glad when I get paid this week. So I can start getting back on my feet.'

'I know how you feel.' Glyn Phillips sat down with Jones and Williams. 'I was skint within weeks of going on strike last year. The council threatened me with an eviction notice. Plus, I was behind on my electric and water bills. What really pisses me off about this strike is the fact that Scargill and his deputies get paid. They're not struggling, are they? The food donations aren't getting through because there are boys on strike not letting them through. Some of us have been donating. But because we are scab bastards in their eyes, they don't want any of our help.'

Williams and Jones nodded in unison.

'While the rest of us are on our arses, the head of the fucking NUM gets to live a life of luxury. Tell me how that's fair.'

'It's not.' Williams said. 'There's been a lot of stuff in the paper about Scargill taking backhanders off Libya and Russia.'

'He wouldn't dare,' Phillips stated. 'If it's true, then he won't be very popular with the union members. Especially when so many of those out on strike have been chucked out of their houses. Not to mention what happened to that woman copper in London last April. That was terrible.'

'The News of the World was going on about it last year.'

'How long d'you reckon this strike will go on for?' Jones asked.

'They reckon it could be over in the next few weeks.' Philips answered.

'But nothing has been achieved. I was watching the news last night about the latest talks. They still haven't reached a settlement. Scargill isn't budging. He's telling those still on strike to keep on striking. Thatcher will never cave. The National Coal Board still says it plans to shut pits that are not making any profit.'

'ACAS and the TUC have had enough of Scargill,' Williams explained. 'They've been trying to convince him to let the miners go back to work for months.' Williams shook his head. 'He's refusing to budge. He seems blind to what's going on up and down the coalfields. Striking miners are getting kicked out of their homes, while he's sitting pretty in his.'

'Perhaps the government has a point with all these pit closures.' Phillips remarked.

Jones glanced at Phillips. 'What d'you mean?'

'Think about it. If a pit is losing money, then there's no point in keeping it open.'

'Now you sound like that bitch Thatcher.' Williams said.

'I'm not trying to sound like her,' Phillips argued. 'Coal isn't going to last forever. We're relying more on coal and oil imports. They reckon within ten years everyone will have gas central heating.'

'I like a nice coal fire,' Jones said. 'The turkey at Christmas cooks lovely in the oven by the fire.'

'I reckon all the pits will shut within ten years,' Phillips speculated.

'What are we going to do? Go on the dole for the rest of our lives,' Williams asked.

'If Six Bells closes, then I might try the Royal Ordinance factory in Ty-Affan. A mate of mine, Terry Lapin, works there. Shit loads of overtime and its shifts. Terry is taking home good money.'

'Fuck that,' Williams stated. 'It's dangerous enough working down the pit. Let alone what they make at that bomb factory at Ty-Affan. A bloke was killed there ten years ago.'

'I don't know what I'm going to do if Six Bells shuts.' Jones sighed.

'No one does,' Phillips remarked. 'Thing is, what the government doesn't see is that if they shut the pits, then it's going to devastate the local communities. The local shops and everything. Everyone relies on the pits for work. There's no work anywhere else. It's not just the mineworkers who Thatcher is targeting its other factories. The ship yards are also being shut. Many people rely on them.'

'Thatcher is trying to destroy the working class. She doesn't give a fuck how she goes about it. Mark my word, all the youngsters will be on the dole within five years. There'll be no jobs anywhere in the Valleys. Those who want to work will have to travel. I was talking to Roger Crawshaw the other day. He's actually thinking about going to college if Six Bells shuts.'

'Yeah, but Roger can afford to do stuff like that. Plus, he's a bit of a clever clogs,' Jones said. 'I asked him why he was working down the pit once. He said he likes the people.'

Phillips gulped down the remaining beer in his glass. 'Well, whatever happens, we'll find out about it soon enough. I read last week if the pits close, then there'll be a decent redundancy package for the miners.'

'Yeah, but if the strike continues, then those still out won't get as much.' Jones said. 'It's another reason I went back to work.'

Phillips stared towards the pub entrance, spotting four men. 'Fuck, here we go.'

Cooper strolled through the pub entrance.

Jones felt like his heart had leapt into his mouth.

The landlord pointed at the group of men. 'Out!'

Cooper glared back at him. 'I thought I'd pop in for a pint.'

'No, you fucking haven't. I know you well enough, Cooper. You started that fight at the Vivian the other week. Your convenor, Lloyd Bevan, said that wouldn't happen again.'

Coper took a step forward. 'Who said I'm here to start a fight?'

'That's what you usually do, Martin.' Williams said.

Cooper directed his gaze towards the trio of men sat at the table. He spotted Malcolm Jones. Cooper's expression morphed into a menacing grin. 'Just the man I was looking for. I heard you started to drink in here.'

'Out, now Martin.' The landlord ordered. 'And take your mates with you, or I'll call the police.'

'Shut the fuck up, landlord for the scabs..' Cooper growled, sweeping as glare around the room. 'You should be ashamed of yourselves. Every one of you is a fucking traitor to the cause.'

Some men in the pub looked away, shame and guilt etched into their expressions.

Cooper took advantage of the moment. 'Yeah, that's right, boys. Look away. Most of you walked out with us last year. And now you've joined the rest of the scabs. What's the matter, eh, boys? Lost your backbone, have you?'

'Fuck off, Martin.' Phillips challenged. 'You still live with your mam. Everyone knows how well off she is. Your dad left you a fortune after he died. You don't have to worry about putting food on the table like the rest of us.'

Cooper marched over to the table where Williams was sitting. 'You were one of the first to abandon the cause, you scab bastard.'

'What was the alternative, Martin, eh? You're too stupid to realise how many of the boys have lost their home because of this fucking strike. You lot who have the means to stay out of work are living in fucking dreamland compared to the rest of us. Families are being kicked out of their homes. Children being taken away. While you and those two arseholes, Collier and Bevan continue to peddle the bullshit that Scargill has been spouting for the last year.'

'I'd show some respect for those of us who are fighting to keep the pits open. You scab twat.'

Williams let out a snort of derision. 'You really think coming in here and threatening us is going to convince any of us to fall in line? Most of us still support the cause. Just because we are still working doesn't mean we've turned our backs on you. Thing is, Martin, you're too stupid to know. All you are is an attack dog for Collier and Bevan. How are they managing when others are losing their homes? I don't see them struggling.'

'We've made our sacrifices over the last year.'

'And where has it got you? Nowhere, that's where.'

'We're making progress. The government is on the verge of caving.'

'Is that what those two dimwit union reps are telling you?' Williams smirked. 'You honestly think Thatcher is going to give in to the demands of the NUM? Jesus Martin, you really need to watch the news now and then. Instead of listening to the crap, you and your mates are being fed. Look around you. There are more of us back at work than there are still on strike.'

'That's because you're all a bunch of scab bastards.' Cooper sneered.

'Martin, either you fuck off, or I'll call the police.' The landlord warned.

Cooper fixed a steely glare on Jones. 'What about you, Malcolm? Are you going to stay with these scabs?'

'What choice have I got, Martin?'

'You can join the rest of us and fight, that's what.'

'For what?'

Cooper stared down at him for several seconds.

The landlord clutched the phone receiver. 'Martin, I'm about to dial 999. What's it going to be?'

Cooper hesitated for several seconds. 'Come on boys, let's leave these scab bastards.'

Jones drew a breath of relief as the door shut behind Cooper and his associates.

'That Cooper is fucking braindead. It was never about the strike with him. He's always looking f an excuse to start a fight all the time,' Phillips criticised.

CHAPTER 21

Newport Central Police station
Present day

'What a load of bollocks.'

'You'll get no argument from me, boss.' Watkins remarked.

'We're back at square one. I can't believe the bullshit that Warren pulled.'

'Martin Cooper is ready to be interviewed. Although the officers making the arrest said he was a handful.'

Fagan reached into his pocket to retrieve his buzzing phone. 'You go ahead, Sean. I'll be right behind you.' The message on the screen was from the same unknown number that had texted him earlier. Fagan studied the message. *'They don't want you rocking the boat.'* Fagan tapped on the keyboard. *'Who is this?'* Several seconds passed before a response came back. *'An ally.'* Fagan dismissed the message and slipped his phone back into his pocket.

Martin Cooper glared at Fagan as he entered the interview room. 'Oh look, it's another pig wrapped in a blanket.'

Fagan glared back at Cooper. 'Excuse me?'

'That's what we called you back in the day. Plain clothes coppers, pigs in blankets.'

Fagan sat down. 'We're off to a good start, aren't we, Martin.'

Cooper slouched in his chair, arms folded. Like a sulking child. Wearing a green camo jacket that had seen better days. Scruffy grey hair with hints of blonde from his younger days.

Watkins started up the interview process. 'Four months ago, Martin, you were arrested outside the home of Alwyn Collier.'

'Scab bastard.' Cooper seethed, spitting saliva. 'Betrayed the cause.'

'What cause would that be, Martin?'

'We should have won,' Cooper replied. His tone was thick with resentment. 'But the scab bastards betrayed us.'

'Is that why you threatened to kill Alwyn Collier four months ago?'

'I didn't threaten to kill him. He made that shit up.'

'According to his wife and daughter, you threatened to shoot him.'

'They would say that, wouldn't they? Fucking scab. Even his own boy wants nothing to do with him.'

'According to Alwyn's statement, you said, and I quote. You were going back home to get your gun, and you'd be back to finish a job that should have been done forty years ago.' Fagan glanced at the information he had. 'It says here you're a registered firearms user. You own a Bereta 1301 comp pro 12-gauge shotgun. Plus a Beretta BRX1 rifle.'

'I had my annual inspection last month.' Cooper interrupted. 'Couple of pigs in uniforms turned up at my house. I keep them in a locked cabinet. Plus, I have updated my shotgun licence. It's all legal.'

'So what were you going to do? Go back and get one of these firearms before returning to kill Collier.'

'Look, my bark is worse than my bite. I'm no Michael Ryan. Sometimes I say things I don't mean.'

'So why did you turn up at his house?' Watkins asked.

'Because he's a fucking scab.'

Fagan could sense his patients wearing thin. 'What do you mean, scab?'

'He betrayed the cause forty years ago. He didn't stand with the miners. Him and other scabs throughout the Valleys carried on working.'

'And you've held a grudge against him for all this time.' Fagan said.

'You've no idea what that bitch did to the miners in Wales. And the working class.' Cooper sneered.

'What bitch are you referring to, Martin?'

'Thatcher, of course.'

'Margaret Thatcher, as in the prime minister?'

Cooper rolled his eyes. 'Of course. Her and that twat Ian MacGregor destroyed the communities throughout the South Wales Valleys. She hung the lot of us out to dry. Alwyn Collier was a bloody Tory, just like her. And a fucking scab. As far as I'm concerned he got what he deserved.'

'You hated him that much, eh, Martin?'

'Everyone hated him for what he did. And then he goes and forms that union for all his scab mates. He betrayed the National Union of Mineworkers.'

'Do you know anyone who hated him enough to kill him?'

'Every miner who went on strike, that's who.'

'Can you account for your whereabouts two nights ago?'

'I was lamping.'

'Where?'

'On my own land and it's perfectly legal.'

'Our records show here Martin, you were arrested for badger baiting a few years ago.'

'I wasn't badger baiting. You pigs couldn't prove anything.'

'Got a grudge against us pigs, have you?'

'You're all the fucking same to me, bent bastards. As well as useless.'

'And why are we bent?'

'Because of what you did to me nearly forty years ago. Your lot beat the shit out of me and made me to confess to something I didn't bloody do.'

'Are you talking about the murder of Dafydd Collier and Sean Price?'

'Yes.' Cooper answered. 'I was in hospital for two weeks and then after that, slung in jail for six months. And when they finally released me, those bastards at Six Bells Colliery sacked me for being on strike. Bastards, total bastards.'

'So you maintain you were out lamping the other night?' Watkins said.

'Yes.'

'And you do not know who might have had a motive to murder Alwyn Collier?'

'He had loads of people who wanted to see the back of him.

Including his brother, Bryn.'

'Do you know his brother well?'

'Yeah, we have a pint together at the Garndiffaith rugby club.'

'Has Bryn ever talked about his brother, Alwyn?'

'All the time. That scab bastard should have never have got where he has.'

'What do you mean by that?'

'He used his fucking scab redundancy money to buy his way into a good job. While the rest of us were thrown on the slagheap.'

Fagan tested out a theory. 'Do you ever meet up with Lloyd Bevan?'

A broad grin stretched across Cooper's face. 'Lloyd's going to change the world. Soon Wales will belong to the Welsh again and we'll kick all the English bastards out. Then all the pits will start opening and the people from the Valleys will have well-paid jobs again.'

Fagan looked at the tape machine. 'Interview ended.'

Cooper exhibited a look of surprise. 'That's it, is it? You're just letting me go.'

'Yes Martin, you can go.'

Cooper didn't hesitate.

Fagan looked over his shoulder to make sure he was gone.

'How come you're letting him go, boss? I reckon he would have given us something.'

Fagan nodded. 'He would have, and he will still be useful to us. But I think this goes beyond Cooper.'

'How do you mean?'

'Collier's body was found at the Keepers. It's in the middle of nowhere. But still public enough for the body to have been discovered relatively quickly.'

'What's the next move, boss?'

'Text Andrew. Tell him to get his arse down to the office. We'll pull the file on the murders of Dafydd Collier and Sean Price.'

'You sure that's wise?'

Fagan smiled. 'No, but it's all part of my plan, Sean.' Fagan handed him a twenty-pound note. 'Shoot down to Greggs and get something to eat. I'll have the usual.'

Fagan consumed the last of his custard slice. He strolled over to the whiteboard. 'Right, let's reflect. Alwyn Collier was found dead in the Keepers. We've yet to name any suspect. Despite interviewing two people. The coroner says he'd been assaulted. We know Collier caught the train to Cardiff. He met with Delwyn Horlor in the morning. Then he went back to the Senedd and was picked up by a car with fake plates. He then disappeared for two hours before returning in another car, also with fake plates. He has to face a committee regarding his staff and their behaviour and his lack of action. When I interviewed Bevan, he was reluctant to talk about it. He was being very evasive with his answers. Collier had his satchel stolen last month. All evidence points to Tanya Glover, who was picked up by CCTV outside the BBC building close to the train station, holding the satchel. Our interview is interrupted by Griffiths and Warren.'

'You think they're covering for Bevan?' Watkins asked.

'I'm bloody well sure of it.'

'Why?'

'He's the First Minister for a start. The last thing he wants is one of his staff being connected with the murder of Collier. CCTV evidence shows her with the satchel. Which links her directly to Collier's murder.'

'She'll probably be able to provide an alibi.'

'Glover didn't murder Collier. I suspect she's being used.'

'Who by?'

'Right now, my money is on Bevan. The question is why. Martin Cooper was arrested four months ago for threatening Collier. Both men have known Collier for decades. Ever since the miners' strike.' Fagan glanced at Brooks. 'Andrew, pull the file. It's about to show up on radar, but right now I don't give a shit.'

Brooks stared at his laptop. 'Martin Cooper, Lloyd Bevan, Amlod Llewellyn and Bryn Collier were arrested on the 6th March 1985 in connection with the murder of Dafydd Collier and Sean Price. According to the accident report, on the 1st March 1985, a scaffolding pole smashed through the windscreen of a taxi heading towards Six Bells. The pole impaled Price through the upper chest, killing him instantly. The car flipped over three times. Dafydd Collier suffered a fractured skull, a broken leg and a broken collarbone. He was also trapped in the car for two hours. He died on March 5th.'

'A day later, Bevan, Cooper, Llewellyn and Collier are arrested.' Fagan said. 'So it took four days to apprehend these men. Did any of them go on the run?'

'No, they were all arrested at their addresses.'

'Why did it take four days to arrest them?'

'It says here police received an anonymous tipoff, naming all four suspects.'

'I've got a couple of articles here, boss.' Watkins said, swiping the screen on his tablet. 'The trial fell apart almost immediately when it was discovered that the police officers in the cars behind signed false statements. All four officers claimed they saw Martin Cooper drop the pole from the bridge. All four statements were signed on the 5th of March.'

'The day before all the men involved are arrested. Andrew, what's the names of the detectives on the investigation team?' Fagan asked.

Brooks clicked on his mouse. 'The names have been redacted.'

'Obviously to protect those involved in the investigation. Which means it's going to be impossible to get any names.'

'Plus, it was forty years ago, boss. Who's to say any of them are still alive?'

'Good point.' Fagan sighed.

'Just come across this, boss,' Watkins said. 'There was a massive write up in the South Wales Argus ten years ago to mark the thirtieth anniversary of the death of Collier and Price. Dafydd Collier, a miner who worked at the Six Bells Colliery in Abertillery, and Sean Price, a taxi driver from Abergavenny, were both victims of a senseless act of violence that shook the community to its core. On St David's Day in 1985. During the dying days of the miners' strike, tragedy struck in the form of a scaffolding pole dropped from a bridge, directly onto the taxi they occupied. The taxi, under police escort, was impacted. Leading to a catastrophic crash that claimed the lives of both Dafydd and Sean. Two others in the vehicle, Gethin Roberts and Tony Morgan, sustained injuries that would leave lasting physical and emotional scars.'

'I want you to run a check, Andrew. Find out if Roberts or Morgan are still around.'

Watkins continued. 'The aftermath of the incident was marred by confusion, corruption and heartache. A police investigation followed. Four men were arrested for the murder of Dafydd Collier and Sean Price. Bryn Collier, brother of Dafydd, Amlod Llewellyn, Martin Cooper and Senedd member, Lloyd Bevan.'

'We also need to find out if Llewellyn is still alive. According to Cooper, Bryn Collier lives in Garndiffaith and coaches a team in the local rugby club.'

'You think it's worth talking to Collier, boss? His wife reckons they haven't spoken in decades.'

Fagan suddenly remembered something. 'Cooper said Alwyn Collier's son wanted nothing to do with him. Sean, when you next talk to Stacey, ask her to see if she can get anything information about why Collier was estranged from his son.'

'Will do. The arrests sparked controversy after it was revealed that investigating officers had forced a confession out of them. One of the men arrested, Martin Cooper, was severely beaten. Cooper suffered four broken ribs and was taken to hospital on the 7th of March. In a statement, Cooper said he had been repeatedly beaten by a detective investigating the murder. The defending barrister, Lord Malcolm Barry, represented the men who later became notoriously known as the Blaina Four. The prosecution quickly fell apart when it was discovered police officers had lied on their statements. After initial examination of the crime scene it was determined the officers in the escort cars were too far away to get a clear identification of the person responsible for dropping the scaffolding pole.'

Fagan rubbed his hands together. 'So Lord Barry was their defence.'

Watkins tapped Barry's name into Google. 'According to this

article, Barry donated five thousand pounds to the miners' strike fund. He's quoted as saying, the plan Thatcher had for the South Wales Valleys was nothing short of class genocide.'

'Barry is a nationalist. Very proud to be Welsh. We discovered this during the Robert Turner murder investigation. His family stretches back several hundred years. It wouldn't surprise me if he supports this referendum.'

'He does.' Watkins held up a tablet. 'Bevan visited Monmouth last year. He gave a talk at the Agincourt hotel about the importance of our national identity.'

Fagan studied the picture of Barry shaking hands with Bevan. A thought exploded in his thoughts.

'You okay, boss?'

'Collier was just about to be bumped up to Welsh Secretary, wasn't he?'

'Yeah, so.' Watkins shrugged.

'So what if he had the power to block the referendum?'

Watkins mused over the notion. 'Certainly a motive for murder.'

'When they voted to stay part of the UK in Scotland, Sturgeon still pushed for another vote. In the end everyone got pissed off with her. Everyone was glad to see the back of her when she resigned. And then the expenses scandal unfolded, sealing her fate. Bevan is pushing for a vote on independence for Wales. We need to find out if Collier was going to block the referendum. Perhaps that's why the committee he was due to face was so important to Bevan.'

'The sooner they kick Collier out of office, the better chance they have of securing a referendum.' Brooks suggested.

'Exactly.' Fagan glanced at Watkins. 'What else does that article say about the murders of Dafydd Collier and Sean Price?'

'It mentions the wife of Sean Price, Sally. And how she campaigned for the truth about the death of her husband. As the years passed, her health deteriorated, and her efforts were eventually taken up by her son, Adam. Yet, pursuing truth and justice was not without its perils. Threats and intimidation were wielded as tools to discourage any further investigation into the incident. Despite these obstacles, Sally's son valiantly pressed forward, driven by a desire to honour his mother's memory and the memories of the innocent lives lost.'

'So, in their quest for justice, they were threatened along the way. Andrew, pop to Morrisons in Abergavenny tomorrow and ask Adam Price about what threats they received.'

Brooks nodded.

Fagan stared at the whiteboard. 'And so the plot thickens. We need to find out how and why Collier ended up at the Keepers with fifty grand stuffed into a satchel that was stolen a few weeks back. The satchel was thrown into the centre of the pond. Why did he do that?'

'It was a bribe.' Watkins said. 'Collier was just about to be bumped up to Welsh Secretary. He had the power to halt the referendum.'

'Someone lures him up to the Keepers, presents him with the fifty grand. Collier is not impressed, so he throws the satchel into the middle of the pond.'

'Annoying the murderer.' Watkins added. 'A fight breaks out. Collier is assaulted and falls into the pond. Our murderer moves in to finish the job.'

Fagan frowned. 'The coroner at the scene said that the bruising on Collier's face wasn't severe enough to cause any kind of damage. After we've been to Talgarth to speak with Victoria Armstrong, we'll go to Prince Charles in Merthyr tomorrow and speak to the coroner.'

'Do you think Armstrong will reveal anything useful, boss?'

'She may give us some insight into Collier's thoughts on the referendum. She could also give us useful information on the inner workings of the Senedd.. Armstrong may be a little more forthcoming with what she has to say.' Fagan's phone pinged. 'Shit.'

'What's up, boss?'

'It's Warren. He wants to meet with me tonight. I was planning to take you along to talk to the members of the Valleys Colliery Union.'

'What's the deal with Warren, boss? Why is he being a dick to us?'

'Good question.' Fagan sighed. 'Warren is old school, very old school. Should have been put out to pasture years ago. But he's clung on. Listen, we'll wrap this up for now. Our appointment with Armstrong is at ten o'clock tomorrow morning. Then we'll head up to Merthyr. Andrew will interview Adam Price, then we'll meet up here. I think it's worth having a chat with Lord Barry as well.' Fagan glanced at the whiteboard. 'See if we can make some sense of all this.'

CHAPTER 22

Blaina soup kitchen 1985

Rachel Bessant felt her heart race as she stared through the narrow gap in the shutters. The hall was packed with families waiting to be fed. The hall had been a vital lifeline to the local community. However, because more miners had returned to work, more soup kitchens were being closed around the Valleys. It meant that families had to travel further. This put a strain on the soup kitchens that were still open. Over the past two weeks, Rachel had noticed more families turning up. Hoping for a hot meal and perhaps some groceries they could take home.

Naomi, her sister, came in through a fire exit door. She was eager to avoid the line of people that stretched down the road.

'Where've you been?' Rachel grumbled.

'I've been talking to Kirsty from the corner shop up the road. Guess what happened last night?'

'What?'

'Malcolm Jones was found unconscious two streets from where he lives.'

'No.' Rachel gasped. 'What happened?'

'They reckon he had the shit kicked out of him for going into work. He's at the Prince Charles in Merthyr.'

'What about Tara?'

'Her neighbour told Kirsty she left late last night. Said she was going around her mam's house. The police were knocking on her door and everything. Tara was there first thing this morning. But she wouldn't talk to anyone.'

'Jesus, what is wrong with people?'

'I was talking to Wendy last week. She reckons they're about to be chucked out of their house, because they haven't been able to pay the rent in weeks.'

'Danielle Childs and her husband got chucked out of their house last week. And Social Services took the baby away.'

'Karenza, over the road from us, told me that Daniel was devastated.'

Rachel looked towards the shutters. 'Those lot are going to be really pissed off when they find out the delivery hasn't turned up.' She glanced at her watch. 'Simon is over an hour late. We should be dishing out food by now.'

'Where's Michelle and Pauline today?'

'They couldn't make it. Michelle said she had to help her mam with the shopping. Pauline said she couldn't get a babysitter.'

Naomi looked around the kitchen. 'Haven't we got anything to give anyone?'

'No, ever since the kitchen shut at Six Bells, everyone has been coming here for food. We run out of supplies two days after a delivery. We can't keep up with the amount of people turning up. Simon didn't even turn up last week. People were pissed off because they couldn't have anything to eat.'

'What are we going to do? I can't tell those lot in there, we've nothing to give them. We'll have a riot on our hands.' Naomi considered their situation before spotting a jar of strawberry jam on one of the kitchen shelves. 'I could get a couple of loaves of bread from up the shop and give the kids some toast and jam.'

'We can't just give them toast and jam. I don't know what I'm going to tell them.' Rachel despaired.

'Excuse me.' A woman called out from the open doorway. 'When are you going to serve food? I have a doctor's appointment in an hour.'

Rachel faked a reassuring smile. 'We're just waiting for our delivery to arrive.'

'How long is that going to take? And the kids are starving.' The woman complained.

Rachel walked towards the fire exit door. 'As soon as the van turns up with the delivery, we'll start cooking food. They shouldn't be long. If you join the queue, we'll be with you as soon as we can.'

The woman glanced around the kitchen before turning and

walking away.

'Shit.' Naomi cursed. 'She'll tell everyone we've no bloody food in the kitchen now.'

Rachel glanced up at the clock. 'Where the fuck is Simon with our delivery?'

A loud banging reverberated against the shutters.

Panic gripped Rachel as she stared at the shutter doors.

The pounding on the shutters continued unabated.

'What are we going to do?' Rachel asked in a panicked tone.

Naomi seemed frozen.

The pounding on the blinds became louder. 'Oi, open up, now!'

Rachel grabbed an apron from a hook on a cupboard door. 'Here we bloody go.' She tied the apron and approached the shutters. She glanced at her sister before unlatching the shutters and pulling them back.

'What's going on?' A man questioned loudly.

Everyone in the hall looked towards a terrified looking Rachel.

'Why aren't you cooking food yet? There are hungry kids out here, waiting to be fed.'

'If you would be a little patient, we'll get things moving.' Rachel smiled.

The man looked behind her at the kitchen. 'It doesn't look as if you've made a start yet. When is the food going to be ready? I can't stand around here all day long. I have things to do.' He looked at the crowd behind him. 'So has everyone else.'

Murmurs rippled through the onlookers. Young children with blank and hungry expressions stared back at the two women in the kitchen.

Rachel summoned the strength to address the issue. 'We're still waiting for our delivery. It's running late at the moment. But we will start cooking food as soon as they arrive.'

'When will that be, exactly?' The man's frustration mounted.

'As soon as our delivery man turns up.' Rachel looked beyond at the room of people. 'We are sorry for the delay. But as soon as the delivery turns up, we will start cooking.'

'I've come from Nantyglo, because the soup kitchen has been

shut there.' A woman moaned. She wrestled with an agitated toddler.

'Why hasn't the delivery shown up?' The man who had pounded on the blind asked.

Naomi stepped forward, offering her sister support. 'We don't know, but I promise they'll be here. You just have to be a little patient.'

'Look, I know you girls do the best you can. But there are hungry children out here. Why don't one of you pick up a phone and find out when the delivery is coming?'

A loud horn sounded from the back of the community hall.

A wave of relief engulfed Rachel. 'That's our delivery now. We'll unpack and start cooking.' Rachel grabbed the shutter handle and wrenched it shut.

Simon Chester opened the back door of his van.

Rachel marched out of the entrance to the kitchen. 'Where the bloody hell have you been, Simon? D'you have any idea what we've been through. They're about to tear the place apart in there.' Rachel nodded towards the shutter in the kitchen.

'It wasn't my fault. Some twat slashed the tyres on my van. Stupid bastard strikers are attacking delivery vehicles. I've had my windows smashed at my house because I'm picking up donations from working miners.'

Naomi stared into the back of Chester's van. 'Is this all there is?'

'Yeah.' Chester sighed.

'We'll barely be able to feed everybody in one sitting with this. You usually have a van packed with supplies. There's usually enough for at least four days.'

'No one is donating any more. People are fucked off with having to give all the time. The news was on about it last night. Calling it donation fatigue. This strike has been going on for nearly a year. They're still no closer to sorting it out. They reckon the NUM is close to collapse. There's only a small hard-core group of miners around here still on strike. Most have gone back to work. Everyone is struggling at the moment. Trying to catch up with payments. The local shops aren't being as generous anymore. The bloke at the Spar won't give any more free bread. I've had to pay for this out of my own pocket. Donations from the NUM have dried up.' Chester drew a breath. 'I reckon within a few weeks, no one is going to give any more money or food. It's over for the miners.'

Naomi grabbed two boxes of Walkers crisps from the back of the van.

'The landlord at the Rifleman's in Blaenavon said that's the last time he's donating crisps.'

'Well, at least it's enough to hand out to the kids for now. The grownups won't have an excuse to moan,' Naomi said before disappearing into the kitchen.

Rachel noticed the look on Chester's face. 'You okay?'

'This is the last time I'll be making a delivery.'

'What?'

The former soldier took a moment to explain. 'Rachel, it's like being back in Belfast. Every time I go out and make deliveries, my van gets attacked. I had my tyres slashed this morning. D'you know what happened yesterday to our mam?'

'What?'

'Some twat spray-painted scab supporters on the side of her house. She was devastated by it. After all she's done to support the strike in the past year. The kids throw stones at the van in the areas where miners are still on strike. I'm getting flashbacks, thinking I'm back in Belfast. The doctor is increasing my pills.' Chester ran his fingers through his hair. His face racked with despair. 'I just can't do this anymore. It's too much with the business I'm trying to run.'

'You're the last person in this valley who is still making deliveries.'

'I know,' Chester said. 'Let's face it, Rachel, no one gives a shit about the strike. People around here are fucked off with it. They just want their lives back. That's why most of them have gone back to work.'

'Oi twat!' Martin Cooper shouted as he marched towards the van with two other men.

'Jesus fucking Christ.' Chester groaned. 'This is all we need.'

'What are you fucking doing, Rachel?' Cooper demanded to know.

Rachel folded her arms, staring back at Cooper with an expression of defiance. 'What's it look like we're doing?' She glanced at Chester. 'We're unpacking the van so that I can feed the hungry families in there.'

'No, you're not,' Cooper snarled. 'You can take this lot back to the scabs and tell them to shove it up their arses. We don't want any charity from those bastards.' Cooper glared at Chester. 'You've got a fucking nerve showing your face around here, soldier boy.'

'Back off, Martin.' Rachel thundered. 'Simon is just helping. Those families in there are hungry. It's alright for you. Still living at home. Does your mam still wipe your arse for you?'

Chester smirked at Rachel's mockery.

'You can wipe that grin off your face, soldier boy. Or I'll wipe it off for you,' Cooper threatened.

Chester stepped up to Cooper. 'You can fucking have a go if you think you're hard enough.'

'What's going on?' Naomi barked, stepping out the door. 'People are getting impatient. They want us to start cooking. I've just told them the delivery has arrived.'

'Martin doesn't want us unloading the van,' Rachel explained.

Naomi planted her hands on her hips, fixing a glare on Cooper. 'Why?'

'Because we don't want any donations from scabs, that's why.'

'Okay then, Martin. This is what me and Rachel will do. We'll go back in there and tell those who haven't had a decent meal in days that Martin Cooper says you can't eat today. Then, I'll phone our dad and our Scott and they'll both come down here and give you a hammering. Is that what you want?'

'Don't be like that, Naomi. I don't want to mess with your dad or Scott.'

'Then don't be such a twat. I've got a building full of hungry people. And you're turning everything into a stupid political debate about where the donations are coming from.'

'Wake up, will you, Martin? The deliveries are getting smaller,' Rachel stated, pointing at Chester. 'This is the last time Simon is going to be coming here. No thanks to your lot attacking his van.'

'He's taking donations from the scabs.'

'Who gives a shit where this food is coming from? As long as I can feed those kids in there. I don't care if Maggie Thatcher herself is supplying the food.'

The man who pounded on the shutters suddenly appeared. 'Why aren't you getting the food ready?'

Chester took advantage of the moment, pointing at Cooper. 'Because this twat won't let us unload the van.'

The man knew Cooper. 'Martin, what the fuck are you playing at? There are hungry women and children in there.'

'With all due respect, Layton, this food has been donated by scabs.'

Layton Powell shook his head. 'So, what's your fucking point?'

'My point is, we should only accept donations from striking miners.'

'You dull twat, Martin.' Powell pointed at himself, then at Cooper. 'We're the striking miners. Why d'you think I'm here with the kids?'

'But it's a betrayal of the cause if we accept charity from scabs.'

'And it's a betrayal to our kids if we don't feed them. Jesus, Martin, you really need to engage that brain of yours sometimes.'

Cooper seemed to struggle with his next line. 'But what about what we're trying to achieve here? With the strike and everything.'

'Martin.' Powell shook his head. 'I'm not starving our kids based on your short-sighted principles. There are two dozen blokes in there waiting to be fed. D'you want me to go in there and tell them you're stopping these girls from feeding our kids?'

'No, of course not.'

'Then fuck off.' Powell glanced at Rachel. 'I'll help you get started.'

Cooper scowled at Powell before turning and walking off.

CHAPTER 23

The Rifleman's arms–Blaenavon
Present day

Warren stared at the entrance to the pub. 'I'll take the lead on this Fagan, understand?'

'Perfectly, sir.' Fagan nodded obediently.

Both men entered the pub. The loud conversation that could be heard from outside faded away. All eyes were locked on Fagan and Warren as they walked through the door.

Warren relished the uncomfortable silence. He strolled up to the bar like he owned the place. 'Double Bells whisky please landlord.'

The landlord glared back at him before reaching for a glass.

Warren knocked back the glass in one go, and ordered another, throwing a twenty pound note onto the bar. He turned and faced the men in the bar. 'And how are we this evening, gentlemen?'

Murmurs rippled through the room.

'I take it you are part of this Valleys Colliery Union, so I'll waste no time. My name is Chief Detective Superintendent Warren. This is Detective Inspector Fagan. We're here because we are looking for a murderer.'

'So, what, you think we had something to do with it?' A man asked.

'Not at all,' Warren responded. 'I'm sure every one of you in this room is innocent. But someone knows something. Alwyn Collier was found dead at the Keepers. I know what a small town like Blaenavon is like. Lots of rumours circulating about his death. He was found with a large amount of money in a satchel.'

The men in the bar exchanged looks.

'I thought that would get your attention.'

Fagan shot Warren a hard stare. It was information he shouldn't have been revealing.

'Why should we help you?' Another man questioned.

Warren took the bait. 'Because if you don't help us with our enquiries, I'll get a couple of vans up here. And drag you down to Newport for questioning.'

'You haven't got the authority to do that. This isn't the glory days of the Sweeney anymore.' The man scoffed. 'None of us had a grudge against Alwyn. We are all friends here.'

'Are you?' Warren questioned. 'The large amount of money found with Collier would suggest different.'

'What's that supposed to mean?'

'He was a politician. You know what politicians are like. Most of them are bent.'

'What about you pigs back in the day? You were all bent. Everyone in this room remembers what you lot did at Orgreave and Six Bells.' The man stated.

Warren savoured the taste of a third double whisky. 'Back in the day.' He nodded. 'Let me tell you something about back in the day. Everyone was bent. D'you honestly think the National Union of Mineworkers gave a fuck when you silly bastards walked out nearly forty years ago? They knew you militant twats would obey without question. Jesus, you didn't even hold a ballot. Like lemmings, you just followed the leader. And where did it get you, eh? Long-term unemployment for many of you. The destruction of your precious communities. While the heads of the NUM sit on their big fat pensions. You think the likes of Scargill gave a fuck about your struggle? All he was interested in was his small-minded lust for power. And now he's sat in a nice big house. While you silly buggers struggle on.'

'I think you better leave.' The landlord said, throwing the twenty-pound note back at Warren. 'Your drinks are on the house. I don't accept money from pigs.'

Warren scooped up the banknote before stepping away from the bar. 'We'll find the person who murdered Collier. And if I find out any of you are holding back information, then I'll make sure you do time for perverting the course of justice.' Warren marched towards the pub entrance.

Fagan placed a card on the table. 'My contact details if you have any information.'

'Fagan, let's go,' Warren growled.

'Do you mind telling me what the point of all that was, *sir*?'

Warren looked back at the pub. 'Bunch of dinosaurs stuck in the past.'

'We can't just go wading into a place like that demanding answers.' Fagan protested.

'So what's your suggestion, Fagan? Handle them with kid gloves? Try to understand them?' Warren pointed a nicotine stained finger at him. 'You haven't seen these fuckers in action. I have. I was at Orgreave when it all kicked off. The poor militant miners making out that the police used horses and dogs.'

'I've seen the videos on YouTube, sir. The police shouldn't have acted the way they did. All those men wanted was to save their jobs. Nothing else.'

'Jesus, Fagan, now you sound like one of those wankers in there.' Warren turned and walked back towards his car.

'What are we trying to do here, exactly?' Fagan called after him. 'Catch a murderer or protect Lloyd Bevan's dream of an independent Wales.'

Warren stormed up to Fagan. 'What's your problem DI Fagan?'

'My problem is, we let a vital suspect go today. Why did you storm in to the interview room and end the interview with Tanya Glover?'

'Because she's nothing to do with this.'

'Bollocks, CCTV images prove she stole Collier's satchel. The same satchel that was fished from the Keepers. And let me tell you another thing, *sir*. You shouldn't have mentioned the money found in the satchel. It only muddies the waters when you reveal information like that. And it's against protocol.'

'We're not going to solve this murder by playing it safe, DI Fagan. Do you want to find out who murdered Collier or not?'

'Of course I do.'

'Then you'll do as you're fucking well told. Is that clear, DI

Fagan?' Warren marched off back towards his car.

'Alwyn wasn't bent.' A voice said from behind.

Fagan faced one of the men from the pub. 'That was him saying that, not me.'

'Alwyn was an honest man, wanting to do the right thing.'

'And I believe you.' Fagan said.

The man gestured to the pub. 'We're a mixed bunch in there. Both strikers and scabs. We learnt to settle our differences long ago. We meet once every six months to remind ourselves of the good times.'

'Good times?'

'The old days, when the South Wales Valleys were filled with thriving communities.'

'Can you think of anyone who would want to murder Alwyn?'

'I'll admit, Alwyn wasn't popular with many people. He was determined to heal the wounds of the past.'

'You mean the miners' strike?'

The man nodded. 'After the strike ended, a lot of the boys were disillusioned with the National Union of Mineworkers. Alwyn formed the Valleys Colliery Union, so some of us jumped ship. The Nottinghamshire miners had also formed their own union. The National Working Miners' Committee.'

'I suspect that didn't go down well with others.'

'No. But there were some of us who saw that times had to change. Despite the failure of the NUM to break the Government, Scargill still clung on to power believing in his own bullshit.'

'Did you go on strike?'

The man nodded. 'I thought it was worth it at first. I stuck to my guns.' The man paused. 'Or rather, I stuck to union guns. Back then, we would do anything for the union. For the first several months, we had support. The soup kitchens kept many families fed throughout the strike. Donation flooded in. But, by the time Christmas came, the donations dried up. I couldn't afford anything for my kids. The bills piled up. I was constantly fighting with my ex-wife. But still, I kept believing we were fighting for a good cause. By February, we had run out of money. I had no choice but to return to work. It was Alwyn who told me I was doing the right thing. He was a forward thinker. Alwyn knew the pits would shut eventually. That's why he set up the Valleys Colliery Union. Alwyn wasn't prejudice. He let both strikers and scabs join the union. When the Six Bells shut, we had a good payout. But those who stayed in the NUM were worse off.'

'You just mentioned your ex-wife.'

The man shoved his hands into his jacket pocket. 'My wife's family were diehard supporters of the strike. When I went back to work, my name was mud. The next thing I knew, a load of boys were dragging me out of a pub and kicking the shit out of me. I was in hospital for two weeks. After I came out of hospital, my wife left me and took the kids. That was nearly thirty-nine years ago. In all that time I haven't seen or spoken to my kids. I ended up remarrying and having three more kids. But I couldn't live in the community anymore. So I moved away to Chepstow.' He paused. 'My brother-in-law at the time, was Lloyd Bevan.'

Fagan looked back down the road, half expecting Warren to drive back. 'What's your name?'

'Malcolm Jones.'

'What was Bevan like back then, during the strike?'

'As fanatical as he is now. None of the boys would do anything without his say so.'

'When you would meet up, did Alwyn ever discuss matters in the Senedd?'

'No. Some of us were curious and would ask him about Bevan, but he wouldn't talk. He said it was a security matter. I've seen the YouTube videos, the debates they used to have. There is one thing. Last year, he mentioned he was working on something that would end Bevan's career once and for all.'

'Did he say what?'

'No.'

'And you can't think of anyone who would want to murder him.'

Jones shook his head. 'He had plenty of people who didn't like him, but no one hated him enough to kill him.'

'Thanks for your time, Malcolm.' Fagan handed jones a card. 'If you can think of anything else, please give me a bell.'

CHAPTER 24

The Miners Lamp–1985

Alwyn Collier hesitated. From outside the entrance to the pub he could hear the men inside singing and chanting. The few, determined to go on with the strike, no matter what the cost. Collier felt apprehension. But after hearing what happened to Malcolm Jones, he knew he would have to face those responsible. He could hear his brother giving one of his speeches to the assembled crowd.

'Alwyn.' A woman called his name as she approached.

Collier looked in her direction.

'Where are you going?' She said with a concerned tone.

He gestured. 'In there.'

'Don't say you're about to go on strike.'

'No, of course not. I'm going to tell them a man who was beaten up last night is still unconscious. All because he had no choice but to go back to work.'

'Alwyn, if you go in there, then you'll end up in a worse state than the man they beat up.'

Collier inhaled. 'I know, but it's the right thing to do.'

The cheering and singing stopped immediately as Alwyn walked through the door. Silence draped itself over the room like a suffocating blanket. The clinking of glasses stopped abruptly. Conversations tapered off within seconds, as everyone realised who had just entered. He spotted his brother propping up the bar. Lloyd Bevan was standing next to him.

Bryn stared back at his younger sibling. Not knowing whether to feel a loathing for his brother because he had defied the picket lines. Or admiration for daring to walk into a pub full of striking miners all on his own.

Martin Cooper was the first on his feet. Intoxicated, he

stumbled towards Alwyn. 'You've got a nerve showing your face in here, you scab bastard.' He slurred.

Alwyn stood his ground.

Cooper lunged toward Alwyn but was too drunk to maintain his balance. He stumbled forward, crashing into a table filled with empty glasses.

'For fuck's sake, Martin!' the landlord yelled.

Bryn Collier glanced at his brother, pretending not to be concerned this scab had just walked through the door. He savoured a mouthful of beer before swallowing. 'What are you doing here, Alwyn?'

Alwyn looked at Cooper. Two men hauled him to his feet and dumped him in the corner of the bar. 'You need to control this attack dog of yours.'

'We do.' Bryn said.

'Really, then how d'you explain Malcolm Jones.' Alwyn swept a gaze around the bar. 'That's right, Malcolm Jones.' His tone was calm. Alwyn knew if he even raised his voice a little, it could spell disaster. 'He's lying unconscious at the Prince Charles in Merthyr.' He pointed at Cooper. 'That animal, and a few of his mates, who are probably sitting in this bar, beat Malcolm unconscious last night.'

Alwyn sensed a room full of hard angry stares boring into his soul.

'That scab made his choice.' Lloyd Bevan stated. 'He joined the ranks of you scab bastards that have stabbed us in the back for the past year.'

'Did Malcolm choose to get beaten until he was unconscious, huh? What happened last night was serious. Malcolm didn't deserve that.'

'Yes, he fucking did.' Bevan raised his voice purposely to gauge a reaction from the men in the bar.

A low pitch hum of murmurs broke the deafening silence.

'I spoke to Malcolm the other day when he came back to work.' Alwyn revealed. 'He told me he was so ashamed of having to go back to work. He was days away from being thrown out of his house. The bills had piled up. He had no one to turn to. But here's the thing, Lloyd. You're the treasurer for the union at the Six Bells pit, are you not?'

Bevan stared back, reluctant to answer the question.

Alwyn took advantage of Bevan's lack of words. 'Malcolm told me he asked for a bridging loan three weeks ago, that the NUM is offering to striking miners. You turned him down.'

Everyone focused their attention on Bevan.

'Isn't that what the funds are for? The money that has been raised for the miners over the past year.' Alwyn gazed around the room, making eye contact with as many as he could stomach. 'Let's have a show of hands, shall we? How many in this room have seen financial aid from the NUM strike fund?'

None of the men raised their hands.

'I have spoken to quite a few boys over the last couple of months. Who had no choice but to return to work. They all approached you for a loan just before Christmas last year. You turned them down. Why?'

Bevan swilled a mouth full of beer. 'We can't help everyone who asks for a handout.'

'But you can help yourselves. Is that about the size of it?'

'What's that supposed to mean?' Bryn said in a demanding tone.

'You've just moved into a nice flat.' Alwyn pointed out. 'With that new girlfriend of yours.'

'And?' Bryn fired back.

'How are you able to pay the rent or mortgage?'

'Donna is working. She's supporting me.'

'Bollocks. She's always around our mam's gossiping. Getting our mam to tell her what me and Dafydd are doing. She's always leaving as we're coming home.' Alwyn looked at Bevan. 'Why have you been turning down bridging loans?'

'I just told you, there are others who are struggling. We've been supporting the soup kitchens for the last twelve months.'

'Not anymore, you're not. There's only one soup kitchen left in this area. And that's on the verge of collapse. I was speaking to someone earlier today about it. Their delivery driver isn't delivering anymore because he's constantly under attack from the likes of him.' Alwyn pointed towards Cooper, who was snoring loudly in the corner. 'You're poisoning your own well and you don't even realise it.' Alwyn composed himself. 'Let me ask another question.' He swept another gaze around the room. 'How many of you are on the verge of going back to work?'

A wall of silence met his question.

'I know none of you will admit it. But you're all going back, eventually. When everyone walked out last March, this place was packed to the rafters. Standing room only. Now there's less than half of you. With an exception of a few, most of you here are still living with your parents. Not like the men who have gone back to work. Those who have families to feed, rent and bills to pay.' Alwyn glanced at three men in their sixties. 'You three have less than twelve months left. There's no one left in here with a sense of true purpose.' He looked at Bryn. 'You've no one left to support you, but mindless sheep who will follow without question.' Alwyn pointed at Cooper. 'Or men like him, who just want to start a fight.'

'Do us a favour, Alwyn. Fuck off before you regret coming in here.' Bryn warned.

Alwyn walked up to his brother, standing nose to nose. 'And if I don't leave, what are you going to do? Leave me unconscious, like Malcolm. Is this what we've become, a pack of rabid dogs turning on each other? We're supposed to be work colleagues. Brothers in arms. A workforce community. Instead, we've become a splintered, bitter workforce.' Alwyn turned to face the men in the room. 'We don't need Thatcher to split us. We've already done a good enough job by ourselves.' He pointed at his brother and Bevan. 'Men like them, who are expecting you to follow them no matter what. Even if it leads you to rack and ruin.'

'Don't make us out to be a bunch of bastards, Alwyn. All we're doing is fighting for our jobs. It's you lot who've split the miners. Jumping through MacGregor's hoops. I saw him on the telly last night. Making out he's looking out for our best interest. The only interest that twat has is putting the lot of us on the dole.' Bryn raised his glass. 'We want coal, not dole.'

The room exploded into cheers and chants for several

seconds.

'You don't see it, do you?' Alwyn stated. 'How long do you plan to go on for?'

'As long as it fucking takes.' A drunken Cooper slurred, waking from his slumber.

'Can you afford to go on for another year? The donations are drying up. No one is sympathising with your cause anymore. And you're all too blind to see this.'

'It's you who is blind, Alwyn.' Bryn said, standing. 'You're blinded by that twat, MacGregor, and his lies. Thatcher's determination to put us all on the dole. Shut all the pits and tear our communities apart.'

'Our communities are already being torn apart. All this infighting over the past year has taken its toll. You think I didn't see this coming, Bryn? When the miners walked out ten years ago, they had actual power. The Heath government couldn't handle them. Those were the glory years. But, waiting in the wings, was Thatcher. Even ten years ago she was scheming on how to break the unions, subdue the working class. She's had ten years to plan, and now she is executing her plan with ruthless efficiency. She appointed MacGregor because she knew he would be the man who could do what she wanted. That twat shouldn't be in charge of the National Coal Board. He's a bloody Yank. He destroyed British Leyland, dismantled the steel industry, and now he's got us in his sights. And in the middle you have Scargill and the bloody NUM. Urging you to keep on fighting. Even though there are no donations coming in. There are families throughout the Valleys who are starving, being kicked out of their homes. While Scargill lives in a nice big house. Drives around in a chauffeur-driven car.' Alwyn glared at his brother. 'Just like Thatcher and MacGregor.'

'Scargill deserves it. He's earned it,' Bevan stated.

'Fuck off, Bevan.' Alwyn seethed. 'All Scargill has earned is the disrespect of the miners. That man is not stupid. He knows the end is coming for the miners and the working class.'

'The scab miners.' Bryn added.

'No, not scab miners, but miners who have chosen to work.

Why, because Scargill didn't hold a national ballot for strike action. He was terrified in case he got voted down.'

'He didn't have to hold a ballot.' Bevan said.

Alwyn couldn't help laughing at Bevan's ignorance. 'If Scargill would have held a ballot, he would have been voted down. No one wanted to go on strike, not in this day and age when other industries like the steel industry are being dismantled. Scargill called the miners out because he knew the attention he would get from the media. At the end of the day, he should have asked the NUM to hold a ballot.'

'Why, so all you scab fuckers could vote it down?'

'No one knows what the outcome would have been.'

'MacGregor was shutting Cortonwood and twenty other pits.' Bryn argued. 'The job losses have devastated the local communities in the north of England. How long d'you think it would have been before he focussed his attention on the Valleys?'

'Cortonwood was operating at a loss. Scargill even knew this. D'you honestly think that man is on your side, the side of the working class? He knows the end is near for the coal industry. He's feathering his own nest before Thatcher and MacGregor deliver the final blow. So much money has flooded in for the miners over the last year, but very little has gone to the miners. So where's all the money gone, eh? I'll tell you where. Straight into Scargill's pocket, that's where. And the pockets of his deputies, and the men running the strike.' Alwyn pointed at both Bryn and Bevan. 'Including you.'

'I wouldn't go there if I were you, Alwyn.'

Alwyn locked eyes with some of the men in the bar. 'You lot have already given in to the fear. That's why you're on strike.'

'Thatcher wants to put us all on the dole!' Bevan shouted.

'Is that all your narrowmindedness can see? A bleak future.'

'Okay then, genius brother of mine.' Bryn stated. 'What future have these boys got without coal? After Thatcher and MacGregor are through with us and they've shut all the pits? What then for these boys? What future do their children have?'

'Jesus Christ Bryn, try seeing beyond that tunnel vision of

yours, will you. We are all in the same boat here. D'you think I'm immune from the pit closures because I've chosen to work through this strike? I Won't get any special treatment. But I know I'll get more money than you when they lay me off. Those of you who have been on strike for the past year will be at the bottom of the pile.'

'What good is any redundancy money?' Bevan argued. 'Once you've spent it all, what then, Alwyn? Once that money is gone, it's gone. You'll be left with nothing but dole money.'

'You're as bad as him.' Alwyn pointed at his brother. 'When the end comes, there's no way I'm sitting on my arse and waiting for the dole cheques to drop through the letterbox. I'll be looking for other jobs and opportunities. I'm even considering college and getting some decent qualifications. When we left school, we were all expected to go straight down the pit. It was expected of us. But times are changing, and I'll change with them. Not sit on my arse, bitter and twisted for the rest of my life. It's all about bettering yourselves.'

'Not all of us are cut out for college.' Bryn stated.

'None of you are cut out for the dole, either. You're all working class, for Christ's sake. You all have a choice. Either wait for the end to come. Give into your fear and do nothing for the rest of your lives. Or you can fight for your future.'

'What the fuck d'you think we've been doing for the past year?' Bevan's anger rose.

'And where's it got you? Nowhere.'

Bevan reinforced his defiance. 'We'll continue to fight Thatcher and her government. We're about to do something that will make her sit up and listen.'

Alwyn rolled his eyes. 'Oh yeah, your march on Six Bells on St David's Day. You really think you'll make a difference.'

'We'll make our stand there.'

'Jesus bloody Christ, it's like talking to a brick wall.' Alwyn decided he wasn't going to waste any more of his time. 'Before I go, management at Six Bells has asked me to pass on a message to you two. They want to speak with you tomorrow. I suggest you turn up and listen to what they have to say.' He turned and walked towards the pub entrance.

'That's right scab, fuck off back to your scab mates.' Bevan called after him.

The men in the bar chanted. 'Scab, Scab, Scab.'

Alwyn stopped dead and glanced over his shoulder.

The room plunged into silence.

'For the past year, you have attacked us. Thrown bricks at the buses going into the pits. Smashed windows in houses and cars. Spray painted scab on properties of those who have carried on working. Children of working miners have been attacked at school by other children whose parents have told them to. And now a man is lying unconscious in the hospital. All because he was at the end of his tether and just wanted to feed his family. You don't see us scabs giving you lot a good hammering do you? Most of the boys forced to go back to work still support what you're doing. But they can't live on nothing either. So you tell me, Lloyd, who are the monsters here?'

CHAPTER 25

Talgarth Community Hall – Powys
Present day

'DI Fagan, this is DS Watkins.' Fagan held up his ID.

Victoria Armstrong studied Fagan's badge. 'I thought it would only be a matter of time before the police came calling.'

Fagan glanced out of the window. 'Nice little town. A world away from Cardiff.'

'When the pandemic hit, it made me realise how much I hate the city. I moved out here to get away from everything.'

'I read an article last night about your move to the country. At the time you were still with your husband.'

Armstrong nodded. 'Yeah, we thought we could make a go of it if we made the move out here.'

'Did your marriage end because of your affair with Alwyn Collier?'

Armstrong inhaled. 'My marriage had collapsed before I became involved with Alwyn. When you're someone in politics, Inspector Fagan, it can be difficult to lead the perfect life.'

'The press were quite sensational about your affair with Alwyn.'

'No, DI Fagan. Lloyd Bevan was quite sensational about our affair.'

'Are you saying he was the one who released the CCTV images of you and Collier.'

'Yes.' Armstrong admitted. 'But it was that personal assistant of his that got the most joy out of it.'

'That would be Tanya Glover?'

'Tanya Glover is a dangerous woman. She hates anyone who is straight. Thinks the entire world should be LGBTQ.'

'How did the affair start?'

'That's a question I keep asking. I guess we were both lonely and vulnerable at the time.'

'Despite you both being married.'

'Alwyn confessed he hadn't slept with his wife in over five years. Since moving out to Nantyglo. She didn't want to move. But Alwyn was determined to make things work out there. He thought enough time had passed and that people had virtually forgotten.'

'The miners' strike.' Fagan said.

'It was decades ago. Alwyn was hoping most people had moved on with their lives. But when he moved the trouble started right away. People would target his house and vandalise his cars. His wife had her car spray painted, wife of a scab. He had his windows smashed several times. His wife begged him to move but Alwyn was determined to stay. His marriage wasn't all that brilliant before he moved.'

'Did he reveal this to you?'

'Yes.' Armstrong answered. 'Alwyn met his wife just after he was made redundant. Alwyn told me from the word go she was the controlling one.'

'Controlling?'

'After Alwyn was made redundant, he knew he had to move away from the Valleys. Or as he put it, exiled. When the Six Bells Colliery shut it shattered the community. The strike had split many families down the middle. Many of those who worked through the strike moved away to find other jobs. Those who went on strike went their separate ways. Some moved away and others stayed, but never worked again. The closure of the pits across the South Wales Valleys killed its spirit. That's what Alwyn believed. When he went into local, politics Alwyn's wife pushed him to get a high paid job in the council. She loved the money Alwyn was earning. Loved the holidays and the expensive cars she would buy on HP. Alwyn once told me he considered ending his life because of the debt Elizabeth racked up. When a seat for the Senedd came up, Alwyn took the leap. He was determined to win and start healing the past.'

'Did he ever talk about his brother, Dafydd?'

'I was the only one he would talk to about what happened in 1985. It was St David's Day. Alwyn said it was the worst day of his life. He lost two brothers that day. Dafydd was seriously injured in the crash that also killed a taxi driver. He died a few days later.'

'Did Alwyn ever say how his other brother was arrested?'

'It was a few days after the accident. One of the men on that bridge, Martin Cooper, was mouthing off in a pub. He was drunk and let slip he was on the bridge with Amlod Llywellyn, Lloyd Bevan and Bryn Collier, Alwyn's brother.'

'Did he talk about his brother, Bryn?'

'Only how much he despised him. But this is where it gets weird.'

'How so?'

'When Elizabeth first met Alwyn, she was already having a relationship with Bryn.'

'Really.' Fagan stated.

'For a while, Elizabeth was seeing them both at the same time. But Alwyn was too naïve to see this. He told me he was besotted with Elizabeth when he first met her. I've seen photos of her in her younger days. She was a very attractive looking woman. In the end she chose Alwyn.'

'But?' Fagan said, noticing the expression on Armstrong's face.

'Alwyn told me he wanted to separate from his wife. He'd had enough of her want for a lavish lifestyle. Alwyn said that he served her divorce papers six months ago. But she tore them up in front of him. She knew that if they separated, she wouldn't be able to live the dream life anymore. That's when she dropped the bombshell about his son, Aron.'

'What bombshell?' Watkins asked.

'That Aron wasn't his.'

'He was his brother's boy?' Fagan guessed.

'Yes.' Armstrong confirmed. 'When Elizabeth told Alwyn, it devastated him. He was already estranged from his son. Alwyn said he tried his best to bring him up the right way. But the moment Aron turned a teenager, they drifted apart. But he could never understand why Aron rejected him. Elizabeth revealed to

Alwyn that Aron had found out Bryn was his father when he was fourteen.'

'How did he find out?'

'Lloyd Bevan.'

'That is a twist.' Fagan said.

'What I never understood is why Aron didn't confront his father with the truth.'

'Tell me about Collier's relationship with Bevan.'

'It was turbulent from the start. Alwyn became an assembly member before Lloyd. But Lloyd worked his way up the ladder further. Of course there were rumours Bevan wasn't as squeaky clean as he made out. Then, four years ago he appointed Tanya Glover as his personal assistant. Since then, she's been doing all the dirty work for him. She's carried out several political assassinations over the past few years. Eliminating the competition, or anyone who stands in Bevan's way. She's manipulated and humiliated several female Senedd members. Skilled at luring straight women into bed. She's been responsible for at least four marriage breakdowns. Six Senedd members have been forced to resign over the past four years because of her.'

'Is that another reason why you have stayed away from the Senedd?'

'Yes.' Armstrong sighed.

'Has she made advances towards you?'

'Oh yes, and on more than one occasion. When the pandemic hit, it was a relief to get away from the toxic atmosphere in the Senedd. But when lockdown ended and everyone started to go back to work, the atmosphere was worse than ever. Bevan was more than determined to hold a referendum before the next election.'

'Do you think he's scared he might lose it?'

'He'll lose it by a landslide. The stupid idiot has turned people against him with his barmy policies, including the twenty mile an hour speed limit. Alwyn had a massive argument with him on the Senedd floor about it last year. Saying that it had damaged tourism in Wales.'

'What do you know about Alwyn being bumped up to Welsh

secretary?'

'It was a shock to Alwyn when they changed the law and offered him the role. But I think the Prime Minister did it deliberately. He knew about the rivalry between Alwyn and Bevan. They've had a number of heated debates on the Senedd floor about the vote for an independent Wales over the past few years.'

'Do you think when Alwyn would have been made Welsh Secretary, he would have blocked Bevan's bid to hold a referendum?' Watkins asked.

'That's exactly what he was planning to do.'

'He told you this himself.'

'Yes.' Armstrong nodded.

The pieces of a puzzle started to form in Fagan's mind. 'Can you think of anyone who hated Alwyn enough to murder him?'

'He wasn't popular in the area where he lived. But I don't think anyone hated him enough to do something like that.'

'How long were you having an affair with him?'

'A few months maybe, not long enough to form a strong emotional bond. We were both lonely at the time. Our marriages were going through turbulent times. What we didn't count on was Bevan's number one, as he called her, following us around. When she leaked those pictures to the press, it sent Alwyn into a downward spiral. He considered resigning his position. But I convinced him to carry on.'

'You still had lunch with him on a regular basis?'

'Yes, it's one of those unfortunate necessities of being a Senedd member. Alwyn was very professional. He wouldn't talk about our affair when we were having lunch.'

'What do you know about the committee he was due to face on the day he died?'

'That was a complete set up from the start. Bevan claiming that Alwyn didn't control his staff. Allegations of sexual harassment were fabricated. Although there was the incident where one of his staff was found to have indecent images of children on his phone.'

'Besides planning to put a block on the referendum did Alwyn say he was working on something that would end Bevan's career?' Fagan asked, remembering the conversation he had with Malcolm Jones the night before.

'Come to think of it, he said something to me a few months back. All he said was it would put an end to Bevan once and for all. It was after he had one of his arguments on the Senedd floor with Bevan. But he never went into details.'

'When was the last time you spoke to Alwyn?'

'The day before he died.'

'How did he seem?'

'On edge.'

'Because of the committee?'

'That and something else, but he didn't say what. Alwyn just said he had something to take care of.'

Fagan nodded. 'I appreciate the time you've given us.'

'Alwyn was passionate about Wales, DI Fagan. He thought a referendum on independence for Wales would have opened the floodgates for everything, crime, immigration, social issues. But Lloyd Bevan was too blind to see any of this. All Alwyn wanted was to heal the wounds of the past. That's why he moved back to the area near where he grew up. Despite the hostility Alwyn believed in healing the scars left in the wake of the miners' strike.'

Fagan stood.

'Alwyn didn't deserve this. Now that he's gone, there's no stopping Bevan from going forward with his plans for a referendum.' Armstrong paused. 'Next month I was going to announce that I am stepping down.'

'We'll be in touch as soon as we have a breakthrough.'

'A twisted tale boss.' Watkins remarked as they headed towards Merthyr.

Fagan glanced out of the window at a reservoir. 'I said this was all about politics at the beginning of this investigation.'

'Do we bring in Bevan for questioning?'

'What evidence have we got to prove he had anything to do with Collier's murder? We know they were rivals on the Senedd floor. We know Collier was planning to block a referendum when he became Welsh Secretary. Bevan has an alibi the night Collier was murdered. He wouldn't be stupid enough to do the deed himself.'

'But you think he was directly linked to Collier's murder?'

'Yeah, the question is, how is he connected? I spoke with someone last night about Alwyn Collier. He said that Collier was planning something. And now Armstrong said the same thing. Come to think of it, Delwyn Horlor mentioned something when we interviewed him. He said Alwyn told him he was being forced to play a trump card.'

'You reckon Collier had dirt on Bevan?'

'It's a possibility. When we get back to Newport, we'll have another look through the case involving the Blaina Four. I also want a list of every assembly member who has resigned over the last few years. Let's see what the coroner has to say first.'

CHAPTER 26

Nantyglo community centre 1985

'Thanks for coming in today, girls,' Donna Reynalds said loudly. 'I know many of you here have a lot to do. But this meeting is really important. We're here to talk about the march on Six Bells Colliery on St David's Day. This is going to be a big march. The boys have plenty of support from other collieries across the Valleys and other factories. It should be a good turnout. We are also here to address the difficulties we've faced over the past few months concerning the soup kitchens.'

'There should be more of us, Donna,' Sharon Welsh called out. 'There isn't enough to support the boys anymore. A lot of women have backed out because their husbands have gone back to work. There are loads of police patrolling the villages around the Valleys. The soup kitchens are being shut, Donna. I thought you were responsible for keeping them going in this area.'

'Look, I know donations have dwindled over the past several weeks. But there are a few of us who are doing everything to get more soup kitchens going.'

'Dwindling.' Sharon interrupted Donna. 'There are no soup kitchens left in Nantyglo and the soup kitchen in Blaina is about to go under. I was talking to Naomi. The more men that go back to work, the less need there is for these soup kitchens. The news reckons this strike will be over soon. Is there any point to these marches anymore? If they're not going to get us anywhere?'

'Of course, there's a point to all this,' Donna stated. 'If we let Thatcher do whatever she wants, then the government will shut every pit across this valley. Is that what you want?'

A few of the women shook their heads.

'We've worked long and hard for the boys over the last year. I know many of us have had to go without. But I promise you in a few years' time we'll be looking back on this moment with pride. Let me ask you ladies this. D'you want our kids to have a future?'

More nods.

'There's more than just the coal mines out there, Donna. I'd like my boys to grow up and go to college or university. Instead of being shoved down a filthy mine for fifty years of their lives.'

Donna looked back, shaking her head. 'Dreaming again are we Sharon?'

Muffled laughter rippled through the assembled women.

Sharon looked back. 'You've no right to mock me. Just in case you've forgotten, I started the Blaina women's support group. All you have done is muscled in and taken over. You're not even from this area. You're an outsider. Where did you say you were from?'

'Does it matter? I'm helping to support the miners. We're all helping. What you're trying to do, Sharon, is put a dampener on things.'

'No, I'm looking at the bigger picture here. That's what I'm doing. My Frank has had enough of this strike. We all have. I've barely been able to feed the kids over the past few weeks. I've had to scrounge off everybody. No one is helping anymore. It's getting shameful having to go round to people's houses begging for scraps of food. In the first few months of this strike people had dignity. People helped each other. There was real solidarity throughout the South Wales Valleys. But nearly a year on and no one is helping. The only ones that don't seem to struggle at the moment is the union officials. Our husbands have been promised financial help from the unions, but they've got nothing.'

'Your Frank can ask for a bridging loan from the NUM.' Donna pointed out.

'Why should we borrow money from the NUM and have to pay it back? Our fellas are striking for the NUM. They should be paying us. Not us lending money and having to give it back. D'you have any idea what it's going to be like after the strike is over. I know loads of families who will take years to pay back all the money they've borrowed during this strike.' Sharon looked around the room. 'There are a few girls in here that have expressed their concerns. But they're too afraid to speak. Just in case you grass them up to that boyfriend of yours, Bryn Collier. That's what you did with Tara Jones' husband.'

'Are you saying we should all give up and go back to work?'

'Don't try to make out that my Frank is about to become a scab, Donna. He's supported your boyfriend from the start. He still does. But you have to admit, the situation has become stale. There aren't any negotiations going on anymore. No one seems to know anything. And there's growing rumour this strike is about to end.'

'I don't know who you've been speaking to, Sharon. But my Bryn says Scargill is about to reach a breakthrough with the government.'

'Where did he hear that crap from? Thatcher was on the telly the other night. Saying she's steadfast in her goal to break the unions. What I want to know is what Bryn and Lloyd are going to do?'

'They're planning a march on Six Bells and take the pit. That's what they're planning to do.'

'And you don't think the police will be ready for them?'

'We know they'll be ready. But Bryn has got a few surprises up his sleeve.'

'And what then? What happens if you succeed in bringing the pit to a halt?'

'They'll occupy it. By doing this they will rally the miners who are still striking.'

'Bloody hell, Donna, you can't see it, can you? This strike can't go on forever. Everyone who has been involved is on the brink. You think by occupying Six Bells you can bring the government to their knees? They'll just send a load of bastard coppers in there to drag them out and haul them off to the cells. It will be worse than Orgreave last summer.'

Donna was tired of Sharon's negativity. 'Are you going to support us, Sharon?'

'What d'you think I have been doing over the last year, eh? I have done nothing but support the boys on the picket lines. I have brought them drinks and food every day. My Frank was nearly in the hospital last week because it was that cold. He had a temperature that nearly killed him.'

Donna showed no emotion. 'Is your Frank about to go back to work, then? Is that what you're saying, Sharon?'

'No, he's not about to go back to work. But no one is taking into consideration the mental impact this strike is having on the men, and us girls.'

Some women nodded.

'Not to mention the community. There are families that have been split up because of what has happened over the last year. Some people have had to move away and can never return.'

'Sharon.' Donna sighed. 'We haven't got time to talk about this.'

'Then we need to make the time. Because eventually, Donna, people will start to crack. And what about after the strike? When the boys go back to work. They can't stay out forever, can they? Eventually, the NUM will have to call an end to this strike.'

Sharon looked around the room. 'I started this support group a year ago. We helped each other out. Raised money from jumble sales and other fundraising events. But now everyone is tired and fed up. There are fewer volunteers who are willing to help.'

'So you're throwing in the towel are you Sharon? Giving up on the cause.'

'The cause is dead in the water. Jesus, you're too blind to see it.'

'Let me ask everyone in this room.' Donna said. 'Who here wants to see more pit closures? Thousands of men out of work?'

Some women turned and looked at Sharon to see her reaction.

'There are pits shutting every bloody month. They shut the pit in Blaenavon four years ago. No one gave a shit. Now it's a bloody museum.'

'Every pit across the Valleys will be a museum if we don't take action.'

'The coal industry is no longer making a profit.'

'You sound like that twat, Ian MacGregor.' Donna criticised.

'You really need to go down to the library now and then. You'll be surprised what you will learn.'

Some women were clearly amused by the ensuing argument.

'So what's your solution then, Sharon? Bow to the government and let Thatcher win?'

'I haven't got a solution. Neither have you, Bryn, or Lloyd. Or the idiots running the NUM. But at least I have the guts to admit it.'

'If you're not going to contribute to this meeting, Sharon. Then I suggest you fuck off and leave those who still give a shit about this strike plan.'

Sharon threw her coat over her shoulder. 'Thing is, Donna, I still give a shit, and so does my Frank. There are loads of miners still on strike who are questioning whether we should go on. It's only a minority who thinks carrying on with the strike is a good thing.' She turned and walked out of the room.

Blaina

Tara Jones rushed to the door with a sense of urgency. The hammering on the door was so loud it had upset the baby.

Standing on the pavement outside was a tall, bulky man. Wearing a long black overcoat. He clutched a clipboard. A woman in a smart grey suit was also present. Four large men waited by a parked van. Two police officers accompanied the group.

Four women stood on the other side of the narrow road, gossiping. One of them shouted across the road. 'I hope you're here to chuck those scab bastards out.'

'We don't want any of their kind around here.' Another woman bellowed.

The woman in the grey suit turned, looking towards them.

Tara's fear peaked as she opened the door.

'Mrs Tara Jones.' The man in the black overcoat asked in a stern voice.

'Yes.'

'Where's your husband, Mrs Jones?'

'He's in hospital.'

'I see.' The man sounded unsympathetic. 'The reason we are here, Mrs Jones, is to serve you and your husband with an eviction notice. Effective immediately.'

'I don't understand.'

'You were warned last month, Mrs Jones, about nonpayment of rent, that you will be evicted.'

'My husband has returned to work. He's earning again.' Tara argued.

'But you just said your husband is in the hospital. How can he be earning?'

'He'll be returning to work soon. As soon as he's on his feet again.'

'I'm sorry Mrs Jones. You and your husband have had ample warning. There are families throughout this area who need housing. Families who have money to pay their rent.'

'We've nowhere to go.'

'You will be temporarily housed in a shelter for the homeless. If you say your husband will be back at work, then you will be allocated a new house when he starts earning again.'

'Please, you can't chuck us out. What about my children?'

The man glanced at the woman. 'I am a social worker from the local welfare office. Your children will be taken into care until you get back on your feet.'

'What?' Tears tumbled down Tara's cheeks.

'We will arrange for your daughter to be picked up from school and placed into foster care.'

'Please, don't do this,' Tara begged. 'I promise I'll get the money.'

'When will that be, Mrs Jones?'

Tara was unable to answer.

'We have contacted you several times in the past few months, but you have ignored all the letters.'

'Please, I've nowhere to go,' Tara sobbed.

The man in the overcoat continued to be unemotional. 'I just said, Mrs Jones, you will be rehoused in a homeless shelter. Your children will be put into foster care until you get back on your feet.' The council official nodded to the social worker who stepped forward.

Tara blocked her path. 'I'm not letting you in.'

The two uniformed officers took up position. 'Mrs Jones, if

you don't let these people do their job, then you will be arrested.'

Tara stood firm. 'You're not taking my children.'

The social worker stood aside.

The two police officers lunged at Tara, grabbing her by both arms.

'Get off me, you bastards!'

'That's it boys, get rid of the scab bitch.' The four women across the street laughed.

Tara was bundled into the back of a police car. Terrified and livid, she watched helplessly as the social worker carried her screaming son out of the front door.

CHAPTER 27

Prince Charles Hospital–Merthyr Tydfil
Present day

The coroner handed Fagan the report.

'Where's the body?'

'Released to the family.'

'That was quick, considering he was murdered.'

The coroner frowned, shaking his head. 'He wasn't murdered.'

Fagan looked up from the file. 'But he was assaulted before he went into the water.'

'I carried out a thorough examination of Collier's body. He died of a massive heart attack. Not surprising given his current condition.'

Fagan studied the file.

'According to his medical history, Collier has had four heart attacks in five years. Each one was worse than the previous. He was on a lot of medication for various conditions: blood pressure, diabetes, asthma. I'm surprised he lasted as long as he did. He was severely overweight and his liver wasn't in good condition. This man was a ticking time bomb in health terms. I'll go as far to say that another heart attack was imminent. It could have happened anywhere.'

'His wife mentioned he hadn't touched a drink in a few years.' Watkins said.

'He must have been a secret drinker then.'

'What about the bruising caused by an assault?'

'Not severe enough to cause a heart attack. A more detailed examination on the bruising revealed it was a glancing blow.'

'So Collier was backing away when someone assaulted him?'

The coroner nodded. 'It was a coincidence that Collier had a heart attack at the same time as he was assaulted. Albeit a tragic one. I suspect he suffered a heart attack when he fell backwards into the Keepers. The temperature in the pond was eight degrees. Cold enough to have caused a cold shock to Collier's system. Since his heart wasn't in the healthiest conditions. It wouldn't have been able to withstand the shock of going into cold water. His body was partially submerged. Indicating he may have been alive for a short time before his heart gave out. From the way the body was positioned, it looks as if he tried to claw his way out of the Keepers.'

'Damn.' Fagan sighed.

'Hold on, boss. Whoever assaulted Collier walked away. Surely, they must have seen he wasn't moving.' Watkins suggested.

'Collier was a large man. The splash in the water would have made a noise for several seconds. If the suspect left in a hurry, chances are he didn't realise Collier had stopped moving.' The coroner pointed out.

Fagan considered his options. 'The person who assaulted Collier could be charged with gross negligence or manslaughter. The failure to act.'

'You'll have a hard time proving that, DI Fagan. The defence will simply say their client didn't realise what had happened.'

'Shit.' Fagan cursed.

'I've e-mailed a copy of this report to Detective Chief Superintendent Warren.'

Fagan sensed his heart sink. 'Which means he'll drop the murder enquiry.'

'He contacted me yesterday, wanting a full update.'

Fagan nodded. 'Don't worry, I know you were just following protocol. Thanks for this.'

Fagan slammed his hand on the dashboard. 'Fuck.'

'So what now, boss? Do we contact Warren? Or do we wait for the order to wind down the murder enquiry?'

Fagan considered the question. 'We still have the fifty grand to investigate. Whatever Collier was doing up at the Keepers, it had to be something serious.' His phoned pinged. 'Talk of the devil.' Fagan read the message. 'Cease all murder enquiries into Alwyn Collier immediately. Send all relevant information to the main South Wales police headquarters.'

'That's it then, boss.'

Fagan stared at the message. 'None of this makes sense. You can't just walk away from something like this. You have to tie up loose ends.'

'Sounds like Warren will have his own people doing that down at South Wales police headquarters.'

'Or perhaps he'll sweep everything under the carpet.'

'You think he's bent?'

Fagan looked at Watkins. 'Yeah, I do Sean. I also think he's part of whatever has been going on.'

'So what do you want to do?'

'Like the man said, hand everything over.' Fagan smirked. 'Then make a few follow up enquiries. You know, tie up those loose ends.'

'You thinking of going rogue, boss?'

'No, I merely want to understand all this.'

'So what's the next move?'

Fagan considered Watkins' question. 'Both Malcolm Jones and Victoria Armstrong said that Collier revealed to them he was working on something. That would put an end to Bevan's plans and career. And we have Delwyn Horlor saying that Collier was being forced to play a trump card.'

'An expose, maybe? I mean, it had to be Bevan, exposing Collier's affair with Armstrong a few years back. She certainly believed it.'

'The fifty grand.' Fagan said.

'What about it?'

'It was obviously a bribe.' Fagan grabbed his phone and texted Brooks some instructions.

'A bribe to stop him from doing whatever he was planning to do.'

Fagan nodded. 'Collier took the train to Cardiff the morning he was murdered.' Fagan corrected himself. 'Had a heart attack.

Met up with Delwyn Horlor at Unite union offices. Then he disappears for two hours before having to face the committee in the afternoon. Something happened in that committee. After the committee Collier makes his way from Cardiff to the Keepers. Terry's taxis picked him up at Abergavenny and dropped him off in Blaenavon around seven o'clock. So where was he between Terry dropping him off and him having a heart attack at the Keepers?'

'Uniform went door to door, but no one saw him.'

'But he was somewhere. He obviously didn't walk to the Keepers. Someone would have spotted him. When he arrives at the Keepers, he meets his attacker. The attacker has the stolen satchel with the money in it. They offer it to Collier, who is angered by the offer. He grabs the satchel and throws it into the Keepers. The coroner pointed out that he wasn't healthy and was a ticking time bomb, health wise. Just seeing the money may have triggered his heart. Especially when he saw his stolen satchel was being used to carry it.'

'A lot of speculation there, boss.'

Fagan frowned. 'I know. I tell you what, we'll pop in on Collier's wife and update her on her husband's death.'

Nantyglo

Fagan stopped dead in his tracks. They had parked down the road from where Collier lived. Standing at the front door was Tanya Glover. Fagan and Watkins retreated to their car, slouching in their seats as Glover roared by in her vehicle.

'I wonder what she's doing here?' Fagan questioned as they walked through the front gate.

Elizabeth Collier opened the door.

Fagan produced his ID. 'Mrs Collier, we were here a few days ago regarding your husband.'

Elizabeth stared towards the entrance to the drive.

Fagan looked in the same direction. 'Is everything okay, Mrs Collier?'

Elizabeth nodded. 'You better come in.'

'Where's your daughter, Mrs Collier?' Watkins asked.

'She's away in London.'

'What was Tanya Glover doing here?'

Elizabeth shook her head. 'She was asking about a project that both Lloyd and Alwyn were working on.'

'A project?' Fagan queried.

'The woman is full of it. She insisted Alwyn had information that Lloyd needed. She asked if I knew the combination to his safe.'

'Do you?'

'Yes, but the only thing in the safe was Alwyn's will. Alwyn hated Lloyd Bevan. There is no way they would have worked on anything together.'

'Mrs Collier, we're here to tell you the results of your husband's autopsy. Alwyn apparently died of a heart attack.'

Elizabeth nodded. 'That woman just told me.'

Fagan felt a surge of anger race through him. 'Tanya Glover knew this?'

'Yes.'

Fagan and Watkins exchanged glances.

'Did she say how she knew?'

'No.'

'We need to speak to you about Alwyn.' Fagan paused. 'We've spoken to Victoria Armstrong.'

Elizabeth let loose a snort of derision. 'Oh, aye. That trollop been gossiping, has she? Giving you a sob story about me being a right bitch to Alwyn. Let me tell you, she's no angel herself.'

'She told us about your son, Aron. And how he isn't Alwyn's.'

Elizabeth nodded. 'It was stupid of me in the first place to even pretend Alwyn was Aron's father. Aron looks so much like Bryn. I was young and stupid.'

'How long were you in a relationship with Bryn Collier?'

'Less than two years. My father was a miner. We used to drink in Abertillery working men's club on a Saturday night. I met Bryn in 1986. He just had a bad break up after a short term relationship. I knew he was one of the men accused of those murders.'

'Did he ever talk about it?'

'Not really. I first met Alwyn when the Six Bells shut in 1988.' Elizabeth paused. 'It was stupid of me to think I could carry on a relationship with Bryn. When the pit shut, Bryn went off the rails. He was drinking too much. So I made my choice. When I found out I was pregnant, I decided not to tell Bryn.'

'When was the last time Alwyn actually spoke to his brother?'

Elizabeth hesitated. 'Three weeks ago. It was the first time they'd spoken in nearly forty years.'

'Do you know what they spoke about?'

'No, but yesterday Bryn came to see me.'

'What did you talk about?'

'Bryn said Alwyn had told him he had information that could reopen old wounds.'

'What kind of information?'

'He said was it was something that could bring his world crashing down around him. Bryn also asked me if Alwyn kept anything in his safe.'

'But he didn't say specifically what Alwyn told him.'

'No, sorry.'

Fagan stood and handed Elizabeth a business card. 'I'm so sorry for your loss. If you need anything, please contact me.'

Watkins noticed the look on Fagan's face. 'You want to share, boss?'

Fagan clutched the steering wheel. 'I figured it out, Sean. I think Alwyn Collier was about to expose new information about his brother's murder in 1985.'

'You think he had information that could have triggered a retrial?'

Fagan glanced at Watkins, smiling. 'I'm certain of it. In 1993, when I joined Liverpool CID, I investigated the murder of a twenty-five-year-old mother of two. Jane Harris. A thirty-year-old man, Gareth Fisher, was arrested for her murder. But when it went to trial, the jury couldn't reach a guilty verdict. So Fisher was set free. In 2005, he was jailed for armed robbery. The silly twat boasted to his cellmate he murdered Jane eleven years previous. In exchange for a shorter sentence the cellmate gave evidence against Fisher. He was tried and convicted of murdering Jane Harris in 1993. The only reason it's sprung to mind was because Fisher was released last year.'

'He was convicted because of the double jeopardy law changing in 2005.'

Fagan nodded. 'What's the betting Alwyn Collier had information that could have triggered a retrial of the Blaina Four? It all makes perfect sense now. That's what Jones, Armstrong and Horlor were talking about. Collier told them he was working on something that could bring Bevan's career to an end. Glover and Collier's brother turn up, asking if Alwyn had anything in his personal safe. They're all looking for the information he was about to reveal. And lastly we have Martin Cooper. Who turned up outside Collier's home a few months back, threatening to kill him if he opened his mouth. It wasn't just about him becoming Welsh Secretary and blocking the referendum. It was also about Collier getting justice for his brother Dafydd Collier and Sean Price.' Fagan stared at the road ahead. 'We need to piece all this together.'

CHAPTER 28

Six Bells Colliery – 1985

Bryn Collier and Lloyd Bevan glared at the management team that walked into the meeting room.

'Good afternoon, gentlemen.' Edwin Boyce greeted.

Collier and Bevan remained silent.

'This is John Hunt from the National Coal Board.' Boyce inhaled. 'Let's get down to it, shall we? I know you don't want to be here. So I'll try not to waste too much of your time. Mr Hunt is here to discuss terms of returning to work.'

'That will never happen.' Bevan snorted. 'Not as long as you lot from the National Coal Board plan to throw us all out on the dole.'

'Mr Bevan. Surely you must see the position of the National Union of Mineworkers. They have failed in their aim in the past year to persuade the government into giving in to their demands.' Hunt explained. 'As we speak, there are high-level talks going on between NUM officials and the National Coal Board. This strike has gone on for far too long.'

'And it will continue, as long as you fuckers keep closing pits.'

'Using foul language like that, Mr Bevan will not help your cause.' Hunt maintained a calm manner.

'Okay then, I'll put it in plain English so even you can understand. The members of the NUM will no longer tolerate this systematic slaughter of the coal industry. We will continue to put up resistance.' Bevan pledged. 'As long as Thatcher and her government continue their war on the working class.'

'No one is at war, Mr Bevan. The National Coal Board has to make adjustments in order to keep up with our competitors abroad. We are seeing more coal exports than ever. There is a massive change taking place. Coal is going to be replaced with natural gas and nuclear power. So you see, sacrifices have to be made.'

'Is that what you told the miners at Cortonwood last year, and the other nineteen pits you shut?' Collier asked.

'The pits you've just mentioned were operating at a loss. What you have to understand is the coal industry in the United Kingdom hasn't made a profit in forty years. The British taxpayer has been doling out money for an industry which is haemorrhaging money. It makes little sense to keep subsidising a failing industry. The government is pushing a plan for cheaper, more efficient energy production. Nuclear power is fast becoming the energy production of the future. Both oil and natural gas are cheaper to produce than coal.'

'Doesn't stop this government from importing coal from abroad, though, does it?'

Hunt pursed his lips. 'It is cheaper to import coal from places like Russia than to mine it at home.'

'In other words, cheap fucking labour. What about the jobs that are being lost in this country because of imports?' Bevan pointed out. 'Men who have given their lives to the coal industry. You throw us aside like we don't matter to you bastards at the top. When the end comes for you, they'll give you a massive payout. You'll be able to retire in your fancy house. While those at the bottom are getting thrown out of theirs.'

'With all due respect, Mr Bevan, your union members decided to walk out last year. You didn't even have a ballot to strike. Now you're dealing with the consequences. But instead of looking to yourselves to blame, you are blaming others for your actions.'

'And what about your actions?' Collier fired back. 'Putting twenty thousand men on the dole queue in the North of England. We are fighting for our livelihoods here. The miners of the South Wales Valleys don't have a hope in hell of finding other jobs.'

'There are other sources of employment out there, Mr Collier,' Hunt remarked.

'Where?' Collier shouted. 'This government under Thatcher has waged war on the working class. The car industry, the steel industry, the dock workers. Hundreds of thousands of men tossed aside. Without as much as a second thought from the government. What about the families you have put on the poverty line? Millions struggling to make ends meet.'

'We are aware there is a minority of families finding it difficult.'

'A minority of families. Are you fucking blind or what? There are over four million on the dole, not just a minority. It goes to show how much pricks like you actually care. Four million people, including steel workers, car workers and miners from previous years when you have shut pits.'

Hunt ignored Bevan's insult. 'The workers the National Coal Board laid off have been given support. Training programmes have been rolled out for men who have lost their jobs. They have had a choice, either to train for new industries or spend their lives on the dole. We've also given out generous redundancy packages.'

'Bollocks.' Bevan stated. 'You're giving us all this bullshit to justify yourselves and the Thatcher government. Not to mention that prick running the NCB, Ian MacGregor.'

'We have also given miners the opportunities to move to pits that are more profitable,' Hunt continued.

'Where, those scab mines in Nottinghamshire that are still working? In doing so, you've devastated communities in the north.' Collier pointed out.

'Bryn, Mr Hunt is only trying to make you see how pointless this strike is. Jesus, you lot are still arguing about whether you should have called a ballot.' Boyce explained. 'Even the courts ruled the strike was illegal last September.'

'The courts under the control of that bitch Thatcher, you mean. Over eighty percent of the miners were already on strike.' Collier made eye contact with Hunt. 'Following the National Coal Board's decision to shut twenty pits in the north. There was no need to go to ballot.'

'And perhaps if you would have held a national ballot, the press would have seen you in a different light. Scargill is using the solidarity of the miners as a weapon against the government. But it's not working. Thatcher will never budge.'

'The press are a bunch of wankers. Led by that twat Robert Maxwell. He's been gunning for the miners since this strike started. You all have, including the National Coal Board. Scargill is defending our rights to keep our jobs. We know the press are trying to turn the miners against him. Well, it won't bloody work. We'll stand by him.'

'Bryn, the strike cannot carry on for much longer.' Boyce said. 'You think this is the only meeting taking place right now? Up and down the country there are hundreds of meetings similar to this one. It's time to ask yourself why this is happening.'

'It's happening because you lot have caved to the government. You honestly think the miners will cave? Because management has asked us nicely to go back to work.'

'What do you hope to gain out of this strike, Mr Collier? In the long run that is?' Hunt asked.

'Security for the mining communities throughout Wales, that's what. This country was built on the coal industry. Jesus, the South Wales coalfields fuelled the industrial revolution. Now Maggie Thatcher plans to toss us aside as if the last hundred years didn't matter.'

'I'm aware of the proud heritage you have around here, Mr Collier. But the NCB cannot continue to run pits that are unprofitable.'

'So what you are saying is that the Six Bells pit is unprofitable.' Collier glanced at Boyce. 'That's not what you told me last year when they announced the closure of Cortonwood. You told me Six Bells was in profit.'

'And it still is, however we are planning to reduce our output. Which will unfortunately see the reduction of men.'

'Is that why you dragged us in here today?' Bevan asked. 'To tell us you plan to reduce the workforce. How d'you reckon the boys will react? D'you honestly think they'll come back to work willingly?'

'We need the both of you to convince those who are on strike to return to work,' Hunt said.

Bevan burst into laughter. 'What makes you believe we want

to do that?'

'Because it's the only way to secure jobs for the future.'

'How long will that future be? Until next year, when this pit is up for review. There's another two hundred years of coal left underground through the Valleys. That's enough to secure the future of jobs for the next four generations. But you and that bitch sitting in Downing street want to stop. You just want to chuck everyone on the slagheap.'

'Those who take redundancy will be offered a generous sum,' Hunt said. 'Twenty-five thousand pounds.'

'And after that, what then for the working class of this valley? What is going to happen to the miners?'

'Bryn, this is a limited time offer. Otherwise names will be picked out of a hat, those who are laid off will get ten grand less. Think about it. Twenty-five grand is enough to buy your mam's home three times over. It will secure her future. She won't have to worry about rent anymore. You'll have a legacy to leave your kids and grandkids.'

'The only legacy our kids and grandkids will have is a future robbed from them. A chance to succeed in life. To have a job that will last them a lifetime.'

'Bryn, times are changing. You need to see that. The package being offered is generous. But its only for a limited time. We are giving you a chance to hold a ballot on whether to take it or to take the pit to review.'

'Then we'll take it to review.'

'If you do that, the NCB will still lay off men. Your brother has agreed to a ballot.'

'That scab bastard will agree to anything. There's no way the boys will go to ballot. We're going to fight to keep the jobs of everyone.'

'Bryn listen to me. The head of the NUM is going to order a back to work in the next week.'

'Where did you hear that bullshit?'

'The NUM contacted us this morning.'

'Funny, I haven't had a phone call from them.'

'The NUM feels that it may have lost control of the strike. That there are those who will drag this strike out for years. They don't want that. You're never going to win this fight.'

'We'll win this fight. I can guarantee you that,' Bevan stated with confidence.

Boyce pursed his lips. 'We know about the demonstration you have planned. We know you're going to take the colliery by force. The police are gearing up for a massive operation to stop you. I was in a meeting with the police commander this morning. You will not get near the gates to this pit.'

Bevan smiled. 'Are you that afraid of us? You have to get the bastard police to protect you.'

'Lloyd, you really need to consider what you are about to do. If you march on this colliery and try to take it by force, then the media will have a field day.'

'Good, then perhaps those reading the papers will see how desperate we are.'

'Lloyd, you can't fight progress. It's coming whether you like it or not.'

'Mr Bevan, if you go down the path you are planning, then it will not go well in your favour. You and the union members backing you will lose out on an opportunity to rebuild your lives. Surely you have to see it our way. Coal production in Great Britain is being scaled down. The government is moving towards a more sustainable energy production. Coal production is dirty and dangerous.'

'And what about the nuclear power stations? If one of those blows up, then the entire country is fucked.'

Hunt decided he'd had enough of arguing. He gathered his notes and stood. 'I'm sorry, Mr Bevan, Mr Collier. But I have other things to do. Your reluctance to listen to what I have proposed here is only going to doom your cause.'

Boyce also stood and followed Hunt out of the door.

'You tell that twat MacGregor, the miners of the South Wales coalfields will keep fighting for their livelihoods.' Bevan called out after them.

Hunt stopped, glancing over his shoulder. 'You will lose, all of you will.'

CHAPTER 29

Newport Central police station
Present day

Fagan stared at the text message he'd just received. *'follow the money'*

Watkins and Brooks walked into the room.

'Right then, boys. This is the situation with Collier. The coroner has concluded he died of a heart attack. Which means we are no longer pursuing a murder investigation. Detective Chief Superintendent Warren has ordered all information relating to this case to be handed over to South Wales police in Cardiff. I have spun a story to Chief Constable Griffiths. Saying we need to tie up loose ends before submitting information over to the Cardiff boys. Fortunately, he believed me. We've been given the rest of the day and tomorrow to tie up those loose ends.' Fagan glanced at the whiteboard. 'Despite the fact Alwyn Collier died of a heart attack, fresh evidence had surfaced. Collier may have had information relating to the murders of Dafydd Collier and Sean Price on St David's Day, 1985. Here's where it gets sticky. Collier hid this information, which means we have to find it before tomorrow afternoon. Let's focus on the Blaina Four and their arrest. Andrew, what have you got?'

'Bryn Collier, Martin Cooper, Amlod Llewellyn and Lloyd Bevan were arrested on 6th March 1985.' Brooks explained. 'They were arrested after a tipoff, following a drunken confession from Martin Cooper. He claimed they were on the bridge the day the scaffolding pole was dropped.'

'You say tipoff. So someone voluntarily walked into the police station and gave the police information?'

Brooks studied the information. 'No, someone telephoned Merthyr police station and made the claim.'

'Which means it could have been any silly bugger.' Fagan sighed.

'Or might never have happened at all.' Watkins remarked, staring at his laptop.

'How do you mean, Sean?'

'According to this article about the trial, the defence shot down everything the prosecution threw at the accused. Cooper denied saying they were on the bridge. He provided an alibi for the night he was supposed to have made the confession. His mother, Bronwyn Cooper, said her son was with her all night.'

'What about the fourth man, Amlod Llewellyn?'

'Died two and a half years ago. Cause of death, liver cancer.'

'So that leaves Cooper, Bevan and Collier.' Fagan ran the names through his head. 'Where are they now?'

'Bevan is obvious. He's First Minister for Wales. Bryn Collier lives in Abersychan, Pontypool, on Glansychan Lane. He's got a Facebook profile. Collier is both chairman and patron of Garndiffaith RFC.'

'Patron.' Fagan mused. 'Must have a big pension pot to support a rugby team.'

'According to his profile, after Six Bells Colliery, he worked for Port Talbot steelworks for over thirty years.'

'What about Cooper?'

Watkins stared at his laptop. 'He's no social media presence, a total ghost in that department. It's just his arrest record. He lives up the Varteg.' He tapped away on his keyboard. 'This is interesting, boss. It says here Cooper was first arrested in July 1980 on suspicion of arson.'

'What did he set alight?'

'According to this, a property in Abergavenny, belonging to Welsh Secretary of State Nicholas Edwards, was firebombed. Cooper was arrested on suspicion of arson two days later. A witness said they saw him running away from the property.' Watkins glanced at Fagan. 'His defence lawyer was Malcolm Barry.'

'Cooper has a connection with Lord Barry. Run a check with the registry office. Find out who Cooper's parents were. And what they did for a living.'

Watkins clicked on his mouse.

'What happened after they were all arrested?'

'They were questioned for three days straight.' Brooks revealed. 'They were all charged and put on remand for eight months. On 30th October 1985, their trial began at Cardiff Crown Court. It only took three days for the trial to collapse. Following the statement and evidence given by Cooper. He was severely beaten while in police custody and hospitalised. The trial collapsed because of several elements. The police cars that were escorting the taxi were too far away to see anything significant. Five police officers gave statements relating to the incident. However, after a cross examination, the defence concluded they were too identical. Barry was quoted saying, *There was no unique perspective from each of the officers. It was almost like someone had typed out a report. Photocopied it five times and got the so-called witnesses to sign it.* There was also the forced confession from Martin Cooper. The run up to the trial generated public support for the Blaina Four. Especially in the wake of what happened during the Battle of Six Bells.'

'Got a result on Cooper's parents, boss.' Watkins announced.

'Let's hear it, Sean.'

'Cooper's father, Rhodri, was born November 1930. His mother Bronwyn was born in August 1937. They were married in March 1955. Rhodri Cooper's occupation was a groundskeeper for the Barry estate.'

'There's our connection.' Fagan rubbed his hands, together.

'His mother, Bronwyn, was a housekeeper. Martin Cooper was an only child. Born in 1956.'

'Collier had new information about what happened to Dafydd Collier and Sean Price. We need to go back to St David's Day, 1985.'

Brooks studied the information on his screen. 'The Battle of Six Bells Colliery kicked off around 9:30 in the morning. Around two and a half thousand miners and demonstrators had gathered on the Six Bells road.'

'Jesus, talk about a precursor to Anfield.' Watkins said. 'That road is narrow. Two and a half thousand in such a small area. It's a wonder someone was crushed to death.'

'According to an eyewitness, Bryn Collier gave a rallying speech to the demonstrators. One witness report states the police line, a few hundred yards away, beat their shields and chanted.'

'They were goading the demonstrators into charging the police lines.' Fagan speculated.

'That's exactly what happened. A witness reports claims several demonstrators became angry when the police beat their shields. As soon as a group of men charged the police lines, the rest followed. The police were instructed to fall back and form a line at Lancaster Street. This is where they set their trap. Police blocked off each end of the street, trapping six hundred demonstrators. This was the epicentre of the violence. Demonstrators who tried to break free were beaten with truncheons and thrown into the back of police vans. Three hundred miners had to be taken to hospital that day. Fifty-eight police officers were also injured.'

'The media had a field day.' Watkins said. 'Calling it the last stand of the working class.'

'What about the incident with Dafydd Collier and Sean Price?' Fagan asked.

'The police quashed the demonstration within four hours. There were running battles with the police in other areas. Including Six Bells park, Richmond Road and.' Brooks smiled at the report he was reading.

'What?' Fagan asked.

'There's a street in Six Bells called Coronation Street.'

Fagan saw the funny side. 'I expect Hilda Ogden gave some of the demonstrators a good hiding with her rolling pin.'

Brooks continued. 'According to the prosecution in the case against the Blaina Four. Cooper, Bevan, Llewellyn, and Collier evaded the police. They made their way to the footbridge that spanned the newly built A467, Aberbeeg road. At approximately 1:21pm, a taxi was travelling along the A467 under police escort. Nineteen-year-old Dafydd Collier, sixty-three-year-old Gethin

Roberts and fifty-one-year-old Tony Morgan, was heading to Six Bells Colliery for the afternoon shift. Fifty-three-year-old Abergavenny taxi driver, Sean Price was at the wheel of the vehicle. At approximately 1:22pm, a scaffolding pole was hurled from the footbridge. Sean Price was killed instantly when the pole smashed through the car windscreen, impaling him through the chest. The vehicle rolled three times before coming to rest by the side of the road. Dafydd Collier sustained a fractured skull, two broken legs, and a broken collarbone. Gethin Roberts suffered a broken arm and two broken ribs. Tony Morgan was left paralysed below the waist. None of them were wearing seatbelts. Dafydd Collier died on the 5th March 1985.'

'How far were the police behind the taxi?'

'A good few hundred yards, according to one of the officers in the panda cars. They were told to keep their distance behind any vehicles they were escorting to the Six Bells Colliery. This is how the defence, Malcolm Barry, determined, they were too far away to make an identification as to who actually threw the pole. A manhunt was immediately launched following the incident. On 6th March 1985 all four men were arrested.'

'The police interrogate them. Beating the shit out of Cooper and forcing him to sign a confession. They're remanded in custody until the trial, which collapsed because of the way the police behaved.'

'They arrested seven hundred people on the day.' Watkins said. 'There's plenty of conspiracy theories floating about.'

'Conspiracy theories?' Fagan sounded doubtful. 'What about?'

'It's been claimed the only way the police could have turned up in force like that is if the army helped. One witness account claims that while they were being thrown into the back of a police van, they pulled on a police tunic. The witness claims he was wearing an army uniform underneath.'

'We need to focus on what information Alwyn Collier may have had to bring the murders into the public domain again.'

'It has to be a deathbed confession from Amlod Llewellyn.' Brooks suggested.

Fagan nodded. 'That's the only thing the CPS will take notice of. For a double jeopardy trial to take place, concrete evidence has to be presented There can't be a shred of doubt. The information Collier had must have been enough to trigger a retrial.'

'I found an article in the Guardian, boss.' Watkins said. 'According to this, Martin Cooper, Bryn Collier, and Lloyd Bevan received compensation in 2016. For wrongful arrest and imprisonment. They each received a quarter of a million quid. Thirty years after their arrest. Thing is, the Guardian refers to them as the Blaina three.'

Fagan leant back in his chair, running the information through his mind. 'Llewellyn wanted nothing to do with getting a payout.'

'Why?' Brooks asked.

'Because he knew the payout was based on a lie. What if they were all on that bridge and one of them threw that scaffolding pole? Killing Dafydd Collier and Sean Price. And because the police at the time fucked up, they walked free. I've seen loads of footage from the Battle of Orgreave. The police not only charged at the miners on horseback, but they unleashed police dogs. Can you see that happening today?' Fagan shook his head. 'I'm guessing Amlod Llewellyn had a conscience about what happened that day.'

'Why didn't he come forward sooner?' Watkins asked.

'He may have had a conscience about it, Sean, but Llewellyn wasn't stupid. If he would have come forward, it would have meant spending the better half of his life behind bars. In 2016, Bevan won a seat in the Assembly. Steadily working his way to the top. He influenced the way the media published the story. Llewellyn refuses the payout and in 2020, he's diagnosed with cancer. 1n 2021, towards the end of his life, he makes a deathbed confession. It could be a signed statement, or a video confession. Either way, it's enough to trigger a double jeopardy trial. Shit.'

'What's up, boss?'

'We need to get hold of the information Collier had. But it could be anywhere.'

'If Llewellyn made a deathbed confession and Collier had hold of it, then why didn't he go to the police?'

'Good question Sean, one we'll have to put on the back burner for now.'

Brooks' phone pinged. 'Labs have come back with an analysis of the fifty grand. Apparently, whoever handled the money treated it with bleach.'

'Trying to get rid of DNA and fingerprints.'

'That's what labs reckon. They've also found a print on one of the notes. But it will take time to run it because the bleach has damaged it. The satchel has also been treated with bleach.'

'Reply to labs and tell them to keep us informed. Under no circumstances do they hand over the information to those lot down at Cardiff nick.'

'That's going to piss Warren off, boss.'

'What Warren doesn't know won't hurt him, Sean.' Fagan grabbed his jacket off the back of the chair. 'Come on, let's have a chat with Lord Barry.'

Skenfrith

Fagan looked out across the Monmouthshire landscape. Skenfrith castle keep towered above the surrounding trees.

The door opened and Barry hobbled out on his walking stick. He recognised the man standing in his driveway. 'If you are here to talk about the murder of Robert Turner, DI Fagan, then may I suggest you contact my solicitor.'

'Actually, Lord Barry, I'm here to talk about a different matter.'

'I've no interest in talking to you about anything. Good day, Inspector Fagan.' Barry turned back towards the main door to his manor house. His Barbour wellingtons crunched on the gravel.

'I'm here about the Blaina Four.' Fagan called after him.

Barry stopped and slowly turned to face Fagan and Watkins.

'You represented them at their trial in 1985, did you not?'

'Yes, I did. Thanks to you bumbling buffoons, I dispatched the prosecution with ease.'

'Despite the fact they could've all been guilty.'

'Based on what evidence, Inspector Fagan? A forced confession. Corrupt police officers who had a hatred towards the miners. If you want to look into corruption, then I'd suggest you look in your own backyard.'

Fagan held up his mobile phone. 'I have been doing a little research. You came out of retirement and represented Collier, Bevan and Cooper in their claim for compensation.'

'Those men went through hell in 1985, Inspector Fagan. They were imprisoned for several months for a crime they didn't commit. They had to endure trial by media. Marginalised by a government that cared little about the livelihoods of families throughout the South Wales Valleys.'

'Why didn't Amlod Llewellyn receive compensation?'

The question seemed to rattle Barry. 'What are you trying to achieve by dragging up the past, Inspector Fagan?'

'All I'm doing is trying to establish facts.'

'The facts are this, Inspector Fagan. The police were corrupt. They lied about everything that had happened that day. Hundreds of miners were rounded up, arrested, and subjected to barbaric treatment. Similar to what happened at Orgreave. Now, if there is nothing else, I'd appreciate it if you'd get off my property.' Barry turned and headed towards the front door.

'Why did Amlod Llewellyn refuse the money in 2016, Lord Barry? Was it because he wanted nothing to do with the lie that has carried on since 1985?'

'Good day to you, Inspector Fagan,' Barry said, slamming the door.

Watkins puffed out through his cheeks. 'Waste of time, boss.'

'No, it confirms what I suspected. Llewellyn wanted no part of a lie.'

'But without the information you believe Collier had, we're nowhere.'

'I know.' Fagan admitted.

'What now?'

'We'll wrap up for the day, but I'll have a chat with Bryn Collier later on.'

'Do you think he'll speak to you?'

'No, but Collier's wife said he confronted his brother about something. It has to be the information Alwyn had. Plus, Bevan's assistant was at their house asking for information. Spinning Collier's wife a bunch of bullshit about a project Alwyn and Lloyd Bevan were working on. Collier's wife knew Alwyn hated him. I'll do a little digging first, see if I can find something that will rattle his cage.'

'Watch your back, boss.' Watkins warned. 'They can be very passionate in that part of the world.'

Fagan started the engine. 'Let's try to figure out where the missing information is.'

CHAPTER 30

Tudor Street Police station–Abergavenny 1985

'Good morning sir,' Benson greeted as chief Constable Merlyn entered his office. Commander Terry West followed behind.

Benson stood.

'We thought we'd give you one final briefing today regarding events tomorrow.' West revealed. 'There's been a slight deviation from our primary plan.'

'How so?' Benson enquired.

'As you know, we plan to establish roadblocks all over the South Wales Valleys. To stop demonstrators from reaching the Six Bells Colliery. Management at the Six Bells pit had a meeting with union officials yesterday. They made it quite clear they have no intention of returning to work. The stubborn militants want to drag this strike out as long as possible.'

'There's a lot of rumour the unions want to order a back to work for all striking miners.' Benson remarked.

Merlyn nodded. 'I was in a briefing yesterday with regional chief constables. A majority of men have returned to work. However, we still have to deal with the militant few. Still causing disruption to the supply chain of coal. There was a major incident yesterday afternoon when a few picketers got inside Llanwern steelworks and halted the furnaces. It took two bloody hours to drag them out of there.'

'What's this new strategy you have in mind?' Benson asked.

'We will put a large amount of resources into protecting the Six Bells pit from being overrun by strikers. Our intelligence has revealed that's exactly what they plan to do. The silly bastards will probably go for an all-out assault on the pit. Thinking they'll have the numbers to overrun our police lines. They are keeping their cards close to their chests so we don't know the exact plan of action. We already have officers guarding the main gate. The pickets have been there every day, and it's been mostly peaceful. Any sign of trouble and the gate to the pit will be closed. However, the union officials, Lloyd Bevan and Bryn Collier, plan a show of strength tomorrow. We know there are several rallies planned around the Abertillery and Six Bells area. We believe this is a diversionary tactic to split our forces. However, we have reserves on standby should things get out of hand.' Merlyn revealed. 'We know there are men from other industries who plan to join the rally tomorrow morning. Three coaches are due to leave Port Talbot steelworks around ten o'clock tomorrow. There are two coaches coming from Lucas Girling in Cwmbran. And one coach from the Royal Ordinance factory just outside Monmouth. There are also coaches that have been organised from other pit heads around the Valleys. Our intelligence in the North of England has revealed five coaches are travelling from North Yorkshire late this evening.'

'It will be a wasted journey, sir,' Benson said. 'With all the roadblocks we have planned, we should be able to quash this demonstration. It will only be a few hundred men.'

'We're allowing coaches to get through.' Merlyn said, glancing at West.

Benson stared back at Merlyn. 'Can I ask why, sir?'

'The government is determined to crush the union movement once and for all. Over the past week there has been high-level talks between NUM union officials and the government.' Merlyn smiled. 'Mr Scargill may be coming to his senses and ordering a back to work for all remaining striking miners.'

Benson chuckled. 'Stupid bastards have finally realised they've lost. Well, serves them right. Perhaps now this country can get back to normal.'

'Indeed.' West said. 'it has always been the intention of the government to break this stalemate. Scargill knows he's beaten. Once the miners return to work, the power of the unions will diminish. We've been told to let the coaches through. We'll be using a similar tactic to the one we used at Orgreave last June. Although it will be a scaled down operation. We won't be using horses or dogs this time around. Mrs Thatcher wants to subject those still on strike to one last humiliation.'

'A warning to others planning future action.' Merlyn pointed out. He unclasped a briefcase and pulled out a map of the Six Bells area.

Benson studied the map.

'Our officers have been instructed to let coaches through. But not too many. We have five thousand officers in reserve. When the demonstration starts, we will monitor the situation closely. Let them march on the Six Bells Colliery and have their little demonstration. We'll contain the strikers in a relatively small area. We'll then call on our officers to move in and make the arrests. The stupid bastards won't see it coming.' West smiled. 'We have two coaches of undercover officers who will be allowed into the area. Your man, Owain Lance, will lead the operation.'

Benson nodded. 'Owain is an outstanding officer, sir.'

'There will be a large gathering of press at the Six Bells Colliery. All the main news channels will be there. The BBC, ITV and the new Channel Four. All the major newspapers will be there to cover events. They will cover the demonstrations and make the strikers look like a bunch of tossers.'

Benson smiled. 'Well, I for one will be glad to see the back of this miners' strike. These militants have been a thorn in the side for the past year. Everyone is sick of their constant moaning.'

'Once everyone is in place, our officers will move in an quash any potential takeover of the pit.'

'What about civilians, sir? Women and children have often attended these rallies.'

'We believe the women are planning another rally to distract our officers. They're looking to thin out the herd. But our reserves will give them a nasty surprise. It's a school day, so we're not expecting any children. We'll arrest any women who might decide to get more physical with our officers. Your job, Sergeant Benson, is to supervise the police officers at the Six Bells Colliery. You will have two hundred men at your disposal. They will be equipped with full riot gear.'

Benson nodded stiffly. 'I'm looking forward to crushing those militant bastards once and for all.'

The Miner's Lamp–Six Bells

Bryn Collier put up his hand to get everyone's attention. 'Settle down, boys. Me and Lloyd have some news to tell you.' He glanced at Lloyd. 'As some of you know, we were at Six Bells yesterday. Meeting with their management team and a representative from the National Coal Board. There's no easy way of putting this. They plan to lay off half the pit and go down to one shift. They have also offered a redundancy package for those who vote to take it. The twat we met with from the coal board said that it is a limited time offer.'

The room erupted into shouting.

Collier put up his hand. 'Listen to me, all of you. We are going to fight this all the way.'

'So we fucking should.' A man said, sitting in the audience. 'Otherwise, this past year has been a total waste of time. Many of us in this room have sacrificed a lot. We've lost our homes, and some of us have lost family, because they've sided with the enemy.'

Collier nodded, thinking about his two brothers.

'Those scab bastards who have worked have betrayed the union, their workmates, family and the cause.' Martin Cooper seethed.

Collier could sense the tension in the room. 'Yeah, we've all sacrificed a lot over the past year. But we must remain strong. We must remain resolute in our goals.'

Some of the men knocked on tables.

'The sacrifices we've made over the last year must not be in vain. We cannot let the other side win. Thatcher and her government must not be allowed to go ahead with their plan. That is why we are going to march on the Six Bells Colliery tomorrow. And that's why we are going to take control.'

The crowd in the room responded positively to Collier's words.

'Lloyd, do you want to say a few things? Assure the boys we will stand by them no matter what.'

Bevan composed himself. 'Coal is in our blood. It is the lifeblood of the South Wales Valleys. And I'll be fucked if Thatcher and her government think they can obliterate our history. We need to be strong as a union. We also need to be strong as a community. Our families are depending on us. To fight for our future, and the future of generations to come. When I look at what's happening to the coal industry, it fills me with dread. Hundreds of thousands of jobs have been lost in the steel industry, car plants, docks and the railways. These men have no future now. They've been cast out. Forced to live on government handouts. Which is not enough to feed their families. That's not going to happen to the coalfields of South Wales.'

'How much did the coal board offer those scab bastards who are likely to take it?' Cooper asked.

'The men they plan to lay off will be given a twenty-five grand redundancy package.'

Murmurs rippled through the room.

'I hope none of you are planning to turn scab and betray us,' Cooper seethed. 'If anyone in this room even crosses that picket line, then you'll fucking well answer to me.'

'What about the police?' An audience member asked. 'Surely they'll be out in force, ready to protect the pit.'

'Don't worry about that. We have a plan. We can't tell you what it is, but when it happens tomorrow, it will boost our cause. Especially if the press are there to take photographs.'

'Who do we have coming from other pits?' Another man asked.

'We have about twenty coaches arriving from all over. Tower Colliery is sending four hundred men. And the Hoover factory is sending three coaches. There'll be enough of us to stir things up.'

'I know some boys who will support us,' Cooper offered. 'There's a coach load coming up from Cardiff in the morning. I'm going down to meet them later on this afternoon. I'll arrive back here with them tomorrow. We'll put on a display for the police bastards.'

'Did management say when they plan to lay off half the workforce in Six Bells?' Paul Clarke asked.

Bevan stared back at him. 'No, they didn't go into any details. They just told us about the redundancy package.'

'Well, it must be soon.'

'The National Coal Board was not forthcoming with information.' Collier said.

'When do you think this strike will be over?'

Cooper pointed at Clarke. 'It will be over when we say so.'

Clarke glanced at Cooper before looking at Collier and Bevan. 'Since when did he become a union rep? All I want to know is when this strike is going to end.'

'We don't know.' Bevan answered.

'I'm at the end of my tether now, Lloyd.' Clarke looked around the room. 'Loads of us are. We've supported you for almost a year. But there seems to be no end in sight.'

'Tempted by the redundancy offer, are you?' Bevan's tone was deliberate. All the men in the room fixed their gaze on Clarke.

'Fuck off Lloyd. Don't put me on the spot like that,' Clarke answered in a defensive tone. 'Most of these men in this room are fucked off with the strike. We've followed the leadership of the NUM for a year. This strike is getting us nowhere. Most of the boys in this room are too terrified to tell you they want to go back to work.' Clarke looked at Cooper. 'Why did Malcolm Jones deserve the kicking you gave him?'

'Because he's a scab bastard who betrayed the cause.' Cooper grinned.

'I tell you what, Martin, you'd be a suitable candidate for the BNP. Just shave your hair and you'd fit right in with those arseholes.'

Cooper glared back at him.

'The soup kitchens are almost gone. The donations have dried up. How long do you expect us to go on for if there is no more help?'

'The NUM and National Coal Board are close to a deal.'

'You said that last week. And the week before. In fact, you've been saying it for months. Every time you and Bryn call one of these meetings, it's the same old bullshit. The NUM is close to a deal. We watch the news. We know what's going on.'

'The news is nothing but propaganda,' Collier stated.

'No more than what the NUM is. I can't stand to watch Scargill on the TV anymore. He's as bad as you two. We're close to a deal. The government will give in to our demands.'

'So what, you suggest we give in to the government?'

'But how long can we keep going for?' Clarke demanded to know, dodging the question. 'You both know we can't stay out indefinitely. It's a wonder the coal board hasn't sacked the lot of us. Right now, twenty-five grand is tempting. I don't give a shit how many people are shaking their heads at what I'm saying. I know there are men in this room that would gladly take it. All of us are in debt. Do you have any idea how long it's going to take most of us to pay off our loans? When we return to work, we'll have bills to pay. Jesus, some of us will be working double shifts for the next year to catch up.'

'Listen to me, all of you.' Bevan said loudly. 'We are going to win this fight. We are going to force the National Coal Board to stop closing pits.' He looked at Clarke. 'I promise you, Paul, that you'll look back on this strike with pride.'

Clarke stared back, but said nothing.

Prince Charles Hospital - Merthyr Tydfil

'Your husband has regained consciousness.' The doctor explained to Tara. 'He has several broken ribs and a broken arm. His cheek bone is fractured, and he's still heavily concussed. He also has a fractured leg. Whoever did this to him could have easily killed him if they wanted to. He'll be in hospital for a few weeks.'

Tara shuffled into the small hospital room.

Her husband was propped up in bed. A nurse was helping him drink a glass of water. He winced in pain.

'You're going to be sore for a few days.' The nurse explained. She spotted Tara entering the room. 'I'll leave you alone to talk.'

Tara stared at her battered husband.

His face was swollen. His arm was bandaged up.

Tears streamed down Tara's face as she realised what Cooper and his associates had done to him. 'Mal, it's me.'

Jones struggled to turn his head.

'I'm so sorry, Mal. I'm so sorry they did this to you. I had no choice. I had to tell Lloyd what you had done,' Tara sobbed.

Jones stared blankly at his wife before summoning the strength to speak. 'Fuck off and leave me alone.' He turned his head back towards the window.

Tara ran from the room sobbing.

CHAPTER 31

Garndiffaith RFC
Present day

Bryn Collier clapped his hands together loudly. A group of men were running around the perimeter of the rugby pitch. 'Come on, you lot! Pick up the pace. I'm expecting you to give those Abertillery tossers a good hammering tomorrow night.'

'Bryn Collier?' A voice from behind asked.

Collier briefly glanced over his shoulder. 'Who's asking? Oi Callum, you useless wanker, shift your arse! You run like that tomorrow night, and you're off the team!'

Fagan stepped in front of Collier. Obscuring his field of vision with his ID. 'Detective Inspector Fagan, Gwent Police.'

Collier stepped to the side and shouted at a man on the other side of the field. 'AK, keep pace! Make sure they run an extra two laps.' He glared at Fagan. 'What do you want, Inspector Fagan?'

'I think you know.'

Collier let out a snort of derision. 'If you think I'm going to shed a tear because that scab of a brother of mine is dead, then you can forget it.'

'His wife said you visited her yesterday. Asking for information that may have been in the safe.'

'I wanted to know if he had a will and was going to leave his boy anything.'

'You mean your boy,' Fagan corrected him. 'I know everything, Mr Collier.'

'You know fuck all.' Collier mocked.

Fagan looked about. 'Nice pitch and clubhouse.'

'One of the best in the county, as well as having the best teams.'

'Very generous of you to be patron of the club.'

'What's your fucking point, DI Fagan?' Collier demanded to know.

'Collier's wife said you met with your brother recently. It was the first time you had talked to him in nearly forty years.'

'I'm free to talk to whoever I want. Even if it includes scabs from time to time.'

'Mr Collier, your brother, was found dead up at the Keepers with fifty thousand pounds in cash.'

'That doesn't surprise me. My brother was a bent politician, and a scab bastard.'

'And what about your other brother, Dafydd? Was he a scab as well?'

Fagan's words ignited Collier. 'How dare you show up here and dredge up the past. You have no fucking idea what I went through, what we all went through.'

'Done well out of it though, haven't you? A quarter of a million compensation for wrongful arrest and imprisonment. You've certainly helped this place. I read that in 2015 it was close to collapse.'

'My brother died because of the traitors and scab bastards who betrayed the cause.'

'What cause is that exactly?'

'The fight against an oppressive government. Who wanted nothing more but to wipe out the working class in the Welsh Valleys.'

'That was forty years ago, Mr Collier. Margaret Thatcher is long dead.'

Collier spat on the ground. 'Good fucking riddance to her. I hope she's burning in hell. Her and that twat MacGregor. Together, they sucked the life out of the South Wales Valleys. Entire communities left to rot. It may have been forty years ago to you. But it still seems like yesterday to the rest of us.' Collier looked Fagan up and down. 'And then there's you, the pigs. Who kicked the shit out of us at Orgreave and Six Bells.'

'Why did Amlod Llewellyn refuse the compensation?'

'Stupid twat.' Collier mocked. 'Should have taken the money instead of.' He stopped talking.

'Instead of what, Mr Collier? Growing a conscience about what happened that day on the bridge.'

'We were nowhere near that fucking bridge!' Collier screamed.

One of the men running around the pitch broke off from the group and jogged towards Fagan and Collier.

Collier's face was purple. 'You fuckers arrested us, beat the shit out of us, and then forced us to sign false confessions. After which you threw us into prison.'

'You were acquitted, Mr Collier. A court found you innocent.'

'Because we were innocent. It's you lot who were the bent bastards.'

'Everything okay, dad?'

Collier looked at the man who had peeled away from the group. 'Everything is fine, son.' He stared at Fagan. 'You have no right coming here. I suggest you fuck off back to your trough, join the rest of the pigs.'

'All I'm trying to do, Mr Collier, is find the truth.'

Collier's son stood nose to nose with Fagan. 'Oi, you heard my dad. Piss off back to your trough, pig scum.'

Llanfoist – 1:33am

Fagan jolted upright. The loud banging on the door pounded its way into his dream. He looked towards the window. Immediately spotting why someone was hammering on his front door. The dancing colours on the curtains alerting him to a fire that was raging below on his driveway. He jumped out of bed, flinging open the curtains. His car in the driveway was a mass of flames. Fagan leapt down the stairs and went out through the back of the house.

The distant wail of a fire engine grew louder.

'I called the fire brigade as soon as I saw what was going on.'

Fagan watched helplessly as his Jeep was engulfed in flames. A fire engine screeched to a halt. Five firefighters poured out of the vehicle, quickly setting up a hose. Another fire engine turned into the street.

'Fuck!' Fagan yelled at the top of his voice.

Another car raced around the corner. Jamie Evans spotted Fagan in his pyjamas and dressing gown.

The fire crew had quickly dealt with the blaze.

'Jesus Fagan, are you alright mate?'

'Just about Jamie, thanks.'

'Someone did this deliberately, didn't they?'

Fagan buried his head in quivering hands. 'I don't know.'

'Come on, let's get you to the Cantreff. I've texted Jackie.'

The fire crew advised Fagan to use the back entrance of his house while they dealt with the burnt out wreckage of his car.

'Hang on, Fagan.' Evans spotted something on the window.

Fagan glared at the words that had been spray painted onto his front window. *'Scabs and bent pigs belong together.'*

Several minutes later, Fagan sat at the bar, knocking back a double brandy.

Jackie poured another shot into his glass. 'You can have that one, then a cup of coffee.'

Simon Edwards shuffled into the bar in a dressing gown and a pair of boxers. He pulled on the dressing gown cord.

'Suits you.' Fagan smiled, noticing it was Jackie's dressing gown Edwards was wearing.

'Do you have any idea who would want to do this to you, Fagan?' Jackie questioned.

'No.' Fagan stared into the empty shot glass.

'Are you still investigating that politician found dead at the Keepers?' Edwards asked.

Fagan nodded.

'If this is about politics, mate, then you've obviously pissed someone off.' Evans speculated.

'Ugh, that First Minister is going to give us his speech at the Senedd later on, isn't he?' Jackie mocked.

'Don't want an independent Wales then, Jackie?' Evans asked.

'No I don't. Don't get me wrong, I love being Welsh and living in Wales. But I have never liked that Lloyd Bevan. He's obsessed with breaking away from the UK. He's been shoving independence down our throats ever since he was elected as First Minister. It is possible to be part of something and still keep your national identity.'

Edwards kissed Jackie on the cheek. 'Perhaps you should run for the Senedd, love.'

'There's an idea.' Jackie smiled.

A knock on the door interrupted their conversation.

Watkins walked through the door. 'You okay, boss?'

'I suppose Sean. But I'm pissed off someone torched my car. It belonged to my mam before she died. Whenever I drove it, I felt she was still with me.'

Jackie smiled. 'She's still with you, Fagan.' She looked towards an armchair in the corner of the bar. 'Just like our nan still watches over me.'

Fagan stepped away from the bar. 'I appreciate the offer of you putting me up for the night, but I have to go back home.'

Jackie held her phone up. 'You sure, Fagan? I can give our Tommy a bell and he'll send his two boys up to sleep on your floor.'

Fagan shook his head. 'There'll be plenty of police at my house to protect me.'

'We need to pull everything off the traffic cameras by Llanfoist.' Fagan said, as they headed back to his house. 'There's no way these bastards who attacked me were on foot.' He thought about the message spray painted on the front window of his house. 'Scabs and bent pigs belong together.'

'Boss?'

'It's graffitied onto my front window.'

'It's obviously someone with a connection to this.'

'I spoke to Collier's brother last night. He is a man stuck in the past.' Fagan carried out a search on Google. 'According to this, seven assembly members have resigned, ever since Lloyd Bevan became First Minister in 2018. They've all been replaced by Senedd members who represent the Welsh Independent Nationalists.'

'Sounds like Bevan is trying to manipulate the vote in the

Senedd next week.'

'He's due to address the Senedd later on today. Bryn Collier confirmed my suspicions last night. He came close to admitting Amlod Llewellyn refused compensation because of his guilty conscience. Until we get hold of a confession, then it's all still speculation.'

Watkins pulled up by the side of the road.

A group of residents stood a few hundred yards away gossiping.

A firefighter approached Fagan as he climbed out of the car. 'Well, there's no doubt about it. This was definitely arson. Someone smashed the front window of your car.'

A CSI was taking a swab from the window that had been spray painted.

'Anything?' Fagan asked.

'Whoever did this was stupid enough to spit on your window. This is saliva.' The CSI pointed at a streak running down the window. 'It shouldn't take long to get a DNA match.'

'You want me to stay with you for the rest of the night, boss?' Watkins offered.

'No, it's okay, Sean.' Fagan looked at the uniform stationed outside his front door. 'Let's get some kip, then we'll see what the new day brings us.'

CHAPTER 32

Six Bells Park 1985

'Thank god for that.' Bevan said, assessing the crowd. 'There's way more than what turned out the other day. When the buses arrive, we'll really have a good day. Should be a few thousand. The police won't be able to cope, dull bastards.' He grinned at a line of uniforms that stood in front of the gate.

Some of the crowd was chanting. Others were singing. They looked happy to be there. NUM banners were held high, along with a sprinkling of Welsh flags.

'Yeah, it looks like a good turnout.'

'You don't sound very convinced, Bryn.' Bevan noted the expression on his face.

Collier sighed. 'More men are getting fucked off with this strike. Even I'm starting to question what we're trying to do. Every day I'm getting men telling me they want to go back to work. It's looking as if we are losing this fight, Lloyd. I don't know what to say to them anymore.'

'You tell them to hold their ground. We're going to beat Thatcher and her government and come out on top.'

'Doesn't feel like it.'

'What d'you mean?'

'Haven't you seen the news today? They reckon we'll be called back to work within the next week.'

'This isn't the time to get cold feet now, Bryn. I hope you haven't been speaking to that scab bastard of a brother of yours.' Bevan looked around to make sure no one was within earshot of them. 'These people have turned out for us. They need us to rally them, to inspire them. To make them feel they're achieving something.'

'And what exactly is that?'

'What d'you mean by that?'

'What I mean, Lloyd, is what have we achieved with this strike?'

Bevan stared back at Collier. 'Don't say you're about to fold.'

'No, of course not. What I'm saying, Lloyd, is there's not enough of us still on strike to make any kind of difference. You have to see it from the miners' point of view.'

'The boys will stand by us no matter what.'

Collier nodded over to the crowd. 'Yeah, for now. But what about twelve months down the line? Can you say the same? When we first walked out last March, nearly everyone backed us. But the boys thought we'd only be on strike for a few weeks, two months tops. Now nearly a year on and at least three-quarters have gone back to work. Did you see the looks on the faces of the boys at the meeting? When we told them about the redundancy package the National Coal Board is offering. Some of them looked like they were more than willing to take the money.'

'Look at me, Bryn. We have to stick to the plan if we're going to beat Thatcher and her fucking government.' Bevan said in a commanding tone. 'We need these people to help us in our cause for a united Wales.'

'You don't have to lecture me, Lloyd. I know what we're fighting for.' Collier stated in a defensive tone. 'My problem at the moment is we've heard bugger all from the NUM. They've been silent for nearly two weeks. I think Scargill is about to call it a day on this strike.'

'Don't be daft. Scargill will never cave in to that bitch. He'll back us all the way. He hasn't let us down yet, has he?'

'No, but you haven't been able to get hold of his management team. I'm having to lie to the men about support packages. Pretty soon we're going to look like a right couple of twats. Especially when everyone is struggling. We should have never accepted those payments, knowing full well where the money came from. Even Alwyn mentioned it the other day. He mentioned that copper killed outside the Libyan embassy last year.'

'We've fuck all to do with that. When we met with the Chief Executive of the NUM last year, he told us our conscience was clear.'

Collier glanced at the chanting crowd. 'And if they find out, we're going to be strung up and hung out to dry. Look at us Lloyd, we haven't struggled, have we? Not like the rest of them. Families have been split down the middle because of this dispute. Communities have been devastated.'

'And they'll be totally wiped out if we don't make our stand today.'

'Alright then Lloyd, let me ask you this. What happens if we lose this strike? What happens if the NUM orders a back to work?'

'Then we keep on fighting.'

'For what?' Collier shouted. His voice drifted across the park. A few of the crowd looked in their direction.

Bevan grabbed Collier's arm. 'Bryn, they can't see us fighting like this. The boys are counting on us to win this.'

Collier spoke lower. 'But we're not, are we? Don't you get it? This strike is dead in the water.'

Bevan released his grip. He looked over at the crowd. 'Okay then, you can go and tell them to go home. You can tell them that it's pointless fighting for our jobs. You can tell them there's no point fighting for our communities anymore. You tell them they've no future. That there's no future in the South Wales coalfields. What do you reckon their response will be?'

'I know what the response will be. I'm not that fucking stupid.'

'Right, this is what we're going to do. I'm going to make a speech to our supporters and together we are going to inspire them. Then we are going to march on Six Bells and demand that management shut down all operations. If they do not comply with our demands, then we are going to take the pit by force.'

'See, that's the bit that worries me.' Collier looked over at the crowd. 'They're ordinary people, Lloyd, not soldiers. And if we manage to take over the colliery, what then?'

'We'll hold it until the government gives into our demands.'

'You said we'll only occupy the pit for a few hours. Now suddenly you plan to hold it indefinitely.' Collier shook his head. 'We can't do that, Bryn, there are men underground working.'

'Those scab bastards know the consequences of their actions. They made the choice to betray the cause.'

'For Christ's sake, Lloyd, you can't trap men underground.'

'Once we take the pit head, we'll make sure operations are kept running. They'll have breathable air. What do you take me for, some kind of arsehole?'

'But you said we'll only occupy the winding gear for an hour or so.'

'Well, plans change. You know how it is.'

'You can't prevent those men from coming to the surface, Lloyd.' Collier protested. 'The press will have a field day. What do you think will happen if we take the pit by force? They'll send hundreds of coppers to storm the pit. Jesus, the government may as well label us as terrorists and send the SAS. Just like they did with the Iranian embassy. Sorry mate, I'm loyal to the cause. But I'm not going to give my life for it.'

'So what do you suggest? We tuck our tails between our legs and go home. I'm fucking sick of being labelled as thugs and troublemakers.' Bevan pointed at the crowd. 'All they want is a future, that's all. Thatcher and MacGregor want to rip that away from them. They want to deny us a future. Now you tell me, Bryn, is that fair, eh? Is it fair we won't have a future because of what that bitch and that twat are doing?'

'No, of course not.'

'Then let's stop bickering and do something about it.'

Collier inhaled.

Bevan patted him on the arm. 'We'll get through this and win.'

The crowd of demonstrators watched Bevan climb onto the back of the flatbed van.

Bevan put the megaphone to his lips. 'It is great to see that so many of you have turned up today. We all know why we have gathered here today, don't we?'

Nodding heads rippled through the crowd.

'We are here as a symbol of defiance to a government that wants to destroy our way of life. Maggie Thatcher's plan to shut the coalfields of South Wales is not just an attack on our livelihoods. It's an assault on our identity. The government's plan of mass pit closures through the South Wales coalfields is an insult to generations of miners who've toiled in the coal faces for over a hundred years. Maggie Thatcher and Ian MacGregor refuse to acknowledge the devastation they're about to bring upon us. They see us merely as numbers on a balance sheet. Not as families struggling to put food on the table. Or a community trying to build a future for our children.'

Emotion rippled through the crowd.

'The government speaks of closures as if they're mere business decisions. But we know this isn't true. Thatcher refuses to acknowledge the human cost. The emotional cost. The devastation that will rip through our communities will be unprecedented. The pits they want to close are the lifeline of our towns. These pitheads are the beating heart of Wales. The government and the National Coal Board refuse to comprehend the bleakness that will descend upon the Welsh Valleys. The prospect of long-term unemployment stretching across future generations.'

The crowd jeered.

'Thatcher's vision of a capitalist society, where profit reigns supreme, is a vision that sacrifices the very soul of the working class. Not just across the South Wales Valleys, but the rest of Great Britain. We have all seen the struggles of the miners in South Yorkshire who now face a bleak future. And the betrayal of the Nottinghamshire miners who joined the ranks of the scabs that have betrayed our cause.'

More booing and jeering emanated from the demonstrators.

'Thatcher's vision glorifies greed, while disregarding the plight of hardworking people. But we refuse to succumb to this heartless ideology. We reject a system that values profits over people. Where the few thrive while many face a bleak future of hardship and unemployment. And we do this, because we are the working class of South Wales!'

The crowd erupted into cheers.

'I see in every man and woman who has turned out a renewed sense of determination. To stand up against the threat that both Thatcher and her puppet, Ian MacGregor, represent. After all we've done for the National Coal Board. They stand happily by and let this extermination of the working class continue.'

More cries of anger came from the crowd.

'We stand here in solidarity. United by the same struggles. The same hopes, and the same determination to resist these illegal pit closures. We stand together in this place, representing the backbone of this nation. The working class are the ones who've fuelled its industries. Thatcher treats us as disposable. But we are not expendable!' Bevan shouted, punching the air.

The crowd roared back their support.

'We are not mere cogs in a machine. Our strength lies in our unity. In our unwavering belief in a society where workers have power. Where communities thrive on solidarity and mutual support. It's time to remind those in power that the workers, the miners, the families are the heartbeat of this nation. And without us, it grinds to a halt.'

The crowd cheered, waving banners and flags.

'We will hold our heads up high. Faced with the political butchery of the working class by Maggie Thatcher and her government. We will stand up to the destruction of our communities. By a government that concerns itself, not with the people that helped build a nation. But with lining its own pockets.'

The crowd booed loudly.

'We must resist the dismantling of our communities. The erosion of our values, and the dehumanisation of our struggles. We are not only fighting for our jobs, but for the very soul of our communities. Let us stand firm, shoulder to shoulder. And show the world that the spirit of Wales, the spirit of its people, burns brighter than any coal in our mines. Together, we can build a future where the dignity of the working class is respected. Where the well-being of our communities is paramount. And where the power lies in the hands of the people, not in the pockets of the privileged few.'

The crowd continued to cheer and chant.

'So let us hold our heads up high. Let us wave the Welsh flag with pride. Together, we will show Thatcher that our spirit will never diminish. And the rest of the country will watch as we make our voices heard.' Bevan punched the air. 'The miners united, will never be defeated!'

The demonstrators chanted. 'The miners united, will never be defeated! The miners united, will never be defeated!'

Bevan and Collier jumped down from the flatbed. The demonstrators parted to let them through and take the lead.

A senior police officer stood firmly in front of a row of uniforms.

The crowd surged towards the police line, chanting, waving flags and NUM banners.

The lead constable looked at the line of police and nodded. They stood to one side and let the crowd march through the park entrance.

'Dull twats. They've no idea what they're walking into.' The senior police officer grinned.

The crowd continued to chant as they walked down the road toward the Six Bells Colliery.

CHAPTER 33

Newport Central police station
Present day

Fagan stared at the text message he just received. *'They're trying to throw you off the scent.'* He pocketed his phone before knocking on Griffiths' door.

Warren glared at him as he walked into the room. 'Would you care to explain what you are playing at Fagan?'

'Sir?'

'Don't bloody sir me, Fagan!' Warren exploded. 'I told you to wind down the investigation yesterday. Following the results from Collier's autopsy.'

'That's what I've been doing, sir. Tying up loose ends before my team hands everything over to your team in Cardiff.'

'Do these loose ends include interrogating Bryn Collier last night at the Garndiffaith rugby club?'

Fagan looked at Griffiths before glaring at Warren. Anger simmered deep within. 'I'm sorry, but doesn't anyone want to ask me about the arson attack on my home last night?'

Warren dismissed Fagan's question. 'Kids Fagan, just gangs of kids. It's been happening all over the Valleys.'

Fagan could scarcely believe the crap Warren had just come out with. 'Have grandkids, do you, sir?'

'I beg your pardon?'

'Do you have grandkids?' Fagan raised his voice.

'Yes, I have seven of them,' Warren replied in an equally loud voice.

'Know much about the miners' strike, do they, sir? You know, detailed history about what went on forty years ago.'

Warren returned Fagan's question with a blank expression.

'These weren't kids who attacked my house last night. They

were grown men. They spray-painted scabs and bent pigs belong together on my window. There's no way a fifteen-year-old yob would do that.'

'Why did you question Bryn Collier at the Garndiffaith rugby club last night?'

'Bryn Collier was a loose end I was trying to tie up.'

'Bryn Collier hasn't spoken to his brother in forty years, Fagan. All you've done is to dredge up painful memories for that man.'

'Actually, sir. They both spoke a few weeks ago. Bryn Collier didn't show any compassion for his brother. He even told me he wasn't shedding any tears for him.'

'You were told to hand over all information to Cardiff.'

'And that's what I was planning to do at the end of the day.' Fagan looked at Griffith. 'You gave me the time.'

'Fagan, if there is one thing I can't stand, it's an insubordinate officer. Especially those like you with so many years behind them.'

'What's that supposed to mean?'

'It means, DI Fagan, that you are to cease all enquiries relating to the death of Alwyn Collier. That includes loose ends.'

Fagan had no other choice but to play his hand. 'Okay then. The reason I visited Bryn Collier last night is because I've uncovered evidence the deceased had information to prove that Bryn Collier, Martin Cooper, Amlod Llewellyn and Lloyd Bevan were guilty of the murder they were acquitted of thirty-nine years ago.'

'And what information is that exactly?'

'Collier, Cooper and Bevan all received compensation in 2016 for damages awarded by the police. For wrongful arrest and imprisonment. Amlod Llewellyn, the fourth man accused of the murder, didn't receive any compensation.'

'So?'

'I suspect Llewellyn refused because he had a guilty conscience.'

'You know this for a fact, do you, Fagan?' Warren queried.

'Why would he turn down a quarter of a million?'

Warren deflected the question. 'Fagan, you're clutching at straws. Alwyn Collier died of a massive heart attack. There's no murder investigation to pursue. You're obsessing over this.'

'What about the fifty grand found in his satchel?' Fagan argued. 'A satchel that was stolen from Collier a few weeks back while he was on his way to Cardiff. Lloyd Bevan's assistant is seen plain as day, outside the BBC Building near Cardiff Central, holding the satchel.'

Warren folded his arms. 'Okay then Fagan. Tell myself and Chief Constable Griffiths here what you think you have.'

'I think this is all political.'

'How so?'

'I've spoken to three people who've all said that Collier told them he was working on something big. Something that could put an end to Bevan's career.'

'What do you think this, *something,* is?'

'A deathbed confession from Amlod Llewellyn. Giving a detailed statement about what happened on the bridge the day Dafydd Collier and Sean Price were killed.'

'What's the point of a deathbed confession about a crime that happened nearly forty years ago?'

Fagan almost laughed at Warren's ignorance. 'A deathbed confession could be enough to force a retrial, a double jeopardy trial. Under the 2005 legislation.'

Warren stared back like a rabbit caught in headlights.

Fagan took advantage. 'On St David's Day thirty-nine years ago to the day, two events took place. The Battle of Six Bells and the murders of Dafydd Collier and Sean Price. Following these events the police were exposed for their brutality against the miners. Over three hundred protestors were taken to hospital. Dafydd Collier and Sean Price were killed in the afternoon when a scaffolding pole was thrown off a bridge. Bryn Collier, Martin Cooper, Amlod Llewellyn and Lloyd Bevan were arrested on 6th March 1985. Following an anonymous tipoff. They were interrogated by police for three days before being charged. But because of the way the police treated them, their defence was able to call into question their statements given while they were being interviewed. The trial collapsed, and they were set free.'

'And you think Amlod Llewellyn turned down the

compensation given to Collier, Cooper, and Bevan because he knew they were guilty?' Griffiths said.

'That's exactly what I'm saying, sir.'

Warren shook his head. 'But you've no evidence to prove this, Fagan. Because Collier had nothing in his safe.'

Fagan realised what Warren had said.

'And without no evidence, all you have is a theory. D'you honestly think the Crown Prosecution Service will take you seriously? For a double jeopardy trial to happen, you have to have evidence that proves beyond reasonable doubt all parties are guilty. All the police officers involved in the interrogation of the men accused of these murders are dead. The police officers in the escort cars are dead. All the men in that taxi are now dead. There's no one left to give statements.'

'Except Bryn Collier, Martin Cooper and Lloyd Bevan.' Fagan countered.

'You really think you can take on the First Minister with these accusations?' Warren said. 'He'll end your career in a heartbeat. You'll be the one put on trial for slander and defamation of character, if you accuse the First Minister of anything. The fact you interviewed Bryn Collier last night could be seen as harassment.'

'That's bullshit and you know it.'

'Where do your loyalties lie, Fagan?'

'My loyalties?'

'Let me put it in plain English, shall I. Whose bloody side are you on?'

'The side of the victims. That's whose side I'm on. The side of justice. It's not just a theory I have. Llewellyn must have told someone what happened that day on the bridge. When I questioned Collier last night, I could see it rattled his cage. Alwyn Collier's wife told me that Bryn Collier went to see her the day before yesterday. He wanted to know if his brother kept anything in his safe. I'll tell you who was also there.'

'Who?' Griffiths asked.

'Tanya Glover, Bevan's personal assistant.' Fagan looked at Warren. 'I know how a double jeopardy trial works. I know you have to have evidence that will stand up in court. That's what I'm looking for. If you wouldn't have interrupted that interview I was conducting with Glover, then we might have had shed a little light on what's going on here. Bryn Collier told his brother's wife the information his brother had was enough to bring his world crashing down around him. So you see, it has to be something that proves they were on that bridge. It has to be something that Amlod Llewellyn left behind. That's what Bevan is so afraid of. If this evidence came to light, then it would end his career. He's due to give a speech on Welsh independence at the Senedd later on today. I also find it more than a coincidence last night, after interviewing one of the men accused of murder in 1985, I had my home attacked. This is all connected.'

'Do you realise what you're doing here, Fagan?' Warren rumbled.

'Yes I do. I'm getting justice for two men who didn't deserve to die.'

'No, you're not. You're trying to destroy the lives of three innocent men.'

'That's not the impression Bryn Collier gave me last night. Or Martin Cooper, when I interviewed him. Cooper was arrested four weeks ago for threatening Alwyn Collier. A police witness heard him say to Collier that if he opened his gob, he would live to regret it. Alwyn Collier may have died of a heart attack, but there is still enough here to pursue an investigation. A murder investigation from 1985.'

Warren sighed. 'Fagan, without that evidence, you have nothing. So I suggest you stop chasing rainbows and get on with your job.'

'Excuse me sir, but that's what I've been doing.'

'No one wants to dredge up the past, Fagan. You're talking about ancient times. Where were you in 1984 and 1985? Doing time in Usk prison.'

Fagan stared back at Warren.

'I've seen your file, Fagan. I'm surprised they let you sign up to the police. I also see that you are being investigated regarding your conduct towards a vulnerable man.'

'Oh Jesus, here we go.' Fagan groaned. 'Benny Nelson is far from vulnerable. It's Lloyd Bevan that doesn't want to dredge up the past, because it could expose him as a murderer.'

'I can't be bothered to listen to any more of your fantasies, DI Fagan. I'm ordering you to cease all investigation into the death of Alwyn Collier. Your team will hand over all the information they have accumulated over the last few days.'

'And what about the attack on my home last night? Am I to drop that as well? Someone torched my car and spray-painted my front window. I think that at least warrants an investigation.'

Warren considered Fagan's question. 'If you want to waste taxpayers' money by pursuing something as trivial as that, then fine.'

Fagan clutched the railings outside the main entrance to the police station. His phone buzzed in his pocket. Fagan read the text. *'We need to meet.'*

CHAPTER 34

Guardian of the Valleys memorial – Six Bells

Fagan spotted a man in his late seventies sat on a bench looking up at the massive sculpture of a miner staring out over the valley.

'It was erected to remember those who died in the 1960 Six Bells disaster.' The old man explained.

Fagan glanced up at the statue. 'History is not my thing, sorry.'

'History often defines us, DI Fagan.' The old man pointed at the sculpture. 'This monument doesn't just remind us about who we've lost. But what we've lost. Especially the people of the South Wales Valleys.' The man paused. 'I can help you, Inspector Fagan. But only if it's in my best interest to do so.'

'And what is your interest?'

'The truth.'

'Sorry to disappoint, but I don't think it exists.' Fagan took in a lungful of air.

'Alwyn Collier's death was unfortunate, but not in vain. You can still crack this case wide open.'

'That's the problem. I don't have a case at the moment. Just a theory. I've been ordered to cease any investigation into Collier's death.'

'Because those in power don't want you exposing a lie.'

'Who are you exactly?'

'I'm a former member of British Intelligence, with information that will help you.'

'What has Alwyn Collier got to do with all this?'

'Nothing and everything.'

'I'm in no mood for riddles.' Fagan turned and walked away.

'They're all guilty of that murder, DI Fagan. Bryn Collier, Martin Cooper and Lloyd Bevan. Surely you must have your suspicions.'

Fagan stopped and turned. 'But I've no evidence to prove it.'

'Not yet, anyway.'

'Why have you called me here today?'

'To expose you to a truth that everyone needs to know.'

Fagan walked back towards the man. 'I'm listening.'

'Back in the 70s and 80s, Britain was blighted by strike action. The unions dominated the news headlines. In 1972, Prime Minister Edward Heath was forced to cave to the National Union of Mineworkers. Many of the unions were led by men with communist ideologies.'

Fagan smiled.

The man nodded. 'I can see why you are sceptical, DI Fagan. Waiting in the wings was Margaret Thatcher. She knew what was going on and she was determined to take action. When she took office in 1979, Mrs Thatcher was briefed by both US and British Intelligence. She was given a list of names of union officials throughout the country who supported communism. One of the names on that list was Lloyd Bevan.'

'He was a communist?'

The man nodded. 'Amongst other things. Bevan headed up a group called the South Wales Communist Council. A group that was founded in 1920. The Americans became increasingly concerned these union officials were under the control of the Kremlin. The CIA wanted to break the backs of the unions. Margaret Thatcher agreed with them. And so a plan was put into place to put an end to the power the unions wielded. Thatcher drew up a list of industries and unions she wanted to dismantle once she had formed her government. She believed in a free market and felt the UK's growth was being stunted because of the powers the unions had. The National Union of Mineworkers was high on her list. But first she had to deal with the other unions. The dock workers, car workers, and train unions. Who were constantly bringing industry to a halt with strike action. When Thatcher won the 1979 election, she immediately set her plan in motion.'

'How is Lloyd Bevan connected to all this?'

'Bevan had regular meetings with a man called Jack Jones. He was a powerful union leader, head of the Transport and General Workers' Union. In later years he was exposed as a soviet spy. For over forty years he passed secrets on to the Russians. By the time the miners walked out in 1984 Jones had become less prominent. But he had a profound influence on Bevan. By October 1984, the NUM was realising the Government would never give in to their demands. Money ran out and so was support for the strike. Another problem for the NUM was the number of miners returning to work. Especially in the weeks leading up to Christmas. To keep the strike going in the South Wales Valleys, Bevan reached out to fellow members of the South Wales Communist Council. Asking if they knew anyone who could help.'

'What happened?'

'Bevan was unaware he was under surveillance by British Intelligence. On October 24th 1984, Bevan met with a representative from the Soviet Federation of Miners in Soho, London. The representative was also a colonel in the KGB. Russia was engaged in an attempt to destabilise the balance of power in the UK. They wanted a more socialist Prime Minister running the country. Who would cosy up to the unions. The KGB operative offered Bevan two million pounds to keep the strike going.'

'I take it he accepted?'

The old man nodded. 'Around the same time, the NUM gave Bevan another half a million pounds, which was to be paid into the South Wales branch of the Miners' Solidarity Fund. Bevan gladly accepted more money.'

'I thought you said the NUM was running out of money.'

'During this time, the NUM was under heavy criticism from both the press and the government. I take it you've heard of Yvonne Fletcher?'

Fagan nodded. 'Yeah, the woman copper shot outside the Libyan embassy.'

'I have been working closely with two men who have been promoting a book they have written, called No Ordinary Day. Both Matt Johnson and John Murray were on duty the day she was murdered. They have been campaigning for forty years, to bring those responsible for the murder to justice. On the 17th April 1984, WPC Fletcher was gunned down while policing an anti-Gaddafi protest outside the Libyan embassy in London. Months before the event, Gaddafi gave an order. All anti-government Libyan nationals in London were to be eliminated. Weapons were smuggled into the Libyan embassy. A nine-day siege followed Yvonne Fletcher's murder. After which all Libyan nationals at the embassy, including Yvonne's murderer, were taken to Gatwick airport. They were interrogated by the intelligence services before boarding a plane to Tripoli.'

'I've always wondered why they didn't storm the embassy.'

'The reason they held back DI Fagan, is because the British government had a back door deal with the Libyans. The National Coal Board had been stockpiling coal in preparation for a strike. Thatcher's advisors were worried that if the stocks ran out, the government would be forced to cave to the Miners Union. In 1984, the Americans had placed an oil embargo on Libya. But this didn't stop the British government from importing oil from Libya as a backup plan, should the coal stocks run out.'

'And when Yvonne Fletcher was murdered outside the Libyan embassy, the government could not do anything about it.'

The man nodded. 'Following the murder, Gaddafi's representatives contacted the government and warned if any of the embassy occupants were killed by the SAS, Gaddafi would stop the oil imports.'

'Jesus, he had the British government over a barrel.'

'An oil barrel, to be exact, DI Fagan. But to make matters worse, the only way the government could secure the oil in the first place was to sweeten the deal.' The man paused. 'By supplying the Libyan government with weapons.'

'I don't see how this is connected to Bevan.'

'Because the NUM was running out of money, they put the call out for donations from other countries to support families of striking miners. Libya responded. The chief executive of the NUM flew out to Libya to meet with Gaddafi himself. The pictures were leaked to the press deliberately. Tarring the NUM's reputation. The Libyans gave three million in donations. The president of the

NUM knew he had to get rid of the money after a series of newspaper articles ran the story.'

'So they gave half a million to Bevan?'

'Yes. But Bevan didn't hand the money over to the Miners' Solidarity Fund. Instead, he deposited the money into a bank account in Ireland. But not before he gave a hundred thousand to his second in command, Bryn Collier, who was joint treasurer on the NUM's South Wales branch.'

'Why did Bevan put the money into an Irish bank account?' Fagan questioned.

'Bevan was on the watchlist of MI5 for several reasons. One reason was his nationality. Bevan's mother was Irish and his father was Welsh. His mother came from an Irish family that had links to the IRA. Her brother was a prominent member, as was his son, Bevan's cousin. In January 1985, Bevan took a trip out to Ireland to deposit the money he had received. He also met with his cousin, who was top of a watch list following the murder of a British soldier in Belfast.'

'Alwyn Collier found out about this, didn't he?' Fagan guessed.

The man nodded. 'Three years ago, Collier contacted the National Archives in Kew and asked for information about the role of British Intelligence during the miners' strike. British Intelligence flagged his enquiry.'

'Why?'

'During the miners' strike, the intelligence services and the police ran undercover operations to infiltrate the mining communities throughout the country. Including the South Wales Valleys. Their role was to gather intelligence on the activities of groups within the miners' union. They recruited striking miners who would relay information about the union's plans. One of the men who was feeding intelligence back to us was Amlod Llewellyn.'

'The fourth man on the bridge the day Dafydd Collier and Sean Price were killed. That's why he refused the money handed out to Lloyd Bevan, Bryn Collier and Martin Cooper.' Fagan inhaled. 'Shit.'

'Llewellyn wanted to tell the whole story. His role as an MI5 asset and the money the government was paying him. It would have caused a lot of embarrassment if the truth would have come out. Alwyn Collier persuaded him to hold back.'

'Collier wanted justice for his brother, Dafydd.'

'You have an opportunity here, DI Fagan. To expose a man who is about to change the course of history for this country.'

'The referendum.'

'Yes. I suggest you heed the message I sent you.'

Fagan realised what the man was talking about. 'Follow the money. Bevan has been using the money he got from Libya and Russia to fund his campaign.'

'Over the past few decades, Bevan has been investing that money in various businesses around the world. In 2016 he won a seat in the Senedd. The same year he received compensation for wrongful arrest and imprisonment. And then in 2018 he had that shock election win for the position of First Minister.'

'He's as bent as a butcher's hook.'

'And now he has the highest position in the Senedd. And is poised to convince the people of Wales that an independent Wales will be more prosperous, under a socialist leadership.'

'But I still don't have any evidence to prove this,' Fagan said, with frustration in his voice.

'The evidence has been under your nose all along, DI Fagan.'

'Where?'

'The morning after Alwyn Collier was found, you visited an old school friend, Nigel Thomas.'

'How d'you know?'

'Because Mr Thomas was collaborating on a book with Alwyn Collier. Today, Lloyd Bevan will deliver his speech to the Senedd about Welsh independence. There will be a vote in the Senedd next month on a referendum. Collier was due to release his book a week before the vote.'

Fagan smiled. 'Which would have exposed everything.'

'Including the murders of Dafydd Collier and Sean Price.'

'I think Amlod Llewellyn made some kind of deathbed confession.'

The old man smiled. 'That's why I contacted you today, DI Fagan. I know you pulled the file about the murders out of mothballs. Keep going.' He encouraged.

'I would, but I've been ordered to halt the investigation.'

'Since when has something like that stopped you? I suggest you give your former colleague, Wayne Tanner a call. He has something for you that will help.'

'How d'you know I called Tanner?'

The man smiled. 'When you've worked for British Intelligence, DI Fagan, you never retire.' He looked up at the statue. 'The miners' strike changed everything. A battle of ideologies raged. Capitalism came out on top. But at what cost? This country still has poverty and deprivation. Third and fourth generation families that have never worked.'

Fagan's phone buzzed. He gave the man an apologetic look before answering.

'Boss, where are you?'

Fagan glanced at the stranger. 'I'm, uh, tying up another loose end. What's up?'

'Forensics got a result on the arson attack on your car last night. A member of the public handed in dashcam footage of a car driving erratically on the Keepers road in the early hours. It's a 2014 Land Rover Discovery. Registered to Martin Cooper.'

'It's all coming together now, isn't it?' Fagan smiled.

'Cooper lives in a remote cottage in the Varteg.'

'Get Andrew Brooks up there with a couple of uniform to arrest that twat.'

'Andrew is already on it, boss. He took a couple of uniforms twenty minutes ago.'

'I need you to do something for me, Sean. I want you to run a financial check on Bevan.'

'Boss?'

'I know we've been told to stop everything relating to Collier, but keep going.'

'Okay, Boss.' Watkins hung up.

'I think I've got the breakthrough I have been looking for.'

The old man nodded. 'I wish you well in your investigation, DI

Fagan.' He turned and walked away.

'Wait.' Fagan called after him. 'The other day Collier got into a black Mercedes with false number plates. Was that you?'

'Yes. We were finalising details of his book.'

Fagan nodded.

'Good luck, DI Fagan. I'm sure this won't be the last time we meet.'

CHAPTER 35

Six Bells - Friday 1st March 1985
The police line looked menacing. They blocked the main road leading to the colliery. Two hundred uniforms were dressed in full riot gear. Their riot shields glinted in the morning sun.

Benson stared at the crowd that chanted loudly several hundred yards down the road. Like two mediaeval armies about to face each other in battle. He smirked, talking to the nearest uniform. 'Stupid militant twats. If they think they're going to get anywhere near the pithead, they can think again.'

Although the road was wide, it was still a bottleneck. The only way back was the way the demonstrators had marched.

Collier gazed at the police line. 'So what now, Lloyd?'

Bevan seemed lost for words as he assessed the situation.

Collier glanced back at the demonstrators. 'We can't expect them to charge police with riot gear.' He looked up.

A police helicopter flew low overhead, circling.

The sound of distant horns caught Bevan's attention. He looked back at the crowd that parted. Making way for a fleet of buses that rolled slowly down the road. Bevan breathed a sigh of relief. 'About bloody time.'

One coach stopped and two men climbed down the coach steps.

Bevan smiled, offering his hand. 'Glad you could make it.'

'I'm the union chairman, from the Royal Ordinance factory, Ty-Affan, just outside Monmouth.' Other men climbed down from the coaches.

'Thanks for coming boys, we really appreciate it.'

More men disembarked from other coaches surrounding Bevan and Collier. They had turned up from all over. Merthyr Hoover factory, Port Talbot Steelworks, Llanwern steelworks, various pits from across South Wales. A bus full of miners from South Yorkshire. Buses from ICI, near Pontypool and Lucas Girling in Cwmbran had also arrived. Bevan spotted another coach pulling up.

Martin Cooper stepped down, grinning broadly as he approached. 'Alright boys.'

Collier looked on as men climbed down from the coach.

The men were wearing white and blue scarfs.

Collier grabbed Cooper's arm and dragged him away from the crowd. 'Martin, what the fuck are you playing at?'

'What d'you mean?'

'I mean those lot there.' Collier pointed at the mass of white and blue hats and scarfs. 'That's what I mean.'

'I bought some boys from Cardiff.'

'Martin, they're fucking Cardiff City supporters. What d'you think they're going to do to this place?'

'Lloyd said we need a bunch of hard boys to get into the pithead.' Cooper stated.

'You dull twat, Martin. The only thing they'll do is smash everything up.' Collier pointed at the line of police officers. 'That's exactly what they want. You bringing those fucking idiots is like putting petrol on a naked flame.'

'What's the problem?' Bevan suddenly appeared at their side.

'I'll tell you what the problem is, Lloyd. Martin turning up with a load of football hooligans.'

Bevan shrugged. 'So.'

'Jesus bloody Christ. You don't see it, do you? Our original plan was to get into the pit and climb the pithead winching gear. Occupy it for an hour then give ourselves up to the police. I was fully expecting to get arrested before the end of the day. But what you two are planning is ludicrous. The newspapers will have a field day in the morning when they photograph this lot going on a rampage.'

'At least it will show our desperation to keep these pits open.' Bevan said, looking at the line of police. 'Anyway, looks like those bastards at the pit have sent someone to talk us out of doing this.'

Collier turned and spotted his brother, Alwyn, emerging from the line of riot police.

'Looks like your younger brother wants a word.' Bevan stated.

Collier stared down the road towards his brother. He glanced at Bevan and Cooper. 'Do nothing. I'll go and talk to him.'

Both men slowly walked towards each other. Like two generals on a battlefield. The walk seemed to take forever. Finally, they both stopped several feet apart.

Alwyn looked past his brother at the mass of demonstrators. 'What are you doing, Bryn?'

Bryn glanced behind. 'What's it look like we're doing? We're fighting for our jobs.'

Alwyn nodded towards the Cardiff city fans. 'Do you honestly think bringing a bunch of football hooligans is going to change anything? All you're going to do is make yourselves look like a bunch of twats. If you unleash them on Six Bells village, they'll never forgive you for it.'

'Then tell me what choice we have, Alwyn? How do we make the rest of you scabs see through the bullshit that is the Thatcher government? MacGregor claims all he wanted to do was shut twenty pits in the north. But we all know it's part of a bigger plan. A plan to destroy the working class of this country. To wipe out every Welsh mining community.'

'I'm not blind to Thatcher's plans, Bryn. I know exactly what she plans to do.'

'So why aren't you fighting like the rest of us?'

'What is the point?'

'Fuck me Alwyn, and I thought you were the intelligent one in the family. The point of all this is to show the government that we will never let them close the pits.'

'And how do you plan to do that? It's not like the NUM has a seat in Parliament, is it? You lot have spent the last year on strike. Where's it got you? Nowhere, that's where. Thatcher will have her way. She'll use that attack dog MacGregor as the instrument for your downfall. You have spent the past year marching up and down the country. Getting arrested for what? A lost cause.'

'So what you're saying is that the communities in the South Wales Valleys are a lost cause.'

'Fuck off, Bryn, don't twist everything I say. These communities are the heart and soul of Wales. I know the government wants to destroy all that.'

'Then why the fuck are you lot at the Six Bells not standing by us? Why are you handing everything on a plate to Thatcher and MacGregor?'

'Because what chance to we have against Thatcher? She is unwavering, unrelenting, and determined to destroy everything. The pits, our communities, the working class. You think you've been fighting for the last twelve months? Everyone is about to start fighting for a future. I'm not working because I want to be a scab. I'm working to make sure our mam has a roof over her head. When the axe eventually falls on Six Bells, we'll need every penny to buy that house. The redundancy package management offered is more than enough to make sure our mam doesn't have to worry about rent. So she can live out the rest of her life in security. So she has something to leave me, you and Dafydd.'

'You talk about a future. What about the future of those boys back there?' Bryn pointed at the crowd of demonstrators. 'Some of those boys can't even read and write. The only life they have known is down the pit. When Thatcher is done with us, we'll be tossed onto the slagheap. Future generations will be left to rot on the dole.'

'It doesn't have to be like that, Bryn.' Alwyn pointed at the demonstrators. 'With the packages the coal board is offering, those boys can rebuild their lives.'

'Doing what?'

'They will find other jobs. Those who can't read or write can get educated.'

'Not everyone is clever like you, Alwyn. Not everyone wants to get educated. All I want is a job. A life where I can provide for a family.'

'You can have that life, Bryn. You're not stupid. I have heard you talking to the boys. They rally behind you. You're good with words. That's why I'm talking to you.' Alwyn recalled a memory. 'Our dad hated me reading books. I showed him a copy of the Rape of the Fair Country once. One of the old miners gave me a copy when I first started at the pit. I tried to explain what the book was about. Do you know what our dad did?'

Bryn shook his head.

'He snatched the book out of my hands and threw it on the coal fire. He said we were a family of miners, not intellectuals.' Alwyn looked about. 'Most of the boys working down the pit are fourth generation miners. And most of them don't even realise the English kick-started the industrial revolution. But at what cost? Yes, we've built a life in the Valleys, yes we've built communities. But these communities have their roots in slave labour. At the hands of English ironmasters and industrialists. And now, at this very moment, the Rape of the Fair Country is happening all over again. Only this time, it's not the landscape that's being stripped of its natural beauty. It's the South Wales communities that are being stripped of their dignity. And their will to fight.'

'Then why aren't you back there? Fighting for our way of life?' Bryn's tone was one of anger.

Alwyn inhaled. 'Because like the industrial revolution, there is no stopping Thatcher and her government.'

'Look at you,' Bryn mocked. 'You've already given up before the pit has even shut.'

'No, I haven't,' Alwyn insisted. 'When the end comes for Six Bells, d'you think I'm going to sit on my arse and wait for the dole cheques to roll in? No. I'm going to prove to that bitch sat in Number Ten that she'll never extinguish the fight in me. I'm going to use that money to go back to the education our dad denied us and do something with my life.'

Bryn glared back at his brother. 'Dad never denied us anything. We never went without. He worked his bollocks off all his life to provide for us.'

'Yes, he worked all his life. But at what cost? Retirement, black lung and death. All in that order. And that's most miners' story throughout the Valleys, isn't it? You leave school, you go down the pit. You work for forty years, retire and you're dead within five years. Did it ever occur to you, Bryn, that I never wanted any of that? When we were growing up, the stories I heard about the coal mines used to terrify me. Then when I first went down the pit, the old miners used to tell me ghost stories. It never entered dad's head that perhaps one of his sons didn't want to go down the mine. I used to hide books away I bought home from school. Because dad used to come home and talk about work. It was always, when you boys start at the pit, you'll be doing this that and the other. I didn't have the courage to tell him I didn't want to work down the pit.'

'You always were the bright one in the family.' Bryn admitted.

Alwyn took a deep breath. 'Scargill is going to order everyone back to work in two days, Bryn. Why d'you think they've let me speak to you?' Alwyn gestured towards the demonstrators. 'To convince you that what you're about to do is pointless. All this is a waste of time. You need to go back there and tell everyone to go home.'

'No.' Bryn said defiantly. 'You need to tell those ignorant fuckers at Six Bells we're about to march on the pit.'

Alwyn stared back at his older brother. 'I've said all I can say. Tried to make you see sense.' He looked up towards a wall that ran along a road above the Six Bells road.

Hundreds of uniformed police were looking down on the two men.

Bryn glared at his younger brother. 'You piece of shit. You've really proved whose side you're on, haven't you? You set us up.'

'No.' Alwyn said calmly, shaking his head. 'You set yourselves up when you decided to do this. The powers that be wanted to do this so they can make one last example of you. The police have had their own men who have infiltrated your ranks. They know everything.'

Bryn sensed his heart rate quicken at the sight of all the extra police that had suddenly appeared.

'Bryn, don't do this. Don't let this end in chaos.'

'It's you who's brought the chaos, not me.' Bryn spun on his heels and headed back up the road, back towards the demonstrators.

'Shit.' Alwyn cursed before walking back towards the police line.

CHAPTER 36

Present day
'Fagan, that's a weird coincidence. I was about to phone you.'
'I take it you've run those names?'
'I did, but I hit a brick wall, until this morning?'
'Why's that?'
'Your mate Warren is a hard man to research. I've run his name and only a small amount of information has showed up. The same can be said for the First Minister of yours, Lloyd Bevan. There's a reason background checks are hard to do.'

'Go on.'

'For starters, Bevan is a politician. Most politicians, when they're in office, have information redacted. You know, in case some nosey journalist wants to dig up dirt. This Bevan of yours is dodgy as fuck.'

Fagan recalled his meeting with the old man at the Six Bells memorial. 'Okay, dish the dirt Wayne.'

'For starters, he has a long arrest record. He was arrested at Orgreave in June 1984.'

'That doesn't surprise me. He was a striking miner.'

'Here's where it gets juicy. He was on the security services watch list as far back as 1979. Are you familiar with Operation Tân?'

Fagan vaguely recalled a mention of it during the Robert Turner murder investigation. 'Yeah, a police operation set up to track down Welsh radicals. They were setting fire to holiday homes owned by English residents. But it never amounted to anything. The investigation died a death. Several groups came out and claimed responsibility. A group called Meibion Glyndwr were the frontrunner for the attacks.'

'Lloyd Bevan was arrested twice in December 1980 as part of

Operation Tân. Following a spate of fires in the Monmouthshire area.'

'I looked into it a while back. Thirty-four properties were attacked throughout Monmouthshire, from April 1979 to December the same year. The police were stumped on this. That's why the investigative team was disbanded. The attacks were too random to form any connections.'

'Bevan was first arrested on the 6th December 1980. Following a demonstration in Cardiff led by that group you mentioned.'

Fagan smiled. 'Meibion Glyndwr.'

'Ha bloody ha, Fagan. We can't all speak the language of the Taff.'

Fagan chuckled. 'Sorry mate, carry on.'

'He was charged with disturbing the peace. On the 13th December 1980, he was arrested and questioned about an arson attack on a house just outside Monmouth. He was held for two days at Tudor Road police station in your hometown. I couldn't get any information about the actual police interview. However, I came across an interview with Bevan from a website called Welsh Independent Nationalists.'

'That's the party that Bevan leads.'

'I had to translate the interview because it was all in Welsh.'

'What did Bevan say about his arrest?'

Tanner read aloud. 'It all started with a loud banging on the door at three o'clock on Sunday morning in December in 1980. I went downstairs in my pyjamas, really annoyed that someone was knocking on the door that time of the morning. At first, I thought it was my sister. And that she'd walked out on her husband for the umpteenth time. When I opened the door, I was confronted by four police officers. One of them showed me a warrant. He said he was charging me with criminal damage in relation to holiday homes. At first, I thought they were joking. I didn't take it seriously. I asked them what they were on about. One of them replied I was being arrested because I was suspected of several arson attacks on holiday homes. I demanded to know what evidence they had to prove this. That's when the arresting officer got angry. He said, *shut your fucking mouth, get dressed, or we'll drag you down the station naked.'*

'The police didn't beat about the bush back then Tanner. Do you remember when we were bumped up to CID. Smokey incident rooms and old school coppers.'

'The good old days.' Tanner remarked.

'Does it say where he lived at the time of his arrest?'

'Abertillery.' Tanner replied. 'Bevan says he was bundled into the back of a police car and driven to Abergavenny police station. An unpleasant desk sergeant called Bob took my details before I was slung into a cell for twenty hours. They gave me a bit of food during my incarceration. All day long, they had the radio blaring through a tannoy speaker in my cell. They would check on me every half an hour. Every time I managed to nod off, they would bang on the door to wake me up. It was after eleven o'clock in the evening before I spoke to anyone.'

'Sleep deprivation.' Fagan remarked. 'A tactic used to get someone to confess to something they didn't do.'

'Looks that way, doesn't it?'

'What happened at the interview?'

'Bevan claims he was questioned in his cell by the leading officer. A Detective Chief Inspector Pat Molloy. Bevan claims when Molloy interrogated him in his cell, he refused to answer questions. He then claims that Molloy threw him onto his cell bed and screamed at him. He shouted, *You fucking Nashie arsonist cunt! Get this into your head. When you get out of here, you'll get the most unforgettable interrogation you ever got in your life.* Bevan still refused to answer questions until he had legal representation.'

Fagan's curiosity kicked in. 'Was he allowed a solicitor?'

'Yeah, the next morning his brief turned up.'

'By any chance, was he called Malcolm Barry?'

'Yeah, how did you know that, Fagan?'

'Let's just say me and Barry have crossed paths a few times.'

'Bevan claims the interview lasted for twelve hours. He praised Barry for sticking to his guns and believing in the cause. As late afternoon turned into evening, a young constable came into the interview room. He informed Molloy there'd been another arson attack while he was in custody.'

'Where?'

'A place called Talybont.' Tanner answered. 'Bevan goes onto say that Malcolm Barry had a go at Molloy for wrongful arrest. Following his arrest Bevan was taken back home. He said it was just me and a young detective constable who had sat in on the interview. The detective did nothing but apologise all the way home. When he dropped him off at his house, he offered to take him for an apology pint. Bevan accepted.'

'Wayne, do you have a list of names of coppers who were part of Operation Tân?'

'That's the strange thing, Fagan, until an hour ago I didn't. Then I got an e-mail which was sent anonymously. With a full list of names of the team on Operation Tân.'

'Go on.' Fagan's thoughts dwelled on the old man at the Six Bells memorial.

Tanner rattled off a list of names. 'First off, you have Detective Chief Inspector Pat Molloy. Then there was Detective Inspector Ioan Reece, Detective Inspector Ivor Robinson and finally newly appointed Detective Constable Clive Warren.'

'Who is currently Detective Chief Superintendent Clive Warren.' The penny dropped. 'Jesus, it all makes sense now.'

'What does Fagan?' Tanner asked.

'The other day, when I was interviewing Bevan. Warren basically shut me down at every turn. I doubt his head could have been shoved up Bevan's arse any further. My guess is they went for that drink and formed a friendship. Listen, Wayne, do me a favour. E-mail me everything you have. I am about to talk to someone about Bevan.'

'Will do, Fagan.'

'Keep me up to date on the Foetus Snatcher. And when you see Jack Daw, tell him I said hello.'

'Will do Fagan, take care mate.' Tanner ended the call.

CHAPTER 37

Six Bells – 1st March 1985

Bevan surveyed the mass of police that seemed to appear out of nowhere. Many of them were in riot gear.

Cooper glared at the police line down the road. He gripped the baseball bat he had brought with him.

Bryn Collier walked towards them.

'We're pinned in.' Bevan pointed out. Panic was clear in his tone. 'They've got us surrounded. Where the fuck have all these police come from?'

'We've been fucking set up,' Collier revealed. 'They knew what we were planning.'

'Some fucker has grassed us up.' Cooper seethed.

One of the men who had come from the Royal Ordinance factory approached. He pointed at the police that had just arrived. 'With all due respect, boys, we didn't sign up for this. None of us from the Royal Ordinance factory can afford to get arrested. We'll lose our jobs. We thought it would just be a march, that's it.'

'Don't be such a gutless twat.' Cooper barked.

'Hey, I'm not gutless.' The man stated, glaring back at Cooper. 'I'm not stupid either. There's enough police here to throw the lot of us in the cells.'

Collier surveyed the crowd of demonstrators. He could clearly see the expressions of panic and fear on their faces.

'Sorry boys, but I'm about to tell my men to get back on the bus and go home.'

Collier spotted the megaphone in Bevan's hand. He snatched it away. 'Listen to me all of you!' His voiced boomed through the speaker of the megaphone.

The demonstrators looked in Bryn's direction.

'My fellow miners, workers from other factories and all others who have turned up today. We stand not just in protest. But in unity and defiance against a government that seeks to tear apart the very fabric of our lives. The planned closure of our coal mines and the annihilation of our jobs. By the iron-handed policies of Maggie Thatcher and her government.'

The demonstrators jeered.

'Their decision isn't about pits and profits. It's a merciless blow aimed at the heart of the South Wales Valleys. The soul of our communities, and the futures of our children. The Thatcher government views the mineworkers as figures on a ledger. Not men who merely wish to put food on the table for their families. And let's not forget past generations who've bled and died at the coalfaces across the South Wales Valleys.'

The noise from the crowd increased.

'These pit closures aren't just shutting down mines. They're sealing the fate of generations to come. Condemning our children to dole queues and shattered dreams. Thatcher and her government are paving the way for a future where prosperity will fade. This landscape will become dotted with ghost towns. Shadowy reminders of the thriving communities that once prospered. Thatcher's vision of a capitalist society is a blueprint for the destruction of our unity and the annihilation of our solidarity. It champions profit over people, leaving us disposable and discarded like yesterday's coal. But we are not expendable. We are not disposable!'

The crowd cheered.

'Our strength doesn't lie in the depth of the mines, but in the heart of our communities. In the unwavering resolve that courses through our veins. Together, we are an unbreakable force. A force that will not bow to the whims of a system that values wealth over well-being. We stand in solidarity today, to defend a way of life. Built on the principles of mutual support, solidarity, and collective power. We refuse to be crushed under the weight of Thatcher's capitalist machine. We refuse to let our spirit be extinguished by her greed.'

The demonstrators roared.

'The future we seek is one where every worker is valued. Where every family thrives. Where communities flourish with dignity and respect. It's a future where power doesn't reside in the hands of a select few. But in the hearts of hardworking individuals like us.' Collier glanced up at a Welsh flag, gently fluttering in the breeze. 'Today is St David's Day. Let us stand tall, as one people, one voice, one community. And if this is indeed the last stand of the South Wales miners, I promise you this.' He pointed at the Welsh flag. 'Like the dragon, the voice of the working class will roar through this valley, and the valley beyond! And in years to come, the miners of the South Wales collieries will look back with pride and boast. We fought for our jobs on St David's Day!' Collier punched the air defiantly.

The noise from the demonstrators became deafening.

'History will remember this day. A day when the miners of the South Wales coalfields stood up in one voice and declared, we will not go quietly into the night. We will not be intimidated by the attack dogs Thatcher has unleashed.' Bryn indicated to the mass of police officers that surrounded them. 'Our strength is unyielding. Our unity is unbreakable, and our dignity unrelenting. We stand here, not for ourselves. But for every miner who's ever swung a pickaxe. For every family that calls these Valleys home. Together, we shall persevere. Together, we shall overcome! For our mines! for our families! For our communities! And for the Wales we love!' Collier punched the air again.

The demonstrators cheered, clapped and yelled support.

'Solidarity forever! United, we stand, and together, we will triumph! The miners united, will never be defeated! The miners united, will never be defeated!' Collier began to march towards the police line.

The army of demonstrators followed. Chanting loudly. 'The miners united, will never be defeated!'

Benson glared at the oncoming mob. He glanced behind. 'Beat your truncheons against your shields, boys. Let's show these militant bastards who they're dealing with.'

The very air seemed to vibrate.

CHAPTER 38

Llanover
Present day

Nigel Thomas opened the door as Fagan marched up the path. 'Fagan, before you arrest me, at least let me explain.'

'I'm not going to arrest you, Nigel, but I am pissed off with you.' Fagan rumbled.

'I know. I should have said something when you came to see me the other morning, but I couldn't. Collier swore me to secrecy. Look, I couldn't have predicted he was going to be murdered.'

'He wasn't murdered.' Fagan sighed.

Thomas stared back. 'Wasn't murdered?'

Fagan glanced around. 'We need to talk.'

Thomas handed Fagan a cup of coffee. 'What do you mean, Collier wasn't murdered?'

'He had a heart attack while he was up the Keepers.'

'So what does this mean exactly?'

'It means we have to drop the murder investigation and hand over everything to Cardiff.'

Thomas noted Fagan's expression. 'Something tells me you don't want to do that.'

'Because of what I've discovered over the past few days. At first, it was just a theory. I think Collier was given new information regarding his brother's murder that could have triggered a retrial. An hour ago, I had that confirmed.'

Thomas nodded. 'I know.' He confessed.

Fagan glanced at his watch. 'Nigel, I don't have much time. You need to tell me everything.'

'Alwyn Collier first approached me three years ago. Because of the pandemic, we communicated via Zoom. He had read my book, Rape of the Working Class. He told me he was researching a book himself, but he wanted a co-writer. He praised my book and asked me if I was interested in his project. When he told me about it, I jumped at the chance.'

'Was it a tell all biography?'

'It was more than that, Fagan. It was an expose of Lloyd Bevan and his past. Everything from his roots in Meibion Glyndwr, to having family connections to the IRA. But most of all, Alwyn wanted to expose Bevan. And his involvement in the murders of Dafydd Collier and Sean Price. In 2020, during the height of the pandemic, one of the Blaina Four contacted Alwyn. He said he wanted to get something off his chest.'

'This someone was Amlod Llewellyn.' Fagan guessed.

'Yeah. Llewellyn was dying of cancer. When he contacted Alwyn, he said he wanted to make a full confession about what happened that day, on the bridge.' Thomas picked up a tablet. 'Alwyn was so desperate to get answers. He broke the lockdown rules to meet up with Llewellyn, who was in his last weeks of life.'

'What did Llewellyn say?'

Thomas handed Fagan the tablet. 'See for yourself.'

Fagan tapped the play icon.

Amlod Llewellyn lay on his bed, surrounded by medical equipment.

The voice of Alwyn Collier could be heard. 'First of all, Amlod, thanks for doing this. It's been nearly thirty-five years since our Dafydd was murdered. This has been a long time coming.'

Llewellyn removed his oxygen mask. 'I know.' He rasped. 'I've been wanting to talk about this for nearly four decades.'

'Can I ask why you didn't come forward before now?'

'I was afraid. We all were. Bevan was afraid the most. He's tried so hard to bury his past. Now that he's First Minister, he will do everything he can to push for a referendum.'

'What happened that day, you know, the day my brother was murdered?'

'It was chaos. The police were everywhere. They had rounded up the miners who had picketed the Six Bells Colliery. The town had been turned into a battleground. There were windows smashed everywhere. Someone had even thrown a petrol bomb at a group of police officers. We all gathered in a pub called the Miner's Lamp to regroup. Bevan was there, like some kind of army general. Wanting us all to have another go at the police. A lot of the boys had already had a hammering. They knew it was only a matter of time before the police raided the pub. One of the boys said that it was over and that they were all going back to work.'

'What did Bevan think of this?'

'He called them a load of scab traitors and let them go.'

'And after that?'

'There were just four of us left in the pub. Bevan suggested we should go to the bridge over the new road and hang the NUM banner. We avoided the police, who were mopping up pockets of demonstrators around Six Bells.'

'What happened when you got to the bridge?'

'Bevan became angry. He started shouting and screaming about how everyone had betrayed the cause. He was fuming about the police, and how they had stopped him from storming the Six Bells Colliery.'

'What happened next?'

'I suggested we should all go back home. Bevan became more pissed off. He looked around for stuff he could throw off the bridge. There were coaches heading into the colliery for the afternoon shift. Then he spotted the scaffolding pole, just lying there.'

'What did he do?'

'He tried to hand me the pole, ordering me to throw it off the bridge when a bus was approaching. I refused. He called me a gutless cunt.' Llewellyn clasped the mask to his mouth, sucking in oxygen.

'Take your time, Amlod.' Collier said.

'Bevan didn't have the guts to throw the pole himself. That's when he gave it to Martin Cooper.'

'Are you saying it was Martin Cooper who threw the pole?'

'Yes.' Llewellyn gasped. 'I begged Martin not to do it. Bevan was furious. He threatened to throw me off the bridge. Both your brother and Bevan were egging on Martin to throw the pole.

That's when Bevan spotted the police escort in the distance. He ordered Martin to wait until the car they were escorting was in range, then throw the pole.' Llewellyn coughed. 'Martin did exactly as he was told. He waited until that taxi was in range before throwing the pole. I didn't see it hit the car. But I remember the sound of the car turning over. The sound of crunching metal.'

'And then what happened?'

'I saw the look of panic on Bevan's face. The realisation of what had just happened. Martin Cooper was jumping up and down with excitement, shouting, we got the scab bastards.'

Fagan tapped the stop icon on the screen.

'That interview goes on for another hour and a half,' Thomas said. 'Llewellyn goes into detail about the arrests and the interviews and the trial leading up to their arrest.'

'Why didn't Llewellyn accept the compensation handed out to Bevan, Cooper, and Collier's brother?'

'Because he knew the truth about that day. He couldn't believe it when they were cleared of murder. Following their acquittal there was a massive celebration. But Llewellyn wanted no part of it.'

'Because he knew they were all guilty.'

Thomas nodded, pointing at the tablet. 'There are another five interviews with Llewellyn.'

'Five.'

'All recounting Bevan's career as a fundamentalist. Llewellyn and Bevan had been friends since they were children. When they worked together at the Six Bells, Llewellyn described Bevan as fanatical. He always used to say how much he hated the English. I subscribe to one of those family tree websites. I did research on Bevan's ancestors. His ancestor was a man called Lewis Bevan. In 1831, he led a small army of workers in a revolt against the English ironmasters in Merthyr. It's known as the Merthyr rising. Llewellyn claims it was Bevan who set up Meibion Glyndwr in the late seventies. Llewellyn was part of the movement. He even admits to setting some homes on fire during their campaign. But it wasn't enough for Bevan. He wanted to set fire to the homes while they were being occupied.'

'He wanted to kill people?'

'That's what Llewellyn reckons. Bevan was so fanatical he and Llewellyn travelled to Ireland once to meet with his Irish relatives. They were sat in a pub just outside Belfast. Bevan's cousin gave him advice on how they can launch a guerilla style warfare on English people who owned houses in Wales. When Bevan was first arrested and accused of launching arson attacks on several properties, he said the police couldn't prove anything. Llewellyn attacked a home in Talybont because he found out about Bevan's arrest. He knew if another home was set on fire while Bevan was in custody, then the police would have had to let him go. When they released Bevan, he formed a friendship with one of the coppers who were on the team who interviewed him.'

'He turned one of them.'

Thomas nodded.

'I want a name, Nigel.'

'At the time, he was Detective Constable Clive Warren.'

'And Amlod mentions him by name on one of these videos?'

'Yes.'

'Bloody hell.' Fagan stated. 'No wonder Warren has been a pain in my arse. What else is there in these videos?'

'Llewellyn speaks about the money Bevan got from the NUM. Which they got from Gaddafi, and the Russian Mining Federation.'

'What about the man I met earlier? What's his role in all this?'

'He was part of the undercover operation to infiltrate the miners' unions across the South Wales Valleys. When Alwyn contacted the national records office in Kew four years back, he wasn't expecting to be contacted by the intelligence services. Then, out of the blue, this bloke contacts Alwyn and gives him information about Bevan. When you came to me the other morning, I contacted him. I told him he could trust you.'

Fagan stared at the tablet. 'This is enough to force a retrial. But Bevan will just dismiss everything Llewellyn has said. He could claim that Llewellyn could have said anything because he was at the end of his life.'

Thomas picked up a file and handed it to Fagan. 'This is everything Alwyn had collected over the past few years. This is a copy. The original files are in a safe place.' Thomas handed Fagan a USB stick. 'This stick contains all the interviews with Amlod Llewellyn.'

Fagan took the file and the stick.

'What happens now?'

'You tell me.' Fagan shrugged.

'Alwyn Collier wanted to set the record straight.'

'What about?'

'The miners' strike. He didn't defy the picket lines because he thought the miners were in the wrong. He was fed up with the bull in a china shop tactics of Bevan and Scargill. Who ordered everyone to down tools and walk out. Most of the men who followed him weren't told the complete story of why they were striking. They just followed orders. Beyond the strike there were the wider ambitions of Thatcher. She wanted to usher in a new era for Britain. Alwyn hated everything she did to the mining communities. That's why he ran for the Tory party. He was trying to change its image in the Valleys.'

'Didn't have much luck did he, from what I've seen.' Fagan fished his buzzing phone out of his pocket. 'Sean, I was just on my way back to Newport.'

'Boss, we've got a situation up at the Varteg.'

'What's happened?'

'Andrew arrived at Martin Cooper's cottage to arrest him. Cooper has taken him hostage. He's fired on the uniforms who were with Andrew.'

'Shit.' Fagan growled.

'An ARV is on route.' Watkins paused. 'And so is Griffiths.'

'Text me Cooper's address. I'm on my way.'

CHAPTER 39

Varteg Fawr

Fagan screeched to a halt. In the distance, an array of police vehicles blocked the dirt track leading to the remote cottage. Surrounded by scrubland and a scattering of weathered buildings.

Four armed officers were carrying out a weapons check. Over a dozen uniforms were making sure no members of the public could get near the area.

Watkins spotted Fagan trudging towards him.

'What happened?' Fagan asked.

'Andrew knocked on the door of Cooper's cottage. It was obvious he knew they were coming. So he snuck around the back of his cottage and surprised them. He held the gun to Brooks' head and told the other two uniforms to back away. Cooper fired a round at the patrol car, shattering the window. The two uniforms took cover before calling it in. He's got Andrew hostage in the kitchen. And that's all we know. He's been shouting out of the window. Demanding to speak with the pig who interviewed him the other day, the head pig.' Watkins pointed to a Land Rover Discovery. 'I took a peek in the back before the ARV got here. There's a large jerry can and a lump hammer on the back seat.'

Griffiths and Warren were talking to the lead armed officer.

Warren spotted Fagan approaching. 'This is your doing, Fagan.' He seethed, pointing an accusing finger.

Fagan pointed at himself. 'My doing, and how exactly did you reach that conclusion, sir?'

'If you hadn't had questioned Cooper a few days ago, he wouldn't have snapped like this.'

'Dash cam footage from last night shows Cooper driving his car erratically towards the Keepers.' Fagan nodded towards

Watkins. 'DS Watkins said Cooper has a jerry can and a lump hammer in the back of his car. It's obvious he set fire to my Jeep last night. We were in our rights to arrest him on suspicion of arson. Plus, he was arrested a while back after turning up at Alwyn Collier's house, threatening to kill him. At the time Collier's death was still being treated as murder. So yes, we had cause for the arrest.'

'You obviously put yourself into a corner, haven't you, Fagan? Dredging up the past.'

'What I have been doing, sir, is my bloody job.' Fagan pointed at the cottage. 'Cooper wants to speak with me.'

Warren shook his head. 'Armed police will storm the cottage and shoot that stupid twat.'

'Andrew Brooks is in there. The likelihood of Cooper shooting him before an armed response team can deal with him is very high. You do not know what you are facing in there.'

Griffiths stood close by, listening to the unfolding argument.

'I will not let you risk one of my officers when there are other options on the table.' Fagan looked at Griffiths. 'We have an opportunity to talk Cooper down. I am trained in negotiation techniques. I did two years with the northern anti-terrorism unit in Liverpool. Plus, I'm firearms trained.'

'There's a maniac in there who needs to be dealt with. And all you want to do is go in and whisper sweet nothings into his ear. Hoping he will comply.'

'I think Fagan should talk to him.' Griffiths suggested.

Warren glared at him. 'You can't be serious. The only thing that will happen is Cooper will have two hostages to bargain with.' He shook his head. 'No, it isn't happening. These men will go in and deal with the threat.'

'And what about my officer?' Fagan demanded to know. 'Martin Cooper is obviously unstable.'

'Which is a perfectly good reason to deal with this threat.'

'No,' Griffiths said in a firm tone. 'Fagan will go in and talk him down.'

Griffiths' words seemed to enrage Warren. He stared at Fagan for several seconds before deciding. 'Very well. If you want to talk to that psycho in there, then be my guest. I will let your loved ones know. About the stupid and reckless act you did before he blew your fucking head off.'

'Chief Superintendent Warren. I am the senior officer here. If there is a way to end this in a peaceful manner, then we have to consider it.'

Fagan took a few minutes to get dressed in a flak jacket. He made sure his bodycam was out of sight, but in a position to record events.

'You sure you want to do this, boss?' Watkins asked.

Fagan made sure Warren and Griffiths were out of earshot. 'I have an opportunity here, Sean. To get Martin Cooper to confess to a double murder forty years ago. Plus implicate Lloyd Bevan and Bryn Collier.' He glanced at Warren. 'And I know for a fact that twat is bent.'

Watkins nodded silently.

'Are you ready, DI Fagan?' Griffiths called out.

Fagan returned with a stiff nod. 'As ready as I'll ever be, sir.'

CHAPTER 40

The Miner's Lamp- Six Bells 1985
Collier and Bevan entered the bar. Collier held a bloodied rag to his head after being struck with a truncheon.

The room was packed with men who had clashed with the police. The scene looked more like a field hospital than the bar in the local pub. Wives and girlfriends tended those who were battered and bruised. Mopping their bloodied wounds with whatever material was at hand.

One of the men spotted Collier and Bevan and walked over. His arm suspended by a temporary sling. 'Jesus Christ, Bryn, we've just got our bloody arses kicked. Have you seen the amount of police they've sent? We haven't been able to get anywhere near the pithead, let alone hang a banner from it. It's Orgreave all over again.'

The landlord placed two pints of beer on the bar.

Collier took a large swig from his glass.

'Bryn, what are we going to do?' Edwin Lewis' voice cracked with despair.

'We're going to regroup and try again.' Collier stated calmly, taking another swig.

'Bryn, no offence mate, but there's not enough of us to march on Six Bells. Have you seen how many police are out there? Hundreds of the boys have been arrested. It's just like what happened to us when we went to Orgreave last summer. You were there Lloyd. You saw what those bastards did. The others have run. And then there's us lot in here. The walking wounded. You can't expect us to go back out there and try to march on the pit.' The man pointed at his arm. 'They broke my bloody arm. I'm too afraid to go to a hospital just in case I get arrested.'

'What d'you want from us, sympathy?' Bevan snapped.

'You're not the only one who's had a beating today.'

'What we want is for you to tell us what to do.' Lewis looked at Collier. 'Guidance, is that too much to ask?'

Collier finished his pint. Before he could speak, Martin Cooper staggered through the door.

Cooper's bat was snapped in half. 'Bastards!' He seethed. 'Every one of them bastards!'

'Where's your Cardiff mates?' Collier asked.

'Where d'you think? The bastard police have slung them in the clink.'

'But you managed to get away,' Lewis pointed out.

'What's that supposed to mean?'

'I saw you, Martin, on Richmond Road. Running into your Aunty Beryl's house. While the police were throwing all your Cardiff mates into the back of vans. Look at you. Unlike the rest of us, you're still in one piece. Not a scratch on you.'

'Fuck off.' Cooper spat, holding up the remains of his bat. 'I'll drag you outside and beat the shit out of you with this.'

Lewis grinned before bursting into laughter. 'Martin, you couldn't even swing a whole bat at me, let alone half of one. I could have two broken arms and still beat you in a fight. How did you break your bat? Did you have a hissy fit and smash it against the back wall of your Aunty Beryl's house?'

Laughter rippled the room.

Lewis refocussed his attention on Collier and Bevan. 'So what's the plan then, boys?'

Bevan swigged from his glass, glancing at Collier. 'it's like Bryn said. We regroup and try to take the pithead.'

'Lloyd, no one wants to do that anymore.'

'What d'you mean?'

'What I mean, Lloyd, is no one wants to strike anymore. We've all had a guts full. It's been a year and still Thatcher hasn't budged. And Scargill sounds like a stuck record. Repeatedly telling us to stand firm. There aren't enough of us anymore.'

'Planning to go back to work, are you?'

'Every fucker is,' Lewis stated. 'Don't you get it? It's over! The NUM is ordering a back to work next week. It's all over the news.'

'So we'll stay out.' Bevan said.

'The NUM won't support you.'

'Fuck the NUM. If they order a back to work next week, it just goes to show they're a bunch of gutless twats.'

'I can't believe I'm hearing this from our union reps. It's our role as union members to support the decision of the union. If they tell us we have to go back to work next week, then that's exactly what we'll do.'

'And betray the cause.' Bevan said.

'Jesus Lloyd. You're obviously on a different page to the rest of us. What cause?'

'The plan to save our communities!' Bevan exploded. 'To stop our way of life from being decimated by that English bitch Thatcher. She'll destroy us all. If you go back to work, then you're just handing her the coalfields on a plate. English bastards arrived four generations ago. Not wanting to go down the mines themselves. So they sent boys. Generations of Valleys men have toiled in the mines, bled in the mines and died in the mines. And now our communities are about to die. And you're talking about going back to work, you traitorous scab.'

'Oi, I'm no fucking scab. But if the unions say we have to go back to work, then even they can see it's pointless carrying on.' Lewis pointed at Bevan. 'If you take action without the backing of the union, then you're no longer a union member. What are you playing at, eh, Lloyd? The lot of us in here have had a hammering off the police. And you want to go back out there and get another hammering. No, thank you. These boys might be too afraid to say it, but I'm not. When the call comes, I'm going back to work. I'm up to my neck in debt. Having to turn up at a soup kitchen every bloody day, begging for food. It's not right. I want to stand on my own two feet. And I'll tell you something else. When the redundancy offer is announced, I'll be taking it.'

'Scab twat.' Cooper growled.

Lewis pointed at Cooper. 'In the end, all you will be left with is dicks like this to support you. We're tired, Lloyd. If you can't see that, then it's you who's lost sight of the cause. Everyone wants to just go back to work. Rebuild our lives while we still can. Before the pit shuts.'

'Go on then, fuck off.' Bevan snapped. He glanced around the room. 'Is there anyone else here who wants to give up on the cause?'

A man with a bloodied face stood. He looked at Lewis. 'I've had enough. We all have.'

One by one, the men stood up and made their way towards the pub entrance.

'Bastard scabs!' Cooper bellowed as the last men left.

Bevan finished his pint.

'What do we do, Lloyd?' Collier asked.

Bevan took his time answering. He stared into his empty glass for several seconds. 'We'll head for the bridge over the new road. We'll hang our banner from there.' Bevan spotted Amlod Llewellyn, who had stayed with them. 'Amlod, you coming?'

Llewellyn nodded. 'Yeah, I'll come.'

CHAPTER 41

Varteg Fawr
Present day

Fagan stared at the cottage in the distance as he walked up the dirt track. A stiff breeze swept across the Varteg landscape.

Cooper was staring out of the window, pointing his shotgun at Fagan as he approached his property. 'The front door is open. Close it behind you, put the wooden bar across and come into the kitchen!'

Fagan approached the front door, grabbing the handle.

'Close the door and put the bar across.' Cooper ordered as Fagan stepped through the kitchen door.

Fagan noted the thick wooden piece of wood he had just put in place. Together with the wooden bar on the front door, it would take too long for the police to force their way into the cottage and the kitchen.

Brooks was sat at the kitchen table. Cooper had made him handcuff himself.

'You okay, Andrew?'

Brooks glanced at Cooper before nodding. 'Yes, sir.'

Fagan could see the terror etched into Brook's expression. He focussed his attention on Cooper. 'Martin, there are armed officers outside who will come in here and kill you. You need to put the gun down and end this peacefully.' Fagan's tone was calm and even, despite the fact his heart was pumping away fiercely.

Cooper shook his head. 'Good luck to them. You'll both be dead before they get anywhere near me.' He looked at the back door of the cottage. Another reinforced wooden bar was across the door. Wooden shutters covered the window, which faced the mountain behind.

'Martin, please put the gun on the kitchen table and step

away. This doesn't have to escalate.'

'I'm not going back inside.' Cooper's tone was defiant, laced with anger and fear.

'Who says you're going to prison, mate?'

'You lot, that's who. That's why you arrested me the other day. You want me to go down again because of what happened.' He aimed his shotgun at Brooks' head.

'Martin, point the gun at me, mate. It's me you wanted to talk to, right? You know, the head pig.'

Cooper sounded as if he was hyperventilating. 'I'm not going back to prison. I'm not spending the rest of my life in clink.'

'No one is talking about you going back to prison, Martin. It's just you. Now, please point the gun at me. Who says you have to go to prison?'

Cooper looked towards the window. 'That fat bastard out there.'

Fagan looked in the same direction. Warren stood a few hundred yards away in plain view. 'Chief Superintendent Warren?'

Cooper nodded. 'He said, I'll go back to prison, if I open my gob.'

'Do you know what he means by that?'

'He knows.'

'Martin, look at me. What does he know?'

'Bevan told him everything.'

Fagan maintained his breathing. 'What did Bevan tell him, Martin?'

'It wasn't my fault.' Tears trickled down Cooper's cheeks. 'I was just doing what I was told.' He started to cry. 'I didn't mean for anyone to get hurt. It wasn't my fault. It was just a stupid accident.'

'Okay, Martin. I want you to focus. I want you to calm down. Are you talking about what happened forty years ago, at Six Bells?'

Cooper nodded. 'Yeah.'

'Martin, in your own words, I want you to take your time. All I want to do is talk.'

Cooper glanced out of the window.

'Martin, I'm here for you, mate. Don't worry about them out there. Just tell me what happened forty years ago.'

'The police were everywhere.' Cooper began. 'We'd been set up. Lloyd thought there'd only be a few hundred coppers. All we wanted to do was occupy the pithead winding gear at Six Bells. You know, let that bitch Thatcher know she'll never beat us. The miners, united, will never be defeated.'

'Martin, what happened that day? The day of the Six Bells demonstration.'

'We had a plan. Take the Six Bells Colliery and occupy it. It was a show of strength, that's all.'

'But it didn't go according to plan, did it?'

'No.' Cooper whimpered. He wiped tears away with his sleeve. 'The bastard police were ready for us. They were beating on their shields, chanting at us.'

'They wanted you to fight them. Is that what you're saying?'

'Yeah.' Cooper nodded. 'Bryn Collier had just spoken to his brother.' Cooper inhaled. 'Fucking scab, Alwyn Collier. He betrayed the cause.'

'Martin, you're doing fantastic. What happened?'

'We got the shit kicked out of us, that's what happened!' Cooper suddenly exploded, causing Fagan to jolt. 'The bastard police, with their truncheons, beat the shit out of everyone. It was the beginning of the end for the working class. That bitch Thatcher and her pet attack dog, Ian MacGregor, wanted to put an end to the miners and the South Wales coalfields.' Cooper stared at Fagan. 'They succeeded, didn't they?'

'But you still have the spirit, Martin. The fighting spirit of the working class. She didn't take that away from you or the other miners.'

'What fucking good is the will to fight if there's nothing left to fight for?' Cooper sobbed. 'She took everything from us. Entire communities wiped out. We lost our jobs, our dignity, our communities.' Cooper stared out of the window at the village below. 'The Varteg used to be vibrant and alive. A sense of true spirit and community. Now, it's just kids on crack. It's the same everywhere you go across the Valleys.'

'Martin, tell me what happened on the bridge.'

'It wasn't my fault. I was just following orders.' Cooper cried.

'So you were on the bridge?' Fagan coaxed.

'We hung the NUM banner off the railings.' Cooper sniffed hard and swallowed. 'I was proud to hang the NUM banner over the side of the bridge. I was proud to be a member of the NUM.'

'And then what?'

'Bevan totally lost it. He was shouting and screaming. Saying people had betrayed him and he was going to get revenge.' Cooper paused briefly. 'He picked up the scaffolding pole and handed it to Amlod Llewellyn. He told him to throw it at a bus that was about to pass under the bridge. It was carrying scabs on their way to Six Bells. But Amlod refused. He said it was. Bevan shouted at him, calling him a traitor to the cause. Then he handed me the pole.' Cooper became emotional. 'I didn't mean to do it. I was just following orders. I didn't think anyone was going to get hurt. I thought the pole would land in front of the car. I didn't even see it hitting the car.' Cooper sobbed.

'Did Lloyd Bevan order you to throw that pole off the bridge?' Cooper nodded. 'Yeah.'

'When was the last time you spoke to Bevan?'

'Last week. That's when he gave me the money to give to Alwyn Collier.'

'The fifty thousand pounds?'

'Yeah, he said I had to give it to Alwyn to stop him writing that book about us.'

'It was you who was with him at the Keepers the other night, wasn't it?'

'Yeah. Lloyd gave me Alwyn's phone number and told me I had to meet him and give him the money. He said I had to tell Alwyn he would get another fifty thousand if he kept his gob shut. If he didn't write that book about us.'

'Did you pick Alwyn up from Blaenavon and drive him to the Keepers?'

Cooper nodded. 'We talked for ages. I begged Alwyn for his forgiveness. I tried to tell him I didn't mean for that pole to hit the car.' Cooper took a deep breath. His tone darkened. 'Fucking scab bastard wouldn't accept my apology. He said I'd spend the rest of my life in prison.'

'Martin, what happened when you offered Alwyn Collier the money?'

'He went loopy. Grabbed the satchel and threw it in the Keepers. Told me I can shove the money up my arse. He said he was going to write that book and tell the entire world what happened.'

'You became angry?'

'I was fuming.' Cooper seethed. 'I turned around and threw a punch at him.' He started to hyperventilate again. 'I, I didn't mean to kill him. It was an accident.'

'Martin, you didn't kill him.'

Cooper stared back with an expression of surprise and relief.

'Alwyn Collier had a massive heart attack. It was just poor timing on your part.' Fagan took a step forward.

Cooper raised his shotgun, pointing it at Fagan. 'Don't,' he growled.

'Martin, listen to me. I can help you. But I need you to put the gun down on the kitchen table. Then I want you to sit down in the armchair.'

'I can't.'

'Why Martin?'

'Because I've confessed my sins to you.'

'No, Martin. What you've done is tell the truth. You've done the right thing. You've stood up to the lies Bevan has been telling for the last forty years.'

'But I'll still go down. There's no stopping that.'

'Martin, I can help you. I promise, if you testify against Bevan, it will go in your favour.'

'But I'll still go to prison.'

'I can't lie to you, Martin, you will. But the jury will be lenient with you. When they find out you finally stood up and told the truth. You said it yourself. You were just following orders, right? You were just doing what Bevan told you to do. You're loyal to the cause.'

Cooper took a few steps back, his gun trained on Fagan. He backed into a Welsh Dresser. Hard enough to dislodge a framed black-and-white photo that clattered onto the stone tile floor. The frame's glass exploded, scattering shards of glass everywhere.

Fagan's heart leaped somersaults.

Cooper turned the gun on himself, tucking the barrel under his chin.

Fagan put his hands together. A tear trickled down his cheek. 'Martin, don't do this. Don't let it end this way.'

'What choice,' Cooper panted. 'What choice do I have?'

'You have a choice, Martin.' Fagan pleaded. 'You can walk away with your head held high. Proud that you stood up and told the truth.'

'No.' Cooper gasped. 'It's over.' He glanced down at the black-and-white photograph at his feet. A young boy stared out from the picture. A cheeky smile, flanked by doting parents. Cooper sobbed. 'Mam, Dad, I'm so sorry. I let you down.' Cooper closed his eyes, his finger poised on the trigger of the shotgun. 'For the cause, for Meibion Glyndwr.'

'Martin, No!' Fagan yelled.

The sound of a single gunshot echoed across the Varteg landscape, reminiscent of distant artillery fire. A murder of crows fled their tree. Cawing, as they rose into the inky grey sky.

CHAPTER 42

Fagan wrapped a paramedic blanket around Brooks. 'How you doing, Andrew?'

Brooks sipped a hot coffee. His hands shook violently. He glanced down at his shirt. Speckles of blood were dotted all over it.

Watkins approached. 'Armed response is packing up and heading back to Cardiff, boss.'

Fagan inhaled, looking towards Warren who was talking on his phone. 'I guess we'd better head down there ourselves.'

'You planning to arrest Bevan?'

'You're damn right I am.' Fagan looked at Brooks. 'I want you to take the next month off, Andrew. I'll make sure you have the support you need.' Fagan nodded to three uniforms who stood close by. 'Follow me.'

'Well, Fagan, you handled that beautifully. A man blows his head off while you're trying to talk him down. Some negotiator you are,' Warren mocked. 'I can't wait to watch your hearing when you get kicked off the force for gross negligence and misconduct.'

'With all due respect, sir, fuck off.' Fagan rumbled as he marched towards Warren.

Warren chuckled softly. 'I've had my eye on you for the past week, Fagan. You're a shit excuse for a copper.'

Fagan looked back at the cottage. 'It's all worked out for you, hasn't it? Or should I say, Lloyd Bevan?'

'What the fuck are you babbling on about, Fagan?'

'Don't act like you're stupid.' Fagan glanced at Warren's phone in his hand. 'Was that Bevan on the phone? Were you telling him Cooper had shot himself? I bet he leapt for joy, didn't he? I mean, Cooper was still the loose cannon you had to deal with.'

'Do you ever stop to hear yourself? Eh, Fagan?'

'Amlod Llewellyn,' Fagan stated. 'He was another loose cannon, wasn't he? I bet you were glad when he popped his clogs. He had secrets to reveal about you and Bevan.'

Warren stared back.

Fagan reached into his pocket, pulling out the USB stick Thomas had given him. 'Llewellyn confessed everything to Alwyn Collier before he died. Including your connection to all this. You were part of Operation Tân. You were the cuckoo in the nest. Feeding information back to Lloyd Bevan and his band of arsonists. You even went out with Llewellyn and set a few fires with him.'

Warren's face turned to ashen white.

'All the little secrets are on here, ready to be exposed. And Alwyn Collier was about to expose them in his book. That's why you had to take charge of the investigation. You knew about the book he was writing. You had to get your hands on information that could have implicated you. In what would be classed as a terrorist group by today's standards. When the coroner concluded Collier died of a heart attack, it must have come as a great relief to you. You didn't have to deflect the attention away from Bevan anymore. This is what it's been all about, hasn't it? Protecting Bevan's precious dream of an independent Wales. He's so close to achieving it, isn't he? And that's why he was so desperate to make everything go away.'

Warren was like a deaf mute.

'When Collier died, it sent the lot of you into a panic. At first, it looked like he'd been murdered. Which meant you had to tread carefully. Distance yourself from Cooper. Who was unpredictable. Bevan thought he was the loyal foot soldier he's always been. So he was stupid enough to give him the money. Hoping Cooper would talk Collier out of releasing his book. And then there's Bevan's assistant. Another loyal puppy dog who thought she had got away with stealing the satchel.' Fagan paused, stepping up to Warren. 'You told me the other day you despised insubordinate officers. Do you know what's worse than an insubordinate copper? A bent copper. But thankfully that's something I can deal with. Chief Detective Superintendent Clive Warren, I'm arresting you under the 2021 Counterterrorism and sentencing act. I'm also arresting you for perverting the course of justice. You do not have to say anything. But it may harm your defence when questioned something you later rely on in court. Anything you do say will be used in evidence against you.' Fagan glanced at the three uniforms. 'Take him down to Newport. Come on, Sean. Let's go and arrest that twat of a First Minister.'

Griffiths put his hand up. 'Fagan, where are you going?'

Fagan rolled his eyes. 'Where do you think I'm going? Bevan is guilty of murder. Not to mention the fact he's a bloody terrorist.'

'He's about to make the most important speech of his career. The least you can do is let the dust settle.'

'Let the dust settle.' Fagan exclaimed. 'Jesus bloody Christ. A man has just blown his brains out because of what Bevan is trying to achieve. He's lied for the past forty years about what happened on that bridge. He accepted compensation money that should have never been given to him. And that's just the tip of the iceberg. He's been scheming for years, investing money that was donated by the Russians in 1985. He took money that came from Libya. Money that should have been given out to the miners during the strike, but wasn't. It was not only morally corrupt money. It was blood money.'

'Blood money?'

'Jesus, I can't believe how ignorant you are,' Fagan stated. 'April 1984, WPC Yvonne Fletcher was gunned down outside the Libyan embassy while doing her duty. Several months following that, the chief executive of the National Union of Mineworkers is shaking hands with Colonel Gaddafi. All smiles after Gaddafi agreed to donate millions to the miners' strike fund. Millions that didn't see the light of day. Instead, it was divided between men like Bevan, who kept it to themselves. Paying off their mortgages and buying luxury cars. While a morally bankrupt government looked on and did nothing. Because they were also doing dodgy deals with Gaddafi. And then there's us. The police, who beat the shit out of the miners who just wanted to keep their jobs.' Fagan pointed out over the Varteg and Garndiffaith.

A group of locals were standing outside the police cordon.

'Look out there, will you, sir. Is it little wonder why people across the Valleys still see the police as bastards? Forty years on from the strike and they still view us as a bunch of bastards. Can you honestly blame them? I don't. Because we're still complete bastards. Especially what we did at places like Orgreave and Six Bells.' Fagan looked at Warren, who was climbing into the back of a police car. 'Bent coppers like Warren who hide in plain sight for decades. Coppers who join the force and abuse the powers given to them. Kidnapping young women off the street and murdering them. And those of us who are just trying to do our jobs properly are getting tarred with the same brush. I'm sick of it!' Fagan looked Griffiths up and down. 'Then there are senior officers like you. Your only concerns are reputations, pension pots and promotions.'

'Don't lump me in with the likes of Warren and Cousins, Fagan,' Griffiths protested. 'I'm nothing like them.'

'Then why are you asking me to let the dust settle? While Bevan gives his little speech. I'm sorry, sir. But you can bloody well kiss my arse on that.' Fagan glanced at Watkins. 'Let's go, Sean.'

Griffiths watched as Fagan marched towards his car. 'Fagan!'

Fagan stopped and looked over his shoulder.

'You do this, and you change the course of history.'

'This isn't about history, sir. This is about justice for two men who didn't deserve to die nearly forty years ago. Justice for a man who just killed himself for a warped ideology. And justice for all those miners who were fighting to keep their jobs.'

CHAPTER 43

The Senedd – Cardiff Bay
Lloyd Bevan swept a gaze around the circular Senedd chamber. All Assembly Members were present. Waiting for him to begin a speech he had been dreaming of for decades. At that moment, it seemed as if the eyes of the world were focussed on him. He looked down at the speech he had prepared.

'My esteemed colleagues, fellow politicians, people of Wales. Today is St David's Day. A day of national celebration when the people of Wales come together and embrace their culture. It is also a day that I want to speak to you about a way forward for the people of this nation. For the past few years, I have been working hard campaigning for a referendum. In which the people of Wales are given the opportunity to choose their future.'

'Today, I stand before you not just as a politician but as a voice for the dreams and aspirations that have been etched into the very hills and valleys of this land we call home. Wales, a nation of poets, warriors, and dreamers. A tapestry woven with the threads of our history.'

The Senedd members all applauded.

The convoy of police cars peeled away from the M4 motorway, speeding towards Cardiff bay. Fagan sat in the passenger seat.

Watkins was staring at the road ahead, with his foot hard on the accelerator.

Fagan had copied the video from the USB stick onto his laptop and was watching one of the videos Amlod Llewellyn had made shortly before his death. He removed an ear piece. 'I can't believe it. It's all here, Sean. Llewellyn saying he was on the bridge the day Dafydd Collier and Sean Price were killed. Bevan ordering

Cooper to throw the pole off the bridge. The aftermath of the trial. How Bevan and Bryn Collier celebrated after being acquitted of murder in 1985. Llewellyn said that he'd distanced himself from Bevan in 1995. He claims that the death of Collier and Price started to eat at him.'

'His guilt didn't stop him from coming forward, did it, boss?'

'I guess, like Cooper, he didn't want to spend twenty years in prison. Because the police fucked up by beating the shit out of Cooper, they got away with it. Bevan must have thought he was invincible following the trial. He kept all the money meant for the miners' strike fund.' Fagan looked out of the window, watching the landscape streak by.

'You okay, boss?'

Fagan thought back to the events at the cottage. 'Cooper didn't deserve to end his life that way. He may have been guilty. But he's as much as a victim as Dafydd Collier and Sean Price.'

'How d'you mean?'

'Bevan used him. He didn't care about Cooper. To Bevan, he was just another person to manipulate. Cooper thought he was doing the right thing, following Bevan. Doing what he was told.'

Bevan continued with his speech. 'Members of this Senedd. As we consider the prospect of Welsh independence, it is crucial to reflect on the historical struggles that have shaped this nation of ours. The trials endured by our forebears during the era of the English ironmasters and the Industrial Revolution. The clang of machinery and the billowing smoke of industry once dominated the Welsh landscape. In this crucible of industrialisation, the Welsh workforce toiled under harsh conditions. Welsh labour fuelling the engines of progress. While often exacting a heavy toll on their well-being. As I stand before you today, and put forward the case for Welsh independence. I stand as a proud descendant of those who not only shaped this world. But also built this world.'

More rapturous applause.

'The industrial revolution, a force of transformative power, brought undeniable economic growth. But also unleashed social and economic injustices. And many of these economic injustices endure to this very day. The ironmasters' dominion saw the exploitation of workers, the suppression of wages, and the degradation of living conditions. Our ancestors, the backbone of the industrial engine, faced not only the physical hardships of gruelling labour but also the indignity of systemic inequalities. In the face of such adversity, the Welsh people rose in various revolts, their voices echoing through the Valleys. The Merthyr Rising of 1831, a poignant chapter in our history, saw ironworkers and coal miners unite in a collective cry for justice. Their demands were clear. Fair wages, reasonable working hours, and an end to the oppressive conditions that shackled them.'

Some of the Senedd members stood up and applauded Bevan's words.

Fagan stared at his phone, watching Bevan addressing the Senedd. 'Arrogant twat. What's the betting Warren was on the phone to him the moment he heard the gunshot that killed Cooper?'

'Bit of a shocker, Warren being bent and all.'

'Not to me it wasn't, Sean. I've encountered many like Warren before. I'll say this for Bevan. He's delivering a killer speech to the Senedd.'

Bevan composed himself. 'The twentieth century marched hand in hand with technical advancements in the industrial world. But a shadow also loomed on the horizon. This shadow took the form of the Conservative government. Under the rule of the Iron Lady, Margaret Thatcher. The legacy of those decisions, made over four decades ago, still echoes through our towns and valleys. Leaving scars that bear witness to the struggles endured by the hardworking people of Wales.'

More applause.

'The industrial heart of South Wales, once vibrant with the hum of collieries and the clang of steelworks, suffered a devastating blow during the 1980s. The coal industry, which had long been the lifeblood of our communities. Became a target of ruthless economic policies that sought to dismantle it. The closures of mines, the loss of thousands of jobs, and the subsequent erosion of the social fabric inflicted wounds that, even now, have not fully healed.'

'It's going to cause a bit of commotion when you just burst in and arrest him, boss.' Watkins commented.

Fagan maintained his stare on his phone. Watching Bevan deliver his speech. He grinned. 'I know. I can't wait to see his face.'

Bevan glanced at his speech. 'Communities that had thrived on the collective spirit of hard work and solidarity grappled with unemployment, poverty, and a sense of abandonment. Families that had for generations relied on the mines as a source of livelihood were left without a clear path forward. The social cohesion that had been a hallmark of South Wales unravelled as the very foundations of these communities were shaken. The aftermath of Thatcher's policies are still felt today. With high levels of unemployment persisting in some areas. And a generational impact on the social and economic landscape. The scars of deindustrialisation run deep. Leaving a legacy of economic hardship and social dislocation that demands our attention and commitment to healing. Once again, history is being repeated. With the loss of nearly three thousand jobs in Port Talbot steelworks. The last corner of Welsh community spirit is about to be extinguished under another Tory government. An independent Wales would mean no more job losses. No more meddling by an outside power that cares nothing for the people of Wales.'

More applause from the audience.

'We find ourselves at a crossroads. The time has come to chart our own course. To unfurl the banner of Welsh independence and let it flutter in the winds of self-determination. There are uncertainties and challenges that lie ahead. But let us not forget the strength that resides in unity. The determination that still burns in the heart of our communities.

Together, we are a force that can shape our own destiny. A destiny woven from the dreams of generations past and the aspirations of those yet unborn.'

Tanya Glover stood in the viewing gallery, looking down at Bevan. Smiling as he addressed the Senedd. The distant sound of wailing sirens grew louder. Glover turned and looked out of the window, spotting four police cars that raced towards the steps of the Senedd. She rushed out of the viewing gallery and headed towards the main entrance.

'He's full of himself, isn't he, boss?.' Watkins commented as he listened to Bevan.

'I've got a speech of my own when I clap eyes on him.' Fagan responded, staring at his phone.

Glover raced down the front steps of the Senedd as the first car came to a halt. Anger simmered as she spotted Fagan climbing out of a car. 'You've no right to come here and try to stop this!'

Fagan rolled his eyes. 'Sean, deal with *Miss Glover,* will you.'

Watkins was flanked by a uniformed officer. 'Tanya Glover, I'm arresting you for perverting the course of justice. You do not have to say anything, but it may harm your defence when questioned something you later rely on in court. Anything you do say may be given in evidence.'

'Get off me, you piece of shit!' Glover screamed as she was led away.

Inside the Senedd as he delivered his speech, Bevan realised time was running out. He heard the sirens of the police cars as they approached. His heart pounding as he continued to address the Senedd floor. 'One of the undeniable advantages of charting the course towards Welsh independence lies in the abundant business opportunities and jobs that await our people. Let us envision a future where economic prosperity is not just a distant hope, but a tangible reality. Where the decisions that shape our economy are made right here. Within the borders of our beloved Wales. Independence heralds a new era of economic empowerment for our nation. The potential for job creation and business growth becomes a beacon guiding us towards a brighter future. Imagine a Wales, where local entrepreneurs, fuelled by the spirit of independence, drive innovation and establish enterprises that resonate with our cultural identity. These businesses, deeply rooted in Welsh soil, have the power to create jobs, stimulate economic growth, and contribute to the vibrant tapestry of our national economy.'

The main doors to the Senedd opened.

Everyone looked in Fagan's direction as he strolled towards Bevan. Fagan could hear the whirring of camera lenses as they focussed on him. He held up his phone, maintaining his stare on Bevan. 'Wonderful speech. A bit long winded for my liking.' He glanced around the Senedd floor. 'These people will find out who you really are.'

Bevan stared back, devoid of words.

'Lloyd Bevan, I'm arresting you for the murders of Dafydd Collier and Sean Price in March 1985. You do not have to say anything, but it may harm your defence when questioned, something you later rely on in court. Anything you do say may be given in evidence.'

A shocked and bewildered audience looked on as Bevan was led from the Senedd floor.

Garndiffaith RFC – 6:39pm

'Yes, come on!' Bryn Collier shouted across the rugby pitch. Watching his son score the winning try of the evening.

The crowd or spectators joined in, cheering.

'Nice one, Aron! I'm proud of you, son.' Collier clapped.

'Good game?' A voice said from behind.

Collier turned to face Fagan, who was accompanied by Watkins and two uniforms.

Collier breathed in. 'Yeah, we're top of the league now.'

Fagan stepped up to the line and watched the team of players hoisting Collier's son into the air. 'I'm surprised you didn't run.'

'I've been running for almost forty years, DI Fagan.' Coller shoved his hands into his pockets. 'It's time to atone for sins of the past.'

Fagan nodded to Watkins, who stepped forward flanked by the uniforms.

'Bryn Collier, I'm arresting you in connection with the murders of Dafydd Collier and Sean Price in 1985. You do not have to say anything. But it may harm your defence when questioned something you later rely on in court. Anything you do say, may be given in evidence.'

Collier looked at his son for the last time.

'Don't worry, I'll make sure his mam looks after him.' Fagan promised.

Collier was cuffed and led away.

CHAPTER 44

Newport Central police station
Two days later

Bevan glared at Fagan, who had gone through the interview start up sequence. Watkins was sat at his side with a notepad.

Fagan pointed at a monitor on the wall. 'I'm playing a video recording featuring Amlod Llewellyn shortly before his death in 2021.' Fagan tapped the play button on the remote.

Bevan watched Llewellyn's deathbed confession.

'As you can see, Amlod Llewellyn gives a detailed account of the events of March 1st 1985. He clearly states you ordered him to throw the scaffolding pole off the bridge. When Llewellyn refused, you handed the pole to Martin Cooper.' Fagan called up another video on the monitor. Filmed on his bodycam. 'I'm now showing Mr Bevan the video of Martin Cooper. Mr Cooper insists you ordered him to throw the scaffolding pole off the bridge. That resulted in the death of Dafydd Collier and Sean Price in 1985.'

Bevan watched as Cooper recounted his version of events.

'Directly after his confession, Martin Cooper committed suicide.'

Bevan stared back. 'No comment.'

'Had plenty to say the other day, when you were delivering your speech to the Senedd.' Fagan smiled. 'It's all over the news, Lloyd. Your grand dream for Welsh independence gone down in flames. Everyone is talking about you. Questioning your past.'

Bevan smirked. 'Dreams don't die, Inspector Fagan. They merely take on a different form.'

'What were you thinking when you were on that bridge that day? You must have been livid. Especially after you failed to take the Six Bells Colliery. That's what you were planning to do, wasn't it? Bryn Collier has told us everything. The man is in pieces. He said that he wanted to come forward years ago. But you made him stay loyal to your cause. You, Bryn Collier and Martin Cooper carried the illusion you were innocent. That the police had forced you to sign a confession.'

'They did!' Bevan hit back. 'Bastard bent pigs.'

Fagan nodded. 'I won't argue with you there, Lloyd. They were bent. But so were you. You were on that bridge. You ordered Martin Cooper to throw the scaffolding pole at the approaching car. Did you see the pole hit the taxi? Did you see the pole smash through the window, killing Sean Price instantly?'

'No comment.'

'Must have affected you. Especially when the news of Dafydd Collier's death came a few days later. Must have sent you into a panic.'

'I didn't know.'

'You didn't know what, Lloyd? That your orders resulted in the deaths of two innocent men that day?'

'They weren't innocent!' Bevan shouted. 'They were scabs.'

'But Sean Price wasn't a miner, therefore wasn't a scab.'

'But he was taking them to work.'

'That's your justification, is it? For killing him. Your reasoning for ordering Martin Cooper to throw that pole at the oncoming car.'

'I just told Martin to lob the pole, that's all. How could I have predicted what was going to happen?'

'When you found out Sean Price had been killed, what was your reaction?'

'No comment.'

'You were on that bridge. You ordered Cooper to throw the pole. The same pole that killed Sean Price instantly. What was your reaction when you discovered he had died?'

'My client has stated he did not throw the pole, Inspector Fagan.' Bevan's solicitor pointed out, glancing at the TV monitor. 'The two videos you've just played prove that. Amlod Llewellyn states my client wanted him to throw the pole before he gave it to Martin Cooper to throw. Martin Cooper also confirms this. My client was not responsible for Martin Cooper's actions.'

'He ordered Cooper to throw the pole off the bridge. He could have easily have told him not to.'

'I had to do something.' Bevan blurted out.

'What is that supposed to mean?'

'To fight back.'

'Against who?'

'Thatcher and her fucking government, that's who.'

'You ordered Martin Cooper to throw the pole because of Maggie Thatcher?' Fagan leant back, folding his arms. 'Help me understand this, Lloyd. What did Thatcher have to do with what Martin Cooper did?'

'Because of what happened that day.'

'You mean the Battle of Six Bells?'

Bevan nodded. 'I had to do something. To send a clear message to the government, they would never win.'

'But they did win,' Watkins pointed out. 'All your efforts were for nothing. And two men died for nothing.'

'No,' Fagan said, looking at Watkins. 'There were more than two casualties that day. Sean Price's wife was pregnant when her husband was killed. The impact of his death caused her to miscarry twin girls she was pregnant with.'

'DI Fagan, you are jumping to conclusions. Since we don't have access to Mrs Price's medical records.' The solicitor explained.

'Okay, we'll move on.' Fagan opened a file, pulling out a photograph, before sliding it towards Bevan. 'We've been looking at your financial records, Mr Bevan. This CCTV image was taken of you just over four weeks ago at the Bank of Ireland, in Dublin.' Fagan produced a sheet of paper. 'Your schedule states you visited the Republic of Ireland for trade negotiations. Your statements from the Bank of Ireland revealed you withdrew seventy thousand pounds on that day.'

A look of panic flashed across Bevan's face.

'CSI pulled a satchel out of the Keepers the morning Alwyn Collier's body was found. This satchel contained fifty thousand pounds in cash. Close examination of the notes revealed fingerprints. This was despite the fact someone had taken the time to treat the notes with bleach. In an effort to remove any fingerprints. The fingerprints found on the notes are yours.'

'No comment.'

Fagan pointed at the photo in front of Bevan. 'The man you are standing next to in this photograph has been identified at Declan O'Brien. A representative of Sinn Féin.'

'As you just pointed out, DI Fagan. My client was on a trade negotiation trip. Mr O'Brien was a trade representative Mr Bevan was due to meet.'

Fagan glanced at the piece of paper. 'And it says so here. But let's go back a few decades, shall we, to 1984? Because that's when you first opened up that account, isn't it?' Fagan glanced at his notes. 'October 14th 1984, to be exact. You boarded a ferry laden down with cash donated to the miners' strike fund. Money that should have gone into the South Wales branch bank account of the NUM. Isn't this true, Mr Bevan?'

'No comment.'

'So why did you keep the money? The three million pounds in total. You received from the Russian Mining Federation and the money given to you by NUM executives. Money donated to the National Union of Mineworkers from Libya. You talk about Thatcher being the number one enemy. What about Gaddafi? Look at what he represented.'

Bevan stared at the photo before speaking. 'Do you honestly think we were the only ones taking bribes and back handers? Engaging in back door deals with foreign enemies. The Tories were masters in that sort of thing.'

'Are you freely admitting to keeping funds that should have gone to the miners?' Watkins said.

'What fucking harm did it do?' Bevan challenged.

'The money should have gone to the Miners' Solidarity Fund. To support the miners throughout the strike.' Fagan pointed out. 'As for the harm it caused. What about the families that went without? Those who lost their homes. Parents who had children taken away from them. The families who were split down the middle because of the strike. I spoke to your former brother-in-law a few nights ago. He told me he hasn't seen his kids in nearly forty years. And you have the nerve to sit there and make out that it didn't do any harm.' Fagan sensed anger rising.

'We weren't in a position to ask where the money was coming from.'

'You were the head of the NUM for the South Wales coalfields. You had every opportunity to question where the money came from. My only assumption is you knew the strike was going to fail. That's why the NUM was desperate enough to accept money from Gaddafi. By the time he made his offer they were out of money. Scargill knew the strike was lost. That's why he was willing to accept money from anywhere at that point.' Fagan pointed at another file in front of him. 'It's all here in Alwyn Collier's notes. Notes he was turning into a book.'

Bevan stared at the file.

'That's what you wanted. The information he had on you and the activities of senior members of the NUM during the strike. Financial records from whistleblowers who have come forward. Alwyn Collier had compiled a book that would have buried you and your political ambitions.'

'Alwyn Collier was a scab!' Bevan yelled. 'He betrayed all of us to a corrupt system.'

'And what about your way of doing things, Lloyd? You weren't exactly squeaky clean, were you? By the time the miners' strike ended your pockets were lined. You were in prison, but knew the police couldn't charge you with anything. Because of what they did to Martin Cooper. How many times did Lord Barry visit you in prison? To tell you that you were home free. Then you had the audacity to accept the compensation given to you in 2016. Knowing full well you were guilty of murder.'

Bevan stared straight ahead.

'Is that when you decided to put your plan into action? To run for the Senedd. To push your dream of Welsh independence. The money you received for compensation was more than enough to fund your campaign. You didn't have to use the money you kept in your Irish bank account.' Fagan glanced at his notes. 'Two days before you travelled to Ireland, you made a statement to the Senedd. About what trade would look like for an independent

Wales. You travelled to Ireland to meet with Declan O'Brien.' Fagan tapped on the photograph. 'Declan O'Brien, the modern face of Sinn Féin. But what is he in reality?'

'No comment.'

'Declan O'Brien is a former member of the IRA. Suspected of the murder of British soldiers during the 1970s and 1980s. He was on the watch list of British Intelligence back then.'

'No comment.'

'And then there's you. Founder of Meibion Glyndwr. A group suspected of dozens of arson attacks from the late 70s to the mid-90s. It must have been a dream come true when you recruited Warren.' Fagan pointed at the file. 'You found a sympathiser in the form of Clive Warren. A supporter of the cause and a serving police officer. Who could give you tipoffs. Advise you on how to avoid getting caught. And someone who could throw the police off the scent.'

'DI Fagan, my client has never been convicted of anything connected to this group. Mr Bevan has also reflected the brutal treatment at the hands of the police. On the occasion when they arrested him with no evidence.'

'See, that's the thing, isn't it, Lloyd? All these years you've been hiding behind police misconduct. While all the time you've been guilty of many crimes. When Alwyn Collier started to research his book, I doubt even he could have predicted the treasure trove of information he would uncover. When you discovered he was due to be given the role of Secretary of State for Wales, you had to get rid of him. Creating flimsy evidence that he did nothing to control his staff. You knew as soon as he was appointed to the role, he would immediately block your plans for a referendum.'

'Alwyn Collier was a fucking traitor to the cause! He would have denied the Welsh people a chance to be free.'

'We're already free, Lloyd. Someone told me the other day that we don't need to be an independent country to identify themselves. Many of us are proud to be Welsh without having to follow the twisted ideology you promoted.'

'Twisted ideology.' Bevan argued. 'Who have you sworn your

allegiance to, DI Fagan? Another corrupt Tory government. You're no better than the scabs that sided with Thatcher and the National Coal Board.'

'I'm not the one sat on your side of the table, Lloyd. All this information, plus the confessions of Amlod Llewellyn, are enough to put you away for a long time. Murder, mishandling of funds.'

'What fucking good would it have done if I didn't keep the money, eh?' Bevan interrupted.

'You could have helped those miners who supported you. Those who were riddled with debt after a year-long strike. It took some miners years to get back on their feet. Some of them used their life savings to support you and your cause. Some had to remortgage their houses just to stay afloat. And it would have vindicated you for taking money from foreign enemies of the United Kingdom.'

'Who gives a fuck where the money came from? It wasn't like I had to kill someone to get it.'

Fagan inhaled, containing his anger. 'The money that came from Libya was blood money.'

'What the fuck are you trying to accuse me of now? You pig bastard, you're still as bent as ever.'

'April 1984.' Fagan maintained a calm tone. 'WPC Yvonne Fletcher was shot dead outside the Libyan embassy in London. Several months later, the chief executive of the National Union of Mineworkers flies out to Libya to meet with Gaddafi. Begging cup in hand, gladly accepting money from him.'

'I know my history.' Bevan shouted. 'The British government was importing oil from Libya. Why do you think they didn't storm the embassy? They let them go because Gaddafi threatened to cut off oil supplies to the UK. The Tory government, under Maggie Thatcher, was so desperate to outlast the miners they supplied weapons to Gaddafi to keep the oil flowing.'

Fagan looked down at the file. 'I've read Allwyn Collier's notes. I can see what was going on. NUM officials lining their pockets while ordinary strikers were on the edge of financial oblivion.' Fagan grabbed the photo of Bevan and O'Brien, placing it back in the folder. 'The courts have granted us a further thirty-six hours to detain you, Lloyd. So I suggest you make yourself comfortable.' Fagan stood and headed towards the door.

'Inspector Fagan.' Bevan called after him.

Fagan turned.

'This isn't over.'

Fagan looked back at him. 'You condemned those who worked through the strike. You kept money that should have gone to the miners. Money that came from sworn enemies of this country. You affiliated yourself with a known terrorist organisation. You've lied about what happened on that bridge for forty years. So you tell me Lloyd. Who's the real scab in the room?'

Bevan glared back. His eyes bulged. 'Long live Meibion Glyndŵr. His children will rise and take back what's rightfully theirs.'

Fagan hesitated before leaving the room.

E P I L O G U E

Prince Charles Hospital–Merthyr Tydfil
Tuesday 5th March 1985
Even from down the corridor, Bryn could hear the harrowing sobs of his mother. He made his way slowly towards the doorway. The flatline tone of the heart monitor pierced the air.

Alwyn clutched his mother in his arms. 'It's okay mam, Dafydd is at peace now.' Tears streamed down his face.

Bertrice spotted Bryn standing in the doorway. She tore herself away. Reaching out for him. 'Where have you been?' She screamed. 'Where have you been, Bryn? While your brother has been lying in hospital all weekend?'

A nurse rushed into the room. 'Please Mrs Collier, sit back down.'

Alwyn stared at Bryn before marching towards him, pulling his brother away from the door. 'We better talk where our mam can't hear.'

They made their way out of the car park.

'I'm sorry Alwyn, I.' Bryn's voice was full of emotion.

'Where have you been, Bryn, eh?' Alwyn shouted.

'I've been.'

'WHERE?' Alwyn screamed, cutting Bryn off. 'Haven't you even watched the fucking news?'

Bryn was lost for words.

'It's been all over the news for the past few days. The police are hunting for the men who dropped that scaffolding pole from the bridge. The police are looking for you, Bryn. They want to know where you were that day of the accident. So where the fuck have you been? A taxi driver from Abergavenny was killed in the accident. And now our Dafydd is dead. He was in the front of that car when the pole hit. All he was doing was going to work, for fuck's sake.'

'I've been organising things with Lloyd.'

'WHAT THINGS?' Alwyn screamed.

'For the strike.'

'Jesus fucking Christ, Bryn, the strike is over. Don't you get it. The NUM called all miners back to work two days ago. You have to return to work. No one has heard from Scargill.'

'We have to keep fighting.' Bryn struggled to say. 'If we don't, Thatcher will destroy our communities.'

'Can you even hear yourself, Bryn? You sound like Lloyd. His obsession with protecting the Welsh culture scares the shit out of me. And then there's Martin Cooper. The police reckon he's been involved in these fire bombings across Wales. Tell me you're not involved with this group, Meibion Glyndwr.'

Bryn failed to answer.

'Are you a member of this group or what, Bryn?'

'No, I swear.'

'Fuck off. I can see it in your eyes. That Bevan has brainwashed you. Making you believe you're on some kind of sacred quest. Do you have any idea the damage you and your mates have done over the last year? Convincing miners to keep on striking. Even if they face eviction. While all along, you lot have been managing just fine. How is that, Bryn? How is it you can afford a nice flat? And Lloyd has been able to live in a nice house. While those who have followed you have been on their arses for the past year. All the boys who've gone back to work don't even want to talk to you. Especially in light of what has happened to Dafydd and that taxi driver.' Alwyn inhaled. 'I just want to know one thing, Bryn. Were you on that bridge last Friday?'

Bryn sobbed.

'Answer the fucking question, Bryn. Yes or no. Were you on that bridge last Friday?'

'No, I wasn't, I swear,' Bryn sobbed.

Alwyn stood nose to nose with his brother. 'I don't believe you. You're a lying twat, Bryn. I can tell by the look on your face. I'm going back to comfort our mam. Don't bother coming, otherwise I'll put you in the fucking hospital. And don't bother showing up at the house either. If I see you at Dafydd's funeral, I'll fucking bury you in a hole next to him. I don't ever want to speak to you again.' Alwyn turned and walked back towards the hospital entrance.

Bryn dropped to his knees, sobbing. 'I'm so sorry, Alwyn. Tell our mam I never meant for any of this to happen.'

Alwyn stopped momentarily, glancing behind.

The end

Detective inspector Fagan will return in, The Dead will find You.

Help an independent author.

Many thanks for buying a copy of The Dead Will Beckon. I would be grateful if you could spread the word about this book, social media, Goodreads, a local book club. Or just have a conversation next time you're in the pub or at work.

I don't have an email list, but you can click on the follow button on my Amazon page. They will email you when I am about to release a new book.
Many thanks
Jason Chapman

Jasonchapman-author@hotmail.com

Hey avid book readers. Why don't you try my other books? They're also available on Kindle Unlimited.

Were you a fan of the X Files back in the day? You'll love my UFO Chronicles books. If you like stories of alien encounters and government cover-ups. Or perhaps you're a fan of fast-paced thriller. My Sam Drake series is perfect for those who like a bit of escapism.

The UFO Chronicles
The fallen
Codename Angel
The Angel Conspiracy
The Angel Prophecy

Detective Sergeant Samantha Drake
Dystopia
Avalon Rising
Signals
Project Genesis

Detective inspector Mark Fagan
The Dead will Beckon
The Dead and the Buried
Melody from the Dead

**OFFWORLD
PUBLICATIONS**

Printed in Great Britain
by Amazon